Condition Noted

FIC
Unger
Win.2024

W9-BDT-718

39098082649111

The new couple in 5B

THE NEW COUPLE IN 5B

Also by Lisa Unger

THE NEW COUPLE IN 5B

LISA UNGER

PARK
ROW
BOOKS

PARK
ROW
BOOKS™

Recycling programs
for this product may
not exist in your area.

ISBN-13: 978-0-7783-3334-0
ISBN-13: 978-0-7783-1028-0 (International Trade Paperback Edition)

The New Couple in 5B

Copyright © 2024 by Lisa Unger

All rights reserved. No part of this book may be used or reproduced in any manner whatsoever without written permission except in the case of brief quotations embodied in critical articles and reviews.

This is a work of fiction. Names, characters, places and incidents are either the product of the author's imagination or are used fictitiously. Any resemblance to actual persons, living or dead, businesses, companies, events or locales is entirely coincidental.

TM is a trademark of Harlequin Enterprises ULC.

Park Row Books
22 Adelaide St. West, 41st Floor
Toronto, Ontario M5H 4E3, Canada
ParkRowBooks.com
BookClubbish.com

Printed in U.S.A.

*In loving memory of my uncle Frederick Davidson,
who was a true Renaissance man, ever at work on his epic poem, my aunt
Phyllis Davidson, who epitomized the glamour of New York City for me,
and for my uncle Mario Miscione, a loving and devoted family man.*

overture

You. Standing on solid ground, reaching. Me. On the ledge, looking down. All around me, stars. Stars in the sky, the city a field of glittering, distant celestial bodies. Each light a life. Each life a doorway, a possibility. That's the thing I've always loved about my work, the way I can disappear into someone else. I shed myself daily, slipping into other skins. Some of them more comfortable than my own.

"Don't," you say. "Don't do this. It doesn't have to be this way."

I hear all the notes of desperation and fear that sing discordant and wild, a cacophony in my own heart. And I think that maybe you're wrong. Maybe everything I am and everything I've done, has led me here to this teetering edge. There was no other possible ending. No other way.

Sirens. As distant and faint as birdsong. It seems as if, in this city, they never stop wailing, someone always on their way to this emergency or that crisis. Rushing to help or stop or save. From the outside, it seems like chaos. But when you are inside, it's quiet, isn't it? Just another moment. Only this time the worst thing is about to happen, or might, or might not, to us. Every flicker of light, every passing second, just a shift of weight and another outcome becomes real.

"Please." Under the fear, the pleading of your tone, I hear it—hope. You're still hopeful. Still holding on to those other possibilities.

But when I look at you now, I know—and you know it, too, don't you?—that I've made too many dark choices, that there is no outcome but this one. The one that sets us both free right here and right now.

Pounding. They're at the door.

You know what's funny? Even on that day we first met, I knew it would end like this. Not really. Not exactly this, not a premonition, or a vision of the future. But even in the light you shined on me, even as you made me be the person I always wanted to be, there was this dark entity hovering, a specter. The destroyer. You were always too good for me, and I knew I could never hold on to the things we would build together.

Sounds rise and converge—your voice, their pounding, that wailing, the endless honking and whir of movement from this place we have lived in and loved.

The weight of my body, I close my eyes and feel it. The beating of my heart, the rise and fall of my breath. I tilt and wobble on the edge, as you move closer, hands outstretched.

"We'll be okay," you whisper. At least I think that's what you say. I can hardly hear you over all the noise. Your eyes, like the city below me, a swirling galaxy of lights.

You're close now, hand reaching.

Just one step forward or backward.

Which one?

Which one, my love?

ACT 1

the inheritance

Look like the innocent flower,
but be the serpent under it.

William Shakespeare
Macbeth, Act 1, Scene 5

one

Sometimes the smallest things are the biggest.

Like the slim rectangular box that sits at the bottom of my tote. Maybe just six inches long and two inches wide. Light, flimsy, its contents clatter when shaken. But it's a whispering presence, a white noise buzzing in my consciousness.

Max, dapper in a houndstooth blazer and thin camel cashmere sweater, peers at the oversize menu, considering. As if he isn't going to order the penne ala vodka and salad he always does. I hold mine, as well, perusing my options. As if I'm *not* going to get the pizza margherita, no salad. The tony Italian restaurant on Broadway across from my publisher's office is packed, silverware clinking, conversations a low hum. Lots of business being done over sparkling waters and tuna tartare.

Outside the big picture window, beside which we sit, the river of traffic flows, horns and hissing buses, the screech of brakes, the occasional shout from annoyed drivers. Beneath all of that, I feel it, the presence of that slim box, so full of possibility.

The waitress takes our expected orders, deposits Max's usual bottle of Pellegrino. I'm a tap water girl, but he pours me a glass, always the gentleman. I note his manicured nails, buffed and square, the white face of his Patek Philippe. No smartwatch for him. Max appreciates timepieces for their elegant union of form and function.

"So," he says, placing the green bottle on the white tablecloth.

I don't love the sound of that word. Max and I have known each other a long time. There's a heaviness to it, a caution.

"So?"

"Your proposal."

That's why we've met for lunch, to discuss the proposal I've submitted for my new book.

He slips my proposal out of the slim leather folder he's laid on the table between us.

"There's a lot to like here."

That's publishing code for *I don't like it*. How many times did I say the same thing to authors I was editing?

I have always been a writer, scribbling in the nooks and crannies of my days, my foray into publishing just a stop on the road to the writing life. But Max never wanted to be anything else more than an editor, the one who helped talented writers do their best work.

"But?" I venture. He lifts his eyebrows, clears his throat.

Max and I met when we were both editorial assistants, fresh out of the Columbia Publishing Course. We were so eager to enter the world of letters, literature geeks seduced by what we imagined was the glitz and glamour of the industry. He climbed the corporate ladder, while I stayed up late, got up early, holed up on weekends to complete my first book.

By the time I had finished my first draft, Max was a young star editor at one of the biggest publishing companies in New York, the first person I asked to read my manuscript; he was the first person to say he believed in me, the first editor to buy something I'd written and to make me what I'd always wanted to be. A full-time writer.

He runs a hand through lustrous dark hair, which he wears a little long, takes off his tortoiseshell glasses. "I don't know, Rosie. There's just something—lacking."

I feel myself bristle—lacking? But underneath the crackling of my ego, I think I know he's right. The truth is—I'm not *that* excited about it. The belly of fire that you need to complete a project of this size, honestly, it's just not there.

"There was so much fire in the first one," says Max, holding me in the intensity of his gaze. He's so into this—his job, this process. "There were so many layers—the justice system, the misogyny in crime reporting, the voices of the children. It really grabbed me, even in the proposal you submitted. I could see it. It was fresh, exciting."

"And this isn't." I try and probably fail to keep the disappointment out of my voice.

He leans in, reaches a hand across the table. "It *is*. It's just not *as* exciting. The first book, it was a success, a place from where we can grow. But the next book *needs to be* bigger, better."

Bigger. Better. What's next? That's the mantra of the publishing industry.

"No pressure," I say, blowing out a laugh.

My first true-crime book was about the violent rape of a young Manhattan woman, the travesty of justice that followed where a man was wrongly convicted and the real criminal went free, then continued on to rape and kill three more women. It took me five years to research and write while working a full-time job as an editor. The book did well, not a runaway bestseller but a success by any measure. The moment was right for that book, post Me Too, where society was casting a new light on women wronged by men, looking at older stories through fresh eyes.

It's been a year since the book came out, the paperback about to release soon. I can't take five years to write another one.

Max puts a gentle hand on mine. His touch is warm and ignites memories it shouldn't. His fingers graze my wedding and engagement rings, and he draws his hand back, steeples his fingers.

"Is this *really* what you want to be writing?"

"Yes," I say weakly. "I think so."

"Look," he says, putting his glasses back on. "You've had a lot on your plate."

I'm about to protest but it's true. My husband, Chad, and I had been taking care of Chad's elderly uncle Ivan, who recently passed away. Between being there for Ivan, Chad's only family, in the final stages of his illness, and now managing his affairs, it's been a lot. Scary to watch someone you love die, so sad, sifting through the detritus now of his long and colorful life. Uncle Ivan—he was all we had. I've been estranged from my family for over a decade. His loss feels heavy, something we're carrying on our shoulders. With the temperature dropping and the holidays approaching, there's a kind of persistent sadness we're both struggling under. Maybe it has affected my work more than I realized.

I think of that box in the bottom of my bag, that little ray of light. I am seized with the sudden urge to go home and tear it open.

"Look," he says when I stay quiet. "Just take some time to think about it, go deeper. Ask yourself, 'Is this the story I really want and need to tell? Is it something people need to read?' Make *me* excited about it, too. We have time."

We don't, actually.

The money from the first book—it's running out. Chad has a low-paying gig in an off-off Broadway production. This city—it takes everything to live here. Our rent just went up and we need to decide whether or not we can afford to renew the lease. It's just a one-bedroom, five-story walk-up in the East Village, and we're about to be priced out unless one of us gets paid a signifi-cant sum. Chad has an audition for another better-paying job, but things are so competitive, there's no way to know if he even has a chance. It's just a commercial, not something he's excited about, but we need the cash.

Today he's at the reading of Ivan's will. But we don't expect to inherit anything. Ivan died penniless. His only asset the apart-ment that will go to his daughter Dana.

Did I rush the proposal because I'm feeling desperate? Maybe.

The waitress brings our meal and I'm suddenly ravenous. We dig in. The pizza is good, gooey and cheesy. The silence be-tween us, it's easy, companionable, no tension even though it's not the conversation I was hoping to have. Writers, we only want to hear how dazzling we are. Everything else hurts a little.

"You said there was a lot to like," I say, mouth full. "What *do* you like about it? Give me a jumping-off point to dive deeper."

"I really like the occult stuff," he says, shoving a big bite of penne into his mouth. It's one of the things I love most about Max, his passion for good food. Chad is so careful about every-thing he eats, either losing or gaining weight for a role. "You kind of glossed over that."

I frown at him. "I thought you didn't like ghost stories."

There were several supernatural elements to my last book—the little girl who dreamed about her mother's death the day before it happened, how one of the children believed he com-municated with his murdered sister through a medium. Both of those bits wound up on the cutting-room floor. *Too woo-woo,* according to Max. *Let's stay grounded in the real world.*

"I *don't* like ghost stories—per se," he says now. "But I like all the reasons why people *think* a place is haunted. I like what it says about people, about places, about mythology."

I feel a little buzz of excitement then. And that's why every writer needs a good editor.

The proposal is about an iconic Manhattan apartment building on Park Avenue that has been home to famous residents including a bestselling novelist, a celebrated sculptor and a young stage and screen star. It's also had far more than its fair share of dark events—grisly murders, suicides and terrible accidents. It's a New York story, really—the history of the building, its unique architecture, how it was built on the site of an old church that burned down. I want to focus on each of the crimes, the current colorful cast of characters that resides there, and tell the stories of the people who died there—including Chad's late uncle Ivan, a renowned war photographer.

I'll still have access to the building, even though we're almost done cleaning out Ivan's things. His daughter, from whom Ivan hadn't heard in years, even as he lay dying and Chad tried to call again and again, is now circling her inheritance. She wasn't interested in Ivan, or his final days, his meager possessions. But the apartment—it's worth a fortune. Anyway, I've befriended the doorman, Abi. He is a wealth of knowledge, having worked in the building for decades. I think he's long past retirement age but doesn't seem to have any plans to hang up his doorman's uniform. *Some folks don't get to leave the Windermere, Miss Rosie,* he joked when I asked him how much longer he planned to work. *Some of us are destined to die here.*

"And I like the crimes," Max says, rubbing thoughtfully at his chin. "So I think if we can tease some of those elements out, I can take it to the editorial meeting."

The truth is I'm more excited about revising the proposal than I was about writing the book when I walked in here. He's right. It's not the architecture, the history of the building—it's the darkness, the crimes, the people. The question—are there cursed or haunted places, some energy that encourages dark happenings? Or is it just broken people doing horrible things to each other? A mystery. That's what makes a great story. And story is king, even in nonfiction.

"I'll get right to work," I say. "Thanks, Max."

"That's what editors are for, to help writers find their way to their best book." He looks pleased with himself. "Now, what's for dessert?"

Outside, a loud screech of tires on asphalt draws my attention to the street just in time to see a bike messenger hit by a taxi. In a horrible crunching of metal and glass, the biker hits the hood. His long, lanky limbs flailing, flightless wings, he crashes into the windshield, shattering it into spider webs, then comes to land hard, crooked on the sidewalk right in front of the window beside us. I let out an alarmed cry as blood sprays on the glass, red-black and viscous.

Max and I both jump to our feet. I find myself pressing against the bloody glass as if I can get through it to the injured man. I'm fixated on him, then remembering Ivan, those last shuddering breaths he took.

The biker's eyes, a shattering green, stare. His right leg and left arm are twisted at an unnatural angle, as if there's some unseen hand wrenching his body. I reach for my phone, but Max is already on his. *We've witnessed an accident, on Broadway between Fifty-Fifth and Fifty-Sixth, outside Serafina. A man is badly injured.*

He's dead, I want to correct him. But I don't. Once you've seen the look of death, you recognize it right away. It's a kind of vacancy, a light lost, something fled. Those green eyes are empty, beyond sight. A stylish young woman in a long black coat and high heels runs up to the twisted form and drops to her knees while she's talking on the phone.

She puts a tender hand to his throat, checking expertly for a pulse. Then, she starts to scream. Her screaming, so helpless, so despairing—does she know him? *Help. Help. Somebody help him.* Or does she, too, recognize that look? Does it connect her as it does me to every loss she's ever known?

I'm still pressing against the glass, transfixed.

A crowd gathers, blocking the man from sight. In minutes, an ambulance arrives. There's a frenzy of angry honking horns, people frustrated that their trips have been delayed by yet another accident. Max moves over to me, puts a strong arm around my shoulders.

"Are you okay? Rosie, say something."

I realize then that I'm weeping. Fat tears pouring down my cheeks. Turning away from the scene on the street, and into Max's arms, I let him hold me a moment. I take comfort in his familiar scent, the feel of him.

"I'm okay," I say, pulling away finally.

"You sure?" he says, face a mask of concern. "That was—awful."

We sit back down in stunned silence. Time seems to warp. Finally, the man is shuttled away in an ambulance, and the crowd disperses. We're still at our lunch table, helpless to do or change anything. How long did it all take? Someone from the restaurant steps outside, dumps a bucket of soapy water over the blood that has pooled there. Then he uses a squeegee to wash the blood from the window right next to me but instead just smears it in a hideous, wide, red swath.

I get up quickly, almost knocking over my chair. The rest of the diners have gone back to their meals. The show is over; everyone returns quickly to their lives. As it should be, maybe. But I am shaken to my core. So much blood. I feel sick.

"I have to get out of here. I'm sorry."

Max rises, too. He tells the hostess he'll come back for the bill, then shuttles me outside and hails a cab. The traffic is flowing again, and one pulls up right away.

"You're so pale," Max says again, opening the door. He presses a hand on my shoulder. "Let me pay the bill and run you home?"

"No, no," I protest, embarrassed to be so rattled. "It's fine."

I just can't stop shaking.

"Call me when you get in," he says. "Let me know you got home safe."

Then I'm alone in the back of the cab, the driver just a set of eyes in the rearview mirror, city noise muffled, Max's worried form growing small behind me. My pulse is racing and my mind spinning.

What just happened? What *was* that?

An accident. One of hundreds that happen in this city every single day. I just happen to have been unlucky enough to witness it.

My father would surely declare it an omen of dark things to come. But he and I don't share the same belief system. I haven't spoken to him in years; amazing that I still hear his voice so clearly.

The cab races through traffic, dodging, weaving, the cabbie leaning on his horn. I dig through my tote and find the little white, blue and purple box, pull it out so that I can put my eyes on it. A pregnancy test.

In the face of death and loss, what do we need most?

Hope.

Life.

I can't get home fast enough.

two

I let myself in through the heavy grated metal street door, check the mail, which contains only bills and useless fliers. Then I walk up the five stories to our apartment. I'm still a bit shaky, but the bike messenger accident is already fading some.

I guess that makes me a real New Yorker, now indifferent to the misery of others. New York City, as much as I love it, is an assault, a daily punch in the face. You do have to shut down a bit to survive its noise, odors, catcalls, lurking predators, its violence. I find myself revising the event. It wasn't that bad. Maybe he was just stunned, not dead. He'll be injured, of course, but ultimately live to messenger another day. Right? Right.

By the time I've reached the fifth floor, I almost believe it. I unlock our apartment door and push inside. I am hoping Chad will be home already, but he's not.

The apartment is sun-washed and tidy, and I feel some of my tension drain as I kick off my heels and pad across the wood floor. Despite my desperate revision of the event, I'm still flashing on the sight of the man hitting the windshield, hearing that crunch of metal, seeing that spray of blood. Underneath that, there's a current of deep disappointment that the meeting didn't go the way I had hoped.

After hanging my coat and tote on the hooks in the hallway, I carry my little box right into the bathroom.

I'm two weeks late.

This is it.

The absolute worst time to have a baby—when we're both broke, our futures uncertain. But I don't care. This is the thing I want more than I want any other thing—a baby, a family. My whole body, my heart, aches for it. I stalk playgrounds and offer to babysit the children of our friends. I browse baby names online and gaze longingly at images of stylish nurseries on Pinterest. It's not just me; Chad wants this, too. We so badly hope to create the family neither one of us have. I'm estranged from mine; Chad's parents both died too young in a car accident. Now that Ivan's gone, we're alone.

We'll make this work. This baby. This life. We will. He'll get this commercial. I'll rework my proposal and Max will love it.

In the dim yellow light coming in from the thin frosted bathroom window, I lay out the kit on the porcelain sink. I read the instructions carefully, just to be sure I'm doing everything right—even though I've done this plenty of times, the enterprise always resulting in another disappointment. In the end, though, it just comes down to peeing on the stick. I do that, place the little lid over it and lay it down.

I catch sight of myself in the mirror, which has a little chip out of the corner. My face, framed by wild dark hair, frowns in concentration, squinting a little from staring at the tiny type. My resting worried face. When left to its own devices, my brow wrinkles; the corners of my mouth turn down. I force a smile at my reflection.

"You've got this," I tell the girl in the mirror. I am not sure she believes me.

Fifteen minutes. Not more. Not less.

In the living room, I sink onto the couch we bought with my first big advance payment. It seems a silly expense now, more than some people might pay for a used car. But it is as plush and ensconcing as a hug; it embraces me. I grab the cashmere throw, another aspirational purchase, and wrap it around my shoulders.

Breathe.

I check my phone. No word from Chad. I wonder how the audition went. I envision him waiting in a room with other similarly handsome, charming actor types. But he's the best. He has real talent, and it's just a matter of time before someone sees that. From there he was going to the reading of Ivan's will. His location is unavailable. I refresh. Refresh. Nothing.

A text from Max: You home?

Sorry, I shoot back. I'm home. I'm fine. You?

That was horrible. I keep thinking about that poor guy. His leg. You think he's okay?

No, definitely not. Instead, I type: I'm sure he is. The ambulance got there so fast.

I flash on the twisted form of the biker, the swath of blood on the window, push it away. No, I don't want that image in my head.

Outside the old, mullioned windows there's a view of other apartments, the fire escape, the alleyway between buildings. Most of the windows across from our apartment are empty, dark, spaces occupied by people with actual jobs that require them to be gone during the day.

But she's home, the young mother with her toddler. He's in his high chair; she's on the phone. Dark hair up, dressed in a yoga tank and tie-dye leggings, she's graceful and swift. She's talking to the baby now, though I can't hear her through the closed window. She taps his nose with the tip of a delicate finger. The baby looks up at her, adoring, laughs. I feel a pang. I watch them more often than is reasonable.

Seven minutes.

I jump when the buzzer rings. Once. Twice. Three times. Urgent. Angry? Probably just some weirdo. I wait. Maybe they won't ring again.

Again, long and loud.

This time I answer. "Who is it?"

"It's Dana."

Dana? Chad's cousin? Why is she here? She and I have never even met in person.

"Oh, hey," I say into the intercom box. What does she want?

Eight minutes.

"Can I come *up*?" There's a churlish edge to her tone.

"Uh, sure." A quick glance around the apartment. It's neat enough. "But Chad's not here."

She doesn't say anything, so I press the buzzer and open the apartment door. I hear the gate clang and she hoofs it up five flights, footfalls echoing loudly. Finally, a striking redhead, dressed in a sweeping blue coat, tight jeans, thigh-high boots, arrives on the landing. She's panting after the exertion.

"Fuck," she says between breaths. "That's a lot of stairs."

"Yeah." I step aside so she can enter the apartment. "You get used to it. I'm Rosie, Chad's wife. He's not here."

She stays in the hallway, looks me up and down, makes some kind of an assessment that I can't read. Then, a smirk. "You're just his type."

I smile uncertainly. What does that mean? Like she knows him, knows me. She doesn't.

I steal a glance at my phone. Ten minutes.

"Come in." But she stays rooted.

"Well," she says, looking around. "The Windermere will be a *big* upgrade for you two, won't it?"

The flush on her cheeks, I'm getting, is only half from effort. The other half is from anger.

"I'm sorry. What?"

But she doesn't seem to hear me.

"You know what my father gave me in this life?" she asks. Her mineral-blue eyes blaze, but her bluster doesn't fool me. All I see is sadness, loss.

"Nothing," she says when I don't answer. "Absolutely. Fucking. Nothing."

Join the club, I want to say, thinking of my own father, but it doesn't seem like she's looking to bond. Her stare is hard and unyielding.

"Do you want to come in? Have some water?"

But she's obviously lost to her anger.

"Ivan was a drunk," she goes on. "He beat my mother. Did you know that?"

I shake my head.

"Then he left us. Like with nothing. My mom struggled all her life to take care of us. The whole world lauded him, you know, for *his art*. But you know what he gave us? Nothing."

"I'm sorry," I say. And I am. Ivan was good to me—kind, loving, a father figure even though I didn't know him that long. But he wasn't my father; we didn't have any history, any baggage. "He regretted it, that he wasn't a good father to you. Deeply."

He *had* admitted his failings as a father and a husband. I don't know if he regretted it necessarily. He was practical about his flaws. But it seemed like the right thing to say to her now. Wrong.

She lifts a pale, hard palm. "Don't."

Dana is a beauty with high cheekbones and a wide, full mouth. I can see Ivan's cool intelligence in her eyes. Her brows are perfect arches, crinkling now in anger and sadness.

"He was a monster," she says.

I want to tell her that he wasn't. But I stay quiet, look down at the black-and-white tiles on the ground. I could say the same thing about my father. And I would fight anyone who disagreed with me.

She glances up at the ceiling, still breathing hard, then gives a slow shake of her head. "Do you ever look at them? His photographs. All those images of mayhem and gore. His portraits of war criminals. The battlefield shots, the corpses of children, the burned villages."

"He was a *war* photographer," I say. "But no, I haven't spent a lot of time looking at his work."

"Right, because you're a decent human being. You turn away from images of violence. But think about it. He was there, watching, doing nothing, just taking pictures. He was a voyeur, someone who gazed upon disaster, murder, death, and did nothing but watch."

I never thought about it that way. Maybe she has a point. Or maybe she's just demonizing him because it's easier to hate him than it is to be the sad, abandoned little girl of a man who couldn't love her.

"I think he saw it as bearing witness, reporting the truth," I venture.

"Sure," she says with a derisive laugh. "That sounds like him."

I smell the light floral of her perfume, notice a simple wedding band on her left hand.

"Do you know what my father left me in death?"

I shake my head. She planned this, obviously. It's not hard to predict what she's going to say.

"Absolutely nothing."

"The apartment—" I start.

"Is *yours*." She stares at me hard.

"What? No."

Uncle Ivan didn't have much. His savings had dwindled to almost nothing. We knew that because we helped him pay his bills, even as we struggled to meet our own. Toward the end *we* were buying his groceries, helping to cover the building's exor-bitant maintenance fee, even though he'd paid off the apartment long ago. Luckily, Ivan served in the military before his career as a photographer, so he had decent health insurance, and all those bills were covered. Dana, his angry daughter, contributed nothing toward the end, even after repeated calls from Chad, asking for her help.

"I came in for the reading of the will. I expected that he'd leave the apartment to me since I'm his only living child. It was the very least he could do, but it seems he left it to you and your husband jointly, that he *very recently* changed his wishes."

This is not possible. Ivan told me himself that he wanted it to go to Dana.

I'm about to say so when the door downstairs squeals open, then clangs shut. There are footfalls on the stairs. The gait is brisk and sure. It must be Chad.

Twelve minutes.

"I don't know what to say, Dana."

She takes a step forward, and I retreat, her energy pushing me back. "How about you say that you'll sign the apartment over to *me*? That would be the right thing to do."

"Dana?"

We both turn to see Chad jog up the final flight.

He's golden, with a thick mane of straw-colored curls, faceted hazel eyes. He's broad in the shoulders, fit and lean through the body. He has a strong jaw, just the smattering of stubble, styl-ishly left behind. My husband—he's a movie star. He just hasn't been discovered yet. Still, most women swoon in his presence. Even I do—his wife who knows all his faults and foibles.

Dana glares at him, puts a hand to her throat.

"What are you doing here?" he asks. There's that little notch between his eyebrows that he gets when he's angry or worried.

She takes a step back to let him walk by.

"I was just leaving," she says. "And you'll be hearing from my lawyer."

"Don't do this, Dana," he says, sounding weary. "I'm as surprised as you are."

Chad is clutching a big manila envelope. I'm starting to connect the dots.

"Like you *didn't know*," she says, seething. "Like you didn't plan this *all along*."

"And where *were* you?" he asks, angry now. "When Ivan was *dying*?"

She shakes her head, jaw tensed, looking back and forth between me and Chad. Her eyes fill with tears, hands shaking.

"Do you have any idea who you married?" she hisses at me. "Run while you still can, Rosie." So much sadness, rage. I take another step back, wrap my arms around my middle.

With that, she turns and heads toward the stairs. "Trust me, this isn't over," she calls back.

"Dana," Chad says as she storms away, her heels tapping a staccato beat. He walks to the banister and yells down, "Dana, let's talk about this."

But we hear the clang of the door downstairs carry up. She's gone. We both stand a moment, stunned. Finally, he drops an arm around me and ushers me inside the apartment.

"What was that about?" I ask. I'm antsy to get to the bathroom. Fifteen minutes have passed.

He drops onto the couch, staring at the envelope in his hands.

"Rosie," he says, a smile tugging at the corners of his lips. "Ivan left us the apartment."

All our luck has been bad lately. It doesn't seem possible that we could receive such a boon, this change of fortune. If you can consider it good fortune to take what probably truly belongs to someone else. I don't allow myself to accept it, push away, still focused on my other hopes.

"Give me a second," I say. He nods, opening the envelope, lifting out the documents. Two sets of keys clatter to the distressed wood coffee table.

In the bathroom, I lock the door and close my eyes. *Please, please, please.*

But when I open them again, my heart sinks hard into the pit of my stomach. Just one blue line. I bite back my tears of disappointment, brace against its powerful waves. We haven't been trying that long, I tell myself. It shouldn't hurt this much. We're young. It's *really* not a good time to be having a baby.

I sit on the toilet and focus on my breath.

Then, I wrap it all up—the test, the wrapper, the box—in tissues and toss it into the wastepaper basket. I haven't told Chad that my period is late. No reason to bring him on the roller-coaster ride with me. I stare at myself in the mirror, look into my own dark eyes, run my fingers through the thick waves of my hair and put on a smile worthy of my actor husband. *Pull yourself together.*

When I step back outside, Chad is staring at the keys in his hand.

"It's ours," he says. "It's all right here. The keys, the deed, the co-op documents."

"That's—wow," I say, sitting beside him.

"Oh, my God, Rosie," he says, grabbing both my hands. "That place. It's worth a fortune."

A two-bedroom apartment with stunning views and washed with lights in a prewar building with a doorman. Hardwood floors, towering ceilings, a working fireplace. I can hardly bring myself to imagine us there.

"It's hard to celebrate this," he says. "Because Ivan's gone. But—wow."

I don't want to say what I'm thinking because I'm the pragmatist and he's the dreamer. But what are the taxes on an inheritance like that? That maintenance—it's huge. Can we even afford to inherit something worth that much?

"What about Dana?" I think about the angry flush on her cheeks, the sadness in her eyes.

He lifts his shoulders. "What about her? Where was she when Ivan was dying? I mean, she never even called. He hadn't spoken to her in over a decade."

It's complicated, I want to tell him, when you're estranged from your parents. Would I go home if I learned my father was on his deathbed? I can't say. Maybe not. But then again, I wouldn't expect an inheritance, either.

"She's going to sue us for it," I say, thinking about the angry flush on her cheeks, her parting threat.

He seems to consider, looking at the documents that are spread out, the two sets of keys that catch the meager light coming in from the window. "Let her."

"Rosie," he says, pulling me closer, leaning in. His eyes search my face. "It's okay to be happy about this. Be happy for us."

Then we're making out, the apartment and everything else forgotten. The heat between us comes up fast; it always does. We haven't been married that long, less than a year, just a simple affair at city hall, a gathering of friends at our favorite bar afterward. We keep promising each other a honeymoon, but we've been hustling so much to make ends meet, to take care of Ivan, it hasn't happened.

His lips on my neck, his hands tearing at my white silk blouse. It falls to the floor and then I'm unzipping his jeans, hiking up my skirt and climbing on top of him. He slides easily inside me, hard, hungry. I let the passion take me as he puts his lips to my breast. It's fast and intense, hot. I push myself deeper and he drops his head back in pleasure, groans, helpless. I put my lips on the soft flesh of his exposed throat. His arms close around me. Everything but this is gone.

"Rosie," he whispers. "I love you so much."

Bottle rockets of pleasure shoot through me as he climaxes with a moan that sounds like pain, and my body answers with a shuddering orgasm. I drop against him, my gaze falling outside. I forgot to pull the shades. All the windows are dark except one. The yoga mom is standing there watching us. She must have seen the whole thing.

Luckily, I'm not the shy type. When she sees me looking, she turns away, embarrassed, and shuts the shade hard. I giggle to myself, tell Chad about the yoga mom, remark how we should be more careful.

"Authors gone wild," he says. We both get a laugh out of that one.

I keep my gaze out the window, wondering if anyone else saw. There's a painter on the top floor; sometimes he works all night. There are a couple of young women on three who look like they have office jobs. They always have friends over, or they're on their big couch, sweats on, hair up, Netflix, Uber Eats. They seem sweet, young. They usually go to bed around ten, are gone for the day by seven. The rest of the windows are shaded most of the time.

"I'm going to call Olivia."

"That's a good idea."

Olivia is one of our few friends with a real job. The rest are writers, actors, artists. Olivia is a lawyer at a big firm uptown. She's on the partner track and is always coming late or leaving early from events, performances, signings. She and Chad used to date a hundred years ago, but it's not a thing. At least not for me. She was the first of his friends to become my friend, too. Sometimes I do catch her watching him wistfully or watching me—I don't know how. Not jealous. Just sad maybe. Like maybe she shouldn't have let him go. But she did.

Chad picks up his phone and I head into the bathroom for a quick shower. I sit on the toilet to pee and when I pull the tissue paper back, it's dark with blood. Any clinging hope that the test was wrong is dashed. A hard cramp almost doubles me over. And the afterglow of making love to my hot husband fades fast.

I think of that smear of blood on the restaurant window, the angry red of Dana's cheeks. The pain passes as I dig through the cabinet for a pad.

"You know," yells Chad from outside. "I really think our luck is about to change."

But I don't believe in luck—good or bad. Life just happens. It's a roller coaster; you hang on tight and ride.

three

Chad drifts off as we watch *Blade Runner 2049* for about the millionth time. He knows Ryan Gosling's every line, sometimes stands up to perform it for me in unison with the screen. It's cute that my husband is a huge science-fiction geek and that his dream role is to be like Gosling in *Blade Runner*, or Harrison Ford in *Star Wars*—those kind of space swashbucklers, but with layers. He's currently on off off-Broadway playing a witch in a musical, gender-bending version of *Macbeth*—which is actually quite good and getting some nice early reviews. He has his Shakespeare chops having earned his MFA from Columbia University. He still goes to acting class on Thursday nights, always honing and deepening his craft. But his boyish heart dreams of space adventures.

He's asleep on the couch, snoring. I watch him for a minute because he's so sweet when his face is relaxed like this. When he's awake, he's in constant motion, always hustling from this thing to that, ambitious. I suppose the same is true of me, and sometimes our days are so full that it's as if we're always rushing past each other, barely connecting. I push a lock of hair from his eyes, touch the softness of his cheek and he stirs, eyes opening.

"You were sleeping."

"I was dreaming—about Ivan. About the apartment." An uncharacteristic worry wrinkles his brow.

"We can talk about it more tomorrow."

He nods, rising, lifting his arms in a stretch, exposing those taut abs.

"Coming?" he asks, sleepily, heading toward the bedroom. He trails a hand back for me.

"I'm going to work a while."

This is my time and it's a known thing between us. He's an early bird. But my creativity peaks when the day is done, and others sleep.

"Don't stay up too late," he says, then leans in to give me a kiss on the head before disappearing into the dark of our bedroom.

I pull my laptop from my tote and get to work.

Once I'm in the document, the revisions come easily, and the structure is clear to me in a way it wasn't before. I can see it.

Time clicks by. The pages fly.

Dawn is less than an hour away by the time I'm done, the sky already lightening. I'm exhausted but I'm happy with the revisions on my proposal. I just know that it works—I can feel the tingle on my skin.

Maybe Chad is right. It's kismet that we've inherited this apartment. I was meant to write this book and meant to live at the Windermere while I do it. I feel the high-energy vibration.

I draft an email to Max and to my agent Amy, then send it off with the new proposal attached. The time I note is 5:55— that must be a good sign, right? Ivan's apartment is 5B at 55 Park Avenue.

I am about to turn in, when the glint of our new keys catches my eye. I sit back down and sift through the apartment documents, think back on our conversation with Olivia.

"First," said Olivia when Chad put her on speaker, "you'll want to find out how much the apartment is worth."

"I looked up the last apartment to sell in the Windermere," Chad told her. "It was bigger, more up-to-date, than Ivan's— but it went for five million."

I puzzle at this. When did he look it up? On the way home from the reading of the will? Probably.

"Wowza," Olivia said. "How much is the monthly maintenance?"

"Well, it's an old building so they have a lot of expenses, including that full-time elevator operator, so it's over $2000 a month. But, you know, we're paying more than that now for rent."

Olivia's silent a moment, and we can both hear her tapping her phone, the swish of a text going out.

"I'll check into it with our probate guy, but I think the exemption is up to ten million. So if all the documents are in order, the language of the will is clear, you guys just got seriously lucky."

Chad and I looked at each other.

Holy shit, Chad mouthed.

Okay, maybe I do believe in luck.

But it wasn't just luck, was it? We'd been there for Ivan in a way no one else had. He'd been our Christmas, Thanksgiving, birthday, everything for the years Chad and I have been together. He stood up for us at our wedding, was our witness on the certificate. When he fell ill so suddenly, we were there. He never had a moment alone and uncared for, up until the very end. He died in that apartment, in his own bed, with us by his side.

He never once mentioned leaving the apartment to us. And it had never occurred to either one of us to ask for anything. We did what we did out of love. That simple.

"Why didn't he leave it to his daughter?" I asked out loud, though I didn't really mean to. "Dana said he'd changed his will very recently."

Chad gave me a look. "Who cares? He made his choice. And he chose us."

I told Olivia that Dana planned to sue us, that she'd come here making threats.

"I mean—she can try. But if the will is good, and he has a lawyer that oversaw the change, she doesn't have a legal leg to stand on. People cut their kids out of their wills all the time. It's not pretty, but there's not much you can do about it."

We were both silent. I weaved my fingers through Chad's.

"Hey, guys?" Olivia's voice crackled over the speaker. "Congratulations. Celebrate this, okay? You deserve it."

"Thank you," I say. "Olivia, you get the first dinner we cook in our new place."

"I'm holding you to that," she said. I could hear the smile in her voice. "Seriously. Good for you guys."

It takes a big person to be genuinely happy for your ex and his new wife when they inherit a fortune they didn't expect. I've always admired her—her sense of style, her success, her dedication to her job. But she went up a few more notches in my estimation.

Now, sitting alone in our living room, I pick up the keys, jingle them. They are cold and heavy in my hand. I try to envision us there, happy in Murray Hill, a real old New York neighborhood. Maybe it lacks the glitz of SoHo, or the understated swank of Tribeca, the gritty cool of our current East Village abode. But it's quiet and beautiful. There we are, pushing a baby stroller down Park Avenue. I can *see* us—happy, safe.

But Chad's wrong about one thing: the maintenance is nearly $4000 a month, almost double what we're paying now. With what we have, what we'll get back on our security deposit from this place, we can afford to live there for approximately six months—if we eat a lot of ramen. Unless I get a book deal. Unless Chad lands this commercial.

I'm thinking all of this as I slide into bed next to my husband.

He turns to hold me, and I move into his arms, drift off right away into a deep and dreamless sleep.

When I wake up, Chad is long gone. He has rehearsal all day, and tonight is opening night. I probably won't see him again until I go to watch him on stage. No small roles, as they say. But this one *is* tiny. I think he's on stage a total of twenty minutes.

I get up and brew some strong coffee. It's almost ten. Once I've poured my cup, I head straight for my laptop. There's already an email from Max:

> Wow. I don't know how you did this so fast. But it's—amazing. I love the new structure organized by each crime—I'm excited to bring it to the team today. More soonest.

I allow myself a whoop of excitement and drop Chad a quick text with the good news. But my husband doesn't answer, and I didn't expect him to. His phone is probably in the dressing room and he's on stage all bubble, bubble, toil and trouble.

But there's still money to think about.

I dial our East Village landlord's office and get his secretary.

"Hey, Mira," I say. "It's Rosie Lowan on First Avenue? I just wanted to let you know that we won't be renewing the lease. So, we'll be out by the end of the month."

There's a brief silence on the end of the line, then, "Yes, I know. In fact, I'm just processing your security deposit return today."

"Oh," I say, confused.

"Your husband. He called a couple of weeks ago, asked if we could expedite the return of the deposit, that you needed it for your new place."

"When was this exactly?" I ask.

"Let me check." I hear her clicking on her keyboard. "October fifth."

Just a few days after Ivan died. Had Ivan told Chad that we were getting the apartment?

"Well, I guess he's one step ahead of me," I say, covering my confusion.

"If you want to pick up the check, it will be ready this afternoon."

Okay, that's weird, right? Chad, who literally never does anything administrative, has called the landlord and asked for the return of our deposit. Which—I guess is a good thing? Money sooner rather than later, another deposit in our meager accounts rather than a withdrawal. But does that mean he knew we were getting the apartment? Would he not have told me? That he was sure enough we were moving to request our security deposit back?

I flash on something Dana said: *Like you didn't plan this all along.*

Then, *Run while you still can, Rosie.*

But I push thoughts of Dana away, a hurt person, spewing her rage. There's an explanation for it, I'm sure. And I have more important things on my mind.

The project is tugging at me. I'll get to work today, head up to the Windermere and spend some time in the apartment. *Our* apartment.

I shower and get dressed, silently saying goodbye to all the annoying things about our place—the slant in the floor, the leak in the bathroom, the cracked Formica floors in the kitchen. I am about to head out the door when my cell phone rings. I pull it from my pocket and see a number I don't recognize but an area code I do.

Don't answer, Chad would surely say.

But I do.

I don't say anything when I engage the call. Standing by the front door of my apartment, I just listen.

Finally, a young female voice asks, "Rosie? Are you there?"

"Sarah?"

"Hi," she says, blowing out a breath. "It's so good to hear your voice."

My little sister. It is good to hear hers too and it also hurts.

"I miss you," she says.

Since I left for New York City ten years ago, a runaway essentially, fleeing abuse, chaos, madness, I haven't talked to my parents at all. But I do occasionally speak with Sarah and my grandmother. I send them real paper letters, telling them about my life. When I got married, I wrote to let Sarah know. I always make sure she has my address and a way to reach me. In case she ever wants to leave, too.

"Everything okay?" I ask, a knot in my stomach.

"You know," she says. "Life."

"Mom and Dad?"

"The same."

That doesn't surprise me. I block my memories of my time growing up, the isolated house, the feeling of always being afraid. I got a free ride to New York University, and they gave me a job in the bursar's office to cover my other expenses due to my condition of extreme poverty. Even though I have struggled to survive in this city, to leave my difficult childhood behind, I never once looked back. And I did it. I'm a survivor, if nothing else.

"Rosie," she says. "I'm getting married. To Brian Jenkins."

"That's—great," I say. She'll be twenty in June. Brian was a boy from our Ozarks town; I don't remember a thing about him except his father drank with mine, that they sat on plastic chairs out on the lawn in front of a bonfire and sometimes drank all night, laughing at nothing, sometimes fighting.

"I'm pregnant."

Surprise, surprise. Still, it's a bit of a knife in the gut. "I'm happy for you, Sarah."

"Are you?"

"Of course."

The silence between us is tense, heavy. It goes on too long and I think maybe the call has failed.

"I had a dream last night," she says then, voice soft. "A bad one."

Sarah and her dreams. We used to share a room, and the kid was plagued by nightmares, which was no surprise since our waking life was not a safe or secure one.

"It was about you," she continues when I don't say anything.

"Okay." I should tell her I have to go. But instead, I sit at the small kitchen table, put down my tote.

"I dreamed that you were trapped in a castle, and that there was a monster drinking your blood. Except you didn't know it. He was drinking it slowly, little by little, taking it while you slept. And you were just wasting away, getting thinner and paler, weaker, until you couldn't even get out of bed. You couldn't even move to save yourself."

A chill moves through me even though I've donned my coat and the apartment is overwarm.

"I'm fine," I assure her. "I'm happy and safe."

You're fine, I used to whisper to her in the dark. *You're safe. I'm here.* It wasn't true. She wasn't safe, neither of us was. And I left her the first chance I got.

"You are?"

"I have a good marriage, a good career, a nice place to live. There's no monster. No castle. I'm okay."

It helps to say it and maybe it helps her to hear it. She breathes softly on the other line. I strain to listen for other sounds but there's nothing.

"If my baby is a girl, I'm going to name her Rosie," she says. "And I hope she'll never leave me."

Wow. That one really hurt. The knife twists; I bleed out.

"I'm sorry, Sarah. But when you're ready to leave there, I'll help you find your way."

"This is my home," she says, sounding a little angry now.

"Then I wish you all the best."

A heavy silence pulses on the line. My sister, my childhood, the place where I grew up—just hours away by plane, but the distance seems uncrossable. That she could come here, or I could go back there—it doesn't even seem possible.

"Be careful, Rosie, please. If there's something you're planning to do, someplace you're planning to go, don't do it. It's wrong. It's bad."

I push out a little laugh. If I don't believe in luck, or justice, then I most certainly don't believe in Sarah's dreams. In fact, what I believe is that you are the author of your life. That you write your own story. That you are the hero and the villain and everyone else.

"Okay," I say gently. These calls, or the letters that come from her or Grandma, they always sting. I know she's reaching out for me, trying to make a connection in this way. Sharing her dreams, which she thinks are prophetic. But it only serves to make me want to get farther away. "Thanks for calling, Sarah."

A bigger person would be able to give her more. Some love, some words of encouragement, some laughter even. But when it comes to my family of origin, I'm all dried up.

"Rosie," she says. "I love you."

She hangs up before I can say it back. Which is fine because maybe it's not even true. The heaviness I always feel after contact with my family, a deep fatigue, a kind of weighing down of limbs, a dullness of mental acuity, pulls at me. Abuse, it lives in your body, haunts like a demon. If there was a monster drinking my blood, I've already defeated it. Or escaped it anyway— through years of therapy and active work on myself.

I stand and shake the phone call off.

I'm going to the Windermere, our new home, to get started on my new book.

Life—it's ahead of us, not behind.

★ ★ ★

Abi, the Windermere doorman, always pressed and polished, unfailingly proper, seems to be waiting for me when I arrive. In fact, he *always* seems to be waiting, as if he never leaves his post. Which he must. But I've rarely walked in through the varnished wood doors without his having opened them for me. He's a romantic apparition of New York past, an upright, polite and helpful doorman and elevator operator.

"Ms. Lowan," he says, swinging the door open. "Wonderful to see you as always."

I've asked him to call me Rosie many times, but he never does.

I step into the small, well-appointed lobby. Marble floors, a polished doorman station, dark wainscoting, ornate red-and-gold wallpaper. All the finishings in the building, from the crown molding to the polished brass doorknobs, are original. The residents are dedicated to preserving the history of the building infused in its rich details. When things need to be replaced or repaired, a committee meets to make sure the grandeur of the Windermere is maintained.

"Good morning, Abi," I say.

He tugs on the lapels of his maroon uniform blazer, looking more soldier than doorman, straight-backed and clean-cut, at the ready. He takes his cap from the doorman station and puts it over his thick black hair. He's ageless, his accent unrecognizable. I asked him once where his family was from and he waved a hand, saying, "I've lived all over the world. But now I'm just a New Yorker."

I didn't press. I don't like to answer that question, either. My family is of Scots-Irish descent, not that I feel any connection to those places, and I was raised in the Ozarks of North Arkansas, my childhood a time and place so distant from where I am now that it might as well be in another galaxy. I might be from those places, but I am not *of* them. Like Abi, I consider myself a New Yorker now. This is the place I chose.

Abi strides gracefully toward the elevator. "Shall I give you the tour?"

"The tour?" I ask with a smile. "I think I know the place pretty well."

Should I share the news with him? But I hold it back because, honestly, it still seems too good to be true. What if Dana *does* sue us? What if she gets the place back? Sometimes it's better not to attach in the first place than suffer the pain of loss.

"All new homeowners get a tour, Ms. Lowan." He offers a slight bow, which seems silly and antiquated and sweet all at the same time.

"Oh," I say. "You heard."

"I think you'll find that news travels fast here. In any case, Mr. Lowan told me when he came by this morning. Congratulations and welcome."

"Thank you," I say. "Chad was here?"

"He came very early. To take some measurements, I think."

That's news to me. "Oh, right," I say. "Slipped my mind."

Abi is so tall that his cap nearly grazes the top of the elevator door as he steps inside. The manually operated elevator—a piece of New York charm that sets the Windermere apart from other buildings. Also, a huge expense and part of why the maintenance is so high on a building with few amenities. According to Ivan, there was talk at one point of modernizing. But it was decided that the elevator man was part of the Windermere's elegance. Also, the shaft is too small for modern elevators, and the mammoth cost of undertaking that project was prohibitive. Windermere residents, many of them older, do not like change and they do not like assessments.

And there is something lovely about the mahogany interior, the pleasant clicking of the closing gate, the quiet, well-oiled hum of the machinery, Abi's steady hand on the bronze-handled mechanism that controls ascent and descent. Stepping into the lobby of the Windermere, and into this elevator, is like stepping into the old New York of my dreams, reminding me that this building has been here since the late 1920s. All the people I'll be writing about have stepped over these floors, ridden in this very elevator. It connects my present to the building's storied past. It's a time machine.

"The tour, then?" he says.

It seems rude to decline. And I need to know everything there is to know about the Windermere. So why not start here? "Yes, please."

Instead of going up, we go down to the basement. I follow dutifully as he takes me to the laundry room, which is clean, well-lit and a modern finished area within the large concrete and exposed pipes basement labyrinth.

"Most of the apartments have washers and dryers now, but the machines down here are new and state-of-the-art," Abi explains. It's true that everything gleams, white and clean, the look of having been barely used.

As we're leaving the laundry area, I notice something I haven't before. In the far corner of the room, mounted on the ceiling, there's a half dome with a blinking red light.

"What's that?" I ask Abi.

"Oh, that's the security camera," he answers. "The doorman on duty monitors the basement, the roof, the hallways, the elevator, the alley out back, the back staircase. For safety, of course."

How had I never noticed that before? Just a few months ago, Chad and I tiptoed up the stairs to the roof to make love beneath the stars and the city lights. Was Abi on duty? Did he see us? The thought makes me flush. I glance up at him, but his expression is unreadable.

As we move through the rest of the basement, I start to notice the half domes everywhere. That must be a new feature, since the cameras, too, look modern and state-of-the-art.

Abi shows me the furnace room, the hot water heater, the electrical boxes—all the innards of the building.

The Windermere, like many old New York buildings, doesn't have central air; rooms are cooled inefficiently by window units, heating by clanky radiators. Ivan said that the board priced out the prospect of installing central air, but the residents again voted against the huge assessment that would have been required to convert the old building. In summer sometimes the apartment is sweltering, but we'll live with it.

Abi and I snake through the labyrinthian hallways of the basement until we get to a row of metal cages, maybe ten by ten.

"These are the storage units for each apartment," says Abi. "Maybe you've been down here?"

I shake my head. I don't remember Ivan mentioning a storage unit and I've never ventured past the laundry room into the dark of the basement.

Most of the cages are packed to the rafters with all manner of items—bicycles and filing cabinets, old furniture and stacked boxes, skis, easels, a drum kit, shelves of books. I recognize some of the names—Donofrio, a heart surgeon and his wife; Stuart, a painter of some note, his work displayed in galleries around the world; Adamo, the lawyer; Abeling; O'Malley, the medium who I have yet to meet—she's high on my list of people to connect with; Campbell, the professor. It's a diverse group, all nationalities, mostly creatives and professionals. I think we fit in here—the writer and the actor. Surely, we'll be the youngest by a decade, the least established. Maybe it will be good to be surrounded by people who are successful in their chosen profession. It will rub off on us.

"Did Ivan have one?"

"Of course," Abi answers, motioning for me to follow. "Your husband has been down here a number of times."

"Has he?"

"Ivan's daughter, Miss Dana, sought access yesterday, but I couldn't allow it. She was—quite irate."

Interesting.

"What was she looking for?"

Abi's dark, heavy brow wrinkles. "I'm not sure. I told her to connect with you or Mr. Lowan. Did she not?"

"We saw her, but we didn't discuss the storage unit. She's angry with us, that Ivan left us the apartment. Don't take it personally."

Abi smiles at that. "In my line of work, you learn to never take anything personally."

I wonder what that means.

"The owners," I say. "Do they treat you well?"

"Generally, yes," he says vaguely. Strangely, he glances up at one of the cameras and doesn't go on. I nod, sensing that I shouldn't press further.

We've come to stand in front of the storage unit, which unlike the others, is meticulously organized. Just boxes lined on metal shelves, each labeled by year or by place. I scan the boxes—Berlin, Paris, London, Iran, Afghanistan, Belarus. I notice right away that a box is gone, a blank space in the neat rows like a missing tooth.

"There's one missing."

"So there is," says Abi, not offering more.

Did Chad take it? Is it up in the apartment somewhere?

I hunt through my tote and fish out my new ring of keys. One of the smaller mystery keys fits right into the lock with a satisfying click.

"I might take some time down here if it's okay."

"Of course," says Abi. "Let me know when I can finish your tour."

A red blinking light catches my eye again. "Those cameras. Who monitors the video feed?" He's already told me—but it's the journalist's way. Ask the question again to see if the answer is the same.

"The doormen," says Abi. "There are monitors in the office behind the desk on the ground floor. It's just for security, of course, to make sure all of our residents are safe."

"Of course," I say. "Are the feeds recorded?"

Is there a flicker of hesitation? "No, Ms. Lowan. No recording."

I let myself into the storage unit, and Abi leaves so quietly that it's a moment before I notice that he's gone and I'm all alone.

It feels like an invasion of privacy to start lifting lids on the mottled boxes—portfolios and loose photographs, books of negatives, journals. But what difference does it make now that Ivan's gone? Besides, we cleaned out his entire apartment—donating things like books and clothes, pots and pans, keeping a box of correspondence and photographs, journals, things we thought Dana might want. Ivan was a minimalist. He wanted little when he lived and had almost nothing of any material value when he died.

A shuffling noise behind me catches my attention, but when I turn there's nothing. The unblinking eye of the camera stares back at me.

Is it odd that Chad didn't mention the storage space? I wonder, as I sift through the boxes. He's notoriously absent-minded. It's not out of the realm of possibility that he simply forgot. And yet, he's been here multiple times, according to Abi. Why?

When I come to the empty space for the missing box, I stand staring. A rectangle of black dust had gathered around the box that used to be there, the space where it sat clean and gray. I feel a tingling curiosity to know what box is missing, where it is. I stand a minute, staring in frustration, as if I might will the box back to its rightful place, then finally moving on.

I slide off the lid with Dana's name on it, and see that there is a letter to her, sealed, on top. I move it aside and sift through a collection of pictures that must be Dana as a child—fair skinned and strawberry blonde, laughing, on a bike, on horseback, running joyfully through what looks like the Tuileries in Paris. Graduation, her wedding announcement, some articles about her work as a photographer—art and fashion in her case. I think she'd want to know that he'd kept all of this.

Chad doesn't seem in the least concerned about Dana's loss. But it's nagging at me. I decide to call her and offer her this olive branch. This idea is easing my guilty conscience some when the lights go out and I'm plunged into total darkness.

"Abi?" I call out, fumbling for my phone, finally finding it. The flashlight feature is no competition for the darkness and shadows all around me. The blackness seems to swallow the meager beam.

Power outage? No, I still see the blinking red light of the camera.

"Abi?" I call again. Is there audio surveillance, too?

"Ms. Lowan, everything all right?" It's Abi's disembodied voice, coming from an unseen speaker.

"The lights went out."

"Oh, the circuit box. I'll be right down. Stay put."

So audio and visual surveillance. Good to know.

After sliding the box back, then shining the phone light in front of me, I leave the storage unit and lock it behind me.

A noise from behind causes me to spin. I expect to see Abi.

But instead, the beam of my flashlight catches a small, slim figure slipping around the corner.

"Hello?" I call, following. "Hello?"

Ahead of me, there is the light pattering of footsteps. But every corner I turn, there's nothing, just blackness that dissipates in the beam of my light. My heart starts to thump.

When we were little, I used to chase Sarah into the woods, where she would hide until I found her. She was impossibly fast and could make herself invisible, snuggling into the crooks of trees, crouching behind rocks. She was like a fairy or an elf, one with the forest, where I always felt like an interloper crashing and tripping, getting whipped by branches.

Around the next corner there's a crouched form. I almost say her name. *Sarah.* It's not Sarah, of course, but a little boy, in a smart school uniform, crisp white shirt and black leather shoes. He's on the ground, his arms wrapped around his legs, resting his forehead on his knees. I can see the rise and fall of his breath. The blond of his hair glints in the light from my phone.

He must be scared, maybe playing in the basement when the lights went out.

"Hey," I say. I didn't think there were any children in this building. Must be a visiting grandchild. He could have come down the service elevator or the stairs. "It's okay. The lights will come back on and Abi's on his way."

I move in closer, reach out a hand to gently touch his back, but as I do, he turns. I reel back in horror.

His eyes are gouged out, and his throat is a hideous blue-black. He opens his mouth wide and it's a maw, its darkness swirling and endless. He issues a horrible shriek that electrifies every nerve ending in my body.

I back up into the concrete wall, hitting my head hard against an exposed pipe. My own scream is an echo of his. He moves closer, closer, and I turn to run from him.

But the lights come on as suddenly as they went off, and I run right straight into Abi, who comes fast around the corner looking as scared as I feel.

"Ms. Lowan," he says. "Are you hurt? You were screaming."

"There's a boy," I say.

But I spin and there's nothing there. "He was right here."

I follow the path of the blood that must be dripping from my own head. But the hallway dead ends at the laundry room—which in the light, looks about as crisp and white and unscary as a place can look.

I put a hand to the side of my head. When I draw my fingers back, they're wet with blood. More blood—the accident, my period, my sister's warning of a monster drinking from my jugular.

"There was a boy," I say again.

"There are no children in this building, Ms. Lowan. Not anymore."

"Someone's grandchild?"

"No, no one visiting at the moment."

Abi's face is a mask of concern. "Let me help," he says. "Please.

THE NEW COUPLE IN 5B • 49

You must have just given yourself a fright in the dark. I promise you there's no one down here."

I know what I saw. "Abi," I say more firmly, "there was a boy. I saw him."

"Let me take you to the Aldridges' and I'll go back to check," he says with a nod. Is there the slightest tone of condescension?

We get into the waiting elevator and take it up to the semi-private foyer of apartments 5A and 5B, which is shared with next-door neighbors, Ella and Charles Aldridge. She is an heiress, he a retired architect, an urbane, art-loving, world-traveling couple in their seventies. We've grown quite close to them; they were a big support when Ivan was sick.

I am about to protest that we don't need to bother them, that maybe there are bandages in Ivan's—in *my*—apartment. But Abi rings the bell and Ella comes to the door, all dressed in black— a narrow tunic and flowing pants.

"What's happened?" she asks, as if already sensing something wrong. A glance at my head. "Oh, my goodness."

She ushers me inside and Abi says to call if he's needed, that he's off to inspect the basement and try to find out why the lights went out, then disappears behind the elevator doors. Probably glad to escape the drama.

Soon, Ella's tending to the cut on my head as I sit helpless and embarrassed at her dining room table.

Their apartment; it's aspirational. Every object, every stunning work of art, each elegant piece of furniture, chosen, curated, designed. I think of our East Village place, nice enough, but just a step above college-student chic. We have champagne tastes, Chad always quips, and a wine cooler budget.

"Not as bad as it looks," she says, wiping away the blood with a cloth.

I'm still shaking, wondering if Abi will come back and tell us what he found in the basement. "Ella, I saw a boy."

She keeps her eyes on my wound, puts some Neosporin on it.

"For goodness' sake those stupid basement lights. It's like a horror movie down there when they go out. Something—I keep telling Charles and the board—must be done. No wonder you got spooked."

Expertly, she butterflies what turns out to be just a small cut at my hairline—though it is tender to the touch.

"Is there a boy in the building?" I press.

Abi has already told me there isn't. But maybe he's wrong.

"Not to my knowledge, dear." She's so close I can smell the clean scent of soap on her skin. "There," she says. "You're all fixed up."

She bustles off and then returns with a glass of water, which I drink, grateful for the coolness of it, the comfort. The city noise from five stories below is faint through the thick windows.

"Between Ivan passing, all the stress you two are under with work, I'm not surprised that your eyes are playing tricks on you," she says.

I bristle at this. Our eyes don't play tricks on us, do they? Unless we're mentally ill, unstable. If this had happened to Chad, would anyone imply that he hadn't seen what was right in front of him? I think to argue, but the truth is that when the lights came up there *wasn't* anyone in the basement. Just me. And Abi.

So then, what *did* I see?

"I hope you don't mind," says Ella now with a smile. She folds long, elegant fingers together. "I bumped into Chad this morning and he shared the good news. We're over the moon that you two are moving in. And I promise we won't be your nosy, meddling, elderly neighbors."

I return the smile. "And we won't be the raucous, party-all-night newlyweds."

We both share a laugh, and she leans in to give me a hug—she's thin, frail, where Charles is enormous, a powerhouse who exercises daily, beats Chad at racquet ball with embarrassing frequency and seems twenty years younger than he is.

I rise, thanking her for taking care of me as she escorts me toward the front door.

"I'm an idiot," I say, peering into the mirror in her foyer. The cut is so tiny; how could there have been so much blood? "I'm so sorry."

"Don't be silly," she says, tucking an errant strand of her snow-white bob behind her ear. "You two have been through a lot. And that's what friends are for. I hope you'll always come to us. For anything."

I give her another quick hug, grateful for her friendship.

When she closes the door, I take a moment, breathe deeply, before sliding my key into the lock and turning it. I've been here so many times. But this is the first time it's mine—ours.

I step inside and it's all white, empty of furniture, the gorgeous wood floors gleaming, the crown molding, the tall windows that let in expansive views of the city. I wander into the kitchen, which needs updating and won't get it for a while. The kitchen ends in a back door that leads to the service hall and elevator, where we'll take out our trash.

Finally, I go into the room that will be our bedroom, maybe where we'll conceive our first child? I am aware suddenly of a deep wanting for this place to be our home, where we start our family. It feels stable, solid, a space where we can build the life we want.

It feels like ours already.

When I walk into the second bedroom, I stand at the door and issue a little gasp.

By the window, there's a white parson's desk, and a too-expensive ergonomic chair. On the desk is a simple glass vase of pink sweetheart roses.

My husband.

He snuck out and came up here to set up this writing space for me. He knew I would come here today and find it. That's how well he knows me. My heart swells with love and gratitude.

And next to the desk is a box I recognize as being like the ones in the storage unit. The missing box. It must be.

Scribbled on the outside in Ivan's scrawling hand: The Windermere.

Walking over to the desk, I can barely allow myself to believe that this beautiful place will be mine to write my book. On the gleaming white surface, there's a note from Chad.

Welcome home, my love. I feel a rush of emotion and tears well.

But curiosity soon overwhelms sentimentality. I drop to my knees and lift off the lid of the box. The first thing I see is the *New York Journal* article about the people who lived in this apartment before Ivan. Paul and Willa Winter, the young novelist and his Broadway dancer wife. As I start to read, the present moment disappears.

four

Willa
1963

I wait until his breath is heavy and deep. My husband is a sound sleeper. Once he has drifted off, it's difficult to rouse him.

It's a joke between us that the building could burn to the ground, and he'd find himself among the ashes in the morning. I watch his profile against the dim light coming in from the window, touch a tender hand to his cheek. The ticking Westclox Big Ben alarm clock on the bedside table glows, telling me that it's late, nearly midnight. The warm air drifts in from the slightly open window. The city, its music, calls to me.

I'm the restless one, the one who can't settle. I have trouble with sleep. It doesn't always come for me.

"I'm sorry," I whisper. He stirs, turns on his side and issues a soft snore. I *am* sorry.

But still, I slip from bed, naked from our lovemaking. I wash in the small bathroom, slip into my shimmery black dress and kitten heels, grab some money from his wallet on the dresser and go out the back door, taking the service elevator to the street.

I never dreamed that I would be an unfaithful wife.

Especially not to such a kind and loving husband.

But here I am, scurrying up Park Avenue, like a teenager sneaking out of her parents' house.

The spring air is warm, and people are out, strolling, laughing. They've been to bars and clubs, restaurants. They're walking arm in arm. Someone's singing, out of tune but having fun. New York City. Every dancer's dream, the place we all come to reach for stardom. So few of us find exactly what we were looking for when we were young, told by our small-town teachers and well-meaning parents that we had talent. We *may have* had something that others didn't, back in the sticks where people were dull and so few had that creative spark inside.

But here, everyone who made it this far has that something special—a big talent, voracious ambition. Here, you compete with the best. And it's brutal.

My ankle aches as I turn onto Thirtieth Street, this street quieter than the avenue, darker.

At the door to the Delmar Hotel, I hesitate, remember Paul as I left him, sleeping soundly, faithful, content in our life. I look back down the path I've taken, so easy just to turn around. But I don't go home; I let the bellman swing the door wide, follow the sweep of his hand, nod at his *good evening, miss.*

A jazz piano in the corner fills the room with an unfamiliar but lighthearted tune, the young singer's voice smoky and full of secret laughter.

He's waiting at the bar. I see him right away, though the room is only dimly lit by candles on bistro tables.

You are the one for me, the singer croons. *There's no one else.*

Again, before the man I've come to meet sees me, I almost turn and go back to my husband. Paul will never even know I was gone. And if he did, I could just say I slipped out for cigarettes, and he'll be glad for it because he wanted a smoke after dinner, and we were out. It's not too late to be the wife I wanted to be.

Paul, my husband. I love him. I *do.*

It's just that he wants to stay in always, and I want—no, I *need*—to go out. I want to move my body on stage, or anywhere, the music pulsing, desiring eyes on me. He's quiet, a writer, always thinking about the stories in his head. And me, I don't come alive until I'm out in the world—talking, laughing, drinking, dancing. He wants to sit by the fire, like we're old and gray. But the city—with its nightclubs and bars, its stages and bright lights, fancy restaurants and glittering people—it calls to me, especially when the sun goes down.

I want to devour this place, this life. And he wants to watch it from the windows of our safe and lovely home.

My dreams. They're slowly fading. It's not much of a surprise. I've always known that I am a good dancer but not a great one. My beauty is an asset, but my bust is too big, my legs too thick.

My last role was as a burlesque dancer, part of the chorus in a small off-Broadway play; it got good reviews, had a solid run, but it has closed. I have a few auditions this week—a dancing part in a commercial and another chorus spot in a much bigger play—but my ankle is sore and I'm not getting any younger.

Back at home, they think I'm a star. But the truth is that I'm just one of a million young dancers not quite good enough to be the very best. Because here, that's what you *must* be to be anything at all.

I was in despair when my last show closed, part of me feeling—knowing—that this was the end, my last chance to be seen, discovered. But then on that last night I saw *him* in the audience. A familiar face but someone who's always just been on the edge of life.

I've never met anyone like him; his olive skin and his deep dark eyes, his exotic accent, and mysterious gaze. That night he was waiting for me backstage.

You are the most beautiful woman I have ever seen, he said as I approached him.

That's all we want to hear, those of us reaching for the stars and falling, falling, falling instead.

And Paul, it should be said, was not there. He was on deadline, couldn't get away. Even though he must have known I needed the support that night.

But the page always comes first.

Don't leave me. Please stay, the jazz singer begs now.

I should go.

I will go home to the husband who loves me, who provides for me and who truthfully has been in the audience of nearly every performance, cheering the loudest and looking at me with eyes full of adoration.

I am about to go home when he turns, and his gaze hooks me. His smile, easy and knowing, is like a rope around me, tugging me across the floor to him.

"You are stunning," he whispers when I'm beside him.

Not an hour ago I was in the arms of my husband, and now I let this stranger put my fingers to his lips.

My mother had a word for girls like me.

You're always looking for something just out of reach, Willa. But everything you need is right here. She was right; I *am* always looking for something. I am not sure what. But I know I haven't found it yet. Maybe tonight.

"Let's paint the town," he says. His voice is hypnotic. His arm snakes around my waist.

"Yes," I say, hearing the city night calling. "Let's."

five

Max is waiting for me on the street outside the theater on Lafayette.

A light drizzle falls, coating the sidewalk, cars, umbrellas, in a glassy sheen. My head is pounding from the cut on my forehead, and I'm still reeling from the basement encounter, the romantic gesture from my husband.

Max leans against the building holding his umbrella in one hand, staring at his phone in the other. He pockets his cell as I approach, face brightening. I'm washed with a kind of relief—for the safety and comfort of his enduring friendship.

"Hey, you're late," he says, taking me into a warm embrace. "I was starting to worry."

Max is my date for all of Chad's opening night performances. He's the calming influence I always need. When Chad goes on stage, I'm more nervous for him than he is for himself, which is not helpful and something I keep from him.

"Busy day," I say, trying for a smile.

He gives me a frown but doesn't push, stows his umbrella. We go to the will-call window and grab our front-row tickets, and then bypass the crowd gathering outside.

The warmth and light of the theater, the murmur of the crowd, is a welcome contrast to the wet, chilly night outside. There's that buzz of excitement that always precedes a performance. The energy of anticipation; it's electric.

"So," Max says as we take our seats, shift off our coats. "I have some good news."

I feel a little jolt of excitement. "Oh?"

He goes on, "Everyone loved your proposal, Rosie. Your changes were spectacular—the Windermere, wow, what a scary place."

The encounter in the basement comes back to me. I put my hand to my head; it's still tender.

"Rosie?" says Max. He takes off his glasses, puts a hand on my arm.

"More good news," I say, my voice sounding falsely bright to my own ears. "Uncle Ivan left us his apartment. We're actually moving in at the end of the week."

His reaction is not what I expected. He freezes for a second, and then looks stricken. Kind of like he looked when I told him I was marrying Chad. *Wait, you're* marrying *him? I thought it was just a fling.*

And I thought you'd be happy for me, I'd said then, wounded. To be truthful, I never imagined that he'd be overjoyed that I was marrying Chad. There's always been an undercurrent between Max and me. So while I didn't think he'd be *happy,* much in the way I wasn't exactly thrilled when he was seeing someone, I hoped he'd at least be friend enough to fake it.

I am. It's just—Chad. He's kind of a player, isn't he?

What is that supposed to mean? You don't even know him.

We didn't talk for a couple of days after that, but in the end our friendship was too important to each of us to let it drift. He apologized, celebrated with us at our wedding and has never said another bad word about my husband.

The small orchestra starts tuning, that thrilling flutter of winds and strings. I have butterflies in my stomach for Chad, but Max's face gone pale is a distraction.

"You're moving *into* the Windermere?" he says.

"We inherited Ivan's apartment," I say, keeping my voice low, my eyes on him. "So, yeah. I mean, this is a once in a lifetime opportunity."

"You could sell it," he says. "It's probably worth a fortune."

I'm surprised at a powerful rise of resistance, even though of course we've discussed and considered it as anyone would. "I— *we*—don't *want* to sell it."

"But Rosie, its history," he says, worry etching around his eyes. "All those murders. Those suicides."

I push out a laugh, annoyed now, disappointed in his reaction. "I thought you didn't believe in ghost stories."

"I don't," he says. "But I believe in energy—good and bad. The Windermere has—a dark past."

Another flash on the incident in the basement—what happened, really? The lights went out; I panicked; saw something that wasn't there. Right?

"That's irrational," I say, partially to myself. "Bad things happen everywhere. Especially in this city. Is the sidewalk out in front of the restaurant cursed now because we saw an accident there?"

He seems to consider this, looks down at his Playbill.

"I thought you'd be happy for us," I say when he says nothing.

I can tell he hears the echo of our last friendship-threatening conversation about my life choices. Max presses his mouth closed, as if he's physically trying to shut himself up.

"I am," he says with a hand on my arm and an apology in his eyes. "Of course I am."

He laughs a little. "See," he says, pulling me in and giving me a squeeze around the shoulders. "That's how good your proposal was. You scared the bejeezus out of a nonbeliever like me."

An awkward silence swells between us. I look around the buzzing theater. It's packed, with the usual eclectic mix of Manhattan artsy types, young and old, swanky and grungy, tattooed, pierced, bejeweled. My eyes fall on a woman in the front row across the aisle, her eyes heavily ringed in dark shadow, her bare arms sinewy thin, wrists bangled in silver, clad in a slim black tunic. She's staring at me. I offer her a smile, but she just watches me another moment, then turns back toward the stage. She reminds me of someone. Do I know her?

"Hey," says Max, drawing my attention back. "I'm *sorry*. I'm happy for you. Truly. I can't wait to hang out in your haunted apartment."

I give him a look, but then we both start to laugh.

He's right. The proposal—it *is* dark. Truthfully, I'm not certain that I would have chosen to live at the Windermere, either. But that's life, right? A twisting helix of choice and chance. Sometimes you choose, but only within the constructs of your current situation. Anyway, it's short-term. I'll write my book, and after a while we'll sell, make a fortune and then move out to the burbs to raise a family like everyone else.

And—p.s.—despite my upbringing, I'm with Ivan. I don't believe in ghosts.

The houselights go down and the music solidifies. The curtain draws back, and the play begins. It's thrilling—the darkness of the theater, and the wild production of *Macbeth*—alive with gorgeous costumes, the quirky but excellent and original score, the talent of the actors. In a pre-opening review, *The Stage* had called it "a fresh, exciting and darkly funny rendering of a Shakespearean classic." And so it is.

I get more tense as we approach Act One, Scene Four, where Chad plays Third Witch.

Finally, it's time.

Thunder reverberates through the theater, and everything goes black.

When a spotlight comes up center stage, there's a huge cauldron glowing green from within. The three witches enter, two from stage left, one—Chad!—from stage right. He's unrecognizable in his hooded robe, hooked nose and monstrous makeup.

The theater is small, and Max and I are right on the edge of the stage. I'm so close, I can hear the hems of the actors' costumes brushing the floor, see the lighting apparatus behind the cauldron.

Thrice the brinded cat hath mew'd.

Thrice and once the hedge-pig whined.

Harpier cries 'tis time, 'tis time.

Chad delivers his line perfectly and I suppress the urge to cheer. I search the hunched figure for signs of my husband, but he is transformed. A monster, a ghoul.

Smoke crawls eerily across the stage. Chad mentioned that they were having issues with the smoke machine, but it seems to be working, filling the stage, fog coming to our feet. The creeping smoke morphs from white to blood-red. As it does, an uncomfortable heat crawls up my neck into my cheeks.

The witches keep chanting.

Round about the cauldron go: In the poison'd entrails throw—

Sweat comes up on my forehead, and I shift away from Max, who is like a furnace giving off heat.

Double, double toil and trouble; fire burn and cauldron bubble.

Suddenly, I can't get a lungful of air, my throat constricting, my breath growing ragged.

The witches keep chanting.

Calm down. I know what this is. It hasn't happened in years. I do what my therapist tells me to do, count backward from ten, ground myself in the moment. Breathe. I hear myself start to wheeze, drawing a look from Max.

"Rosie?" he whispers.

He's seen this before. Once on the subway, once at a crowded publishing event. Please, not now.

As if through glass, I hear Chad's voice.

Adders fork and blind-worm's sting. Lizard's leg and owlet's wing.

I look up and he seems to be pinning me with his strange gaze. The smoke is making its way through the whole theater like a thick fog. A sickly sweet and acrid smell fills my nose, my mouth.

I look away from Chad. The woman from across the aisle is staring at me again, this time with a ghoulish smile. Who is she?

I can't breathe. At all.

Oh, God.

Finger of a birth-strangled babe, Ditch-delivered by a drab, make the gruel thick and slab.

Panic sets in hard. I grab for Max, who grips my hand.

When Hecate enters, the audience gasps. She's hideous, with a giant nose and straggling black hair, taller than the other witches, her face a mask of sagging flesh covered with warts.

Oh, well done! I commend your pains. And every one shall share in the gains.

I'm gasping, the room around me fading to gray. Then I'm on my feet, Max shuttling me toward the door.

A cackling voice, impossibly loud, follows us out the door.

By the pricking of my thumbs, something wicked this way comes.

Out on the street, I lean against the building, struggling for air, to hold on to my consciousness. Max leaves me to get water but comes back quickly with a bottle, cracks it open.

It's not just me; other people have left the theater, too. I see a young man breathing off an inhaler. Another woman coughing uncontrollably. I look around for the strange woman from the theater, having the unexplainable feeling that she followed us out. But she's nowhere to be seen.

"I think it was the smoke machine," says Max.

It wasn't. Not for me. I had a panic attack. I can count all the things that might have brought it on. Ivan's death. Our money worries. Dana's visit. The apartment. The call from my sister. The incident in the basement of the Windermere. All moments, as my therapist and I have identified, when I've felt out of control, at the mercy of things larger than myself, powerless, helpless.

Chad comes rushing out the side door, still in costume, his makeup still terrifying.

"Rosie," he says, coming right to me.

"I'm so sorry," I say, looking past his wrinkles and warts, right to his eyes. "You were amazing."

"Was it a panic attack?" he asks, pulling me tight to his body. I take in the familiar scent of him.

"Or the smoke machine?" I offer, embarrassed to have my issues be ruining his night. "I couldn't breathe."

My airways are opening, fear has passed, leaving my hands still slightly shaking, adrenaline still pulsing.

He pulls back to put a hand on each cheek, his gaze searching. "You're under too much stress, Rosie. This happens when we're not looking out for you."

"I'm okay," I say, eager for it to be so. "The desk, the box, the flowers...thank you."

"Ah, you found it," he says, pleased.

His fingers lace through mine. Everything around us disappears. It's only us.

"I saw it, Rosie," he whispers, leaning in close. "The pregnancy test in the wastepaper basket."

I shake my head—sadness, embarrassment, welling. His eyes search mine with love, compassion.

"It *will* happen, Rosie," he says. "I promise. When it's our time, it will just happen."

I nod, wanting to believe him, glad not to have to hide it from him.

"Remember," he whispers. "I care about one thing in this world. You."

We press our foreheads together, the rubbery nose of his horrible mask rubbing against my cheek. Finally, reluctantly, he pulls away.

After he disappears back inside, I take a few minutes to pull myself together.

"Let me guess," says Max, who knows me too well. "You skipped lunch."

He magically produces a bag of nuts from his pocket, and I gratefully scarf them down and drink the water as we walk back inside. The usher lets us in between scenes.

When we take our seats again, I look across the aisle to find with relief that the woman is gone, her seat empty.

I barely see the rest of the play, so lost am I in the chaos of my thoughts.

six

It's moving day.

The bright morning is fresh and cool in the way of new beginnings. But I am groggy with lack of sleep, and Chad's chipper mood is not doing anything to improve mine.

I seal the final box and look around the empty space, the scuffed wood floors, the big windows. It was the first place that belonged to me alone until Chad moved in. I've been happy here. *We* have. I'm sad to say goodbye to the life we lived within these walls, on this slanted floor.

Chad's banging around in the bedroom, humming one of the songs from his play. My head is aching and I'm trying not to be cranky.

The truth is that instead of being excited about the move, and thrilled that Max has made a big offer on the new book— bigger than I expected—I've been tense, sleepless. When sleep does come, I've been having nightmares.

I chase the boy from the basement through a labyrinth. I know it's my job to save him, but he keeps slipping around corners, a wraith, laughing.

Chad in his witch costume, holds me down, his grip like a vise, his fingers sharp and hard as claws. He sinks his teeth into my neck and drinks my blood, while the strange woman from the theater watches with that ghoulish grin.

I know it's partially Sarah's call that's to blame. I wish I could say that her prophetic dreams came out of nowhere, that she was unstable or prone to delusions. But this is my family. Sarah, like my grandmother before her, was what my father called a dreamer, the visions she had while she slept very often coming to pass.

In the town where I grew up, my father was known as Preacher. He delivered his fiery sermons in the barn behind our house—his own brand of religion, cherry-picking from all the grand traditions. He spoke in tongues—total gibberish I would later learn as I started to study languages. And people from all over the county brought their sick for my father's healing touch.

Holy Spirit, help us! he'd yell after whispering to the demons that were tormenting the ill. The congregation would respond in kind. And it would go back and forth, back and forth, a strange echo until my father moved on to the next.

I've traveled far in every way possible from my childhood hell, but it's still with me. Since my sister's call, I'm pulled back into that time, that little-girl self where I didn't know what was real and what was lies. Now I keep hearing Sarah's small, frightened voice on the phone, her words.

I'm angry—at my family, at myself. I've moved away from that town, my father and his nonsense. I've traveled and educated myself out of my childish beliefs. Why does it still cling?

Chad has suggested gently that I go back on the sleeping pills I used to take when we first met. But so far, I've refused. I don't want to go back to that crutch. And besides, there's something about the medication that has me mentally dull during the day, making the work of writing and researching feel like dragging a boulder behind me up a hill. Writing a book is struggle enough; I don't need the extra weight.

One last look around the empty space, then I wander over to the window to see the yoga mom feeding her baby in his high chair. I'm going to miss them, as well as the painter, and the young office girls. They're strangers, of course, but a familiar feature of every day. Our views from apartment 5B are expansive—downtown out the south-facing windows from our bedroom, uptown and the gleaming Chrysler Building to the north. We can watch the sun go down from the dining room, which looks west.

It seems like too much of a luxury. But I've done the math. With what we have, including the deposit, which I still haven't asked Chad about, his earnings from the theater, my advance, which should come soon, though publishers notoriously are glacially slow to pay, we can swing it. For a while. Chad didn't get the commercial he'd auditioned for, but I know he'll get something soon. I can feel it.

Chad comes up to hug me from behind. "This was our first place together," he says, surprising me by sounding sentimental now when for the past three weeks he's been singing about how *we're moving on up*, channeling his favorite '80s sitcom. "I carried you over the threshold after our wedding."

"And the bathroom ceiling leaks," I remind him, and myself, because I'm feeling sentimental, too. "And the floor slants. And don't forget about the mice."

"Still," he says, spinning me around. "I've loved it here—with you."

"We could stay," I say, only half kidding.

"Hell, no," he says, leaning back. "Your castle awaits, my princess."

A monster in a castle, drinking your blood.

Stop it.

"What?" he says, laughing, I guess, at my expression, which he says sometimes goes dark. "What are you thinking?"

"Nothing," I say. "Just a lot of work ahead today."

"Today is the first day of the rest of our lives," he says with a dramatic sweep of his arm. He's the king of the well-placed cliché. But he's right. It feels momentous.

"Is that everything, miss?" a mover asks me. The guys from Two Hunks and a Truck are, as billed, quite hunky and as muscle-bound as would be required to do this job.

"I think so," I answer. I release a sigh. "Yes, that's it. Thank you."

Item by item, they've expertly navigated our meager belongings down five flights of stairs. And now it's all gone. It strikes me that if something happens to that truck on the way uptown, we won't own a single thing except the empty apartment and the clothes on our backs.

Abi is expecting them on the other side, has the service elevator ready and waiting.

When Chad joins me in the living room, he holds a little purple fabric pouch in his hand. It's dusty, tied with twine, a small tawny feather dangling from the end.

I suppress the urge to knock it from his hand.

"What's this?" he asks.

I'm embarrassed but I tell him the truth. "It's a charm my grandmother sent to protect me from—"

His hazel eyes are full of love, curiosity. I feel my cheeks burn. "From?"

"From evil."

I practically choke on the word because it's silly, isn't it? There's no such thing as spiritual evil. No pouch of herbs or stones can protect us from the real dangers of this world.

Chad glances back and forth between me and the pouch, then he shrugs his broad shoulders. "Well, we can use all the help we can get."

I don't tell him that it's useless now that he's touched it, moved it from its place over the door. It came in the mail, and I handled it very carefully as my grandmother's note instructed. I never opened it, because you're not supposed to. It's my grandmother's charm, her energy and magic, not to be meddled with. I don't say any of that because that's just more silliness.

"True," I say. "Here, I'll put it in my bag."

He hands it over and I drop it in my tote next to my laptop. It jingles softly. I should just throw it in the trash.

"It holds on, doesn't it?" he says.

I nod. He puts a cool hand to the back of my neck. Chad was raised Catholic, but he's lapsed, both his parents gone in a car wreck while he was finishing high school. He still crosses himself when something bad happens to someone, runs into churches we pass to light candles for his parents. We can try to escape what we come from, but it stays with us in all sorts of ways.

"Let it all go, Rosie," he says, bright, hopeful. "It's a new day for us. Can't you feel it?"

He's been a bit down about the commercial, but he has a big audition tomorrow, this one for the lead in a television series.

I'm about to agree but he moves in fast and sweeps me off my feet. I am laughing and shrieking as he carries me out the door.

He does it again at the threshold of the new place, earning whoops of delight from Ella, Charles and Abi, who have all gathered to welcome us.

"You were never romantic like that," Ella teases Charles, watching from our shared foyer on the fifth floor.

"I was!" Charles says, his voice gravelly, his German accent light from so many years in the States. "I *am*, my love."

He's elegant in a cashmere sweater and pressed wool pants, white hair slicked back dramatically. Tall, powerful.

"Let's leave these two to get settled," he says. "And I'll *show* you how romantic I can be."

I hear her giggling like a much younger woman as the door

closes behind them. Abi, who has ushered us up, says his good-byes, as well, and disappears into the elevator.

"We're home," Chad says when we're alone, putting me down on the shining wood floor of the small foyer.

The natural sunlight is bright and streaming in through the big windows. The hunks have not yet arrived, though they left before we did, so everything is white and new—a blank canvas, an empty page—full of endless possibilities.

I allow myself a rush of joy.

The rest of the day passes in a blur—the hunks arriving and hauling our stuff up in the service elevator, in through the back door, through the kitchen.

Ella and Charles come by around noon with a picnic basket of sandwiches and wave off our offer for them to stay, saying we need the day to ourselves to settle in but come by for a quick welcome cocktail tonight.

"Come as you are!" Ella is stylish in her black jumpsuit and pointy flats. "Do not dress up."

When the movers place the couch, it's perfect for the room. It had been way too big for our place, dominating the space and making it impossible for us to have end tables or shelves.

It's aspirational, Chad used to say. *It's for the apartment we wish we had.*

Well, here we are.

The hunks assemble the bed, flop the mattress on top, lug the dresser in, careful not to nick the newly painted walls or chip those original wood floors.

The only thing we've kept of Ivan's is the dining room table he said had been there from the previous owners. It was, according to Ivan, custom built for the narrow space, which is little more than a passage from the kitchen to the living room but has big windows and an elegant metal chandelier.

"I'm glad we kept this," I say.

Chad puts a palm on the wood, and I do the same. "He liked

it because it was solid, handcrafted, designed to last a lifetime or more," he says. "A piece to be handed down."

I notice for the first time a chip out of the wood at the head of the table. It's a deep gouge that looks as if it has been sanded down and stained over. The flaw only adds to its character. I walk over and put a finger on it.

For some reason, Dana's words ring back to me. *You know what my father gave me in this life? Nothing.* But Ivan gave *us* this apartment. This beautifully made table, I think with a twist of guilt.

When Chad goes to help the hunks in the kitchen, I take the pouch out of my purse, and am happy to find that the ledge above the front door is wide enough to accommodate it. It's nonsense. Of course, it doesn't work. And there are no evil forces working against us in the world.

But Chad's right. We can use all the help we can get.

We tip the movers Bob and Steve generously and wave as the service elevator door closes and they disappear. Then we stand for a moment in the gray, dank hallway that we share with Ella and Charles. This is where we bring our garbage to be picked up by the super, where we come and go when the doorman is unavailable to operate the elevator. Residents pass through the mailroom downstairs to an identical concrete elevator lobby on the ground floor.

Chad wraps his arms around himself, looks around. He peers around the corner and I follow. Charles and Ella's door is closed. "It's cold in here," he says. "Creepy."

"There's a terrible draft." Air moving through the elevator shaft, vents, creates a soft howling.

In the corner, up toward the ceiling, a blinking red light. Another security camera. I find myself staring into it a moment before I follow Chad into the kitchen and push the door shut, and lock it tight.

In the living room Chad takes me in his arms.

"Doesn't it feel like we've already lived here forever?" he asks, holding me.

"It does," I say.

We stay like that for a while, holding each other, swaying as if to music.

He's right. Even with all I know already about the building's dark history, the terrible things that have happened, it feels embracing, as if it's been waiting for us and we've finally come home.

seven

Thank goodness I ignore Ella's advice to *come as you are*—which would have had me in torn jeans, a Rolling Stones T-shirt and tattered Chuck Taylors.

Instead, I decided to shower, do my hair and slip into a simple black shift before we headed over to Ella and Charles's.

This is no casual-welcome-to-the-building gathering. There must be twenty extremely well-heeled people in their apartment when we arrive, only some of whom I've already met.

"Sorry, darling!" whispers Ella as she welcomes me, maybe clocking my surprise. "One thing led to another. And—everyone's so excited to have some fresh young faces in the building. You don't mind, do you?"

"Not at all," I lie. "It's lovely, thank you."

I feel rather than hear Chad issue a low groan behind me as Ella ushers us in. We're both exhausted. But when I turn, he's wearing his most charming smile.

"Our new neighbors," she announces. "Bestselling author Rosie Lowan."

I blush. That's not exactly true. The book did well but I'm not sure I'd call myself a *bestselling* author—though these monikers are all very vague. But I'm not going to correct Ella in a room of her guests, so I swallow my discomfort and smile.

"And Chad Lowan, critically acclaimed actor and soon-to-be movie star. Now you can say you knew them both when," effuses Ella. She's one of those effortless hostesses who knows how to make people feel good. She's managed to flatter both Chad and me, as well as all the discerning guests in the room.

There's a chorus of *welcome to the building*, and *so nice to meet you*, and *Ivan was such a lovely man, so sorry for your loss.*

Chad, who did *not* bother changing, still manages to look sexy—those straw-colored curls stylishly tousled, his plaid shirt pressing against biceps, pecs, faded jeans highlighting toned thighs. He works the room, shaking hands and flashing that girl-slaying grin at the women—who are all older than us by twenty years at least. Still, there are a lot of fluttering eyelashes.

Charles, tall and snowy haired, soft-spoken, takes me by the arm.

"Let me introduce you to a few people, dear."

Ogadinmah Mgbajah is a cardiothoracic surgeon from Ghana, a stocky, serious man, with wire-rimmed glasses, crisp oxford shirt and precisely pressed pants. He shakes my hand, his grip gentle but firm, skin very soft.

"Oga reaches into people and brings them back to life," says Charles. "Isn't that right, my friend?"

Oga laughs with a deep resonance that sounds like a bass drum, and his smile makes his serious face turn boyish. I envision him in an operating room, a patient open on the table in front of him, blood on his gloved hands. That laughter booming.

I shake off the image as Charles swings me over to a much older woman who is beautiful in the way of precious metals—cool, hard. She wears a stunning red wrap and must be nearly six feet. Hair dyed a wiry orange, eyes Freon green. Are those contacts? They must be.

"Anna is a sculptor born in Prague. Her work has been displayed in museums and galleries around the world."

He directs my attention to a piece lit from above, standing on a pedestal by one of their south-facing windows. It's a twisting piece of metalwork, a woman's torso shredded, no head, no arms. It gleams in the light, stunning, mesmerizing.

"We commissioned this from Anna many years ago. One of the best investments we've ever made."

It looks razor-sharp, as if it would cut deep if you lifted a finger to it.

"It's magnificent," I say. She's staring at me hard, like I'm an equation she's trying to solve. "You're so talented."

"And you," she says, her accent thick, voice throaty, "are so young."

"Well, I'm not as young as I look," I say, for lack of a wittier retort. She reaches out a twisted finger and touches my cheek.

"Just a baby."

It's not mean, but it *is* creepy, and I find myself taking a step back, which earns an enigmatic smile from the sculptor, like I've failed a test I've been given.

I look around for Chad, but he's surrounded by Ella and two other women, all of whom seem to be hanging on his every word. I'm used to this, how women react to Chad. How he plays to it, *laps it up*, really. If he gets more famous, it will get much worse, I'm sure. But it's okay. I know his heart. And it belongs to me alone.

"You're overwhelming her, Charles. Poor thing, she's probably wondering what she's gotten herself into."

I may have seen the speaker in the elevator once, the dark-haired, bearded man wearing a black blazer and gingham shirt, stylishly ripped jeans.

He offers his hand.

"Xavier Young," he says. "I'm the least interesting person here. Just a lowly anesthesiologist—no accolades or awards or fame at all. And, until you arrived, the youngest person in the building at forty-one."

His deep-set dark eyes are smiley and sad at the same time.

"Xavier is too modest," says Charles. "He just published an article in *The Lancet*, the magazine of the American Medical Association."

Xavier offers an assenting nod. "Sure, okay. There's that."

The door buzzer rings. More people?

"Charles and Ella are the most magnanimous people alive," Xavier says as Charles leaves us to answer.

"In addition to being the youngest before you arrived, I was the only one in the building to still be working for a living," Xavier continues. We talk about how he works at Mount Sinai, how he paid his way through school by working as an EMT. "I used to wake people up. Now I put them to sleep."

It seems like such an odd thing to say; it piques my curiosity.

"Do you miss it?" I ask. "The adrenaline of emergency work."

Again, I look around for Chad but now he, Ella and Charles all seem to have disappeared. Ella's mellifluous laughter carries from the kitchen.

"Honestly, I think I reached a kind of adrenal burnout. I stopped caring. After you bring a certain number of junkies back from the brink, you start to wonder—does everyone deserve this type of extreme saving? Or even want it?"

I am at a loss for words, but it makes a kind of dark sense. After seeing so much damage, you must start to desensitize, to preserve your own sanity. He's moved in too close. I take a step back.

"What do you think?" he asks, gently inquiring. "Do you believe everyone deserves to be saved?"

Are you saved? my father used to ask. *Have you accepted the Holy Spirit into your life and your heart?*

"I don't know. I hope so," I say. "Excuse me."

The room suddenly seems overwarm and I move down the long hallway past the gallery of Ella's watercolors. *They were inspired by the Rorschach tests*, she told me. *What do you see?* A butterfly, a mountain, two women staring at each other in anger, a ghostly figure in the window of a haunted house.

I lose myself a moment in the images, Chad's voice carrying from the kitchen. Staring at one of the black inkblots, I flash on something—a moment, a memory—a crowded nightclub, a man and woman pressed against a wall, kissing passionately, groping. It's vivid; I can almost feel the music pulsing. But then it's gone.

The kitchen door swings open, startling me, as Chad, Ella and Charles are all walking in my direction.

"Oh, we were just coming to find you, lovey," says Ella. "I don't think you've ever met my daughter, have you? Lilian?"

The stranger and Chad are laughing as they approach.

I know her.

The woman with them is striking with an ink-black mane, shelves for cheekbones, patrician thin—nails done blood-red, eyes smoky. Her spindly legs are pale through fishnet stockings, and she teeters on precipitously high heels. A skintight leather dress keeps no secrets. Her hip bones jut, slender arms cuffed with Tiffany bangles.

The woman from the theater, the one who was sitting in the front row across the aisle from me.

"Oh, my God," she gushes, coming in for a quick hug like we've known each other for ages. "Rosie, I just loved your book. The research, the layers. I want to talk to you about it for hours."

I'm flustered, not sure what to say. For some reason, it feels wrong, awkward, to say I saw her at the theater. "That's so kind. Thank you. Lovely to meet you."

Charles whispers as we all head back to the living room, "Our Lilian is an actress, like your Chad."

"Oh? Theater?"

But Charles doesn't answer as we join Chad and Lilian, who are chatting with another woman I haven't yet met. Chad drops an easy arm around my shoulder. And I can't stop looking at Lilian, her bony thinness, her eyes ringed with dark glittering shadow.

"Have the documentary rights been sold to your book?" she inquires. Her gaze is intense. "I've been looking for a serious project to produce."

"We've had some interest, but nothing solid," I say.

"Well, let's not talk business tonight," she says with a jingling wave. "Will you give me your agent's contact information before you leave?"

"Of course," I say.

She's looking at me curiously, almost wolfish. Chad has drifted off, so I lean in and say, "Didn't I see you? At Chad's opening night?"

"Oh," she says, a musing frown. "I don't think so."

I am about to protest. I know she was there. She looked right at me. Why would she lie?

But then she's off, hanging on Oga, who laughs that booming laugh and snakes a thick arm around her tiny waist. Anna the sculptor joins them, and their voices go low. They're not looking at us, but I feel like they must be talking about us.

Maybe I'm just paranoid. Tired. With lots of pent-up questions for my husband.

I wonder how soon we can leave without seeming rude.

I'm about to ask Chad when he leans in to whisper, "This is quite a group."

Before I can answer, Charles clinks his glass, and all eyes turn to him and Ella in the center of the room. I'm struck again by their sophistication, how attractive they are even in their seventies, the apartment telegraphing their taste, style and wealth. I wonder what it takes to be so settled, secure in your life. To have achieved what you set out to accomplish, to have defined your taste, refined your likes and dislikes, earned the money to honor that.

"It's been too long since we've had fresh faces in this old building," says Charles, raising a champagne flute. Chad hands me one, and he's holding one, as well.

"Ivan was a good man, a wonderful neighbor and friend. Rosie and Chad were right by his side through his illness and passing. Just look at them—so young, so talented, all the best of everything ahead of them. It's a blessing to have that new energy in the building, even as we mourn the loss of dear Ivan."

I feel the heat come to my cheeks. I look up at Chad and he's wearing that movie star smile—its wattage is blinding. This is the essential difference between my husband and me. He's an extrovert, drawing on the attention of others as a kind of rocket fuel. I am an introvert; interaction, even when it's wonderful and positive, drains me of all my power, all my energy. I feel myself shifting closer to him, his arm wrapping around my waist. He knows. He gets it. We honor this difference in each other.

"Chad and Rosie," says Charles. "We wish you a long and prosperous life here. We hope you'll view us all not just as neighbors but as friends. Welcome to the Windermere!"

Everyone raises their glasses and repeats in chorus, "Welcome!"

"Thank you so much," says Chad, speaking for us both, as always. "We're so happy to be here and thrilled to be surrounded by such warm and welcoming people. We're honored that you'd gather to welcome us."

More raised glasses and then Charles and Ella are at our side again, the party continuing, low voices, laughter, clinking glasses.

"So what do you think of the new intercom system?" asks Charles with a smile.

"I hate it," puts in Ella. "It's creepy if you ask me."

I shake my head and glance at Chad. "Intercom?"

"Oh," says Chad. "I forgot to tell her."

"It's best demonstrated," says Charles, with a wink.

"Hey, Abi," he says, raising his voice. The other guests turn to look at him, and look around for Abi, who I did not see come in.

"Yes, Mr. Aldridge?"

But the voice is disembodied, as it was in the basement, coming from some unseen source.

"Why don't you lock the street door and come help us welcome Chad and Rosie?"

Oh. Is he still downstairs? I realize that they're speaking over the intercom, which I don't remember ever using as long as we've been coming to the apartment.

"That's very kind, sir. But I'm unable to leave my post at the moment."

"Nonsense," says Ella. "Abi, please do. Just for a bit."

I feel bad for him; probably the last thing he wants to do is spend time with the people he waits on all day. But what's the deal with the intercom? Is it voice-activated? That's pretty high-tech for a building that doesn't have central air.

"Very well," he says with a good-natured chuckle. "I *do* have a package for you. I'll be up shortly and thank you."

"Did you know about this?" I ask Chad. "Do we have it, too?"

I can tell by the way he casts his eyes down to the floor that he did know. He clears his throat. "I think they installed ours last week."

"Isn't it fantastic?" asks Charles. He goes on. "Oh, don't worry about the assessment, that was a year ago, before Ivan even got sick. We've all paid. And it's such a convenience. And a comfort to know that Abi is just a shout away."

Ella meets my frown with her own.

I try to contain my dismay. I am a privacy freak. We don't have an Alexa, never use Siri. Chad and I might turn on location services for each other. But other than that, we're not into tethers. No Apple Watch tracking my heart rate, steps, notifying me of every call, email, no Oura to monitor my sleep patterns. No disembodied voice to take my order for toilet paper or the latest bestseller. People love their devices—they telegraph wealth, fitness, virtue, the idea that they are so important and must be connected every moment. But I see them for what they are—the tools of corporations to keep you wanting, buying, unable to be present, shackled to their plans for you and your money. It's a con, a scam, and the whole world has bought right into it.

"I don't understand. Can he hear inside the apartment all the time?" I ask.

"Oh, no," says Charles with a wave. "It only comes on when you say, 'Hey, Abi.'"

"What if Abi is not there? He does have days off, doesn't he?"

"Then the other doormen answer." I remember again that I've rarely seen another doorman. That no one has even referred to one by name.

"But no, no. It's perfectly private," says Charles easily. "It's just like the intercom that was there. Only you no longer have to press the button."

Charles takes my hand. "You're too young to worry about falling and not being able to call for help. But this gives me so much comfort to know that Ella or I can just call for help if we're alone, if something terrible happens."

Well, I think but don't say, *we'll be disabling that feature.*

"I understand," I say. Always better not to argue about things like this. "It is a great convenience."

It's just that *I'm* not willing to trade my privacy for convenience.

Then Abi is at the door, still in his uniform. I clock the time—it's nearly ten. We arrived early this morning and Abi was at the door in his uniform then, too.

He enters the apartment and hands a package to Charles. Everyone gathers around him like he's a celebrity. He waves off a glass of champagne, offers words of welcome to Chad and me, then slips away quickly.

"What would we do without him?" asks Ella after he's gone. But there's something odd about the way she says it.

People begin leaving, saying their goodbyes, wishing us well.

I notice that Lilian whispers something to Chad as she goes and he gives her an easy nod, glancing at me.

"Tomorrow is game night," says Ella, as Chad and I move to the door, thanking her profusely for her kindness. "Rosie, you must join us."

Game night. The introvert's worst nightmare. Small talk. Competition. Salty snacks. Booze, always. Layers of energy from multiple strangers.

"Sounds fun," says Chad, the extrovert. "I'm going to be on stage every night next week so I'm sure Rosie would love the company."

As if I sit around and pine for Chad when he's working. Like I don't have my own life, career, friends, plans. I give him a look, and he raises his eyebrows at me, mischievous. Like, *come on*.

"Sounds wonderful," I lie, as convincingly as my actor husband would. "Thank you for inviting me."

Ella looks so pleased, that I feel bad for not actually wanting to come to game night.

"We play Rummikub. Do you know it?"

"I don't but I'm a quick study. What can I bring?"

"You'll love it. Just bring yourself."

No one ever means that. I'll make something shareable. My grandmother's chocolate chip cookies are always a hit.

Back in the apartment, we wolf down the rest of the picnic lunch we had in the fridge from Charles and Ella earlier that day. We eat in silence; all the questions I have for my husband are jammed up in my throat. We open the bottle of wine we'd been planning to share, and sit on the couch with our glasses.

"Wow," says Chad.

"Yeah," I say. "Wow."

I think we're saying it for different reasons but we're both a little dazed. He has his hand absently on my knee.

"When did you know?" I ask.

"About the intercom?" He gives me an apologetic wince. "I'm

sorry. I knew you wouldn't like that. We'll figure out how to disable it."

I glance over toward the foyer where the speaker and microphone are. Yes, there's that. I wonder if Abi can hear us now. If he's listening.

No. That's stupid. Why would he want to?

"About the apartment," I clarify.

"Oh," he says, looking down, his big tell. Finally, he leans forward. "Ivan told me a while ago. That he wanted us to have it."

Outside, the city noise is very faint, five stories down. We have the lights out and the windows glow all around us. *A while ago?*

"Why didn't you tell me?"

I recount for him my call to Mira, how she already knew we weren't staying. He rubs uneasily at the crown of his head.

"You know," he says, not looking at me again. "I worried that he didn't mean it at first. So I didn't want to get your hopes up. Then, when I realized he was serious, I felt bad about it. I didn't want people to think that's why we took care of him, that we were angling for the apartment. Even though I wanted it—I mean of course I did—I tried to convince him to give it to Dana. I knew how heartbroken, how angry, she'd be."

I wonder at this. He hadn't talked to his cousin in years. He'd been angry that she hadn't helped with Ivan, hadn't been there for him or for us. Chad's a great guy but I'm not sure I believe that he was sensitive enough to worry about Dana's heartbreak.

"Then," he goes on. "I wanted to surprise you after the reading of his will. But Dana beat me to it. And I had to act shocked because I didn't want you to think I'd been keeping it from you."

Which he had been.

This is not the first time I've been unsettled by how well my husband lies. Not that it was truly a lie. But he was so convincing as someone who'd received a surprise boon that I never even considered that he'd already known about it. In that moment, he'd perfectly captured the essence of someone shocked, pleased, but still feeling guilty that he'd taken something from someone else. He is an excellent actor.

He reaches for my hand. "I'm sorry, Rosie. That was shitty. I should have told you when he first mentioned it. I just—"

He lets out a sigh, his brow wrinkled with worry.

"What?"

"I didn't want you to talk us out of accepting it. You're so— ethical, so sensitive to others. And I love that about you. It's rare. *So* rare in this world. But I just wanted this. For us. We deserve a break, don't you think?"

Would I have talked him out of it, or declined it if Ivan had offered it to us both? I don't know. I can't stop thinking about Dana, how sad she was, the box I want her to see so that she knows her father loved her in the way that he could. The letter addressed to her. Maybe there are some healing words there. I know what it feels like to be estranged, alone.

"The Aldridges' daughter—Lilian. I've seen her before." I flash on her wolfish stare, her deep red lips.

Chad lifts his eyebrows. "Do you know who her husband is?"

I shake my head.

"She's married to Robert Dunham."

Oh, wow. Dunham is one of the biggest director-slash-pro- ducers of all time. He's a star-maker. How did we not know this? Or maybe Chad did. Maybe he invited her to his opening night. She left before intermission, which probably isn't a good sign if she'd been scouting for her husband.

"Did you know that?"

He shrugs. "Ivan mentioned it. That they were good people for us to know. Anyway, I think she's more interested in you than she was in me."

Another omission. Why?

"I doubt that very much," I say, recalling how she looked at him, like he was a filet on a plate. "I saw her. She was at your opening night."

He shakes his head, frowns. "I don't think so."

It's an exact echo of what she said. How odd.

"She was in the front row, across the aisle from me," I press. Those knobby wrists, silver bangles, her stare.

He runs a hand through his curls, considering. "If she went, she must not have been very impressed. She didn't mention it when I met her tonight."

I don't tell him that she left before intermission.

"Anyway, Charles and Ella have mentioned her, but this is the first time I'm meeting her. If she was there on opening night, I wouldn't have known her." He takes my hand, face earnest. "Besides, she asked for *your* agent's contact, so I gave her Amy's number and email."

"You did?"

"This could be a good thing—a great thing, Rosie. For both of us."

Releasing a sigh, I sink back into the couch, search my husband's face.

Why would he lie—about the apartment, about Lilian?

I decide to accept what he says at face value and allow myself to be happy about it, all of it. I take in the space, really absorbing its beauty, our good fortune. It's more than I ever dreamed of. And even though I don't know how long we'll be able to afford it, I decide to be in love with it.

But I'm still not thrilled about the secrets. I search for the right words, chose them carefully because that's what writers do. "I don't want us to keep things from each other. Anything. Lies, omissions—they're toxic."

He looks away. I stay silent. The place is so quiet. Distantly, I hear the elevator moving through its shaft.

"I haven't been able to give you very much," he says finally, still looking down at the floor. "And you never *ask* for anything. We didn't have a princess wedding. Your ring—is tiny. We didn't even have a honeymoon. We're always hustling—for this part, for that assignment."

I reach for him. There's an electric connection between us. I felt it the first moment we met, and it has never diminished even a little. When he looks into my eyes, it's lightning.

"I don't need anything," I whisper. "I love our life. I love my ring."

I do. I don't care if we have to hustle. We're young; it's exciting, all the possibilities ahead of us.

He hangs his head. "But I want to give you *everything.*"

"All I need in this world is you, your love and your honesty. Don't lie to me, Chad. Don't keep things from me. Let's make the big choices together, okay?"

His faceted eyes search my face, brow still knitted with concern. "I'm sorry. I *promise.* Never again."

"Okay," I say, holding his gaze.

"What did I do to deserve you?"

"Well," I say with a smile, rubbing my hand up his leg. "You have a huge—"

He moves in quickly, his kiss hungry, interrupting my dirty talk.

Then we're tearing at each other's clothes, and they fall softly to the wood floor.

There is nothing but skin and desire, as he enters me hard and deep. I think to stay quiet—how thick are the walls? But I don't—I hear myself moan, deep, over and over. I wrap my legs around his, and lose myself in the heat between us, feeling like I could never be close enough to him. That even this is not close enough.

Rosie, Rosie, oh, my God. Rosie.

When he puts my breast in his mouth, I experience a seismic orgasm and his body answers. We're both loud, too loud. And when we realize it, we start laughing.

"I wonder if they heard us," I say, still giggling as he lies against me. His weight, the scent of him, his warmth so soothing.

"The walls are thick," he says. "I've never heard them."

"Heard them having sex?" I ask, mock horrified. As if older people weren't romping like teenagers on the couch. Maybe they were. I hope so. I hope we're still going at it when we're Charles and Ella's age.

"No!" he says, widening his eyes. "At all. I've never heard them at all."

He props himself up on his elbow and we lie naked for a few minutes, just our breath, his arm across my middle, both of us lost in our thoughts. I haven't told him about the boy in the basement. But I have made an inner promise to call Dr. Black, my shrink. I wish I could say it's the first time I've experienced anything like this. But it isn't. Even though we've just promised to tell each other everything, I keep this to myself. I know. I'm a hypocrite.

When he gets up to go take a shower, I lie in the dark for a while, putting my hands to my belly, wondering if that was it, the moment we conceived, our first time in our new apartment. I like the narrative of that, that we conceived a baby our first night here. We'll call him Parker, for Park Avenue. Silly.

A noise from the foyer catches my attention. What was that? I listen again. It was a hiss, like white noise. I think about the intercom and Abi, and how weird that is. As softly as I can, I say:

"Hey, Abi?"

Just silence and I'm relieved. Maybe you need to be right in front of the intercom, which is in the small foyer, otherwise he can't hear you.

But then: "Yes, Ms. Lowan."

A little jolt of surprise has me sitting up, pulling the throw blanket around my shoulders. Holy cow. It works. And it must be nearly eleven. Is he *still* on duty?

"Oh," I say, embarrassed like a kid caught making a crank call. "Just checking the intercom."

"It's working very well," he says. Is there a smile in his voice? "Is that all, miss?"

"Yes—thank you. Good night, Abi," I say for lack of anything else to say. *Were you listening to us, Abi? Did you hear us having sex?*

"Good night, Ms. Lowan."

ACT II

the windermere

The world of god and spirits is truly "nothing but" the collective unconscious inside me.

Carl Jung
The Collected Works of C.G. Jung,
Psychology and Religion: West and East

eight

Willa
1963

Paul says that this apartment is haunted. In fact, he thinks the whole building is. He's writing about it in his new novel, a couple in a building populated by ghosts. He says it will be a love story of sorts, but he won't let me read a word. Not yet. But of course, the apartment, which is lovely and full of light, could never be haunted. He's a writer and prone to flights of fancy.

Sunshine streams in through every window. At night we light a fire, and the space is cozy and warm. I remind him that it's the place where our love lives, and where we will raise our family. He just smiles and says that the city is no place to bring up children, that soon we'll move to the country.

And I try to smile back. I don't say how I can never leave this place, how all my dreams are paved into these streets. And all the glittering lights, and the parties, and auditions and opening nights; these things are the blood in my veins.

I am trying to be a good wife. Truly, I am. I cook and clean. I answer his correspondence, take his messages when he's working. I keep myself beautiful for him so that when he emerges from his study, there's something to entice him back to the real world and away from that too vivid, consuming imagination.

He's been cranky. The writing is not going well. He's been frustrated with his publisher, says they're not doing enough for him. And the truth is, I'm not happy, either. Since my show has closed, I've not had another callback from any of my auditions. My ankle is so painful, that some nights it keeps me awake.

And month after month, my period comes with unforgiving regularity. I'm even failing at that, the one thing that should come easily to me. It seems that I can neither be the star I wanted to be, nor the wife and mother that Paul hopes for.

There's only one thing that fills me with joy. And it's another thing I know I'll have to give up.

Tonight Paul was up late writing, and when he emerged from his office, he was a bear. We fought. But like so many of our arguments, it ended with passionate lovemaking—this time on the floor in front of the fireplace.

"I'm sorry. I'm sorry," he whispers as I lie in his arms. Whatever we bickered about already forgotten. Just a way to blow off steam for both of us.

"Love means never having to say you're sorry," I tell him, even though I'm not sure that's true.

He sighs and kisses me on the head. "I'm not good enough for you."

"You're everything," I tell him.

But that's not entirely true, either. I wish it were. I wish he was enough. That this quiet life was enough.

Later in bed when he starts to snore, I slip into my red cocktail dress with the sweetheart neck, fitted bodice and flouncy skirt, and the heels that will make my ankle swell later.

I told my love that I wouldn't come out to meet him tonight.

He said he would wait in case I changed my mind. I check the hour and it's almost midnight. Surely, he'll be gone by the time I arrive.

Still, I sneak down the back staircase again, and out the side door, so no one will see me. And the street is quiet, as quiet as a city street ever is. In the town upstate where Paul hopes to move us, it is as dark and quiet as a tomb. Surely, that will be my fate—a grave of domesticity. Like my mother—hands raw from cleaning, slumped from cooking, body soft from childbearing. No music or hot stage lights, or the wild thrill of applause. Just a task list with no end.

When I arrive at the hotel lounge, the singer is still crooning despite the late hour, and my love is waiting for me in our favorite corner booth. My heart is a soaring bird in my chest. Do I ever feel this way about Paul? It's a question I can't consider. Won't. There are all different kinds of love, I tell myself.

I've barely sat across from him when he reaches for my hand.

"Leave him," he says, urgent. I can tell he's been sitting here, ruminating. There's an empty glass in front of him, a second in his hand. "He can't love you the way I do. He doesn't even *see* you."

The lounge singer mourns her unrequited love, voice dripping with sorrow.

"I can't," I say, leaning in. "You know that."

"You *won't*," he counters, eyes darkening.

Lately, what I can give him is not enough. This man, too, wants a home, a family with me. But that's exactly what I am trying to escape by being here with him now. My life is with Paul. Even if my heart, my soul, is with this man.

"You think I can't give you the things you want," he says. There's anger in his eyes.

Paul is wealthy; our life is secure. No, my love is right. My life with him would not be the same as the one I share with Paul. We'd struggle. And I don't want that, either. My mother would say all that glitters is not gold. I'm smart enough to know this is true.

I try to draw my hand away, but he grabs my wrist. Too hard, his fingers digging painfully into my wrist.

"Stop it," I say, feeling a flutter of fear. Everything has been light and easy until now—late nights dancing, stolen moments, too much champagne.

"I'm sorry," he says, drawing back. His accent is thick when he drinks too much.

But the mood is ruined. And now in this dim room, at this late hour, I finally see clearly how wrong this is, what a mistake I am making in this affair. My husband loves me, and I'm a fool to risk what I have with him.

I rise.

"Please," he begs. He's so handsome with high cheekbones and smoldering eyes, thick, dark hair.

"I have to go. This is so wrong. I love Paul and I won't leave him. Not even for you."

"Willa," he calls as I rush away. His voice is too loud, and people stare. I run from the bar, back up the avenue home, thinking about men and how they always want you to be what *they* want. When, I wonder, do you get to choose who you are?

nine

I am up before Chad, sifting through Uncle Ivan's box labeled "The Windermere."

It's a treasure trove, filled almost to the top with old photographs, the original architectural drawing, apartment layouts. No amount of time in any research library would offer me this wealth of primary sources. As the sun comes up, debuting white golden through the east windows, I am way down the rabbit hole, with the contents of the box spread around me in a great arc—one pile for photos, one for notebooks, one for schematics and drawings.

I unfold a large drawing of the fifth floor—our floor. Our apartment and Charles and Ella's unit used to be one much larger space. Now, Charles and Ella are 5A and we're 5B.

I spread open the layout, the blue-and-white paper whispering, staining my fingertips. Someone—maybe Ivan—has drawn a big red line where the apartments were divided. To my right is the wall of the second bedroom I'm using for my office, but which I hope will one day be a nursery. A big built-in bookcase spans the length of the wall, still holding many of Ivan's old volumes on the shelves.

Staring at it a moment and envisioning the place next door, I deduce that this wall butts up against the back wall of Charles and Ella's kitchen. Was it hard for them to give it up? Did it feel like a loss? They've never even mentioned it.

I have come to recognize Ivan's handwriting, and along the red line he's written: *apartment divided by the Aldridge family in 1960.*

Ivan bought this place in 1965. Paul and Willa Winter lived here before that.

I look around the sunny space and try to imagine them. What were they like? Where did he write? Were they happy? Did they laugh and make love and fight, right here in this room? But my office, with its rows of shelves and gleaming floors, the window looking out at the building across Thirty-Seventh Street, my new desk, is quiet and serene. There's no echo of the past. The space is too bright and beautiful, too *now.*

I sift through the photographs and pull out the one Ivan has of them. Paul is slim with ridges for cheekbones and deep-set, dark eyes, serious in round specs. Handsome, I suppose in a book-ish way, wearing a simple white oxford and pressed black pants. Willa is petite, a glowing beauty, looking up at him with a mischievous smile, wearing a clinging blue dress. He snakes a possessive arm around her waist, and they lean against a gleaming new Buick, the avenue behind them, the trees in the median in spring blossom. I lose myself for a few moments, staring back in time through the black-and-white photograph, think how unchanging is Park Avenue. It looks almost exactly the same, only the cars and the style of the people on the streets have changed.

When Chad starts clanging around the kitchen, I'm snapped back to the present and join him for breakfast, tell him about the apartment, and he agrees that maybe he knew that, too, that the whole floor once belonged to the Aldridge family.

"Did Ivan ever talk to you about Paul and Willa Winter?"

He doesn't answer right away, and I wonder if he didn't hear me. His audition is in a couple of hours; he's probably running lines in his head.

Then, "Why don't you ask Ella? I bet she and Charles know everything there is to know about this building, and especially the apartment."

"They are on my list of people to interview," I say, cracking an egg into the waiting frying pan. As he's setting the table, he drops a fork that clatters on the hard tile floor.

"Sorry."

He's nervous; he always gets distracted and a little dropsy before a big audition.

"You're going to slay," I say, moving over to him and wrapping my arms around his tight middle.

"If only you were in charge of *all the things*," he says, placing a kiss on my head. "I'd be Brad Pitt by now."

"Bigger."

I notice an unfamiliar thin band of leather around his neck and push back his shirt to see what he's wearing. There's a tiny silver hand, fingers pointing down with a blue-and-white stone in the middle that looks like an eye. I know this charm well, a favorite of my grandmother's. The hand is meant to symbolize good luck. The stone in the center is the evil eye charm, intended to cast away negative energy and malevolent intentions from others.

Surprised, a surge of anxiety pushes me back a step. "Where did you get that?"

He puts his hand to it as if he forgot he was wearing it. But he wasn't wearing it last night; I'm sure of that. He must have just put it on as he was getting dressed.

"Oh," he says, pushing out an embarrassed laugh. "Ella gave it to me last night for good luck today."

The sizzling of the eggs in the pan draws my attention. I am grateful for a reason to move away from him and turn my back.

I slide sunny-side up eggs onto waiting pieces of buttered toast. My heart is racing weirdly.

"What?" he says when he brings the coffee to the table. "It's not a big deal, is it?"

I'm searching for my words. The sight of it brings me right back home, the place I fled. My father, the healer. My mother, the tarot card reader. They were tricksters, frauds, con artists, preying on the most vulnerable. My grandmother was not like them. She truly believed in her charms and herbal remedies; her dreams were vivid and eerily prescient. If there is a magical layer to this life, maybe she was tapped into it. But not my parents. They took money from the sick and weak, selling cures, dreams and hopes.

I still haven't said anything, and Chad knows me well enough to know that I need a minute to find the right thing to say. He eats, eyes on me.

"I thought with your grandmother's charm yesterday and how you put it over the door here, that it was just fun. We can use all the help we can get, right? What's our deadline? How many months do we have before we have to think about selling this place?"

I didn't think he was paying attention when we were going over the budget. Chad likes his magical thinking when it comes to money—there will be enough, we'll make it work, something big will happen. He's not interested in spreadsheets and timelines, income and expense projections.

The little eye lying in the notch of his collarbone stares at me.

"You've gotten really close to them," I say. That's part of it, too. It's not just the charm.

He shrugs, looks down at his plate. "I mean, I *guess*. They were here for us when Ivan was sick. If Ella hadn't been sitting with Ivan that last night while we went to the awards dinner, we might not have made it back in time to be here when he passed."

That's true. They cooked for us, stayed with Ivan when one of us couldn't be here toward the end. It's a lot to expect of neighbors and friends, but they did it all without ever being asked.

"I think they care about us, you know? They're not exactly close with Lilian. She's always jet-setting around, doing her own thing, no children."

Lilian. The thought of her staring at me in the theater gives me a little shiver. The way she looked at Chad.

"They *have* been good to us," I admit.

"We don't have any family," he says, voice soft. "Now with Ivan gone—"

"I get it. You're right."

I feel it, too, the emptiness of having lost or moved away from my family of origin. Chad's parents gone; he was an only child. Especially at the holidays, when everyone is rushing around, buying gifts for the hordes, stressing about where to go, who to see, traveling home to be with parents, siblings, aunts, uncles, cousins, and it was just us and Ivan. There's a deep loneliness there, a feeling of not being held, wanted, expected. It's a big driver behind our desire to have children. And maybe he's looking for a kind of surrogate family now that Ivan is gone. A space I suspect Ella and Charles would happily fill.

"This," he says, putting his finger to the charm, "is just for fun. She has a whole collection of them. She even has one for you, was planning to give it to you at game night."

"It's an evil eye charm," I tell him. "It wards off malevolence, jealousy."

"So there you go," he says. "When all those other guys are looking at me, twisting with envy at my talent and good looks, hoping I'll flub my lines or have something in my teeth, *this* will protect me."

He holds it out to me like a tiny shield. We both start laughing.

"Okay, okay," I say finally. "Wear it in good health. But you don't need luck. Talent and hard work will win out. Always. It just takes time."

He gives me a wry grin. "If only that were always true."

"It is," I say with more passion than I intended. "I believe that."

He kisses me and then gets up to leave, clearing our plates, draining the last of his coffee.

I walk him to the door and wait with him at the elevator until Abi comes.

Abi is crisp and upright as ever in his impeccably pressed uniform. When did he go home? He must sleep here. I'm going to find out more about Abi's schedule, though why it bothers me so much I don't know. I remember our late-night conversation, how he answered when I practically whispered his name in my apartment.

"Big audition today, Mr. Lowan?" he says brightly.

Seriously? Either there's a major gossip mill in this building, or Abi really is listening in on our conversations.

"That's right, Abi," says Chad, the extrovert who relishes in all attention. "Wish me luck."

"You won't need it, sir. I have a good feeling."

Chad takes his time kissing me goodbye, not worried apparently about our audience who, to his credit, averts his eyes. *"I love you,"* I whisper.

"Love you."

He blows me a kiss as the elevator door closes.

"Happy writing, Ms. Lowan," says Abi before it shuts completely.

I hear a shuffle behind Ella and Charles's door and wonder if they're watching through the peephole. We've been here less than a full day, and already I'm missing the seedy anonymity of our East Village walk-up.

How am I going to get out of game night? I wonder as I enter the apartment and shut the door behind me. It takes me a second to register that my phone is ringing. Maybe it's Max. We're supposed to have lunch today to go over the outline I submitted. Things have been oddly strained since Chad's opening night, and our conversations have been strictly professional and mostly over email. Though he did send me a funny video of a kitten getting his belly rubbed with a spoon, which I took as a bit of an olive branch. I sent him a heart emoji. I'm hoping lunch will be a reset of our normal, easy friendship.

It's not Max, but I answer anyway because the number looks vaguely familiar.

"Hi, this is Rosie."

"Hey—it's Dana."

"Oh," I say, surprised. "How are you?"

"I'm *sorry*," she says. "About the last time we met. Well, actually—it was the first time, wasn't it? Anyway. I wanted to apologize."

Her voice is raspy and small, like she's been crying or has a cold.

"No need," I say. "This kind of thing—it's hard. There's no roadmap for dealing with grief." Or for being robbed of your inheritance.

A crackling on the line makes me think I lost the connection. The cell service in the building has proved unreliable and we've often resorted to using Ivan's old landline for making calls.

"Dana?"

"Do you have time to get together maybe?"

"Oh." Is that a good idea? She could still be planning to sue us for the apartment. Should I call Olivia? See what she thinks?

"There are some things I think you need to know." She takes a shuddering breath. "About your husband."

My husband? It's a bit of a gut punch, but I try to steady myself. She's unstable, clearly.

"About Chad? Can you tell me now?" I venture. "I have some time to talk."

Honestly, I don't have time to talk. I know it always seems like writers have time to do whatever. But we don't. A small delay—a dentist appointment, an unscheduled call—turns into a wasted morning or afternoon, which can turn into a wasted day where no writing or research gets accomplished. Then you're behind schedule and time compresses, that deadline coming like a freight train.

And what could she possibly know about Chad? They haven't seen each other in years. I'm quite sure I know everything there is to know about him, even his difficult past. We've laid ourselves bare for each other, in every way.

"I'd rather not discuss it over the phone." She's lowered her voice to a raspy whisper, and a tension creeps into my shoulders.

This is a bad idea. There's something wrong with her. I am about to decline when my eyes fall on the box with her name on it; I hauled it up from the basement yesterday. It reminds me that she's a person in pain. That there's a letter in there from a father she thought didn't love her, but who did in his own way. She's family, I guess. Also, I'm looking to repair that bad feeling between us.

"I have something for you, too," I venture.

I expect her to ask me what I have, but she doesn't.

"I'll text you an address," she says instead. "Can you come later this afternoon? Around three?"

"Okay," I agree.

If I called Chad, he'd tell me not to go. But I do want to deliver the box to her. And—what *could* she have to say about my husband?

His childhood was difficult. There's darkness there; I know that much. His parents' deaths, another terrible incident before that—which we almost never discuss. Chad rarely has anything to say about his growing up in New Jersey. It always seems like he'd rather forget that time of his life. Typical. Suburban. Boring. Those are the words he uses most often when strangers ask, even though that's not exactly accurate. Painful. Tragic. That's more like it.

I decide that I'll lug the box to lunch, then meet her after.

"Hey, Rosie. Don't tell anyone in the building that you're

meeting me." She releases a deep breath. "You can't trust the people closest to you."

"Uh," I say stupidly. Before I can ask why and what she means, she hangs up. A second later an address comes through via text—oh, no. Looks like someplace *way* uptown. Like Inwood, or even the Bronx. I do not have long cab rides in my budget, and I'm not hauling that box onto the train.

That's a bit of hike, I text back. Can we pick another place?

But there's no answer. She doesn't pick up when I decide to call.

There it is again, that weird sound from the intercom.

My grandmother used to call it the tingle. That feeling in your nerve endings when something dark is on the horizon. Your body knows; it feels the energy like a dowsing rod.

I glance at the time on my phone and realize the morning is slipping away. Forcing myself to get back to work, I continue to sift through Ivan's box, making notes, writing down questions. There's a lot here and it's going to take more than a couple of hours to read it all.

Near the bottom of the box, I find another photograph—this one of the church that stood here and burned down before the Windermere was built. With its brownstone facade, vaulted doorways, towering steeples, it sits freestanding in its place on Park Avenue, small but stately. The buildings that now sit on either side of the Windermere were not yet constructed.

In the grainy black-and-white image, on the church steps a congregation gathers, well-heeled women in long dresses and elaborate hats, men in suits. I find myself staring at it, trying to discern faces, but the image, taken at a distance, is fuzzy and out of focus.

That buzz, that curiosity that has me digging through the past, is a white noise in my head.

Those people, like the Winters, each of them leading lives that seemed monumentally important—all their dreams, desires, loves, losses, all their pain, joy, children born, wars endured, tears shed, laughter—all gone now. This grainy image is all that remains. More than one hundred years later, no one alive even remembers them. I feel that deep writer's urge to tell their stories. Because in the end, that's what our lives are—stories that we tell ourselves and each other. And those stories are all that remain after we're gone.

I lose myself in my research, forgetting about Dana and what she thinks she might know about Chad. Deep in the flow, my morning passes quickly. When I notice the time again, it's almost noon.

Oh, shit. Max. As I close my notebook, hustle to get ready and head across town for our lunch, I'm still undecided about whether to make the trip uptown to see Dana. Finally, I decide to lug the box in the elevator foyer with me, and press the call button.

Abi comes quickly, and he immediately rushes to pick up the box and carries it to the elevator. He doesn't seem to look at it or be curious about what might be inside. I think about our strange late-night conversation.

"Big meeting with your editor today?" he asks, clanking the metal gate shut.

He must clock my surprise. "Mr. Lowan mentioned it this morning."

"Oh, yes," I say, forcing a polite smile. Another introvert nightmare, to be daily asked about your comings and goings, to have strangers inquiring after things that are none of their business.

"I'm sure it will go well," he says. A scent wafts from him, something fresh and herbal.

Are you? I want to ask. But of course, he's just being cordial. I decide to be the same.

"Thank you, Abi."

As the elevator creeps slowly down the shaft, the silence awkwardly expands. There's a strident ring that indicates someone else needs the elevator. The floor numbers stenciled onto the shaft pass us by—4, 3. Abi brings the elevator to stop on 2.

Xavier steps on looking freshly shaved, stylish in a long black coat and checkered scarf.

"Good morning, Rosie," he says with a little bow. Does he give Abi a look? "Abi."

His cologne is light and pleasant, but I notice when he steps on and the door closes, how small the elevator is. He glances down at the box at my feet.

"How's the research going?" he asks.

I smile. "It's—going."

He offers a polite nod. I breathe a sigh of relief when the elevator opens and we step out into the lobby, Abi hefting the box and Xavier opening the door for all of us. Abi goes to the curb to hail a cab. And I'm surprised when Xavier leans in close, lowering his voice.

"I could tell you a thing or two about the Windermere," he says. There's something strange about his gaze, his tone. He seems a little glassy—his tone almost ominous.

The air is growing cooler and the leaves on the trees in the sidewalk and on the median are starting to turn. When I look at him again, he's smiling. Whatever darkness I imagined is gone.

"Can we get together? For coffee?" I suggest. "I'd love to hear what you know."

"Yes," he says. "Let's do that. See you tonight?"

Oh, game night. Right.

"I think so. Yes, I'll be there."

Then he's striding off down the sidewalk, hands in pockets. I watch until Abi calls for me. He's hailed a cab.

As I climb in, the driver opens the trunk from the front seat, and Abi loads the box, then shuts the trunk, giving the cab a knock to indicate it's time to go.

"Have a good day, Ms. Lowan."

"Thanks so much. You, too!" I call as the cab pulls away. He waves happily.

Had we been in the East Village, I would have had to haul the box down five flights of stairs, put it down on the curb while I hailed a cab, hefted it into the trunk myself. I could get used to this maybe, even with all the game nights and doorman chit-chat, this new uptown life.

I'm thinking on my encounter with Xavier, when I get a text from Chad.

You know what? I think that went well. I'm excited. Maybe the good luck charm worked.

I flash on the tiny hand with the eye in its palm. And I feel that little twinge of what—fear? Yes, it's fear. Anxiety.

Yay! I type anyway.

Heading to the theater for some big meeting about changes to the set. And I'll be late tonight—drinks with Ron after the performance. You going to game night tonight?

Maybe.

It'll be good for you. You can ask Ella all your questions.

We'll see.

Don't be a hermit. See you tonight.

My finger hovers over the screen keyboard. Should I tell him about Dana?

But it seems like too much to text, and then the cab is pulling in front of the restaurant. I stow my phone, pay the driver and ask him to pop the trunk again, which he does.

But when I walk behind and peer inside, my stomach bottoms out with surprise. The trunk is pristinely clean and empty except for the spare tire.

Dana's box is gone.

ten

"Hey," I say, walking around to the driver's window. "Where's the box?"

But how could he know? He never left the driver's seat. Abi took the box, put it in the trunk.

The cabby, a thickly muscled, middle-aged guy with dark, slicked-back hair, shrugs, looks unconcerned. "What box? Hey, can you shut the trunk?"

"The doorman put a box in the trunk. You saw him. He tapped when he was done."

He offers an apathetic eye roll indigenous to New Yorkers. "I don't know, lady. If it's not there I can't help you."

I walk back over and look again, traffic flowing past, drivers leaning on their horns, annoyed at the stopped taxi. Finally, there's nothing for me to do except to shut the lid and step onto the sidewalk.

What the fuck? What happened to that box?

Hey, Rosie. Don't tell anyone in the building that you're meeting me.

I didn't. I didn't tell anyone, not even Chad.

Unless Abi was listening. Over the intercom. Or he saw Dana's name on the box and put it together. Or Xavier did. He did seem— off.

But why would anyone care if I gave Dana things that rightly belong to her? Did Abi *take it*? Could the trunk have popped open while we were driving, and the box fell out? No. No way. Did he make a mistake? Meant to put it in, but left it on the curb by accident? No. I waved goodbye. I would have seen it sitting there. Wouldn't I?

I feel a terrible sense of loss. All those photographs and news clippings, proof positive for Dana that her father loved her, thought about her, kept track of her. Not digital images floating in the cloud—but real paper, vulnerable to damage and misplacement— real things that Ivan touched. The letter. His final words to his daughter. Entrusted to me by the fact that I found them. It was my duty, wasn't it, to broker this meager peace after Ivan's passing? And I lost it.

I watch bereft as the cab disappears into a sea of vehicles and is swept away.

Max is waiting at the table when I arrive, gets up to give me a kiss on the cheek. But I'm rattled and he sees it right away.

"What's wrong?"

I tell him about Dana's call, the box, how it's disappeared. He watches me with a concerned frown.

"Any chance you just left it in the apartment?"

The question is a little annoying. "You mean did I *imagine* carrying it to the elevator, handing it to Abi, watching him carry it to the trunk, hearing him knock to let us know that we could go?"

He pushes up his thick glasses, frowns. "I mean—there's that thing that happens to you, right?"

His words give me a little jolt.

I have been doing a decent job of powering through some of

the weirdness of the past few days—the boy in the basement, the panic attack at the theater. I've been doing my breath work, repeating the phrases given to me by Dr. Black.

The only truth is the moment.

The activities of my mind are a fantasy. I only need to respond to what is directly in front of me.

The past is gone. No one can see into the next moment.

My family of origin felt differently.

My father called me a *seer.* Someone who glimpses into the future, who receives messages or visions—some of them true, some of them just possibilities, some of them deceptions.

But years of therapy have allowed me to understand that for what it was—gaslighting. A way for my family to rope me into their various frauds and schemes, to make me afraid and unstable so that they could keep me in their control, use me to further their reputation as a family of mystics.

While most parents would tell you that your nightmares and imaginings weren't real, your father convinced a creative, imaginative child that her dreams, night terrors or vivid imaginings were a window into the future.

I have an appointment with Dr. Black tomorrow.

I stare at Max, who lifts both palms. "I'm just saying. Remember the whole train thing?"

Of course I remember.

We were editorial assistants working at Pinnacle, a small but prestigious imprint of Vantam Pryce, one of the largest publishing companies in the world. Max worked for Margaret Graul, an iconic editor who had a stable of bestselling and award-winning writers, and who had taken a particular shine to Max. I was struggling to please the imprint's founder and publisher, Peter Mittlemark, who seemed to think my job was to read his mind and anticipate his every mood. While Max was learning how to spot talent, to edit respectfully, to manage big, creative personalities, I was fetching coffee, wrestling with the ancient copy machine, sending out rejection letters and spending all my evenings in the slush pile, trying to find a pearl in the oysters.

Max and I left late together one night; it was our habit to walk to the train together. I was exhausted—worn down from the job, still in therapy, struggling with insomnia and plagued by vivid nightmares when I *could* sleep. I was staying awake on a steady diet of sugar and caffeine.

We chatted as we walked toward the subway platform, the night balmy and busy as the theaters just blocks away were letting out their crowds. The air had a strange smell to it, like something burning. I had my arm looped through Max's and he was doing his best Peter Mittlemark impersonation, complete with the fake British accent that the old man occasionally put on.

Laughing at Max's act, I put my hand on the railing to head down into the station.

And suddenly, I was somewhere else—transported to the platform down below, a train screeching into the station.

A young woman in a red coat with long blond hair was falling away from me, and I was screaming *noooooo* as I reached for her. She'd been shoved by a shuffling, muttering man pushing a shopping cart piled high with garbage. And she was stumbling, slow motion but inexorably, back toward the track. I felt the buttons of her coat on my fingertips as she fell, eyes wide with horror, hands outstretched to me, and then midair she was struck by the train—the horn wailing, people screaming in horror, me on my knees, my right hand still reaching.

Then I was back on the stairs with Max.

"Rosie?"

I snapped back quickly, eager to leave this type of thing behind me forever. Dr. Black said that I had been so gaslit by my family, that I had learned to give myself over to things that for other people might be nothing more than a passing thought.

We all have dark thoughts, Rosie. We all imagine the worst things happening. But most of us know that they're just fantasies that we must push away in favor of the real world that's right in front of us.

"Nothing," I lied, shaking it off. "I'm fine. Just a little dizzy, I guess. I need some sleep."

And that might have been the end of it, except five minutes later, the exact scene played out in front of both of our eyes. We both watched a young woman get pushed onto the tracks, as I reached for her coat—that was blue, not red. Her hair was black, not blond. But everything else—from her terrified scream, the touch of my fingertips to the buttons of her coat, the odor of the man who shoved her—was the same.

I still go back to that crowded platform in my dreams some nights. Max and I were laughing about something; I don't remember what. The platform was crowded, hot. I remember the smell; I caught the whiff of body odor and garbage, turned to see its origin, and the tall, limping man pushing the cart was moving toward us.

The young woman was on her phone, deep in conversation, too close to the edge, her tote pressed to her body. I started to move toward her. But it all happened so fast, the coming train, the man shoving her with his cart, her lost balance. I almost caught her. I *almost* caught her coat. If I had, I could have yanked her back. But the momentum of her fall was too powerful.

Camille Ford. A young magazine editor, new to the city. Gone. Just gone.

That night, crying with my head in Max's lap in his apartment, I told him about my vision, about my parents, about all the things I was struggling to leave behind. He soothed me, heard me.

"It's been in the news so much," Max offered.

It was true, there had been a spate of subway deaths. A suicide, another violent assault that led to a young man being pushed to the tracks. "Maybe you were just thinking about that as we went down."

"Maybe."

Dr. Black calls it confabulation, when the mind takes knowledge and details from other experiences and uses them to make a fantasy more real. But it *was* real—the screech of the train, the smell of urine and filth, voices screaming, the harsh white light.

"Or, I mean—is it possible?" said Max. "You know, that you *are* tapped into something? There's so much we don't understand about the brain."

"No," I said, sitting up fast. "It's not possible."

"Okay," he said, putting a hand to my shoulder. "Okay. I'm sorry."

And that night was the one and only time Max and I were ever together. It started innocently as a kiss and turned into something more. I lost myself in the comfort of his body that night, slept in his arms. In the morning, he apologized for taking advantage of me when I was vulnerable—which was not the whole truth of it. Still, we agreed that our friendship was so important that we didn't want to risk it by introducing sex into the equation. I think the truth of it was that I took advantage of *him*, his warmth, his solidity, knowing that I didn't feel for him what I suspected he felt for me.

We haven't talked about that night—any of it—since.

"So I *imagined* Abi putting the box in the trunk?" I say now. "No."

The waiter comes with Max's sparkling water and we both place our orders—penne for Max, pizza for me. The usual.

"Maybe it was a—prediction? Kind of like that night. I think about it sometimes, what happened. How you saw the girl falling before she fell."

I force myself to drink some water, to take a long, slow breath. I know he's trying to help, but he isn't.

"That night," he says again. "I wish…"

"What? You wish what?" I say too sharply. My shoulders are hiked, breath shallow.

He pauses a second, takes a sip from his glass. "I wish I had been more honest about my feelings. The very next week you met Chad."

Okay, wow. I did not expect to go there. As if I need *this* on top of everything else.

"I'm sorry," I say, even though I'm not sure what I'm apologizing for. What if he *had* been more honest his feelings? The truth is that I don't feel that way about Max. I love him. But I'm not in love with him, never have been. Our connection is powerful but it's not romantic. Not for me.

"Well," he says, taking off his glasses and rubbing them with the napkin. "What's done is done, right?"

I reach for his hand, and he laces his fingers through mine. "You're my *best friend*," I say.

He pushes out a little laugh. "Ouch."

"That means something, right?"

For a moment it seems like he can't meet my eyes. Then,

"Rosie," he says, with the smile I know so well. "It means everything."

"Look," I say after a moment. "Let's just forget all of this. I don't know what happened to the box and until I confront Abi, I'm not going to know. The train that night. Who knows what happened? I was in a weird place, working through all the lies and instability from my childhood. Can we just focus on the work today?"

"Of course, yes," he says with a nod. "Let's focus on the haunted building where there have been multiple violent deaths and suicides and where you've just moved in. At least that's easier to manage."

It is. The past is always easier to manage than the present. It's gone. Now all we can do is narrate what we think happened, write the stories. Those stories become the truth.

We go through the outline, gorge ourselves on carbs, and by the end of the lunch it's clear that story of the Windermere is the story of the people who died there. An intriguing cast of creatives—an actor, a dancer, a writer, a self-proclaimed psychic, a young boy, a prodigy pianist. A chapter for each, featuring bits about the church fire, the famous architect who designed the building—and who also threw himself from its roof— interviews with historians, psychologists, experts on the supernatural.

But ultimately, the story will end with the idea that of course the Windermere is not haunted. There will be some reason, some explanation, or possible explanations for why so many people have died there. I don't know what the ultimate ending will be—only that it's through the lives and deaths of the residents that I'll find a way to understand the history of our new home and say something larger about life and death itself.

"Ambitious," says Max.

"That's a dirty word," I say with mock indignation. "Like a cliff I'm about to jump off, hoping there are no jagged rocks in the water below."

"It's going to be fantastic," he says. "I'm excited. And your writing, just the early pages. It's magnificent. You've really grown."

I'm childishly pleased to hear it.

"But, you know." He frowns, seems to choose his words. "Just stay on solid ground? Don't follow them down the rabbit hole. I know it's hard when you're digging up graves. But try to stay in the light."

Max is referring to the deep depression I suffered during the writing of the last book. He and my agent Amy both had to hold my hand, a lot. But I'm past that. I've had therapy, lots of it. I've been off my medication for over a year—in preparation for trying to have a baby. I'm happy. I'm solid, not at all in the same place I was last time. I realize that I'm gripping the fork in my hand so hard that it hurts, then relax my stiff fingers.

"I'm good."

He seems about to say more but the waiter brings dessert, a tiramisu that we're supposed to share but which I will hog.

"Oh, before I forget." He reaches into his satchel and takes out an old clothbound book.

It as thick as a doorstop.

"You might like this," he says. "I've had it on my shelf forever."

The Secret History of New York City by Arthur Alpern.

"We've published a number of Art's books," says Max, motioning to the waiter for the check. "He's kind of a treasure, knows everything there is to know about this city, the buildings. I can put together a meeting."

The name is familiar; it probably popped up a couple of times on my initial search for information. "That would be amazing," I say. "There's nothing like a living source."

The spine is loose and the pages whispery thin. Flipping through I see blueprints and line drawings, that it's arranged by neighborhood. It reminds me that I am on well-trod ground. There are lots of books about New York buildings and their colorful histories. A whisper of self-doubt. *Is* there a story here? Something that hasn't been told?

"I'll have Andy arrange a lunch."

"Your trusty assistant. That's very posh of you, dear Max. Have your people call my people."

"That's how I roll now. *Senior* Editor." He presses out both lapels of his nicely tailored jacket. He so looks the part of fancy New York publishing star with his tortoiseshell glasses, and clean-shaven face, his carefully styled hair.

He's in line for executive editor of his imprint now that his boss has moved up the ladder. He'll get it; I have no doubt. He's young but great at his job, and it does seem like things always go his way.

"So—what are you going to do?" asks Max as we fork fight for the last bit of tiramisu. He loses. "Are you going home to confront your weird doorman?"

"No," I say, tapping my phone for the time. "I'm going to meet Dana."

A disapproving frown wrinkles his brow. "Uh—is that a good idea?"

No. Probably not. But I still have her voice ringing in my head. Now there's this strange event of Abi not putting the box in the trunk, and to be honest, my inner divining rod is vibrating. Something's going on, and what true-crime writer isn't going to chase that down? Meanwhile, what *does* Dana know about my husband? Something from their past? Something about the apartment?

"Well," says Max when I don't answer. He takes the napkin from his lap and folds it neatly, placing it on the table. "You're not going alone."

"Don't you have a job?"

"No," he says. "I work in publishing. I'm going home to edit for the rest of the day."

He puts air quotes around the word *edit*.

"Ah, I see how it goes."

He picks up the tab, and I thank him for lunch. I don't protest as he shoulders his bag, holds the door for me and we head out to hail a cab. It will be good to have some company, especially someone as steady as Max, someone with both feet planted firmly in the real world.

Before too long we're headed uptown to the address Dana texted.

Again, I consider and decide against calling Chad. He doesn't need the distraction. But maybe the truth is I don't want him to talk me out of it. And I have Dana's warning in my head.

Max is texting on his phone as the driver pulls onto the West Side Highway and I watch the city recede in the rearview mirror.

eleven

Willa
1963

We leave the theater, and the air has grown cold, a stiff, frigid wind whipping up the avenue. The Paramount Theater is grand, too grand for the movies but the perfect venue for *Cleopatra* with the stunning Elizabeth Taylor. I'm still swooning from the colors and the costumes, her raw power, as Paul and I walk up Broadway, arm in arm. What's it like, I wonder, to be a star like Elizabeth Taylor, the eyes of the world on you in adoration?

"Wasn't it marvelous?" I say, pushing into Paul, who has been quiet tonight. He's struggling with his novel, and it always puts him in bad spirits. The writer is a fragile creature, prone to moods. He probably barely saw the film unfold, working through his own narrative issues.

"*That's* the kind of story I should be writing," he says. "Something sweeping and historical, iconic."

He would have said that about anything wonderful we saw—

if it was horror, or science fiction. "That's where the money is, in great epics."

"You're a wonderful writer," I remind him. "A huge success. And we can only write the stories that belong to us—isn't that what you always say?"

He lifts an eyebrow at me, then laughs and kisses my head.

"You're right, of course. What would I do without you?"

"You'll never have to find out."

Paul is so different from my lover. Fair instead of dark, thin instead of muscular. How can two men be so different and yet still attract the same woman?

Anyway, I have *stopped* seeing him. I have. I have quit my lover for good. I am determined to be the wife my husband deserves. I tighten my arm around Paul's waist, look up into his kind eyes.

"I'm the luckiest man alive," he says.

When I look back to the street in front of us, crowded even at this late hour, that's when I see him. Tall and elegantly dressed, striding toward us purposely.

He won't leave me alone, though I've told him that our affair must end. Paul and I plan to sell our apartment and move to the country—where it's better, safer. My career—if you can call it that—is not going anywhere. The city—it's changing. Violent crimes are up and some of the glitz and glamour is fading, grand places gone to seed, the subway ever more dangerous. This November there was a terrible blackout. We're both ready. At least that's what I tell people. Paul needs more quiet; and I don't know what I need. Fewer distractions, temptations, I think.

I keep my eyes on the man coming closer, nudge Paul to the side.

He's been following us. I've seen him lurking in doorways, dining alone at restaurants we visit. The other day he was waiting for me as I left the building.

"I can't live without you," he told me.

"You must," I said. "I'm sorry."

He grabbed my wrist as I tried to walk away. "I'll tell him," he threatened. "I'll tell him that I made love to you in his bed."

The anger in his eyes, the strength of his grip. It terrified me. "You wouldn't," I whispered. "If you love me, let me go."

He softened, apologized. But he followed all the way to the market, lingering at a distance behind me.

Now he moves toward us quickly.

"Paul," I start. But at the last second, he veers past us, our eyes locking. As if to say, *I'm this close. I can ruin you anytime.*

"Yes, darling."

"I'm freezing."

"Let's get you home."

I'm shaken to the core when, back at home, Paul takes my coat, hangs it on the rack. I wish I could come clean, beg his forgiveness, start again. But no. Paul is so fragile, so prone to dark patches and despair. It would kill him. How could I have been so careless, such a fool? My mother was right about me. Never satisfied. Always looking for the new shiny thing like a crow.

"What's troubling you?" Paul asks. He builds a fire, comes to sit beside me on the sofa. It's warmer now.

"You seem skittish, distracted," he goes on when I don't answer. "Worried."

"It's time you knew," I say, looking up into the clear pools of his eyes. They crinkle at the corners with concern.

"Paul," I start, look down shyly.

"What is it, my love?"

"I'm pregnant."

The moment expands as his expression goes from surprise to joy. He weeps with happiness and gathers me close, and I stare into the flames and pray with all my heart that the child is his.

twelve

As our cab races up the highway, Max is answering emails on his phone, and I'm lost in thought.

The first time it happened, I was three—or so my mother tells the story. In her version, it was an idyllic scene—a bright spring late morning, nearly noon, with the sun shining and a breeze billowing the curtains and bringing in the scent of jasmine. My mother was chopping vegetables, preparing stew for the evening's dinner, while I sat at the kitchen table eating my lunch.

When she glanced over to check on me, I had gone blank, eyes glassy. At first, she thought I was choking, rushed over in a panic. But when she reached me, I was breathing fine, just looking off into the distance. *Like you were watching something that no one else could see.*

She shook me a little, gently. *Rosie, Rosie, what is it?*

I pointed to the stove and said a single word. "Fire."

But nothing was burning. She'd not even yet turned on the stove top. And then I snapped back to myself, continued eating like nothing had happened.

Later that night when my mother was cooking dinner, a dish-rag caught fire on the stove, and the flame quickly spread to the curtains. Only my mother's quick work with the ready fire extinguisher saved it from spreading further.

She told my father and he declared me a seer, which I'm sure he just made up then and there. Another freak for his show: Dad, the healer; Mom, the tarot-card reader; Grandma and Sarah were dreamers; now Rosie, the seer.

And truthfully, as I grew, I *was* prone to vivid daydreams. Because they were tolerated and even encouraged, they became ever more detailed, consuming. Occasionally, the things I saw *did* come to pass, but mostly not. This fact didn't seem to bother my father at all.

This life is a multiverse. You're looking into a kaleidoscope, the facets always shifting, every moment impacting the moment that follows. You're seeing the possibilities.

He believed that I could see the future, even if it was a future that might never come to pass because of the myriad ways in which each moment shifts, impacting the next.

Dr. Black has another theory.

If your family had discouraged these daydreams, recognized them for what they were, eventually they would have faded, Dr. Black posits. Instead, they gaslit you into thinking that you had some kind of prophetic vision.

But I was right sometimes, I counter. *Some of the things I saw did happen. Like that time on the train.*

Dr. Black has an explanation for that, too.

We're all prone to dark imaginings, where we get swept away by vivid fantasies about the future. It's possible that some of these daydreams will later come to pass. When it's positive, some might call it manifestation or creative visualization. But there's no fast forward on reality, no preset version of the future to which you have special access.

His theory about the train specifically was that there had been a lot of stories in the news about the violence on the subway. I had mentioned in my early sessions with him that when I came to New York, after the quiet and natural beauty of where I grew up, I found the city frightening at first, especially the subways. The recent violence had awakened some of those fears. And because I had this propensity for vivid daydreams, that I'd been raised thinking were real, that this was some gift I'd been given by God, I had one of those daydreams. That a girl was just minutes later killed, was simply a tragic coincidence.

It wasn't a perfect explanation. But it was one I could work with.

You can run from who you are, Rosie, my father said when I left home. *But you can't hide from it.*

Those words ring back to me when I have vivid daydreams, when things I imagine come to pass. The only reason I don't hate my father more is that I think he truly believed the lies he told me, himself, everyone. He really did—does—think we've been gifted with mystical powers. That he can heal the sick, and my mother can advise the lost with a deck of cards; Sarah's and Grandma's dreams have prophetic qualities, that Grandma's potions, charms and spells have some special powers, that I can see possible versions of the future. He just happens to be dead wrong.

"Is this it?" asks Max as the cab finally pulls up to the curb. It's an area of the city I have never visited, a neighborhood of warehouses, garbage littering streets, a spider's web of electrical lines overhead. To our right a junkyard of wrecked cars and boats with rotting hulls; to our left a brick building lined with freighter truck bays. I check the address: 1245 Viele Avenue.

"I think so?"

Max runs his card through the slot.

"No," I protest with a hand on his arm. "Let me."

"Let's call it research," he says. "That's not too far off, right?"

"Most of what a writer does *could* count as research. Are you going to pay for my Netflix, too?"

"I'd do anything for you, Rosie," he says. "I think you know that."

He gives me a look I can't read, and I feel the heat come up to my cheeks. I thank him—again—and get out of the cab, wondering how we're going to get another one up here and where the nearest subway stop is.

"Oh." He points off into the distance. "I think the MTA iron shop is up here. Where they fabricate structural steel for the subway."

Max is a bit of a New York City nerd, prides himself on knowing about iconic buildings, hidden alleys, obscure historical facts.

"Over across the East River?" he goes on. "That's Rikers. Did you read the article in the *New Yorker* about all the men who died there?"

Max talks a lot when he gets nervous. I, on the other hand, go quiet.

He goes on about how he and his buddies play paintball up here. Hard to imagine his urbane hipster pals, into craft cocktails, art films and poetry playing war games. He must clock my skepticism.

"What? I do guy things."

"Of course you do, honey."

We are surrounded by squat concrete and brick buildings, and the street is eerily quiet, lined with cars. A guy with a tattooed head and wearing a blue mechanic jumpsuit walks by talking on the phone, oblivious to us. But other than him, the sidewalks are empty, warehouses as far as you can see to the water's edge. A piece of newspaper dances up the street carried by the wind. In the gutter a pigeon coos.

"I don't think we're in Manhattan anymore, Toto," says Max. And he's right; the vibe is completely different up here. Industrial. A strange air of desertion. The wind howls down the street, and I pull my coat tight around me. I can feel the first hint of winter in the air.

We walk until we find the door with the rusty metal numbers nailed above it. There's a simple plaque: Dana Lowan Studios. I took my husband's name without hesitating, eager to leave any piece of my old self, my old life, behind. But I guess Dana kept her maiden name—or was there a divorce?

I press the bell and hear it ringing loud and long like a buzzer off in the distance.

We wait, Max tapping on his phone.

I ring again, check the time. It's exactly three.

"Call her," suggests Max.

My call rings and rings, finally goes to voice mail. *Please leave a message for Dana Lowan.*

"No answer."

When I reach for the heavy metal door, expecting to find it locked, it pushes open with a horror movie squeak to reveal a dimly lit, long concrete hallway.

Is that music, playing from somewhere inside the space?

"Should we go in?" I ask Max, only just now realizing that this was not a good idea. I'm hoping he's going to chicken out and drag me off, so that I don't have to chicken out and drag *him* off.

But he's got that look, that curious researcher look that I know too well.

He leans into the long, dark hallway. "Hello?" His voice bounces on the concrete.

This is not smart, I think. But we're inching forward.

A tinny strain of music carries from deep inside the building. We exchange a look, both hearing it. He shrugs as if to say: *We came this far.* When he walks inside, I follow.

thirteen

Once we pass through the dark hallway, we enter a wide-open, bright white space. In sharp contrast to the gritty, industrial neighborhood, the interior could be on any street in SoHo with matte white walls and artful lighting, hardwood floors.

"Wow," says Max.

Our footfalls echo in the cavernous space.

It's a gallery of presumably Dana's photography—a stunning collection of high-contrast nudes. Bodies of all shapes, sizes, ages—her perspective unflinching. In the huge images, an old woman stands in front of a full-length mirror, boldly baring her sagging breasts, her wrinkled skin, her toothless smile. A young man stands on prosthetic legs, stance akimbo, smile wide. A mother feeds a baby from her breast. Another woman has scars where her breasts would be; she poses in lingerie upon a chaise, her stare defiant.

I am immediately drawn into the faces, the eyes, the differ-ent bodies and skin tones. It's mesmerizing. I see pain, joy, love, anger, daring. There's trembling beauty in the curve of a neck,

in the arch of a back. Even what might be considered ugly becomes strangely alluring here in the loving acceptance of the
photographer's eye.

"These are hypnotic," says Max, similarly having forgotten
our errand and in full art-lover mode.

It's only when I get to the final image on the far wall that I stop.

It's a form I know as well as I know my own. A man, his body
crafted as if by the gods—musculature in perfect symmetry, abs
cut, biceps toned. Shadows gather in the dip of his collarbone.
His skin glows. He sits on a wide sill, gazing out a window,
half his face washed in too much light, the rest swallowed by
darkness. One hand rests on a toned thigh; he dips his forehead
into the other hand as if in despair. No wedding ring, I notice.
He looks younger, boyish. This was before I met him, maybe.
I hope. I think my husband would have told me if he had recently posed nude for his cousin.

"Is that—Chad?" asks Max coming up behind me.

I swallow against the thickness in my throat, give a mute nod.

"Okay," he says. "Wow."

We both stand staring at the nude picture of my husband.
Talk about awkward.

Then a creaking noise off to the right catches our attention.
That music—melodic and echoing—carries from someplace else
in the building. Light floods in the high windows. Outside, a
truck rumbles up the street.

"Dana?" I call, a tingling on my skin. Max and I both stand
frozen, listening. We're in the middle of the city. Why does it
feel like we're on the moon?

But there's no answer. Just that strange creaking noise.

"You know what?" says Max, grabbing my wrist. "I'm suddenly thinking this was a bad idea. Let's just—go."

But I'm already walking toward the sound, past more photographs of cityscapes, still-life images of sharp objects like knives,
scissors, cleavers. There are images of children who look like

Dana—a slim boy with inquiring eyes. A fiery young girl with freckles and a searing, knowing stare. No way they're not her children; the resemblance is so strong. Did I know that she has kids?

To my right, there's a small office with a simple desk, laptop open. On the desk lies what I guess must be her phone. It's ringing, vibrating on the surface. I leave it unanswered.

To my left, a doorway stands open to reveal an old-school darkroom. The light inside glows red. Inside are processing tables, trays filled with liquid. A strong chemical smell emanates. There's a ticking clock, a sign that reads Burn Tools, one that reads Dodge Tools. From the ceiling hang arcs of clotheslines.

Photographs hang to dry, fluttering in the draft.

I move in closer to see what's there.

My shoulders hike with tension. More images of my husband.

He waits on a subway platform, reading a paper. I squint for a date but it's not legible, too grainy. He's smart in slim black jeans and leather jacket. In the next photo, he stands at a light, waiting to cross the street. His brow wrinkles in a frown, which I must say is rare. He seems deep in thought, his hair longer than he's kept it since I've known him. I move closer. He's in a café, sitting in a window seat with a woman whose face is not visible in the frame, their fingers woven together. His ring hand is not visible, either. An ex? They are legion.

The final image brings a gasp to my throat. It's all shadows and purple light, a man leans over a woman who is pressed against a wall, other forms, just shadows, populate the image— a bar or a nightclub. I can't see his face, but I recognize his carriage. The woman is unrecognizable as she was in my brief but vivid vision in the Aldridges' hallway. It's the same scene. I can almost feel the throb of the music. How is that possible?

You've seen this before, my father would say. *The image keeps coming back to you for a reason. It means something.*

Coincidence, Dr. Black would counter. *Perhaps you've seen this image before. It was ingrained in your memory, maybe bringing up your insecurities about how women respond to your husband, a deep-seated worry that you're not enough for him.*

I stare a moment, decide to side with Dr. Black. Reason is solid beneath my feet. All the rest of it is a spiral into madness.

Clearly, Dana was following my husband. For a long time, it seems. She was literally stalking him. Why? What else did she find? What has she called me up here to say?

That strange creaking, it's coming from the end of the hall where a door stands ajar. There's a draft, the cold air touching my skin. The walls seem very white, the floor steel gray, the hard surface echoing beneath my boot heels.

"Rosie, I'm getting an Uber," says Max, still in the gallery. "This place is creeping me out."

I hear his footfalls grow fainter.

The body knows.

My breath grows shallow, and my nerve endings vibrate like guitar strings.

Energy in the air moves through your cells. It's not magic. It's biology.

I keep walking toward that door.

The ancient things—fear, grief, pain, danger—they live in our neurons, respond to those signals on the air.

"Dana?"

At the door, I pause. That creaking, slow and long.

A draft whistles through the opening. Feeling alone, I glance back down the long corridor. No Max. The music is coming from the other side of the door, ambient and electronic, soothing, like something you'd hear in a spa. I push the door open, and it swings wide, air rushing out.

I almost don't see her at first, *can't* see her. As if it's too much for my psyche.

She's stylish in black leather pants and thigh-high boots; an oversize sweater drapes off one pale shoulder. Her hands are frozen at her throat, as if she was clawing against the rope around her neck. Eyes wide in fear and pain, mouth agape.

Dana.

She's hanging from the rafters, dead.

The room starts to spin and there's a siren, my own screaming for Max. Rushing over, I try to understand how she got up there. How do I get her down?

My thoughts are a panicked jumble. The rope around her neck is tied off around a metal piling. There's a ladder beside her. Did she climb up there and jump off? I try to loosen the knot, but it's pulled taut.

"Oh, my God." Shock makes Max go gray as he enters the room. "Holy shit. Rosie."

I drop to my knees, wailing. Max tries to bring me to my feet, pulling me back toward the door. He's already calling 911. *There's an emergency. A woman has killed herself.*

No, I want to say. *That's not true. She didn't. Someone did this.*

I can't take my eyes off her. If we'd gotten here sooner, could we have saved her? She died not knowing how much her father loved her. There's a letter from him that she will never read. Max is still trying to get me away, and I pull back to her.

"We need to get her *down*," I yell. "Maybe we can save her."

"No," he says sternly. "She's gone."

I pull away from his grasp, and go back to her.

That's when I see it.

The leather strap of a necklace around her ruined neck.

A pendant.

A silver hand with the evil eye stone in its palm.

fourteen

I can't take my eyes from her, from the pendant, just like the one my husband was wearing, as Max drags me from the room.

"I have to try to get her down," I manage again through sobs.

"She's gone, Rosie, please," he insists, voice strained with despair, managing to get me out the door. "It's too late. It's too late."

I wrest myself away from him to go back, but he blocks me again.

That necklace, I want to say. *It's just like the one Chad was wearing this morning.*

Instead, I just give in to the sobbing, sink to my knees onto the cold concrete. Max comes down to the floor with me.

The police get there quickly, the paramedics right behind, though Max is right, of course—there's no saving Dana. Max and I sit on the floor against the far wall of the gallery, leaning against each other. My head on his shoulder, his hand on my leg. I am shaken to my core, the image of her hanging there burned into my psyche. I can't stop seeing it. I cry quietly. It's not the first time I've witnessed death, but apparently it never gets easier.

She joins a gallery of macabre images in my mind. When I was a child, a man had a heart attack in my father's church. His face was the strangest gray color, his wife wailing. The girl on the subway tracks. Ivan, his last breath leaving him so quietly, another never drawn. The silence that seemed to fall. The bike messenger twisted on the sidewalk.

Now Dana.

Her face—pain, rage, fear, frozen there forever. I feel a helpless grief for a person I never really knew, and it's a knot in my solar plexus.

I've left a message for Chad, but he hasn't returned it.

I try again. No answer.

Where is he?

I jab out a desperate text: Please call me. It's an emergency.

No response.

The responding officer has asked us to wait for the detective to arrive, so that's what we do. But I want to get far from this place, her disturbing images, all the pictures of my husband, whom she's clearly been following around for years. The sight of her—I'll carry that with me, I suspect. Maybe forever.

"Did she seem unstable?" Max asks unhelpfully.

"No," I say. "Yes?"

She was enraged in our East Village hallway, cryptic and strange on the phone. So yes, maybe. But she seemed too wild, too full of feeling and power, to kill herself. Her immense talent, her beauty, her inner fire. How could she just snuff herself out that way? Why? So violently. On her face—fear, pain. Regret? Did she change her mind too late? Or—

"I don't *know,* Max."

"Okay," he says, soothing. "Okay."

The voices of the police officers carry from the other room, low and serious. More people arrive, footfalls heavy, radios crackling. They wear navy blue jackets indicating that they're from the medical examiner's office. They glance at us, strides purposeful, eyes seeing, but say nothing, disappear through the door at the end of the hall.

"She called me up here to *tell me something*," I whisper. "She obviously wasn't planning to kill herself today."

Max rubs a nervous hand on his leg, nodding slowly, considering.

"Or," he says quietly. "Maybe she just wanted you to be the one to find her."

The idea is unsettling. Could she hate me that much? She doesn't even know me. *Didn't* know me. Strange how tenses shift so soon after death.

"Why? Why would she want that?"

"You said she was angry, right? About the apartment."

I look up at him, incredulous. "You think she killed herself over an apartment? That she was taking some kind of twisted revenge on us by arranging for me to witness her suicide?"

He raises his eyebrows, pushes up on his glasses. "The thing is never the thing, right? Didn't you tell me that?"

Meaning when you're angry, hurt, in despair about something, it's rarely about the situation before you, or not just about that. In Dana's case, her rage about the apartment was about her father not loving her enough, not being there, abandoning her and her family. That was the source of her anger and despair. Not the apartment. Or not just that.

"No," I say. "No one would do that."

But people do all kinds of dark and terrible things for reasons that don't seem sound to others. Max doesn't press the issue, wears his so-reasonable-lets-agree-to-disagree face. He's on his phone now, scrolling.

"'Dana Lowan is a world-renowned fashion and art photographer,'" he reads aloud from something he's found in his search. "'She has photographed celebrities, authors, and world leaders, traveled to fashion shoots and movie sets around the world. Her work has been displayed in galleries and museums in New York, Paris, Prague, and London.'"

This is all news to me. "I didn't know she was so successful. Ivan never said."

Max continues. "'Her upcoming exhibit, *Body and Soul*, will open at Artists Space in SoHo'—looks like Sunday."

Artists Space is a world-class gallery; a show there is a career-maker for any artist or photographer. Even I know that.

"So she had an opening at one of the most prestigious galleries in the city this week and she kills herself?"

He's quiet a second. "You can't apply logic to things like suicidal depression."

He's right about that. I've never been suicidal, but I know how you can sink into places so dark you think that there will never be light again. I wonder if that box would have made the difference, if it would have been healing in some way. If she *did* kill herself.

"Says she's divorced," Max goes on. "Two kids."

She left her kids. I wrap my arms around my center. If a child isn't enough to tie you to this world, what could be?

"Ms. Lowan?"

I look up into the gaze of a man who has dark, watchful eyes, the shadow of stubble at his jaw and deep lines etched in his forehead. Max and I rise quickly, gracelessly, from our place on the floor.

"I'm Detective Grady Crowe." He offers a firm handshake. "You discovered the body?"

My hands are still shaking. My fingers feel like icicles in his warm grip. "I did."

"What brings you up here today?"

I wonder if I should call Olivia. She's famous for saying that no one ever thinks they need a lawyer, but everybody does. A woman is dead; I found her. She had a grievance against us, was threatening to sue. There are pictures of my husband all over her gallery. I glance at Max, who shrugs.

"Dana called me," I say. "Asked to meet."

"She's your—?"

"My husband's cousin."

"Just a family visit, or—?"

That must be his technique, to let his sentences trail, asking you to fill in the blanks. I am about to tell the truth. That we inherited an apartment that rightfully should have been hers. That she was angry, apparently stalking my husband, had things she wanted to share about him. But I realize how odd, how suspicious, that sounds given the circumstances.

"She wanted me to see her work," I say instead. "We've only recently gotten to know each other since the recent passing of her father."

Not a lie, right? Obviously, she wanted me to see her work, or she wouldn't have asked me up here. Those pictures in her darkroom; is that what she wanted me to see? Are there more? Things she didn't display but wanted to reveal. Are they on her computer, or hidden in a drawer somewhere? What will the police find when they start looking?

The detective offers a slow nod. Max shifts behind me, gives me a little poke.

"Was she troubled?" asks the detective. He hands me a pack of tissues from his pocket, and I take one. I must be a wreck. "Was there a history of depression?"

"She was estranged from her father when he passed. So like I say, we weren't close. I don't know much about her history."

"But you were close to her father?"

"My husband's uncle—yes. He was our closest relative. We cared for him through his illness and death."

More tears fall. There's a bottomless well, it seems. I use the tissue he provided, to wipe at them, annoyed that I can't keep a grip on my emotions.

He waits a moment. Then, "I'm sorry this happened to you today."

I don't know how to respond to that; it's so kind, so compassionate. I push back into Max for support.

"Can you just run down the details for me?" he asks when I nod my thanks.

I tell him about the call—sort of. How we made the appointment, and she sent me the address. How we took a cab up here, walked through the gallery, found her body. He listens, nodding, scribbling in a leather notebook he produced when I started talking.

"Who is next of kin?" he asks.

I shake my head. "I'm sorry. I don't know. I've tried to call my husband, but I can't reach him."

He gives me a quizzical look, as if everyone is reachable every second and it's weird that my husband is not. "He's in a play," I add, a little defensive even to my own ears. "He doesn't bring his phone into rehearsals and performances."

"An actor," he says with mild interest. "His name?"

"Chad Lowan."

He writes that down and I have the irrational feeling that I shouldn't have told him my husband's name. Which makes no sense, because there's nothing to hide, and even if there was, this detective is going to know all our names at some point. I am a true-crime writer so I know a thing or two about procedure, and the police will treat this place as a crime scene; the death will be investigated. There will be questions, at least some looking around for motive and opportunity for something other than suicide.

"I saw her phone on the desk in her office," I offer. "It was ringing."

We walk down the hall in that direction. The far door leading to where I found Dana is already cordoned off with crime scene tape. High enough for people to walk under, a reminder that they are entering a crime scene and to take the appropriate care.

In Dana's office, Detective Crowe pulls some gloves from his pocket before picking up the phone. He taps the screen and looks at it a moment. I see something on his face that I don't like—a kind of suspicious squint. He turns the phone around to me.

The lock screen is filled with call bubbles.

Every one of them is from Chad.

"Seems like your husband was trying to reach her."

My throat feels thick, so I just nod. Why would he be calling her like that? It looks like no fewer than five times. I haven't been able to reach him all day. Maybe she called him, too. Told him I was coming up here, that she was going to reveal something about him to me.

"Any idea why?"

"No," I say. "None at all."

"You don't happen to know her lock code, do you?"

I shake my head.

"That's right," he says. "You weren't close."

"Right."

In my pocket, my phone starts vibrating, the ringer off. It must be Chad, but I don't reach for it and the detective doesn't seem to hear it buzzing.

Then, with a tilt of his head, "Are you going to get that?"

We lock eyes, and I have no choice but to take it from my pocket. Max rubs his temples.

It's Chad.

"You didn't go up there, did you?" he says when I pick up. "To Dana's studio. There's a lot you don't know about her. It's not safe. She's got major problems, Rosie."

His voice is taut with anxiety, so different from his usual easy, in-on-the-joke-of-life manner. The detective is staring at me hard. I turn away from him, walk out of the office. I still have a right to my privacy, don't I?

"Rosie, are you there? What did she say to you?"

"Nothing," I answer in a sharp whisper. "She didn't say *anything*. She's dead, Chad."

The silence on the line is deafening, a black hole sucking in sound.

"I found her hanging from the rafters in her studio." My voice breaks with fear, sadness, the horror of this conversation.

"Oh, God," he breathes, shock pulling his voice into a whisper. "I'm so sorry. Are you—okay?"

No, I am *definitely not* okay. "The police are here now," I say, hoping he gets that I don't want to talk in front of the detective.

"Don't say another word to them," he tells me. "I'm calling Olivia and I'm on my way."

I want to tell him not to come—because of the photos, because of the calls to Dana that the detective has already seen. *Chad*, I want to say. *What the fuck is going on?* But Detective Crowe is right on top of me.

And anyway, he hangs up before I can answer. "Okay," I say to dead air. "I'll wait here."

Then to the detective, "He's on his way."

Crowe nods grimly. "Women don't usually hang themselves," he says darkly. "In my experience, it's pills or a razor in the bathtub."

Max puts his arm around me, sensing maybe that I'm wobbling a bit.

"And it took some doing. The ceilings in there must be fifteen feet tall. She made a noose, tied it off, got a ladder and—"

"That's enough," I say, putting up a hand. "I get it."

I swear he smiles a little, but he hides it well. "It's just weird, right? Why would she call you up here and then kill herself so that *you* would find her?"

I had asked the same question myself. But I don't say anything, just look anyplace in the room but at him.

He goes on. "Was there bad blood? Between you and her? Between her and your husband?"

My instinct is to spill my guts—tell him everything about the apartment, about the photographs, but I still have Chad's voice ringing in my ears.

"My husband is on his way with our lawyer." My voice is level and calm, not at all how I feel. "I don't feel comfortable answering any more questions until they get here."

The detective lifts his palms, his eyebrows arching. "No need for all that, is there? You're not in any trouble, Ms. Lowan."

"That's good," I answer, moving toward the door. He backs up a step to subtly block my passage. His voice is low and serious when he speaks again.

"But if there's something you need to tell me, now would be a good time."

There's a bit of a standoff. Finally, I offer him a polite smile. "I am happy to cooperate in the presence of our attorney."

"Wow," he says, bobbling his head a bit. "Okay."

He steps aside and Max ushers me from the office and back to our spot by the door.

"You should go," I whisper. "You don't need to be a part of this. Whatever it is."

"I'm *already* part of this." Max's dark eyes search my face. "But—what is happening here, Rosie?"

Dana is dead. Her studio was full of pictures of my husband. He has been calling her obsessively all day while I have been unable to reach him. He has just asked me not to communicate any further with the police until he arrives with our lawyer. The truth is I have no idea what's going on.

When all of that jams up in my throat and I don't answer, Max pulls me into his embrace, and I hold on tight.

fifteen

On our wedding night, Ivan gave a speech.

Think about all the things that had to go wrong for just one thing to go right.

He's talking about the night Chad and I met. It was a week after the subway incident and my night with Max, a misty, early evening. I had tickets to a performance at St. Mark's Church in the East Village, and usually I would have asked Max, but I didn't—because things had been weird since our night together. Because it seemed too much like a date and I didn't want to lead him on. Instead, I invited another friend, a publicity assistant named Hilary, who was bright and effusive and lots of fun.

But as I waited outside for her, I received a text that she'd had a work emergency and couldn't get away. I thought about bailing but I'd heard good things about the independent play written and directed by one of my NYU professors, so I decided to go in on my own.

But the stairs leading to the church were slick in the mist, and there was a crowd. Just as I was about to reach the door, I was jostled and slipped, spilling the contents of my purse all over the stone stairs, skinning my knee.

Embarrassed, frazzled, I chased after my cheap lipstick, tattered wallet, a smattering of different colored pens, crumpled money, change. Most people walked by, creating a space around me and the shamefully junky contents of my purse. But suddenly, I had a helper, a young guy with a full beard and a wool beanie. He wore a baggy sweatshirt, loose jeans, some beat-up old sneakers.

He moved quickly, helping me get everything while the crowd filtered in through the open doors, finally handing me a shattered compact, the powder just a crumble, the mirror I was dismayed to see was just a spider web of cracks.

"I don't believe in bad luck, do you?" he asked me with a smile.

I shook my head. Those eyes; they were hypnotic, full of light and kindness, laughter. There was a moment of heat, of electricity.

"I am so late," he said, looking toward the doors. "Are you okay?"

"I—I—I'm okay," I stammered, my knee raging, bruised and bleeding. "Thank you so much."

"I'll see you again," he said, but then he was gone, swallowed by the crowd.

His energy lingered, his words feeling more like prophecy than the tossed-away comment that it likely was.

I was still tingling, knee still stinging, as I went inside, looking around the theater for the bearded man. But among the artsy, intellectual crowd, I didn't spot him. The usher took me to my aisle seat near the stage, and feeling frazzled, sweaty, I was glad for the empty seat beside me. The small orchestra started to warm up, and finally after what seemed like a bit of delay, the lights went down.

"Tonight the role of Ben will be played by understudy Chad Lowan," said the announcer. The name meant nothing to me at the time.

The play was about a young girl name Jessie who ran away from home to escape abuse and came to New York City, only to be victimized again and again, before eventually finding her way. The character Ben was her social services counselor—the young, hip voice of reason, who helps her get her GED, get into college and find a job. I knew enough about the acclaimed playwright to know that the story was semi-autobiographical. It was funny, moving and true—and Chad's performance was mesmerizing. He'd been studying and rehearsing for the role, never imagining that he'd actually be on stage. Then, the original Ben slipped and fell down the stairs of his walk-up and broke his leg, only an hour before he was due to report to the theater. Chad had raced on zero notice from his job as a bartender up the street and got there just in time—hence his rush up the front steps.

Hilary had to have cancelled late, otherwise Rosie wouldn't have been waiting there. The weather had to be lousy, or the steps wouldn't have been slick. Rosie had to fall. The actor scheduled to perform had to quite literally break a leg just hours before the performance. Chad had to be racing up the stairs at just the moment Rosie fell and spilled the contents of her bag.

His performance, the play, was a huge hit—a standing ovation and big cheers for Chad. I swear I was in love with him before I left the theater.

You fell in love with Ben, Chad likes to complain. *Because he's so woke, and present, so wise. I don't think I'm as evolved as Ben.*

But it wasn't true. It wasn't Ben; it was Chad. It was always him, from that first moment when he handed me the ruined compact. There was something in his gaze, his energy. Whatever it was, I wanted it in my life.

I don't believe in bad luck, do you?

Those were Chad's first words to Rosie. I don't. I don't believe in good luck, either. But I do believe that certain circumstances might look like bad luck, but then lead to something wonderful.

That night at the theater I didn't linger, though. I wasn't going to be the girl waiting to meet the actors—even though it was a small production and the cast always gathered in the lobby to shake hands and talk with the audience.

When the play ended, I moved toward the exit in the crowd. Just as I reached the doors, I heard my name. It was my professor, Miranda Bright—a brilliant playwright who would go on to win major awards. I pushed my way back to her, and she pulled me into a warm hug, smelling of jasmine.

Tall and elegant, with long dreadlocks and wire-rimmed glasses, she was a dynamic, engaged and joyful teacher of her craft. I never wanted to write plays, but I loved writing them for her.

"Your play," I gushed. "It was magnificent. Wow, so moving."

She put her hands in prayer at her chest, gave a little bow. "It's a journey. It's all the people involved. I'm just a team member. But thank you."

Her grace, her humility, was so inspiring.

"Tell me everything," she said generously, even though it was her night.

I told her quickly about my job in publishing, the book I was researching.

"You're going to do great things, Rosie," she said kindly when I was done.

I blushed at her kindness and hoped I could prove her right. I continued to heap praise on her, the wonderful play, her huge talent, insight, wisdom. And then, there he was.

"Poor Chad," she said, looping her arm through his. "He raced from his bartending job. Wasn't he magnificent?"

"He was. You were," I said. "You were—mesmerizing."

He smiled, gave a bow of gratitude. "I wish you wrote for the *New York Times*."

"Maybe someday," I said.

I still don't remember quite how it happened. One minute we were standing and chatting; Miranda got pulled into another group of admirers. Chad introduced me to some other cast members; there was an easy drift backstage where the champagne was flowing.

And then it was late.

"Do you want to get out of here?" he asked finally. That charm; he was so easy with himself, with me.

There was no way he was going to leave there without getting to know her better, Ivan went on. He told me that she cast a spell on him that night. One look, and he was ruined for all other women.

We left together and found ourselves at a speakeasy on Eighth Street and we stayed there until it closed, just talking. Intimacy was total, immediate. We weren't apart again, not really. There wasn't any on-again, off-again. There were no games. We were living together inside six months. Engaged after a year. It took us nearly five years to get to the altar, only because we were both so young and it seemed right to wait. We've barely argued. Even when I was deeply depressed during the writing of my last book, he was there, my rock, my best friend, dragging me through, never impatient, always by my side.

If just one of those things hadn't happened, we wouldn't be standing here tonight, toasting this beautiful, special, talented young couple. Even so, it takes more to make a marriage than good luck, or bad. A few people in this room can attest to how that initial golden moment can dull, how secrets, lies and bad behavior, jealousy, or possessiveness, can tarnish love. But I've seen how these two love each other, support each other, laugh together, are tender, don't hold back, give everything. Maybe it was kismet that brought them together, but it's their pure loving hearts that will keep them that way.

I'm thinking about Ivan's speech, about the night Chad and I met, as I watch my husband work the room. After he sweeps in the front door with Olivia, petite and impeccably dressed in a tight black suit and heels, looking fierce and official by his side, he speaks to the detective, telling him things I've never heard about Dana. That she was unstable, that she'd struggled with mental illness since childhood. She was obsessed with him, was sick with jealousy over his relationship with her father.

His performance is pitch-perfect—earnest, searching, distraught. I feel like I could be watching him on stage.

"I kept this—a lot of it—from Rosie," he says, looking over at me. The wrinkle in his brow, the set of his mouth—worried for me, for us, but trying to help.

"Why were you trying to reach her today?" asks Detective Crowe.

Chad puts a distraught hand to his forehead.

"You don't have to answer that," says Olivia, stepping forward.

"I don't have anything to hide," he says. Olivia gives him an assenting nod.

Chad blows out a breath. "Dana left a message, saying that she was going to ruin my life if I didn't sell the apartment and give her the money."

Detective Crowe stares at him a moment, seems to size Chad up. There's a slight wrinkle in his brow that tells me he's less than impressed with Chad. "Can you play me the message?"

Chad takes the phone from his pocket, searching for the message, then presses Play.

Dana's voice is icy, slicing with hatred and anger. "You have always been such an operator. Such a liar. Your lovely wife. She's on the way up here, and I'm going to tell her everything, Chad. She deserves to know who she married. *Or* we can make a deal."

A shudder moves through my body. *What* was she going to tell me?

"What was she going to tell your wife?" asks the detective, echoing my thoughts.

Chad shoots me a despairing glance. "I have no idea. Rosie and I have no secrets."

I stand in front of the nude photograph of him. Is the detective going to recognize him?

"Maybe it was this?" Chad points at the photograph and I

move aside, feeling my cheeks color. "That I posed nude for her and some of her fellow students. This was ages ago. Long before I met Rosie."

"You posed nude for your cousin?" says Detective Crowe with a frown. "That's a little weird, right?"

"It's art," says Chad with a shrug.

Crowe is right, though. It is weird. My eyes fall on the photograph again. In fact, we're all staring at it with different expressions. Olivia looks embarrassed, turning away. Max frowns. Crowe squints, amused.

"My client is an actor and a model," says Olivia, her voice cutting through the quiet. "This is not unusual. Students do all kinds of things for money. *And* it's time for us to go. Both my clients have cooperated with you. They are in shock and need to process their loss. If you have further questions of them, please contact me."

Olivia puts her body between Chad and the detective, handing him a card. He offers a wry smile and a nod, takes it from her.

"What did she think you'd lied about?" Crowe asks over Olivia's shoulder.

Chad offers a sad, slow shake of his head. "Like I said—she wasn't well."

Olivia begins herding Chad, Max and me from the room.

"No more questions for the time being. My clients are willing to come to the station if there's anything further that they can provide."

Chad puts his arm around my shoulder to lead me away, but Detective Crowe reaches for my wrist.

"Here's my card," he says, his gaze glancing off Chad before he meets my eyes. "I have a feeling you're going to need it."

Something about the way he says it makes my stomach bottom out. What does he see when he looks at my husband? At me? Maybe it's just his job to be suspicious of everyone. I shove his card in my pocket, turn away from him.

Outside on the street, when Chad goes to talk to Max, I tell Olivia, "There were more pictures of Chad in the darkroom."

She frowns, moves in closer. "What kind of pictures?"

"It looks like she was following him. For a long time—like years."

I open my bag to show her. I took them off the line where they hung in the darkroom, nabbing them before the police arrived. I'm not proud of it, but that's what I did just minutes after seeing Dana's body.

She stares at the photos, still slightly damp, in my bag. When she lifts her eyes to me, she lowers her voice and leans in close. "You tampered with a crime scene, Rosie."

I draw in a deep breath. "I know."

She's about to say something else when Chad interrupts us.

"I'm sorry this happened to you." Chad puts his hands on my face. "I didn't know how unwell she really was. I thought—I don't know what I thought."

"Why didn't you call me back?"

"I did. I tried and tried to call. You didn't answer."

It's not true. I know it isn't. But then when I look at the screen on my phone, there's a red number six on my phone icon. A slew of missed calls from Chad, at least three voice messages.

"It didn't ring," I say. "I didn't get these calls."

"I was trying to reach you, to tell you not to go to see her if she called. Clearly, her demons got the better of her today. It's a tragedy."

His eyes well, and there's true sorrow there. I pull him in and hold on to him.

"That was it," he whispers. "She was my last living family member."

"No," I say, urgently wanting that not to be so. "*We're* building a family. That's the past. We are the future."

The pregnancy test I picked up yesterday is waiting for me at home. Now more than ever I want to give this to him, to us. A family that grows, that supports, that loves.

Max and Olivia have stepped off to the side, talk in low tones. They know each other from events and parties, dinners. But there's something about the way they're standing, how he leans into her, how she touches her hair. I wonder if there's something more between them than just an acquaintance through mutual friends. I am surprised by, and quickly quash, a rush of jealousy.

I focus on my husband. "What did she want to tell me about you?"

Chad shakes his head, looks lost. "That picture," I go on. "There are others. She was following you. Watching you."

The air is growing colder, the day going gray; a light rain starts to fall. Chad pulls me under the awning.

"I know," he says. "She—had problems."

He's about to say something more. But Max has called an UberXL, and the black Suburban pulls up to the curb and we all pile in, eager to get away from this place, out of the rain, which is coming down harder.

Olivia, in the back row, gets on her phone and is talking low and serious. Max sits up front with the driver, staring out the window. What must he be thinking?

"That picture," I whisper to Chad.

He holds up his palms.

"It was a long time ago. She invited me to her school to pose for her class. It was decent money, and I was broke."

I guess that tracks. My husband is not shy.

"And these?" I open my bag. He lifts out the photos and shifts through them, shaking his head.

"They're old." He picks up the one where he holds another woman's hand in a café. Her face is not visible in the frame. His ring hand is not visible, either. "That's Elsa, I think. You've met. We saw each other for a while, but it didn't work out."

He's smooth, always has an answer.

"And this one?" The image from the nightclub, it's all shadows and swirling purple light.

He blows out a breath. "I don't know. That could be us. Look at the hair, those boots. That's you, Rosie. Right?"

I look more closely. Maybe? I'm not sure I'm that short, or that slim.

"When were we at a club?" I ask. I'm not exactly the night-club type.

"We've been to a hundred clubs." He puts a hand on my thigh.

"Not in ages."

"Clearly, she's been following me for years."

"Why?"

Because that's really the question. Why was Dana so obsessed with Chad? Why did she call me up here? Why did she kill herself for me to find? Or did she? Chad has perfected the innocent shrug, or maybe *he is* just innocent. "She's been like this since we were kids. Weird. Jealous of me somehow."

"Anyway," he goes on when I say nothing. "Why would you come up here when she called?"

I tell him about her call, about the box I found, about how Abi was supposed to put it in the trunk but didn't. He frowns at me while I talk.

"Did you really think she could tell you something about me that you don't already know?"

The city comes into view ahead of us. I feel like Max is listening to us, but I don't care.

"No," I say. "But she did pique my curiosity. And I wanted to give her those photos, the letter. I thought I could offer her that, at least. Proof that Ivan loved her, thought about her. I thought it could be healing."

"She wanted the apartment, or the money from its sale," he says, angry now. "That's all she cared about, hurting us because he left it to us. She never cared about Ivan."

"It sounds like he abandoned her, his family. Hurt people hurt people, right?"

Chad pushes a strand of my hair away from my face. "You're a good person. You only see the light in people."

"Why would Abi do that? Not put the box in the trunk?"

He shakes his head. "There's an explanation and we'll ask for it."

We drop Olivia first. On the street, I embrace her.

"Thank you for being here for us today. I don't know what would have happened without you," I say.

"Don't talk to Detective Crowe again," she warns, her voice stern. "If he calls or comes to see you, tell him he needs to make an appointment with me."

She gives us each a hug and disappears into the midtown glass tower where her law firm sits on the top floor. She's the youngest partner at Rinker, Yeager and Young.

Then Max drops us at our place.

"You're a good friend, Max," says Chad. "Thanks for going with Rosie. I hate to think of her facing that alone."

We all stand on the street. "That's what friends are for, right?"

"Are you okay?" I ask him. "That was hard on both of us. Come up for a drink."

"I'm okay," he says, glancing at Chad. "I have a work dinner to get to."

He must see my concern. "Don't worry, I'll just drink away the trauma like all healthy adults. Maybe do some tele-therapy."

I want to reach for him, embrace him. He seems lost, lonely, and I feel bad that he's been cast in this best-friend role when maybe he still wants more. I touch his arm, and he puts his hand over mine.

"Take care of your girl," he says to Chad. It's a challenge; a subtle one.

But Chad is the winner, and he knows it, doesn't need to get ruffled. "Always."

Max pushes up his glasses, smiles at me, then climbs back in the car and is gone.

★ ★ ★

"But, Ms. Lowan," says Abi, looking earnest and sweetly confused. "I'm so sorry. You did not have a box with you when you left this morning."

Anger is a ball in my throat. If there's anything I can't stand it's being told something I know to be true is false. It's gaslighting and I've put up with it all my life. I'm so angry, tears come. Which I hate. I hate it that when I'm at my most mad, I cry instead of rage.

"Abi," I say, trying to keep my cool, my mutinous voice shaking. "You took the box from me in the hallway upstairs, carried it out to the street, asked the driver to open the trunk, then knocked on the cab to indicate you'd shut the door."

He is an impeccable man with manicured nails and clear, dark eyes. His black hair is carefully cut and styled. He seems ageless—maybe he's forty, maybe he's sixty. His uniform is as pressed and pristine as his calm demeanor.

"Ms. Lowan, I'm so sorry. This is not how I remember it. You were flustered, running late. Perhaps you're remembering wrong."

Chad is looking on, brow wrinkling with worry.

"I was not late," I say sharply. "I was not *flustered*."

How often does a woman deal with this kind of shit? Where she's made to feel off-kilter, unstable, unable to trust her own memories? It's downright Victorian.

"Ms. Lowan," says Abi, firmly. "There was no box."

I point up to the security camera in the far corner of the lobby. "Let's look at the footage."

He smiles; it's not my imagination that it's just shy of condescending. "There's no recording, Ms. Lowan. It's just surveillance for the back office so the doorman can see what's happening out here if he's back there."

I look to that closed door again. I've never been in there. It wasn't part of "the tour."

"Where *are* all the other doormen?"

"Ah," he says. "You must have noticed that I seem to be here around the clock?"

"Yes, I have," I say. "Maybe you're overtired, working too hard, Abi. That's why you don't remember how things went earlier."

Two can play at that game. Abi offers a wan smile that doesn't reach his eyes; Chad gives me a nudge with his shoulder.

"Not at all, Ms. Lowan. But thank you for your concern," Abi says smoothly. "It's true, though, that we are having a bit of a staffing crisis at the moment. It's difficult to find good doormen being that the job is so *demanding*, and might seem *thankless* to some. Younger people don't see service jobs as very rewarding."

I swallow. Now he's going to make me feel like an elitist bitch, hassling the doorman, blaming him for my mistake. Nice one.

"But I assure you," he goes on. "I am quite all right. And I *am* sorry for any confusion, Ms. Lowan. Truly. And I'm sure it's my fault somehow, but I do not remember carrying a box out for you."

It's then that I remember Xavier got on the elevator as we were on the way down. I know he saw the box.

"Can you ring Xavier?" I say. "He was there this morning."

"He's not in."

"Will you ring him, please?" I press.

His face a mask of patience, he steps behind the desk, picks up the phone and dials. I can hear a persistent ringing, no answer. He hangs up the phone after the ringing has gone on and on.

We all stand facing each other on the marble floor as rain starts to fall heavily outside. Anger boils in my chest, rises up my throat like acid. I want to scream at him, shake that unflappable demeanor, make him admit what I know to be true.

"Okay, Abi," says Chad, finally ushering me toward the elevator. "I'm sure we'll get to the bottom of this. Rosie's had a terrible day. She needs some rest."

Yes, I need some *rest*. Because I'm having a *spell*. Get the smelling salts! I'm wild, raging inside, but I know my exterior is calm. We're so good at that, aren't we? Hiding the roiling depths of our emotions.

"I know," says Abi, with compassion in his voice. "The news has already reached the Windermere."

"What?" I say. "How?"

He blinks. I see a flash of something; then it's gone. "Miss Dana's suicide was on the news. It's a terrible loss, so soon after her father. You both must be reeling."

That doesn't seem possible. It's been just hours, and was it officially declared a suicide? It didn't seem like the detective was convinced that Dana had ended her life.

I stare at Abi, his kind face, his bottomless eyes. When he returns my gaze, something goes cold inside me.

We all ride up to the apartment in silence and I fume about how I'll be using the service elevator from now on, and will find my way into that back office and get a look at that surveillance equipment.

I expect Charles or Ella to come out, to say they've heard the news, but there's only silence from their place and I'm glad as we push inside to our apartment.

"He heard it on the news?" I say when the door closes. "How can that be?"

Chad shakes his head, mystified. "I don't know. Maybe someone called in a tip?"

I shed my coat, my bag, look at my ragged reflection in the foyer mirror. My auburn hair is wild, big circles under my brown eyes, makeup smudged. A striking contrast to Abi's cool, put-together exterior, I look a wreck—flustered, just as Abi said.

I keep seeing her, hanging there. Her eyes bulging, mouth open in an eternal scream, her throat black-and-blue. Will I ever be able to unsee it? That session with Dr. Black tomorrow can't come soon enough.

I flip on New York One News and I'm shocked to see a reporter broadcasting from in front of Dana's studio. I turn up the volume.

"Renowned photographer Dana Lowan was found dead in her studio today, cause of death not yet determined."

How is that even possible?

"Rosie."

Chad calls from the second bedroom, and I move away from the screen to follow his voice. He's standing by my desk, looking down. Sitting there on the floor near his feet is the box with Dana's name scrawled across the side.

What? No. It can't be. I know I brought that box downstairs.

I move over to it quickly, open the lid.

The letter that sat on top of the items inside, the one from Ivan to Dana, is gone.

sixteen

Dr. Black's office feels like a cozy living room with plush furniture and towering bookshelves, a fireplace that he lights in winter, tall windows that look out onto Central Park. I sink into my usual place on his couch, my phone off.

He's long and lean in his Eames chair, black wool pants pressed, a dove-gray sweater hanging elegantly off his thin frame. He adjusts his thick black glasses, runs thin fingers through his floppy, glossy dark hair.

"That's a lot," he says easily. His notebook sits in his lap, but he hasn't written in it. "For anyone, that would be a lot. Death of a loved one, large inheritance, moving, new book contract, which is a boon and a big responsibility. We can also add the strain of trying for a baby. The traumatic discovery of Dana's body. Honestly, I'd be surprised if you *weren't* experiencing anxiety."

Very faintly outside I can hear the street noise. Beside him on a small pedestal table, there's a picture of a young girl with long, dark hair cascading past her shoulders. His daughter as a little girl. She's a teenager now, getting ready for college.

"Anxiety," I say, twisting at my wedding ring. "I could handle some anxiety. It's the other things that rattle me."

I won't say *visions*. I will not use that word.

"Trauma manifests differently for every person. Nightmares. Insomnia. You've experienced both of those. Panic attacks can feel very real—some people experience them physically, even mistaking them for heart events. For you, I think we've determined, it's these waking daymares. Your subconscious fears rise to your conscious mind, and you experience these episodes. Sometimes that includes visual or auditory hallucinations."

It sounds so logical when he puts it like that. Like it could happen to anyone. But it doesn't, does it? Most people know the difference between what's happening in their minds and what's happening in the space around them.

This space, ensconcing and warm, is one of the first places I felt most safe and understood. I started seeing Dr. Black when I was still in college, when he took me on for nearly nothing, knowing that I was barely making ends meet.

"And what about the box?" I ask him.

He raises his eyebrows, shifts in his seat. "To be honest, that sounds a little off to me."

I was expecting him to have a theory.

"No matter what challenges you face from your past, Rosie," he goes on when I stay silent, "you're a smart, present person. If you say you brought that box down to the street, I believe you."

A sense of relief floods my system. Max, Abi, even Chad seemed to think that I'd been mistaken, or that I had misremembered. Even I was starting to wonder.

"Why would he lie like that?" I ask. Because Chad had asked me the same question.

Dr. Black has this way of looking up at the ceiling when he's considering options. "You said yourself that he's overworked. It's a building full of wealthy people with demands they expect to be met quickly. Maybe he screwed up. Didn't put the box in the trunk. He put it back in your apartment to spare himself the dressing down he expected."

Abi hadn't seemed flustered or embarrassed. He seemed, very convincingly, to believe that he'd never seen the box. I tell the doctor as much.

"He's learned to navigate the world of service. Maybe he's become very skilled at covering his errors."

Something releases in my shoulders; that makes sense. Abi lied because he's afraid for his job, is good at covering his errors because he has to be. He's not just another villain gaslighting me, trying to make me weak so that he can be strong. He's not my father.

"Chad and I fought last night," I tell Dr. Black. That is a complete understatement.

We fought about the apartment, his initial omission of Ivan's wishes, how betrayed and angry I felt about that. More so than I had even realized.

Then, we fought about Dana. What was their relationship? Why was she obsessed with him? What did she want to tell me? Why had he never told me about the posing? That there was a lifetime of animosity between them?

We fought about Max. Why am I always with him when it's known that he has a secret crush on me? Why do I spend more time with Max than I do with Chad?

Which led us to fighting about Chad's comings and goings. Where has *he been*, my husband—so often unreachable, location services turned off on his phone?

The thing is never just the thing.

All the strain of the past few weeks, months, reached an ugly crescendo, culminating in the fact that he seemed to believe Abi's versions of events.

It was probably the worst fight of our marriage. We have rarely argued over our years together—a fight or two about money, maybe, some annoyance on his part about my closeness to Max. But last night was a throw-down. I'm still vibrating.

But I underplay it for the doctor. After all, marriage is a secret arrangement, private to the two people involved. Start spilling all your intimacies, and you invite the world into that bubble.

"I could tell he was *concerned*, worried that I'd had an episode concerning the box. I wanted him to believe me. He said he did, but I could see that he wasn't sure."

"You've both been through a lot."

"You mean he's been through a lot with me."

Dr. Black raises a palm. "Your depression while you were finishing your last book was challenging for both of you."

I nod. I can admit that, how I went down the rabbit hole after the murdered women I was chasing in my book. There *were* episodes. Visual hallucinations—I kept seeing Mara Granta being strangled in front of her children. I heard Julia Dole, the recording artist, singing the song that would release and become a hit only after she was raped and stabbed fifty times by her killer. And Matthew Pantel, their murderer, he was everywhere—lingering in doorways, disappearing around corners. Once I saw his face while I was making love to Chad.

"So now he doesn't, can't, believe my accounts of what I've seen or what's happened?"

That doesn't seem fair. But maybe it is.

"Maybe he knows now how anxiety can manifest with you," offers Dr. Black, always the mediator. "Don't be too hard on him. But it's also important that you feel heard, seen and believed by your husband. Maybe bring him in for a session so we can discuss—if you want."

I nod, weary. Chad and I have come in together over the years so that Dr. Black could coach him about dealing with my depression. It always helps.

"So what do I do? About Abi."

Dr. Black tilts his head from side to side thoughtfully. "Have you tried again to reach your neighbor?"

"I don't have his number." I know there's a website with a

building directory, but I haven't looked there. Part of me is scared. What if Xavier *didn't* see the box? Or says he didn't? I stop short of saying this out loud. Because it sounds like I doubt myself. And if I doubt myself, how can I expect anyone else to believe me?

"Maybe you can reach him through your neighbors—the Aldridges, right?"

I nod, though something in me hesitates. I keep hearing Dana's warning. *You can't trust the people closest to you.* "I'll do that."

I remember then that I didn't go to game night. I wonder if they heard Chad and me fighting before Chad left for his performance. If Abi did.

"At this point, it's just your word against his. But confront him if you feel you need to. Assert your narrative, assure him that it's not about his competence, and maybe he'll come clean. It sounds to me like he's operating from a place of fear."

That's Dr. Black's big thing, that we're either operating from love or from fear. It seemed overly simplistic at first—people act out of all sorts of motives. But the older I get, the more I think it's true. Unless you're a sociopath like my father. And then you're just operating from your own sick agenda, unconcerned with anything but your own delusions and desires.

I tell Dr. Black about my call with Sarah, the things she said.

"Remember that your sister is still in your father's thrall. That he's pulling her strings, coloring her reality. She hasn't broken free the way you have."

I'm not free. I'm surprised at how fast the thought comes up. *I'm running. They're always at my heels, psychologically speaking.*

I look down at my fingers. I keep them carefully manicured, this time in a simple white-and-pink French. If I don't, when things get rough, I chew them ragged.

"She said there was a monster in a castle, drinking my blood."

Dr. Black offers a patient smile. He takes a sip from his water glass.

"She saw that *in her dreams*, which are no more prophetic than yours or mine. Even allegorically, it's not representational."

My phone is buzzing in my bag, but I ignore it. I'm sure I turned it off before coming in here.

"You are a strong woman with a successful career and a good marriage. You have escaped a traumatic past and are building a good life for yourself."

I breathe and close my eyes, let his words sink in.

"You've just received an exceptional inheritance and a new book deal. These are all good things. They are *not* diminished by darkness or evil, despite the terrible toll mental illness took on Chad's cousin."

It's hard not to see it that way, that every light thing has its dark counterpart.

"Even if the Windermere has a dark history," Dr. Black goes on, "that means very little in this city. Bad things happen everywhere, all the time. That's life, unfortunately. But remember, good things happen everywhere, all the time, too. And you won't be *punished* for enjoying them."

He's right; I carry that fear that good things will be followed by bad, that enjoyment of life, success, unexpected joys is a way to make yourself vulnerable to the evil eye, the destroyer, the force that wants to crush and ruin everything golden.

It reminds me of the pendants.

"Chad was wearing a strange necklace," I tell Dr. Black. I describe it, say that it was a gift from Ella and Charles. I tell him that Dana was wearing the same necklace.

"He said that Ella had a drawer full of them, that she often gives them as gifts, even has one for me," I finish.

"So they knew Dana, right?" he asks.

"Maybe? I'm not sure we've discussed it."

He folds his hands together. "Anyway, it's a common enough symbol."

After a moment, he stands up, walks over to his bookshelf.

When he returns, he has a bronze hand figurine in his palm. In its center a blue eye. He offers it and I take it. It's cold and heavy in my grasp.

"The eye is soapstone, obsidian and blue topaz. My wife picked it up at a market in Greece. Many cultures have this belief that success, good fortune, draws bad energy—jealously, malevolence. That those things can hurt us. These types of talismans—like the things your grandmother sends you—ease our anxiety over things we can't control."

"Superstition."

"The world can be a scary place, right? If something helps us to manage our anxiety, I support that."

"Well, it didn't help Dana." The words sound harsh, dark, and I wish I hadn't uttered them but there they are, floating on the air.

Dr. Black takes his seat, draws and releases a breath. I put the hand down on the low coffee table between us; it glints in the light coming in from the tall windows.

"Ultimately, it's our choices and not just the outside forces working with or against us that determine our *fate* or *destiny*. That's what I believe anyway. Dana chose to end her life. It's not as simple as that, of course, because depression, mental illness, can be a trickster, making us think we don't have choices when we do."

But what if she didn't choose? I think but don't say. I know our hour is almost up and I don't want to go down that road with him. Tell him that I'm wondering if someone wanted Dana dead; didn't want her telling me whatever it was she had to say; didn't want her to have that box with its letter from Ivan. Because, even to me, it all sounds a little far-fetched. And I am very invested in seeming—*being*—sane and stable.

"Keep it," he says, nodding toward the icon.

"No," I say. "It was a gift from your wife."

"Keep it as a reminder that these talismans are culturally normal. And that anyone could give you one. There's nothing strange about you having it, even though Chad and Dana were wearing the same symbol. I think you can buy a box of those evil eye necklaces online for a few dollars."

It makes a kind of sense. I thank him, put the hand in my bag even though I don't really want it. My phone is buzzing again; I ignore it.

"Make sure you're taking care of yourself. Remember to eat well, sleep well, exercise, get enough downtime. These things are the foundation for wellness. When they start to slip, for anyone, things get a little wobbly. PTSD and anxiety love to work their way into the cracks in our foundation."

I leave his office feeling stronger, more myself. He's been the voice of reason I never had in my childhood, explaining all the things I didn't understand. It all seems so manageable after unpacking the events of the past few weeks with him. A lot has happened, good and terrible, and my foundation is crumbly, patched together, thanks to my upbringing. But it's getting stronger, thanks to the life I'm building with Chad.

It was probably him calling, trying to make up after the argument that kept us up late and had us not really talking in the morning. He left early and I didn't get up to have breakfast with him, which was mean and childish.

But when I look at my phone, the calls are from Max not Chad, and there are three of them. Which is not like Max.

Walking up the street toward the subway station on Broadway, I ring him back.

"Rosie," he answers. "Where are you?"

"I'm leaving Dr. Black's." Where I grew up, seeing a therapist would be a shameful thing. Here, it's the norm.

"I have some bad news."

My strong and positive feelings fade quickly. "What's wrong?"

"I—uh—got fired this morning." He sounds level, calm.

"What?" Not possible. Max—super editor, beloved by all. "No."

"It's not just me," he says. "The whole imprint is being folded.

Apparently, it's not profitable enough and is being subsumed by Dunham." Dunham, a famously literary imprint that publishes fiction and nonfiction.

"Oh, my God, Max," I say. "I'm so sorry. What can I do?"

"I mean—I'm totally shocked. I've had two books on the bestseller list this quarter. But my boss got fired, and so did I, as well as some of the other senior team members. Some of the junior folks will be reassigned apparently to other divisions."

I've stopped walking and I'm leaning against the facade of a big apartment building, the crowd of people rushing past me. I don't want to ask about my book because it seems so selfish. I'll call Amy when I get off the phone and have her do the dirty work. I stay focused on him as a friend and worry about the blow this will be to his life. I'll worry about mine later.

"You'll find another job, right away," I say. "Of course you will. You have a legion of contacts and friends. You're so talented, Max."

He blows out a breath. "I just feel sandbagged."

"Where are you?"

"I'm home," he says. "They, like, *escorted* me from the building. Security *waited* while I cleaned out my office."

The cruelty and inhumanity of corporations, even publishing, is always shocking to me.

"I'll come to you."

"No," he says, sounding weary. "I just need some time to process, figure out what I'm going to do next. Don't worry about your book, okay? I'm sure they are still going to publish it. You'll just be working with another editor, at another imprint. Probably Dunham. You have a lot of fans there."

My throat constricts with emotion. "I don't want to work with another editor."

But the contract is signed, the payment has already been made; it's cleared my account. Even if Max is gone, the company still owns my book unless I buy myself out of my contract—which I obviously cannot afford to do.

"I don't want you to have another editor, either," says Max miserably.

A bus rumbles past, hissing, impossibly loud. I wait until it's gone before speaking again. "I'm so sorry, Max. This is horrible, ridiculous."

He pushes out a mirthless laugh. "It's business, right. No one is indispensable."

"You're indispensable to me."

"Same."

"Meet me for a drink later, okay? We'll figure this out."

We make plans to connect at a place in my neighborhood later. After we hang up, I leave a message for Amy, then head back to my apartment, feeling bereft for Max, worried for my project, *wobbly* in every way as Dr. Black likes to put it.

At home I use the side door to the Windermere and take the service elevator up to my floor to avoid Abi. Of course, there's the camera in the service lobby, the elevator and in the dim, small space outside our back door. I sense, or maybe imagine, that he still knows my coming and going. That he's watching me, judging my choice to avoid him.

I collapse on the couch, exhausted—by the horror of yesterday, my fight with Chad, who still has not called, my emotionally grueling session with Dr. Black, the bad news from Max.

There it is. The not unfamiliar urge to call my mother, my grandmother, my sister—but I quash it down hard. We're always drawn back to our family of origin, aren't we? No matter how much pain they've caused, no matter how far we've run from them. If only the answers to all life's trials lay in a deck of cards, in visions and dreams. How much easier would everything be?

It all swirls as I lie there in our beautiful new home. I pull the throw blanket over myself and fall asleep hard.

seventeen

Willa
1963

"I saw you."

The small voice distracts me from my novel. I have disappeared inside *The Glass Blowers* by Daphne Du Maurier. Paul doesn't think very much of her, but I love to disappear into the worlds she creates—so full of glamour and darkness. Though it was written before I was born, *Rebecca* is still my favorite. But Paul says that there are rumors that her new book, a huge bestseller, was plagiarized from the work of a Brazilian novelist. I don't believe it. Male jealously, probably.

"I saw you."

I barely hear the little voice over the *swish, swish, swish* of the coin laundry machine, the scent of detergent soapy on the air. This basement, dark and dank, is not my favorite place, and yet I often find myself sitting down here, waiting between the wash and drying cycles. There's another young girl in the building, an artist, and we often do our laundry together, sometimes play cards while we wait. But she's out of town, very glamorously off to Paris for an opening where one of her sculptures will be shown. I envy her—her success, her confidence.

The child inside me is growing. And my career is on hiatus, which is code for being over—because I don't know of a single dancer who has come back to work after having children. Your body changes; suddenly, it belongs to someone else. Still, I'm surprised to find that I'm happier than I have ever been.

"I *saw* you," he says again when I ignore him.

That wicked little boy from next door. He stands over by the cages where everyone stores the things that don't fit in the apartment.

"What did you see?" I ask. He's horrid, always having tantrums in the foyer. Sometimes I hear him through the door, screaming at his mother. Once I saw him pinch his sister in the elevator, then lie about it when she started to cry.

"I saw you kissing," he says. "Not your husband."

My heart flutters and I feel the heat rise to my cheeks. "You saw no such thing."

"I did. Right down here."

He still wears his school uniform, pressed white shirt. His white-blond hair is tousled, eyes glittering with unkind mischief.

"You're a silly little boy."

"I'm not. I saw you. You were wearing a flowered dress, and he had his hand up your skirt."

"Nonsense." The little brat. I'd like to throttle him.

The service elevator doors open and Ella breezes in, as flawless as ever in a long white skirt and oversize top. She can't be much older than I am but she seems to live on another planet of wealth and accomplishment. She and her husband, Charles, are world travelers, often gone for months, leaving the children with a nanny. Maybe that's why her child is such a little monster.

"Are you bothering Willa?" asks Ella.

"Not at all," I say. My heart is still hammering.

She sweeps by me with a simple woven straw basket and tosses in a pile of white clothes that hardly seem soiled at all. Even her laundry is perfect.

"Miles can be such a little chatterbox. And a storyteller. Isn't that right, Miles?" says Ella easily. He drifts over to her, playing shy and clinging to her waist. She pours some soap in the wash, pops some quarters in the slots and starts the load.

"You won't stay down here by yourself, will you?" she asks, turning on her way back to the elevator, leaving the basket on the washer.

"I like to read down here sometimes. And it gives Paul some space to write."

She looks around and wraps her arms around herself. Miles has walked off, is peering around the corner.

"You're brave. This place makes me nervous."

"I'm not afraid," I say with a shrug.

"Come up for coffee instead of staying in this dank place," she offers, glancing around uneasily, dropping a loving hand on towheaded Miles, who has returned to look the part of her little angel, gazing at me innocently. "People say that all the Windermere ghosts wander down here."

I laugh at the silliness of that. But it seems rude not to take her up on it. I follow them into the service elevator.

On the ride up, Miles is watching me again, this time with a mean little grin. How careless to let him see me! How stupid! I stare back at him, stare him down, really. I'm not afraid of a little boy, and besides, he's a known liar. Finally, he looks away.

In Ella's apartment—so opulent, the heavy chenille furniture, the stunning art on every wall, a sculpture on a pedestal, pictures in coordinating silver frames on every surface, the grand piano in the corner. Even the throw pillows seem to exude a kind specialness, an only-for-the-very-rich kind of energy. Paul does well but this is old money, hoarded through generations. The space is much larger than ours. In fact, our apartment at one time was part of theirs, divided and sold off for a tidy profit, I'm sure. There is a universe of difference between 5A and 5B, it seems.

She's effortless as she glides into the kitchen, chatting about the weather, how I must come to game night where they play cards sometimes for penny antes.

"Be right back," she says. "Make yourself comfortable."

Then I am alone with Miles.

"Come here," I whisper, trying to look like I have a wonderful secret, or a hidden toy. He's stupidly trusting, like all children, and makes his way over to me. When he's near, I grab him hard by the arm and put my finger to his lips. He tries to wrest away from me, whimpering.

"You're a little liar and everyone knows it," I hiss. "If you ever tell lies about me, I'll call the police and they'll come and take you away from your family and this pretty apartment forever."

"I'm not a liar," he whispers, lip quivering. "I saw you."

"You're a foolish boy who knows nothing. Keep your mouth shut or go to jail with all the other liars."

His dark eyes grow wide, and he runs from me, footfalls echoing down the hallway, door slamming.

"What's happened?" Ella asks, unconcerned, returning with coffee.

"I have no idea. He just ran off." I am very good, too, at feigning innocence. She offers a sigh and a rueful shake of her head, then joins me.

"So how are you enjoying the apartment?" Ella asks, watching me over the brim of her cup.

"Oh, we love it."

"It used to be ours, you know."

"Oh, yes," I answer. "You split the unit, is that right?"

She glances over toward the door that leaves to the kitchen. Our space is tiny compared to theirs. They kept the lion's share of the place for themselves. "The kitchen wall butts up against your second bedroom, Paul's study, I believe."

I nod, sip at my coffee. She's gone a bit cool. Maybe they sold the place because they needed to. Maybe they are not as perfect as they seem. The thought gives me a kind of dark pleasure.

"Sometimes I try to imagine him in there, writing his wonderful novels."

I smile. People are always curious about writers, how they do what they do. But I'm not sure Paul even knows himself where his stories and characters come from.

"And what about you? Did I hear your show closed?"

"Yes," I say. "Sadly. But I don't know how much longer I would have been able to continue on."

I put my hands to my belly. I'm just barely starting to show, and Ella looks pleasantly surprised. "Oh," she says. "Congratulations. When are you due?"

"In the spring."

We are interrupted then by a bloodcurdling scream from Miles's room. Ella rises quickly and shuttles down the hallway, but I don't follow. I know it's all theater from the little devil.

"You will stay in your room until you can behave yourself," I hear Ella say from down the hall. She returns, shaking her head.

"I have my hands full with that one. It's a good thing Lily is such an angel. He can be a terror. I hate to admit it but he tries my patience."

She says it with a smile, though, unruffled. I can't imagine her losing her temper.

"You seem to handle it all with ease."

She laughs. "I assure you, it's an illusion. Motherhood is not for the faint of heart as you'll soon know, I imagine."

Yes, I think with some mingling of happiness and a sudden trepidation.

I'll know soon enough.

eighteen

It's dusk when a soft knock on the door wakes me from a deep slumber.

Dream images cling. A hallway of doorways, each one a different tarot card. I chase Sarah through the basement maze of corridors. A bucket of blood spilled on our new rug.

How long have I been sleeping? The light outside is already growing dim.

That soft knock again.

My phone is lying on the table next to my head, the screen full of message notifications, emails, texts. I start scrolling through them as I head to the door. Through the peephole there's Ella, standing in our shared foyer, holding a small Dutch oven.

"I made a chicken soup," she says as I open the door. She's chic as always in an oversize camel cashmere sweater and leathery leggings. "I know what happened yesterday, dear. I'm so sorry. Can I come in?"

"Of course," I say, standing aside. "Thank you."

She walks through the apartment to the kitchen, and I follow.

"I'll put it on the stovetop. You can just leave it to simmer on low. Stick it in the fridge after an hour or so if you're not going to eat it tonight."

She knows her way around our kitchen, puts the pot on the burner. I'm always moved by her kindness, her thoughtfulness. The aroma is heavenly. It's the savory smell of comfort.

"It's so good of you, Ella."

She waves at me to indicate it's nothing. But it's something.

Just at that moment, a text from Chad comes in, and I read it while Ella stirs the soup.

I'm sorry. About everything. Let's talk tonight. I love you, Rosie.

Some of my tension and sadness releases, and I text him back right away.

I'm sorry, too. Come home right after the show, okay? I love you.

I am rewarded with a heart emoji.

"We missed you at game night last night," says Ella as we return to the living room.

"Oh, I wasn't up to much of anything—after what happened." The myopia of old age? I found a woman's dead body, a family member, hanging. Someone she maybe knew, as well. And she's calling me out for not coming to game night, an invitation that I never officially accepted?

She stops at the dining room table, rests a hand on the wood a moment.

She puts a heavily ringed hand to her throat, glances around the apartment as if looking for something, then gazes out the east-facing window.

"Poor Dana," says Ella. "She was always so troubled."

It sounds flat, though. Somehow distant. We return to the living room.

"Did you know her?" I venture, thinking about the pendant.

"We met a couple of times over the years, on her rare visits to Ivan. It wasn't a good relationship. Mainly his fault, I think. He wasn't *there*, you know. And she suffered for it, hated him for it. But sometimes there's no chemistry. Don't you think that's true? Even between parent and child."

I motion for her to take a seat and she does on the far end of the sectional. I turn on the lights, the apartment seeming dim and cold.

She's right, of course, about chemistry between parent and child. I immediately think of my father and how we were at odds since before I could remember. My relationship with him was characterized by raised voices and slamming doors, that raging, tearful feeling of being misunderstood, railing against his desires and expectations.

"Are you close to Lilian?" I ask. I am still thinking about her wolfish gaze at the theater, the way she looked at Chad at the party.

Ella gives a little shrug, offers a thin smile. "As close as she wants us to be, I suppose. She was always a free spirit, yearning to break away and be her own person. Separate from us."

She pushes a strand of white hair away from her face. The light coming in from the windows washes her out, makes her look older, sadder. She always seems so together, so effortlessly glamourous. Today she looks frail.

"We battled when she was a teenager. Chemistry, again. She has an easier relationship with her father."

"Did she grow up here? At the Windermere?"

"Yes." She gives a slow nod, looks around the apartment. "It seems we've been here forever."

There's something wistful about the way she says it.

"I thought I saw her at Chad's opening night, before I met her at your place."

Ella raises her eyebrows. "Oh? We told her about Chad's play.

But she didn't mention attending. Maybe she wanted to scout him for her husband. That could be a good thing, right?"

"It could be. I guess we'll see."

"I never know what Lilian's up to. She has her own mind, always has."

She's frowning now. And I can see how much they look alike, those same high cheekbones and deep-set eyes. They each possess a chilly, edgy beauty.

"Can I ask your advice?"

She seems pleased, leans forward. "Of course."

I tell her about Abi and the incident with the box. She listens with a concerned frown, leaning toward me.

"But it was back here when you came home?"

"It was."

"Then were you mistaken?"

"I don't see how I could have been. I mean, I didn't *imagine* carrying the box downstairs."

She nods, squinting thoughtfully.

"Does Abi have a key to this apartment?" I ask.

She draws up a little, surprised. Then, "Maybe Ivan gave him one for emergencies. Some of the residents do that. We do. Abi has a key to our place. We trust him completely. Completely."

But her words again ring hollow, and her voice sounds strained.

"There was a letter from Ivan to Dana. It was on the top of the box and now it's gone."

She seems thoughtful, has gone a bit interior. "That *is* strange. I have to agree with you."

"Would he lie, Ella? Just to cover his mistake?"

Something flashes across her face but then it's gone.

"I can't imagine he would. But who knows? Some people in this building can get a little nasty when things don't go their way."

It echoes Dr. Black's thoughts. "Xavier Young was in the elevator that morning. I'm wondering if he saw anything."

"Oh, Xavier," she says with an eye roll. "He's lovely, but like most men he's only ever thinking about himself. I doubt he noticed a thing."

It seems like another odd thing to say.

"Can you connect me?" I press.

She blinks at me, then, "Of course. I'll run his number over later."

It's then that I notice she doesn't carry a phone with her. If she did, I'd press for the number right there. I'll log on to the building website and see if I can find it that way.

"Was he at game night last night?"

She shakes her head, then puts a hand to her throat again and that's when I notice with a jolt that she's wearing the same pendant that Chad and Dana were wearing.

"Your necklace," I say. I can't help but stare, remembering Dana.

She looks down. "Oh, this silly thing," she says lightly. "I gave one to your husband the other night for good luck."

"Did you give one to Dana?"

I flash on Dana's face again, and push the image away hard. In the foyer I hear that strange crackling noise.

The intercom.

Is Abi listening?

"Oh," she says. "Maybe? Or Ivan did, perhaps? I have a drawer full of them. They're party favors, really. You'll think it's silly, but we have an astrology night. Miranda, our medium, comes, and we talk about our star signs, bring questions, make decisions. Sometimes she brings her tarot cards."

My mother had a beautiful deck of tarot cards. As a child I was fascinated by the images—Death, The Hanged Man, The Lovers. My mother explained each card to me in depth, each layer, the meaning of an upright card, an inverted one. I could probably do a reading myself. Not that I would.

Ella goes on. "I ordered those off the internet as a lark. I give them as gifts all the time. Would you like one? Here, I insist."

She takes off the necklace and lays it on the table. We both stare at it.

"It's lovely," I manage, clearing my throat. "Thank you. It must be my lucky day."

I rise and fetch from my bag Dr. Black's figurine. She takes it.

"This is a nice one." She turns it around, looking at it from all sides. "Where did you get it?"

"My—" I am about to say *therapist* but for some reason I don't. "My friend gave it to me. A good luck gift for my new book."

She regards the hand for another moment, and then places it back on the table.

"Your book about the Windermere."

"That's right. In fact, I have some questions for you when you have time."

"I'll tell you what. Come to astrology night—oh, it's just for fun, of course. Miranda is a true believer but the rest of us are just goofing around. Three of the women there have been at the Windermere more than fifty years. And, of course, Charles knows everything, everything about the building. His grandparents were the original owners of this apartment—yours and ours. And he wouldn't miss an astrology night."

"When is it?" I ask, grappling for any excuse.

"As luck would have it, tomorrow!" she says brightly.

"Great," I say. I have a headache coming on. "I'll be there."

When she leaves, I take the soup off the stove and put the pot, still warm, into the refrigerator. Then I take a long shower, washing off the day. I think about taking the pregnancy test, but it's probably too soon. Besides, I'm wobbly enough.

When I'm dressed again and ready to head out to meet Max, I open my laptop at the dining room table, and log on to the Windermere website. It's a slickly designed portal in shades of purple and gray, "The Windermere" in bold across the top. I click through the menu items, check that Chad paid our first building maintenance fee, which he did. Then I scroll through the minutes of the last meeting. We were not yet owners at the time of this meeting, so we didn't attend. And Ivan was in his last days, never one to attend building meetings at the best of times.

But the meeting minutes look straightforward enough. There's a broken washing machine in the basement. Someone complained about the poor lighting and overburdened electrical box in the basement, which I've experienced firsthand. The fourth-floor foyer needs a coat of paint. There's a leak in the roof, water coming in on ten when there's heavy rain.

I'm struck by the banality of it. This old building where so many dark things have happened, still needs to be maintained and kept by its residents. I wonder if there's a way to work this into the book.

In the chat forum I notice a posting from Ella on our move-in date: *Welcome, Chad and Rosie! Everyone, stop by and greet our new neighbors tonight. They're such a lovely couple.*

I scroll through the comments: Heart surgeon Oga: I'll be there. Creepy sculptress Anna: Wouldn't miss it. A couple of other names I don't recognize giving their regrets, Ella reassuring everyone that they'd have another chance to meet me at game night. Down at the bottom, there's a comment from Xavier. *Poor Chad and Rosie. Run while you still can.*

Maybe that's just his sense of humor, but I flash on his glassy stare, his assertion that he had things to tell me about the Windermere.

I click over to the directory tab. But there's no list of names and contact information. Just a single sentence: *Abi can leave a message for you with any of the building's residents.*

A flash of annoyance. Perfect.

I reply to Xavier's comment on the chat: *Lol! Can you call me?* I leave my number.

Then I'm scrolling through the chat history. Missing packages. Gargoyle maintenance. There's a long argument thread about the cost of maintaining an elevator that needs a staffed operator. Sounds on the roof. People want a roof deck but there's no money in the reserves for that cost. It makes me remember that I requested the budget and financials for the building from Charles, who is the eternal board president, and have not received it.

Then near the bottom of the discussions there's a chat entitled: Ghosts of the Windermere. I click on it immediately. But the chat box is empty except for a sentence in red: *This thread was deleted by the administrator.*

Who is the administrator? I wonder.

I click on the box a couple of times in frustration. It remains empty.

Ghosts of the Windermere. I'm thinking that's the title of my book.

I spend too long down the Windermere rabbit hole and finally come up for air, realizing with a start that I'm late for Max. I grab my things and hustle out the front door.

In the foyer, I call for the elevator before remembering that I don't want to deal with Abi. It's too late, though; the doors are opening.

"Good evening, Ms. Lowan. There's a chill in the air tonight."

"Good evening, Abi. Thank you."

He pauses as if he expects me to go back for a warmer jacket, but I step into the elevator. We ride down in silence. Then just before he opens the doors:

"I truly am sorry about the box," he says. "Can we call it a misunderstanding?"

I marshal my resources, search for the right words.

"Abi, I'm sure you're used to dealing with some difficult personalities in this building. And I understand why you feel the need to cover a mistake. But I'm not one of those people. And I would really appreciate knowing the truth. It means more to me than I can explain."

He stares at me blankly for a moment. The elevator has stopped but he still hasn't opened the doors. "I can't offer you anything other than what I've already said, Ms. Lowan. You did not bring a box down with you yesterday. Not that I saw."

There's a strange blankness to him, a rigidity as if he's cast from metal. We are at an impasse. At this stage, if I want to press, I have to call him a liar. And then what? An all-out battle with the elevator man, a campaign to have him fired? Xavier is my only hope.

I nod. "Okay, Abi. Let's just agree to disagree and leave it at that."

He stares again, dark eyes searching my face. He's good. Even *I* almost believe him.

"Thank you, Ms. Lowan."

"Oh," I say as if the thought is just occurring to me. "Can you leave a message for Xavier Young and ask him to call me? We're supposed to have coffee, but I don't have his number."

He stares straight again. "Of course, Ms. Lowan."

The doors open with their pleasant clicking and I walk through the lobby and am out the door before he has a chance to open it for me. He's acting from fear, like Dr. Black said. He's a man afraid of losing his job.

But what happened to the letter?

Maybe it doesn't even matter. Ivan is dead. And so is Dana. His words, whatever they were, will never find her. There's something painful and sad about that. I carry it with me to Gotham, the restaurant where I'm supposed to meet Max.

I call Amy on the way, and she answers on the first ring.

"Hey," she says. "This must be a blow."

I think she's talking about Dana at first but then I realize she doesn't even know about that. "Max. Yes, it's awful. What happened? The imprint folded?"

There's a pause. "There's more to it than that, I think. But the important thing is that they still want you to write your book. You'll be assigned a new editor and it will be published at Dunham."

Assigned a new editor? That's like saying you'll be assigned a new husband or a new shrink. It's not that easy. But I stay quiet because the truth is I'm not successful enough to make waves.

"It's not ideal," Amy goes on. "I know that. We can cancel. You return the money. And we can wait to see where Max lands. I don't *advise* that, but it's an option."

I wish I were in a place in my life where I could return my advance, storm off in a huff and wait for Max to find a new job. But I can't do that. My contract is with the publisher, not my editor.

"No," I say weakly. "I'll make it work."

"You're a professional. Of course you will."

I'm disloyal, a terrible friend. But the need to support myself is real and this is how I do it.

"What did you mean when you said there was more to it?"

Another pause, which could be Amy considering how to answer or could be her texting with someone else while she's talking to me.

Then, "Maybe you should talk to Max. I gotta go, hon. Let's talk tomorrow."

"Amy?"

But she's gone.

When I get to the bar, I grab a seat in the corner. It's a quiet weekday evening, a sharply dressed after-work crowd, low tones and clicking ice cubes. I wait a half hour, forty-five minutes, drain a club soda—no vodka *just in case*, text Max about a hundred times. He doesn't answer.

I play Wordle on my phone, killing time. My phone pings again. This time, with a text from my sister.

Still dreaming about you. Rosie, I'm worried.

I'm fine. How are you feeling? Remembering that my little sister is pregnant, and I am not, does not improve my mood.

I watch the dots pulse. Then, Maybe I should come for a visit.

Oh, God. That's the last thing I need. I can't even imagine her here in my life. Let's talk about it, I type. Call me tomorrow.

I wait for her to respond but she doesn't. It's a new thing, that she even has a cell phone. There's no way she would ever come here.

The bar gets more and more crowded, and I'm getting crushed into the corner. I've never known Max to be even a moment late. He's almost always the one waiting on me. But my call goes straight to voice mail. Maybe he just needs some time and space. I flash on Dana, hanging from the rafters in her studio.

No. That's not Max.

He's as solid as they come.

But anxiety for his wellness has me considering the schlep out to Brooklyn when Chad texts.

Hey. Come home, okay?

My glass is empty; there's a man with a shaved head and lots of gold jewelry eyeing me from across the bar. Max is my dearest friend. But Chad is my husband, and we need to talk. The call is an easy one. I pay the bill and head home.

nineteen

When I arrive, the apartment is full of roses. Roses in the foyer, on the coffee table in the living room. On the windowsill, by the bed. Chad is waiting on the couch, looking buff in a tight black T-shirt and his favorite worn jeans. He rises when I come in, and I head straight into his arms.

"I'm sorry," he says.

"For what?" I ask into the soft fabric of his T-shirt.

"For everything. For being so wrapped up in work, gone all the time, not honest with you about the apartment. Fighting with you last night when I should have been supporting you."

"I'm sorry, too," I say. "We've been through a lot. You've been through a lot with me."

"No," he says, looking at me intensely. "I'm *nothing* without you."

The air is full of the scent of the flowers he brought. I won't say what I'm thinking. We can't afford so many flowers. Instead, I touch my finger to one of the petals. "These are stunning. Thank you."

He kisses me, on my forehead, on my lips, pulls me in tight again. Dr. Black says that it's not the fight that matters as much as how well you make up, if you understand each other better after.

Do we?

"I have bad news," I say, sinking onto the couch. He frowns.

"Well," he answers, sitting beside me. "I have good news. You go first."

I tell him about Max, and he takes it in stride.

"I'm sorry for Max," he says when I'm done. "But you still have your contract, right? And who knows, maybe you'll benefit from working with someone who's—not so close to you, right?"

I try not to bristle at this. I know he doesn't always love my relationship with Max. And maybe part of him is glad for this change. But it's not a good thing. There's no way to cast it as such.

I shrug. "Maybe. It's just such an intimate relationship, so collaborative."

"You'll work together again," he says easily. "Just not on this book."

He's right, of course. The publishing industry is a small one and shrinking all the time with constant mergers. We'll work together again. And in the meantime, we'll just be friends. I soften and allow myself to hear Chad's point of view. Maybe a fresh perspective will be positive.

I am about to tell him about how Max stood me up tonight, that I'm worried about him and need to call again. But I don't get the chance.

"Okay," he says, beaming. "Now for the good news."

My heart thrums a little, with nerves, excitement. For effect, he gets down on his knees and takes my hands.

"My audition. I got the part, Rosie. And it's huge. I'm the lead in a new series called *The Hollows* about a detective and a medium who solve cold cases together. It's based on a true story.

A major director, writer, network. This is *it*. The thing we've been working for."

I let out an excited *whoop* and we're doing a happy dance around the living room. He dashes off to the kitchen and comes back with a chilled bottle of Veuve and two champagne flutes, pops the cork and fills our glasses.

"This is one of those moments, right?" he says. "When the good thing happens? Like the day we met, or the day I proposed, and you said yes, your rave review in the *New York Times*. Let's be completely present for it."

We clink glasses and drink; the champagne is cold and dry, tingling on my tongue, down my throat. Just a sip won't hurt; I'm probably not even pregnant, the test still unused in the bathroom cabinet.

I draw in and release a breath. He does the same.

And then we're *whooping* and dancing again; he spins me around. We spill champagne on the new rug and don't care one bit. Finally, we collapse on the couch, breathless, giggling.

"It films here in the city and on location upstate, but we don't have to move," he goes on, a little breathless. "And if I need to be upstate you can easily just come with me and write up there, commute into the city as needed."

The details don't matter. We'll make this work, whatever it means.

"I'm so proud of you," I tell him. "You've worked *so* hard for this."

"*We* have. Everything is about teamwork. I would have lost heart so many times if not for you, your support."

You and Chad have something special, Ivan used to say. *There's a selflessness to each of you when it comes to the other. And that's what it takes to stay in love, stay committed, stay together.*

Celebrating his success, I push all the other events of the past few days away so that I can be present for this wonderful moment with my husband. He turns on some music, takes another deep swig of champagne. I'm just taking tiny sips, but he doesn't seem to notice. We dance some more, laugh, then make love on the living room floor.

Afterward, we don't have wood for a fire, and it's not cool enough yet anyway, but he lights the pillar candles we decided to keep in there during spring and summer, and we lie naked, enjoying the moment, the flames dancing, the smell of roses and wax on the air.

"She followed me here," he says out of the blue.

I know who he's talking about because she's not far from my mind, either, as much as I wish I could forget Dana for a while. Just for this moment. "From the town where we grew up in New Jersey. I came to Columbia. She went to Parsons."

Chad nearly dropped out a couple of times, struggling with tuition, even with the money his parents had left him. He started bartending, going to acting classes given by the famous teacher Martin Waldorf. He landed small roles right away, but money was always an issue.

"I *did* think it was odd when she asked me to pose for her class. But I was, like, really desperate, you know? And—I'm not shy about taking off my clothes."

"*That* we know," I say, tracing a finger along those perfect abs.

"Ivan and I got closer during those years," he goes on. "He and Dana got further and further apart. Honestly, I think it's why she came to New York, to be closer to him. But he was gone all the time."

He stares up at the ceiling as if the memories are playing out for him there.

"Ivan was scattered, would make plans then not show up. Her mother was so bitter, and Dana carried that with her. She chased after him for a while. He let her down, time after time. Finally, she just started to hate him."

I think about what Ella said about chemistry, how sometimes it's not there even between parent and child.

"I guess I figured out that she was following me a couple of years before you and I met. I finally confronted her, and she said the strangest thing."

"What?" He's never mentioned this before. I push up on my elbow, watching him.

"She said that she was trying to figure out what everyone saw in me, including Ivan. Why he chose me over her. She said that when she looked at me, she saw someone vain, selfish, ugly inside. A dark heart beneath a beautiful mask."

I can tell he's upset by the tautness in his voice, the stillness of his face. I reach for him, and he puts my hand to his lips.

"That hurt me, you know?" He looks at me and I can see it. "I told her that it wasn't a choice—her or me. That we could be a family. Ivan and I had a close relationship, yeah, my father's brother. He filled the gap my parents left behind. But that didn't exclude her."

I stay quiet just letting him talk, pulling the blanket down from the couch and around us against the cold.

"Do you think it's true?" he asks into the quiet.

"Dana wasn't well. That's clear. Okay, Ivan wasn't a good father. He'd admitted as much. But Dana was angry, bitter, deeply depressed. She'd fixated on you, but ultimately you and Ivan just had something special. That wasn't in his control or yours."

He bobs his head slightly, is quiet for a second. Then he turns his face to me and the candlelight dances there, shadows gathering in the dips and valleys of his face.

"No, I mean that there's something dark inside me."

His forehead wrinkles with sadness. Everything in me wants to comfort him.

"That only *she* could see? No. If Dana saw darkness, it was within her."

His eyes search mine; what he sees there seems to satisfy him, his frown fading.

"Eventually, she just—disappeared. From my life, from Ivan's.

She met someone and they got married. We weren't invited to the wedding. She had children. Ivan never met them. I thought maybe she'd found happiness and I was glad for her, even if she had to separate from us to do that."

I understand making that call, deciding that you can't be well or happy with your family of origin. That you're just so different, so utterly incompatible, that the relationship only brings pain to all parties involved. The idea of the happy family is so ingrained in our culture, that we cling desperately to even the worst origins. It takes a deep, abiding courage to let go.

She always wanted something that I couldn't give, Ivan told me. *And I'm sorry for that. Maybe some people shouldn't be parents.*

"She's gone now," he says. "Ivan's gone."

It's so final. We always think that we'll die with everything resolved, a happy ending to all the challenges in our lives. Not Dana and Ivan. The box of his memories sits in my office; the letter he wrote her disappeared. But I won't think about that now, this thing that's utterly out of my control.

"We'll build our own family," I say. "We'll learn from the mistakes of others. Do better."

The pendant around his neck glitters in the firelight.

Maybe it worked after all. For him anyway. I should put mine on.

Later that night when Chad is sleeping, I sneak into the bathroom and take the pregnancy test I've been hiding. My hopes are not very high because I've been disappointed so many times and I've grown a bit numb to the whole process. As I wait, I stare out the narrow window that looks across Thirty-Seventh Street. All the windows are dark, too far to see inside anyway.

A noise out in the hallway attracts me to the peephole and I stare out into the elevator lobby we share with Charles and Ella.

Standing there is the little boy from the basement. I draw in a deep gasp.

He stares at my door, his face still and pale, wearing the same school uniform, shorts and a little jacket, pressed white shirt. I'm frozen with fear, want to scream but can't.

Slowly, the elevator door opens behind him, but the elevator is not there. It's just a gaping maw. I fumble with the lock, watching in horror as he backs up and disappears into the shaft. I hear his wailing, growing fainter then stopping abruptly.

But when I open the door, my heart hammering, the elevator is closed, the hallway empty, bright and clean. I stand staring at the emptiness. There's music coming from Charles and Ella's, a light piano tune. My heart is a jackhammer, blood rushing in my ears.

I stand there for I don't know how long.

Looking, watching the empty space, heart finally slowing, breath easing. Trauma. Anxiety. These visions are how my form of PTSD manifests itself. That's what Dr. Black says. I cling to that. Repeat the mantras he gave me. Finally, my breath returns to normal, and I step back inside the apartment, mind boggling, grasping at what just happened. What did I see?

Still shaking a little, I remember the posting on the chat forum. Ghosts of the Windermere. What if I'm not the only one who's seen him?

"Ms. Lowan?"

I practically leap out of my own skin. It's Abi on the intercom. What the actual fuck?

"Yes, Abi," I manage, my voice sounding cold even to my own ears.

"Everything all right?"

"Everything's fine."

"I saw you come out into the hallway. You looked frightened."

"That's all you saw? Just me."

I can still see those dark eyes, that intense little face. Who is he? What does he want?

"That's all."

"I thought—I heard something."

"Quiet night tonight. Everyone's in. No visitors."

So he's like the gatekeeper to the Windermere? I still have yet to see another person working the door and the elevator.

"Good night, Abi," I say.

"Good night, Ms. Lowan."

I know what Dr. Black would say about what I saw, but my father's words ring back to me. *Energies linger, they echo. The past, the future, all dwell side by side. It's like a double exposure. You see what was there, what might come, overlaying the present.*

My head starts to ache as I walk unsteadily back to the bathroom. Chad's heavy breathing in the bedroom is undisturbed by ghosts in the hallway, our watchful doorman checking in unsolicited. I'm going to disable that intercom, or lodge a complaint about the invasion of privacy.

But all of these thoughts quickly dissipate as I pick up the pregnancy test lying on the marble vanity top. I turn on the light and stare, a gasp of surprise escaping my lips. Disbelief. Then a rush of joy so intense that it banishes all darkness.

Two blue lines.

I'm pregnant.

twenty

"Let's not tell anyone for a little while."

"Let's tell *everyone*," Chad shouts, as antsy and joyful as a kid on Christmas morning. "We'll go up on the roof and just start yelling."

I put a gentle hand on his arm. I love his excitement. But this—can it just be ours for a little while? It feels tentative, delicate. So much could go wrong. "I want to take another test, see the doctor."

He takes my hand and gives an assenting nod. "And you should do that. But let's tell *everyone*. I can't keep this secret, Rosie."

"Most people wait. Anything can happen."

"Since when are we *most people*? Let's tell Charles and Ella at least."

They wouldn't be my first call—Max maybe. More than anything I want to call my mother. Or Sarah. And not because I need their support. *See,* I want to tell them, *good things are happening for me.*

A deep calm has come over me since I took the test last night, a knowing that this is it. We have started our family. We have a beautiful new apartment. Chad just landed a dream role. Our child is growing inside me. All will be well.

I woke Chad up right away, and we've been up talking ever since. Now the sun is rising and we sit at the table Ivan gave us—Chad drinking coffee, me with an herbal tea. It's going to be hard to give up coffee, the magical elixir of life. But my body belongs to the life growing inside me for a while, so I'll suffer through.

"Okay," he says finally. "You're right. We'll wait. But it's going to nearly kill me."

We watch the sunrise paint the east side of the Chrysler Building a brilliant pink.

"I am the happiest man alive," says Chad.

We don't need to talk about the timing, how he just got his first big role and what that will mean for us. My book. It doesn't matter. We'll make it all work and that's it.

"Do we know a doctor?" asks Chad.

"Hilary has a good one," I say. My friend, the one who stood me up the night I met Chad, has just had twins. She raved about her doctor, a young woman on the Upper West Side.

Where I grew up, babies were most often delivered by midwives. My mother was one of them, often called away in the middle of the night to usher a little soul into the world. *Pregnancy is not a medical event*, she liked to say. *Our bodies were designed to do this.*

Sure, unless something goes wrong.

"I think Charles and Ella know someone, too." He traces the ring of his cup. "In fact, I know they do."

The words sink in.

"Did you tell them we were trying for a baby?"

He looks at me sheepishly, and I try to quash my annoyance when I see that he has.

"I might have mentioned it," he says.

"Did they give you a charm for that, too?"

He leans in close to me. "Don't be mad. I just wanted to share it with—someone. You have people you talk to—Max, Hilary, Amy. I don't."

I guess that's true. Strange that the introvert has a gaggle of friends, varying in degrees of closeness. But the extrovert who has lots of contacts and people he knows has few people he'd confide in other than me. No one really. Ivan was one. But he's gone.

I lace my fingers through his. Will our baby have his stunning eyes, his knock-'em-dead smile? Boy or girl? Creative? I try to feel for the energy of the little life inside me but no—there's just my own joy and excitement.

"Are you going to tell your family?" We're at the point in our relationship where we read each other's minds now.

I don't answer right away, take a sip of my herbal tea.

"Maybe," I say finally. "I don't know."

We sit as the room grows lighter and a wash of well-being and peace moves through me. We're in the right place, doing the right things. Growing careers, a growing family. Not all moments in life feel this right. I let myself enjoy it.

After Chad heads off for a breakfast meeting with his agent, I try to reach Max again, but my call goes straight to voice mail.

Once.

Twice.

I'm worried about him. But it's also selfish. I want to talk to him about the book. I have no idea who my new editor will be or how that relationship will evolve. In the last book, I bounced almost everything off Max.

I call him a third time and leave a message. "Hey, maybe you just want to be alone right now, and I get it. But call me. I'm worried about you."

Finally, I press back my worry for Max, my joy for Chad, for the baby on the way to us. I force myself to sit at my desk and work on my outline.

In 1920, The Church of the Holy Name burned to the ground, a five-alarm fire that all but decimated the structure, leaving just the stone exterior. There were no fatalities. The fire was ruled an arson, though no perpetrator was ever named. It sat fallow for five years until architect and builder Marc LeClerc bought the lot, demolished what remained of the building, keeping the foundation and some of the stones, as well as the gargoyles that stood sentry over the front door.

The Windermere opened and the first residents moved in in 1930 at the beginning of the Great Depression. But these were wealthy people, and the pains of the city and the world did not affect the construction of the building, or keep any of its residents from moving in.

Little did they know that Marc LeClerc was heavily impacted by the stock market crash on October 29, 1929. Black Tuesday. After struggling to recover and failing, in 1932 he threw himself from the roof of the Windermere and fell to his death on Park Avenue.

I am going to start here, with Marc LeClerc's death. With his ties to the occult, a mother who was a psychic medium and the effects of the Great Depression on his life and ultimate decision to kill himself, he is the perfect subject to set the mood for the book—history, psychology and the mystical.

Things were peaceful at the Windermere after the initial tragedy until a promising young actor, Frank Malone, shot himself just weeks before he was about to star in his first major role on Broadway in 1950. Then in 1952, Sylvia Monroe, a self-proclaimed psychic, was strangled in the basement, her killer never caught. In 1958, Roberto Estella, a star pianist, fell from a window. His death was ruled an accident, but there was suspicion of foul play involving his male lover. In 1963, a young boy fell down the elevator shaft when it was out of order.

Also in 1963, tragedy befell the Winters. Right here, in this apartment, once owned by Charles and Ella Aldridge; then Ivan purchased it a couple of years later.

There were several other deaths in the building—a heart attack, a stroke, two more suicides, an overdose, one crib death and an incident of auto-erotic asphyxia.

I go through my notes and decide on sections Murder, Accident, Suicide, Natural Deaths.

Here are my major questions: Are some places cursed? My grandmother would say yes. That darkness invites darkness. Dr. Black would surely have a different perspective. Maybe a historian will tell me that I'll find similar histories in other buildings that have been standing for nearly a hundred years—just microcosms of the human condition. Are there dark forces at work at the Windermere? The burning of the church, LeClerc's ties to the occult, seem to set the stage for a horror movie scenario—cults meeting in the basement, human sacrifice. What does each loss of life tell us about life in general—that it's fragile, that it's a struggle, which some of us can't manage, that it slips away, that it can be wrested from us? How do these crimes, suicides, accidents fit into a larger picture of the city's history, its criminality?

As the morning passes, I flush out and rearrange the outline I went over with Max the other day. When I am done, I can finally see it. The book I am about to write. I have a lot more research ahead, months, maybe a year of digging through archives at the New York Historical Society, the New York City Municipal Archives, the New York Public Library, to get all the details right, to dig in deep to my subjects. I'm still looking for more details on the Winters. But the essence, the bones, as we say, are falling into place.

At lunchtime, I run out for another pregnancy test, still using the service elevator and back door. When I get back, I pee on the stick again and sweat it out, eating Ella's delicious chicken soup for my lunch as I wait. It's savory and with the note of a flavor I can't quite place—something almost sweet. I eat way too much. They're so good to us. Of course it's okay that Chad told them we're trying for a baby.

When I check the test, I'm thrilled to find another positive result. I email Hilary asking for the name of her obstetrician "for a friend." And she zaps it over right away, assuring me that it's just between us, and that she'll call and make sure they fit "my friend" in right away. Still, when I call, the earliest appointment I can get is next week.

I call Max again. No answer. I'm considering a run out to Brooklyn when the intercom buzzes.

"What is it, Abi?" I say, pressing the button.

"It's George, Ms. Lowan. Abi's off today."

Oh, so Abi *is* human, not some undead gatekeeper of my building. Good news. I haven't met George. But I'll make a point to later. Maybe he'll be more malleable, and I can talk my way into that back office. And maybe I can use him to get a message to Xavier, who hasn't responded to the message I left in the chat forum or the one I left with Abi. Nor has Ella come back with his number.

"There's a detective here to see you."

Shit. Olivia said not to speak to him without her. "Ask him to wait, please. I'll come down."

I quickly call Olivia but just get her voice mail. The apartment doorbell rings, and I look out the peephole to see a uniformed doorman who must be George. Short and thick bodied, with a tight blond crew cut, he looks to be in his midthirties, shifting nervously from foot to foot. Detective Crowe stands behind him, frowning, impatient. He must have forced George to bring him up.

I know that I should not be talking to him, certainly should not be inviting him into my home. But I open the door anyway.

"I can't speak to you without my lawyer, Detective."

He gives a curt nod. "Look, I can't reach your lawyer and I have questions. A woman is dead, okay? So either you come with me to the station right now and we can wait there for Ms. Brewer however long it will take, or you let me in, and we can just have a quick chat. You help clear up a few things and I'm gone."

I weigh my options—get hauled into the police station where I might wait all day for Olivia to get out of court. Or talk to the detective in the comfort of my own home, hopefully briefly.

Finally, I stand aside and let him in.

"Anything else, Ms. Lowan?" George has flushed red at the cheeks, wears a worried frown.

"Thank you, George." He gives me a little bow and then disappears into the elevator.

Detective Crowe looks around. "Nice place."

I want to rush in with *we got lucky* or *we can barely afford it.* Instead, I keep my voice cool and ask, "What do you need, Detective?"

"I thought you would like to know that Dana Lowan's death has been ruled a homicide."

I sink onto the couch and stay quiet.

"She died from strangulation, but there is also evidence of blunt trauma to the skull."

I still can't find any words, try to piece together what I know about Dana, about her call to me, the box that disappeared from the taxi, Abi's lies, how he knew she'd died too soon after the fact. I should tell Detective Crowe these things; but I don't. I'll tell Olivia when she calls. I also remember at this time that I tampered with the crime scene, took evidence that might implicate my husband. Those photos are in a file on my desk. I wrap my arms around my middle, protective already of the life inside me, not to mention the one we're trying to build.

"Her ex-husband said that she was in a state of rage over this place." He's still standing, looking around the apartment. "That rightfully it should have come to her when her father passed. You didn't mention that."

I wait a moment, choose my words.

"Her father, Ivan, left it to us. We didn't ask for it. That was his choice. Ivan and Dana were estranged, and we cared for him when he was ill."

"That's a huge inheritance. I looked it up. This place is worth nearly five million."

I clear my throat—it's embarrassing. It feels like a violation, too, that he's looked up the worth of our place. "Not quite, but yes. It was a tremendous gift."

He walks over to the fireplace. I've placed Dr. Black's gift there. He stares at it for a moment. I motion for him to sit but he stays standing. I notice his scuffed boots. Chad and I take our shoes off when we come home—careful not to drag in the filth of the city. I imagine the germs from his shoes invading the new cream area rug we could barely afford.

"Why didn't you tell me that at the studio?"

I shrug. "I was in shock."

He looks around. There isn't much to see. We haven't hung any of our art, our photographs, though there isn't much of that, either. It will take a lot to fill these walls, make our place look like Charles and Ella's—money, time, travels. "If you were in a battle over this place, why would you go up there?"

I shake my head. "There was no battle. Ivan's affairs were in order, so she had no legal recourse to contest his will. She called, wanted to meet. I had something that belonged to her and wanted to deliver it. So I decided to make the trip. I was hoping, if I'm honest, to repair the rift between us."

I immediately regret telling him that I had something to give her. That's why you don't talk to the cops without your lawyer. Crowe regards me for a moment, then takes the seat at the end of the sectional facing me.

"What did you have?"

I hesitate a second, check my phone for any word from Olivia, then reluctantly tell him about the incident with Abi and the box. He sits across from me while I'm talking and, when I'm done, he's watching me.

"That's weird," he says. He runs a hand through thick, tousled black hair, then rubs at his dark stubbled jaw. He looks like a man who doesn't sleep well, who wrestles his demons at night. His wedding ring is tight; cuticles ragged.

"He claims that I didn't have the box when I came down."

He offers a look that's starting to become familiar—that suspicious squint.

"You don't seem like a person to make a mistake like that." He leans back, still with those watchful eyes on me, like he's trying to figure me out, see beneath my surface. But maybe that's just his way, occupational hazard.

"I'm not," I say.

He offers a slow nod. "So what do you think happened?"

"Honestly, I have no idea. Maybe he just screwed up and tried to cover."

"Can I see it?"

I consider it. What would Olivia say? "I'll surrender the box to you after I've consulted with my attorney."

He lifts his palms. "Okay."

"They were just pictures of Dana, though, things he'd collected over her lifetime. A letter, which somehow got lost. I thought she might find it healing, to know that he followed the events of her life."

He steeples his fingers, which I've read is the gesture of someone supremely confident. It tracks. "That thing on your mantel."

He doesn't look behind him but my eyes drift there.

"Dana was wearing a necklace with the same symbol," he says.

Did he notice Chad's necklace, as well? I put the one Ella gave me on my desk.

I decide to channel Dr. Black. "It's a fairly common symbol.

The palm represents abundance. The stones in the center are the evil eye charm, meant to protect you from ill will."

"Doesn't seem to be working."

My phone rings then, and we both look at it buzzing on the table. Olivia.

When the call engages, she's already talking. Well, yelling sort of. "What was it about 'don't talk to the police' that you didn't understand, Rosie?"

He bows his head, digs his hands in the pockets of his bomber jacket.

"Olivia, you're on speaker. The detective is here."

Silence. She clears her throat.

"My client will not be speaking any further without my presence. Please leave her residence. You do not have permission to search without a warrant. Do you have one?"

"No," he says, rising, beaten. He informs Olivia that this is now a homicide investigation. There's another silence, this one surprise I'm guessing, but she quickly recovers.

"Please contact my assistant, and my clients will come in and speak to you at their convenience."

The detective moves reluctantly toward the door, face blank with annoyance, eyes still roving.

"Rosie, don't hang up until he leaves."

I show the detective into the elevator foyer and press the button for George.

"I'll need to speak to your doorman," says Detective Crowe. "Abi, you said?"

I nod, feel guilty for throwing Abi under the bus, but what I told the detective was the truth.

"That's not our problem," says Olivia's disembodied voice, tinny on my phone speaker. "As long as you're not speaking to Chad or Rosie Lowan without me."

The mechanism of the elevator climbing up the shaft can be heard through the doors.

"Just one more thing," says Crowe. "We have access to Dana's phone records. Did you know that she and your husband were communicating no less than three times a day?"

I stay quiet. This does not jibe with what I know about Chad's relationship to Dana. Is it true?

"They were cousins," says Olivia flatly. "There was a relationship."

I marvel at how quickly she comes up with explanations for things. It's light speed.

"She was blackmailing him, wasn't she?" says Detective Crowe. "That's what he said, right?"

Did Chad say that? She was threatening to reveal something about him unless he sold the apartment and gave her the money. I guess that's blackmail? But he swore he didn't know what she was planning to tell me. And now she's dead. My skin starts to tingle.

"Please make an appointment with my assistant." Olivia's voice is stern, even over the speakerphone. "We can settle all your questions at that time. The Lowans are witnesses, not suspects. They have suffered a personal tragedy."

The elevator comes, the door opening with its well-oiled clack. George peers out, looking nervous. Maybe he expects me to be led away in cuffs.

"I'm here for you," Detective Crowe says to me. There's something sincere there, I think. But maybe he's just manipulating me. "If you're in trouble."

I shake my head, back away from him. "I'm not. We're not."

He keeps his eyes on me as George shuts the door, and then they're gone.

Olivia dresses me down, lectures me about throwing away my rights, eventually softens and acknowledges that honest people have a hard time turning the police away.

"Was she blackmailing him?" I ask.

She blows out a breath.

"I mean, she *was* threatening him, trying to strong-arm him into selling the apartment. But what did she really have to tell you? That he posed nude, that he had ex-girlfriends? You knew all of that. And it couldn't come as much of a surprise that Chad would take off his clothes for money, right?"

"True," I concede. "But why were they talking so much?"

"She was harassing him. She was unstable. He was trying to reason with her."

I can tell by the way she says it that she doesn't know that to be true exactly. Olivia is creating a narrative, weaving an explanation for all those calls. That's what she does, create a story about why her clients are not guilty. She's good at it.

"You know your husband, Rosie. You're solid and he's a good guy—a bit of a ham but that's an occupational hazard, right?"

She's right. I do know him, heart and soul. The reality of the situation starts to dawn. Someone *killed* Dana, *murdered* her, very soon before we arrived to see her. Her words ring back: *Don't tell anyone in the building that you're meeting me.* Was she afraid of someone in this building? I didn't tell anyone here that I was meeting her. Abi might have deduced because of the box. And maybe Xavier, if he noticed it. Maybe I should just take the service elevator to his back door and knock.

Abi's words ring back: *I think you'll find that news travels fast here.* Did Abi have something to do with Dana's death? Or Xavier? Did *Chad*?

No. No, that's ridiculous.

Isn't it?

The silence on the line expands, both of us lost in thought.

"Dana didn't kill herself," I say. "*Someone* killed her. Who? Why?"

"We have no way of knowing. It could be about anything, and most likely nothing to do with you. We'll make the appointment with Detective Crowe. We'll share what we know and cooperate. But neither of you did anything wrong. And they have no reason to believe you did. Otherwise, they'd have come with a warrant."

She's so solid, so reasonable. And her words make sense—we don't know Dana, at all. Any number of people could have wanted her dead, for any reason. It doesn't necessarily have anything to do with us or the Windermere. Finally, I thank Olivia and we end the call.

I'm buzzing with anxiety, though. My creative thread is lost; Dana was murdered. Another violent death connected to the Windermere.

My call to Max goes unanswered—again. After fretting about him, and all the rest of it for a while longer, I decide to take the train out to Brooklyn.

But first, I'm going to see what I can get out of George. And with Abi away, I'm going to talk my way into that surveillance room.

twenty-one

"So," I say to George in the elevator. "Abi never finished our tour."

"Your tour, miss?" George is less polished than Abi, stocky where Abi is tall and elegant. His uniform pants do not have Abi's careful crease. There's a fray at the gold edging on his cuff. A tattoo peeks up from his collar.

"The new resident's tour," I say. "We started in the basement. But then I had some work to do, so he never finished." The darkness of that event still lingers. I think of the boy's pale face, in the basement, in my foyer. It tugs at my heart.

"Well," he says with a nod. "Abi should be back tomorrow. I'm sure he'll be happy to finish anytime it's convenient."

"He said he was going to show me the office behind the doorman's station."

We arrive on the ground floor and it's a bit jerky. He doesn't seem to be as skilled and comfortable with the elevator as Abi. He has to make some adjustments so that the elevator is aligned with the threshold.

"Mind if I just take a quick peek?"

"That door is locked, miss."

"You don't have a key?"

"No, Abi didn't leave one. Mr. Aldridge was looking to get in there, as well, to look for a package, he said. But I couldn't help him."

"Did you look around?" I ask. "Maybe there's a spare."

"I did. There isn't."

I stare at the door behind the doorman station. "Don't you need to get in there?"

"Not really," he says. "I'm just manning the door until eight tonight. I can deliver packages as they come in. And I'll lock the street door when I leave. Residents can use the service elevator tonight. Visitors can ring the intercom. And Abi will be back in the morning."

"What about the surveillance?"

His face goes a little tight, like I'm annoying him with all my questions. "Like I said, miss, the door is locked. Abi will be back in the morning, and he can answer all your questions then."

Why was Charles trying to get into Abi's office? I wonder.

"Can you do me a favor, George? Will you leave a message for Mr. Young? Ask him to call me."

I take a notecard from the small pile on the doorman's desk and scribble down my number.

"Of course," he says, seeming relieved to be able to say yes to one of my requests.

It's astrology night tonight and Ella has already texted twice to remind me, saying that I could bring an appetizer if I wanted. I'll go after all, start asking some questions. Maybe Xavier will be there.

Or maybe after George leaves at eight, I'll come down and see if I can't find a key. There's also that second mystery key on my ring. Maybe I'll get lucky, and it will fit in that lock.

George opens the front door for me. "Do you need a cab, miss?"

"No, thanks, George. Have a good day."

I feel his eyes on me as I head to the subway.

The train rocks and clatters its way out to Borough Hall, and by the time I emerge into daylight in Brooklyn Heights, I am feeling nauseated.

I think it's too soon for all that and maybe it's my imagination, but it comes in unpleasant waves. I push through it and hustle up the street, air chilly, sidewalks crowded, until I get to Max's place on Schermerhorn Street, a townhouse converted to apartments. He's on the third floor. I do have a key from our days as neighbors, but I ring the buzzer instead, standing on the pretty stoop. Someone has taken care with potted trees, and the door is varnished with ornate knobs and frosted glass panes.

"Just leave it inside the first door," says Max over the intercom, the outer door unlocking with a buzz.

"I'm not your Uber Eats delivery," I say, pressing inside.

"Rosie." He doesn't sound happy to see me. "What are you doing here?"

"Are you going to let me up?"

I don't hear anything for a moment, but then the inner door opens, too.

I hoof it up the three flights and he's waiting for me at his door in sweats and a tattered Ziggy Stardust T-shirt under a plaid overshirt, house shoes. His hair is wild; he hasn't shaved, and his eyes are rimmed with purple fatigue.

"Wow, one day out of work and you just fall to pieces, huh?"

"Don't judge me."

He stands aside and lets me in; the shades are drawn, and the living room is dim, the television on but muted. Pizza box on the coffee table, jacket slung over the chair, dishes in the sink. Max is a neatnik. This is not like him. It's a blow; I get that. But this seems like a steep descent.

There might be more to it. Isn't that what Amy said?

My internet search this morning didn't reveal anything about his firing, the imprint folding. I haven't heard from Amy about my new editor.

There's a stack of books on the big chair next to the couch; he clears them aside so that I can sit.

"Coffee?" he asks.

"Sure."

The kitchen is visible from where I'm sitting. He brews a dark roast in the Chemex. Usually, we'd be chatting about this thing or that, but the silence is heavy between us. I start rambling about Detective Crowe's visit, how Dana's death has been ruled a homicide.

"Another murder associated with the Windermere," he says when I'm done. He brings my coffee, sits across from me. "Will you include it?"

It feels like an odd question, even though I've considered it myself. A woman has died. This is a hazard of crime journalism, that people get treated like characters in a story, that some of the horror of their victimhood is diminished, nearly fictionalized in its retelling. We need distance to narrate, but too much distance and we lose our humanity.

"Maybe," I say. "But I'm more concerned right now about what happened to her. Did it have something to do with us? The apartment?"

"You don't know with what or whom she was involved."

Something about his phrasing makes me think of Olivia. And I remember how intimate they seemed at the gallery. I try to imagine them together, but I can't. She belongs to the hard city of crime and punishment; she's prickly, edgy. He's a craft cocktail, art gallery, history geek; he's—Max. He froths some milk.

"I talked to Amy last night," I say into the silence that falls. "She said that they are going to publish the book at Dunham and assign me a new editor."

Max tries for a smile. "I'm glad. I knew they would."

My eyes fall on his bookshelf. I see several copies of my book there. It feels like our book, because he was so much a part of the process. It's a loss I'm already grieving.

"If I were in a different place in my life, I'd walk away with you," I say.

He looks at me across the distance between us, pushes up his glasses. "I know you would. I know that, Rosie. I would never ask that of you. I wouldn't *want* you to do that."

I sink deeper into the plush chair. My nausea has subsided some, but the stale, greasy odor coming from the pizza box isn't helping.

"I don't know if I can do this without you," I admit.

He clangs around the kitchen some more, tidying up, putting some beer cans in the recycling. Then he comes over with our coffee cups, sits across from me.

"You don't have to," he says, watching me. "We're still— friends. Best friends, right?"

"Of course."

"So that doesn't change. We'll still talk about the book all the time." He sweeps his arm around the apartment. "And I'll have loads of time to help with research."

Outside, an ambulance wails up the avenue, someone issues a shout, followed by the bleating of a car horn.

"What else?" I ask.

Amy's words are knocking around my head. And he just looks wrecked. Getting fired is tough, but I can feel the heaviness, the darkness of his energy, that there's something he wants to say.

"There was an assistant," he says. "A couple of months ago, she claimed that I made unwelcome advances at a book party."

I sit up in the chair, stare at him. He takes off his glasses and cleans them on his shirt, a thing he does when he's embarrassed or buying time to think.

"No," I say quickly. "You wouldn't do that."

Most men, yeah, okay. But Max is a gentleman, kind, chivalrous—a door opener, a coat holder. No. He's not one of those handsy, oblivious men who thinks his needs and desires are the only thing to consider in a sexual encounter. He doesn't use his power position to subtly seduce, to imply his favor might make a difference in a woman's career.

He pushes out a laugh and runs a hand through his hair, puts his glasses back on.

"I don't know," he says, surprising me. "I *was* really drunk that night. I thought she was *into* me. She clearly wasn't."

He puts his coffee cup down next to the pizza box, looks up at the ceiling. "Anyway, she told some people about it. And it got back to my boss. There was a conversation with human resources."

I'm not sure what to say.

"So that, combined with profits being down and—yeah. Here we are."

I realize that I'm leaning toward him, my shoulders hiked with stress for him.

"There's a stain on my reputation now," he goes on. "I don't think I'm going to get another job in publishing."

"What can I do?" I ask.

He shakes his head, lifts a palm. "I talked to Olivia about it. She says to do nothing, learn what I can from the encounter. And check my instincts moving forward."

Olivia. So they do talk independently of us. I feel a little rush of something unpleasant—that feeling you have when your friend is spending time with another friend. Jealousy? Possessiveness?

"When did you talk to Olivia?"

"I called her when this first went down, to ask her advice. And she's been helping me, free of charge."

I nod, not knowing what to say. I take a long swallow of my coffee. I'm glad she was there for him when he obviously didn't want me to be.

He leans back on the sofa, looks off toward the window. Outside, the sky is going gray, threatening rain again.

"Rosie," he says softly, still not looking at me. "Just work on your book, take care of your husband and live your life."

There's something so sad about it. When he turns to look at me, we lock eyes. "Be the excellent friend that you have been since the day I met you in the break room. That's what you can do."

I don't want to tell him about Chad's new role, my pregnancy. I *do*, but I wouldn't. No one struggling needs to hear how great everything is going for someone else. It will be a while before Chad can post about the series on social media, or it will be announced. Maybe Max will be on his feet again by the time I start to show.

"I can do that," I say. "Of course. But are you okay? Like *truly* okay?"

He rolls his eyes at me. "Like—are you going to find me hanging from a ceiling fan?"

"Jesus, Max." The image of Dana hits hard, and I dip my head into my palm as if I can block the vision that's inside my head.

"Sorry," he says, wincing. "Really. I'm sorry."

I gaze at him through my fingers. "Max."

"I'm okay," he says, sitting up from his slouch. "I have savings, a couple of author friends who need a freelance editor. So I'm good for money. Maybe I'll take this time to regroup, take a long, hard look at myself, you know? Make amends. Figure out the next *chapter*."

He smiles at his own wit and so do I. "That's very evolved of you."

His grin wanes a bit. "I try. What about you? Everything okay? You look tired, a little pale."

The truth is I am still a bit wobbly since the train ride, headachy and still vaguely nauseated. Morning sickness isn't instantaneous, is it?

"I'm good." We talk about my research, the structure that's evolving. We get right into it, as if nothing has changed.

Max looks a little sad. "Keep me in the loop, okay? I want to be involved even if I'm not your editor anymore."

"You'll be sorry you said that."

He walks me to the door and takes me into an embrace. We stand there for a while, both of us knowing that our relationship is about to change, but neither of us knowing how. It's as if it will be a long time before we see each other again. It won't be, I hope. Why does it feel like a kind of goodbye?

twenty-two

Willa
1963

I can't quit him. I tried. I *tried*. He haunts me like a specter. Invades my dreams. It's *his* face I see, heaven help me, as I make love to my husband. This baby that grows inside me. It's his; I can feel it. We are connected now; his draw is magnetic, irresistible. Though I said I wouldn't, we keep meeting—while Paul sleeps, writes or studies. My husband is so good, so kind. He suspects nothing, dotes on me, rubs my feet as we lie by the fire at night, talks about our future. He wants to leave this building, this city, buy a house in the country—far from the mayhem of urban living.

Far from the excitement, the glitz and glamour, the culture, the art, my career, any dream I ever had of who I was or what I would become. If we move to Greenwich, my life as a young aspiring dancer is over and my life as wife and mother, shackled by her domestic *bliss*, begins. The idea, the very thought, robs me of any happiness I felt at being a mother, and fills me with dread.

Won't you miss it? I nudge Paul gently. *All the energy, all the excitement, your literary community, the salons, the readings, the parties.*

The noise, the heat, the crime, he counters. *This city is in decline; it grows more dangerous every year. We can't raise our children here.*

Children. Our children.

What about me? I venture. *What about my work?*

He smiles, holds my hand tenderly. *There's enough, Willa. You don't have to work. You can devote yourself to motherhood.*

As if this is the thing all women want. The only thing. A rich husband, a litter of children, a big house in the country. Men can have their careers and their families, too. Women must choose, it seems.

Maybe when the children are older you can teach. Or perhaps there's a community theater.

He means it so lovingly. He has no idea that it's a death sentence.

He's going away tomorrow, a writers' retreat in upstate New York, a prestigious one to which few are accepted. I'm glad he's going. I wish he weren't. I don't trust myself with him away. I am too much myself when I don't have to please him—too wild, too reckless, too in love with another man, too yearning to be young and free and dancing.

I help him pack his brown leather valise.

I'll miss you, he says, coming from behind and putting his hands on my emerging belly. It won't be long before I start to really show. Already my pants are tight, my skirts straining at the seams, the life inside me expanding, seeking to take up more space in my body, in my life.

You always want more and more, my mother used to say. *You're never satisfied with your lot.*

She was right. I did want more than the life she had, little more than a domestic, tending to husband and children, always bending over a hot stove, or wash bin, hair wild, her prettiness fading, shoulders growing hunched with the strain of it all, the endless labor. She, too, wanted to dance once. I've seen the pictures of a young ballerina—erect and slim on pointed toes. She'd been stunning, that young girl, beautiful with eyes of fire. Where did she go? I wanted to ask my mother but didn't dare. How could you just let her die?

On the street, I wave goodbye as he rumbles away in his new black Buick Riviera. The day is crisp, autumn turning the few leaves yellow and orange. I want to call him back. And then I'm overwhelmed by the thought that maybe he won't come back. That he'll have a terrible wreck and die, and I'll be free, inheriting all his money and my freedom.

You're a wicked girl with a dark soul, my mother used to tell me.

She was right.

In the lobby, I run into Ella, Miles and Lilian on their way to school. Each of them perfect in their own way. Ella svelte in a slim skirt and tweed jacket, stylish flats. The children crisp and scrubbed in their school uniforms.

Miles cowers from me, hiding behind his mother. Let's say we understand each other a little better now after the chat I had with him during my visit.

"Is Paul off to his retreat?" asks Ella.

"Yes," I answer, pulling a sad face. "I'll be on my own for a couple of weeks."

"Lucky you," she says, giving me a wink. "You must come for dinner."

I put a gentle hand on Miles's head and he yanks away from me, earning an eye roll from Ella.

"That's rude, Miles," she chastises.

He opens his mouth to say something but then we lock eyes, and he presses his lips together. Smart boy.

When I look back at Ella, she's watching me with something

like mild suspicion, curiosity maybe, but it quickly fades into her practiced polite smile.

"Enjoy your freedom while it lasts," she says, eyes drifting down to my belly. I put my hands there in answer. "And do call us if you get lonely."

Then she sweeps them all out to the street and they're gone.

twenty-three

Astrology night. I balance the warm tray of baked ziti as I ring Ella's buzzer. The aroma wafting up is heavenly. I can't take credit—this is baked ziti I picked up from the Italian restaurant and pizzeria that was Ivan's favorite. A bit of a cheat, but oh, well.

I hear laughter from inside the Aldridges' apartment, ring the buzzer again.

My nausea has subsided some, but I'm aware of a low buzz of anxiety—the pall cast by Dana's death, the detective's unsettling visit, even the simmering joy of my positive pregnancy test.

I'm about to ring again when Ella opens the door, resplendent in a green Pucci shirtdress and Ferragamo flats, her hair back in a thick headband.

"Oh, dear, how long have you been waiting? I didn't hear the bell. What is this now?" she says, taking the ziti. "Silly thing, you went overboard. For appetizer, you could have brought cheese and crackers."

She says it lightly with a kind smile. But as we move inside and approach the table of food, it's clear I've screwed up. My aluminum tray of gooey pasta looks like a poor relation amid the spread of elegant glass platters, ceramic roasting dishes, wood charcuterie trays. Ella makes room for my contribution on the dining room table. Voices drift from the living room.

"I'm sorry," I say.

"Nonsense," she says, uncovering it. "It looks divine."

"It's from Sal's," I admit, chronically honest.

She smiles, puts a hand on my shoulder. "Of course. You're a busy working woman, while the rest of us just sit around all day coming up with things to do."

There's an undercurrent to the statement. It's somehow a compliment and a dig, isn't it? As if I haven't earned or fallen into a life of leisure. As if that's a goal all people have, to do nothing.

"I'm just happy you found time to join us tonight," she says.

We enter the living room where some of the people from the welcoming party have gathered again—Anna the sculptor, Oga the heart surgeon: Charles is standing by the mantel. I look around for and finally spot Xavier, chatting in the far corner of the room with a man I don't recognize. I'll corner him before I leave here tonight.

A woman with wild steel-gray curls and icy eyes sits in one of the big wingback chairs. She is as erect as a dancer, but full bodied, a voluminous skirt spread around her. There's a small table in front of her; another woman in jeans and oversize white shirt, with long blond hair, sits on a colorful pouf before her.

"When we want something different to happen," the gray-haired woman is saying, "we have to do something different." Her voice is smoky and soft.

"For Virgo, this month is a time of changing, shifting, growing. We let go of the things that no longer serve, invite in more of what nourishes this month. Does that resonate?"

"It does," says the younger woman. "I've been thinking of changing jobs. My workplace has grown toxic."

"That's Miranda," whispers Ella. "She's our medium, astrologer and card reader."

I nod, smile inside at Miranda's generic advice. My mother said most everyone is looking for the same things. They want to be loved. They want to be safe. Some people think they want to be rich, or famous or powerful. But it's really the feeling they think those things will give them that they truly crave. And everyone broadcasts a thousand different things about themselves, easy for a certain type of person to read. What you wear, how you carry yourself. Do you bite your nails, dye your hair, wear too much makeup, none? The little details speak volumes to someone who knows how to read people. It's not psychic to be observant, to have a deep knowledge of the human condition. It's just that so few people are paying attention, it seems like something otherworldly.

"The time is now," says Miranda. "I'm picking up that there's an opportunity or dream. One that is tempting. But something is holding you back."

"And that leggy blonde is Jasmine." Ella puts a musing hand to her necklace. "I'm not sure what she does, truly."

"She's an escort," Xavier whispers as he approaches. He rubs at his neatly trimmed black beard and smiles wolfishly.

"Oh, stop it," says Ella.

"It's *true*," he says. "She escorts wealthy businessmen to events, dinners, parties. It's perfectly legitimate."

"Huh," I say.

Jasmine rises gracefully from the pouf, gives a bow of thanks. I didn't hear the rest of their conversation. Her hair is like spun gold, features delicate—high cheekbones and almond-shaped dark eyes, a charming mole by her lip. She moves with the grace and perfect posture of a runway model.

"The money is very, *very* good from what I understand," says Xavier. "And to hear her tell it—she's quite open about it—there's no sex involved at all. Unless—"

"Xavier," chastises Ella, coloring a bit and taking a sip of her drink.

"Unless she wants," he finishes. "And then the money's even better."

We both giggle a little at that until Ella silences us with a disapproving frown.

"Everybody, this is our new neighbor," she says, raising her voice a little. "The very talented and bestselling author Rosie Lowan. Some of you have met."

Anna gives me a cool smile and a wave. Oga salutes me. And everyone else offers a chorus of *Hi, Rosie!* and *Welcome!*

"Rosie and her husband, Chad, are the most delightful people," says Charles, who looks to have had more than usual to drink, a bit red in the face, words slurry. "We're so lucky to have them here at the Windermere."

Which strikes me as an odd thing to say when we're only here because Ivan has passed. And then of course the fact that the apartment should have been Dana's. But maybe I'm just being sensitive. The image of Dana comes back to me again, bringing with it another wave of nausea. The truth is I haven't felt totally well since my ride out to see Max, that nausea coming and going. I am a bit wobbly. Maybe I'm coming down with something. What did I eat today?

I am about to ask Xavier about the box when Ella loops her arm through mine and ushers me to the pouf.

"Miranda," says Ella. "Why don't you do Rosie next?"

"Oh," I say, lifting a palm. "I don't want to cut in line."

"Nonsense," says Ella, pushing me forward. This is the last thing I want. If I needed my fortune told, I'd call my mother. I remember Chad's encouragement to call my family, let them know our news. Maybe.

I can't reasonably refuse to sit with Miranda, so finally, I sink down.

All eyes are on me, the heat of embarrassment coming up to

my cheeks. Anna's searing blue gaze is especially intense. It's not unkind exactly but has the quality of an inspector looking for fault. I am aware of my shabby appearance, that I need a haircut, that the past few days have taken their toll in the form of dark circles under my eyes.

"Hi, Rosie," says Miranda. "Lovely to know you. This is a safe space."

Something about her voice, her words, the warmth of her palms as she takes my hands and I feel some of the tension leave my shoulders. There's an aroma coming off her that I recognize as sage, smoky and sweet. The other people in the room have gone back to their conversations, the chatter low and easy.

"What is your star sign?" she asks. "Let me guess. You're a Taurus."

"That's right."

"Dependable, inquisitive, headstrong," she says with a smile. I offer an assenting nod.

"What's your birthday?"

"April twenty-sixth."

"A true bull, then," she says. "Ruled by Venus, the divine feminine, lover of all things sensual but grounded by your need for stability and security."

"Fair enough." Cookie-cutter Taurus. Everybody knows that.

"Big things are happening for Taurus this year, lots of explosive energy in career and family, big changes, tremendous progress toward your goals."

I can't help but think about Chad, my book, the life inside me.

"My husband is also a Taurus. May seventh."

She closes her eyes and squeezes my hands. "Yes, I can feel it. Big things for both of you this year." She opens her eyes again. There's kindness there, empathy, wisdom. My mother always said that if you look at people with compassion, they bare their souls. Everyone wants to be seen, to be known.

"People born on your day often have had a lot to overcome. Maybe as a child your family didn't understand you, or you were given too much responsibility too soon. Your childhood was not carefree. You were not protected."

I acknowledge this with a nod.

"But this has made you responsible and competent. You have found your way. And—" she pauses, pulls me in and lowers her voice to a whisper "—you'll be a wonderful mother."

She smiles when I look at her in surprise. "It was just a guess," she says, voice still low. "I can see it sometimes. It's something in the eyes."

"I just found out yesterday," I whisper.

"Motherhood will be a healing journey for you. And for others."

"Others."

She shrugs. "Just a vibe, an energy."

We talk more about career and Chad. She's warm and funny and engaging. "I know you've suffered some losses recently," she says. "Your uncle and Dana."

"Did you know her?" I ask. But she shakes her head.

"I didn't know Ivan well, either," she says. "Not a believer."

I look around the room. The rest of the group seems to have moved into the dining room. I am hoping Xavier doesn't leave early. I hear voices and clattering plates. The nausea amps up; my stomach turning a little at the thought of food.

Only Charles remains in the living room, sitting on the couch with his eyes closed. Is he sleeping? He's normally so powerful, so engaged, the life of the party. Tonight he seems a bit fragile, older. "I'm not sure I am a believer, either," I admit.

"Maybe not. But you have an open and questioning spirit. And there's nothing to this life but mystery. Questions to be asked and not all of them answered."

It's an echo of something my father used to say, that he lived in the mystery, letting power move through him without questioning.

"Sad about Ivan," Miranda says. "A tragedy about Dana. Murder, I hear. Not suicide."

"That's what the police have said," I concede, not wanting to say more. "How long have you lived at the Windermere?"

"Twenty years now," she says.

"I'm writing a book about the building," I say. The real reason I'm here.

"Ah, yes, I've heard. About the murders, the suicides."

"Do you know the stories?"

She nods. "It was all before my time. But I will say I feel the energy sometimes. There's something sad on the roof deck—have you been up there? Almost no one uses it. I avoid the basement at all costs."

"I saw something down there," I say without meaning to.

She gives me a satisfied nod. "I knew there was something about you."

I tell her about my family, in the broadest possible strokes—my father the healer, my mother the card reader, my sister and grandmother with their dreams.

"And yet, you don't believe?"

"I guess I'm not sure what I believe."

She shifts in her seat, glances over at Charles, who is snoring softly.

"Have you seen him?" she says quietly.

"Who?"

"In the basement. Have you seen the little boy?"

I hesitate. I don't want to tell her. But finally, I nod.

"His name is Miles," says Miranda softly. "He was Charles and Ella's son. The elevator was broken. He fell down the shaft. This was back in the sixties."

I put my hand to my mouth. I had no idea they'd lost a child, that the little boy who died here was their son. How had I missed that detail? "That's...*horrible.*"

Had I never come across a name for the boy? This tragic detail adds another layer to Charles and Ella. That they could still be so lovely and caring after such a tragic loss is remarkable to me.

"What about Willa Winter?" she asks. I startle a little at the name, but shake my head.

Miranda leans in close. "I've seen her here. In the kitchen usually."

I think about how the schematics I found show that the kitchen is where our apartments were split.

"Such a tragedy," she says. "I feel her energy. So sad, such long-ing."

"Tell me what you know about the Winters." I only know the broadest strokes of their story. I'm eager for more details but they've been elusive. Even the smattering of news articles I've unearthed, including the one in Ivan's box, are vague and unsatisfying.

She's about to say more but then Charles stirs awake.

"Oh, my goodness," he says. "Did I doze off? It's hell getting old. Let's eat, ladies. The stars will still be there when our stomachs are full."

"Can I interview you?" I ask Miranda. Then I look to Charles. "And you, too, about the building."

"Of course, of course," says Charles, looking pleased. "I've been here as long as our gargoyles. Do you know I named them when I was a boy—Fred and Ethel? You're both probably too young to get the reference."

"Well, I haven't been here quite as long, but I know a thing or two. Just pop down to 303 any midmorning," says Miranda. I thank them both, and Miranda holds me back as Charles goes on ahead.

"He wasn't a nice boy from what I understand," says Miranda in a whisper. "Miles. And whatever piece of him lingers at the Windermere is not very nice, either. When you see him—or anything—be careful."

She says it so easily, so practically, as if it's the most natural thing in the world. And maybe it is. My grandmother says that the dead and the living dwell side by side. Dr. Black might call it delusion or psychosis, the manifestation of trauma. Regardless, I saw something in the basement, in my elevator lobby. Ghost or imagination, I'm not sure, maybe some combination of both. But whatever it was, Miranda's warning rings true. It wasn't nice at all.

"I saw a post on the forum that was deleted about the ghosts of the Windermere," I say. "Was it yours?"

She nods. "The administrator deleted it." She rolls her eyes. "Said it was bad for resale to imply that the building was haunted."

"Who's the administrator?"

"Charles, of course. You'll find him running most things at the Windermere." The way she says it, there's a note of warning.

Before we separate in the kitchen, she whispers, "Come see me. We'll talk more. But don't worry. You—and your family— you're perfectly safe here."

I flash on the boy in the basement, in my foyer. I hope she's right.

Astrology night is surprisingly enjoyable. Xavier, it seems, is going to find love; Oga will reconnect with old friends; Charles and Ella will travel; and Anna is about to enter the most creative time of her life. Miranda is a force of positivity, spinning the negative and accentuating the positive. *While Charles is struggling with some health challenges, there is grand travel abroad for you both.*

The food is excellent, and the wine is flowing. It's a strange feeling to be so new here and yet to feel ensconced, welcomed.

Miranda reminds me of my mother, and the urge to call home, broken and toxic as it is, is strong again. As the party thins out, I ask Charles what he knows about Marc LeClerc.

"Ah, yes," he says. "I remember him from when I was boy. An unhappy man. He always frowned, looked hunched by the weight of the world. My grandfather was one of the original investors in the Windermere. I might have his old archives in my storage unit. Shall I look for you?"

I struggle to do the math in my head. If LeClerc died in 1932 and Charles was a boy at that time, he would now have to be over 80. He looks twenty years younger than that.

"That would be so helpful," I say. "I'll check in with you at the end of the week."

He gives me a stately nod, and Ella hands me the nearly empty tray of pasta. Maybe not such a screwup after all.

"I told you it would be a hit!" she says.

I see that Xavier is about to leave, and I hurry toward the door to catch him. We say our goodbyes and thanks to Charles and Ella. And then the two of us are alone in the elevator lobby.

"I have an odd request," he says, before I can jump on him with my questions.

"Oh?"

"Can I come through your place and go out your back door to the service elevator?"

"Oh, that's right," I say. "George is off duty. Of course."

We walk through, and he admires the wood floors, the fireplace, the views, says his place is a bit smaller, and Chad and I must come down for drinks one night.

"Why didn't you use the Aldridges' back door?" I ask as we walk out the back door to the service elevator lobby.

"Oh," he says, glancing down the hallway toward their back door. "I didn't think of it until we were outside, then I forgot Abi wasn't on duty."

The hallway is drafty and damp.

"Are you avoiding Abi?" I ask.

"I make it a habit to avoid Abi," he says.

"Really?"

"Abi knows way too much about the people in this building," he whispers.

"Like what?"

He lifts his eyebrows.

"I mean, think about it. He knows *everything*—all our habits, the company we keep, when we come and go. There are cameras all over the building. He takes all our packages, sends out and receives our laundry. Doormen know all our little secrets, don't they?"

I press the button for the elevator, and we stand in the drafty hallway. I close my arms around myself against the chill.

"Which leads me to a question I've been meaning to ask. I left a message with Abi for you. And George. Did you get it?"

He looks surprised. "No, I would have gotten back to you right away."

"And I tried on the chat."

"Oh, I never go on that anymore. Too much chatter, bickering, complaining. It's tiresome."

He looks at the elevator door, presses the button again. Does he seem suddenly uncomfortable?

"The other day when we bumped into each other in the elevator," I go on. "Did you happen to notice a box?"

"A box?" he asks, frowning. I notice his carefully manicured nails, the stylish cut of his dark hair, the drape of his cashmere sweater.

"I had something I was bringing to Ivan's daughter. It was in the elevator on the floor beside me."

He seems to search his memory banks and come up empty, shakes his head. "I don't remember seeing anything."

I feel a squeeze of desperation. "Are you sure?"

He must hear the despair in my voice, seems to soften. Xavier gives an uneasy glance up at the camera, puts a finger to his lips, then leans in.

"Maybe we can talk about it over coffee."

"I'd like that," I say. We exchange numbers.

"I heard you had a run-in with him," he says, still whispering.

I nod, give him the abridged version of what happened.

The elevator comes and he blocks the door from closing with his foot. "I'll just say this. Don't trust him. And don't tell him anything you don't want the whole building to know."

Oh, I think, so this is about gossip.

"Gossip can be toxic," he says, as if reading my thoughts.

"You're right."

"I was sorry to hear about Ivan's daughter. You found her body? You must be reeling."

"It was awful. We're still in shock, I think. Did you know her?"

Something passes across his face, but it's gone before I can name it. "No," he says. "We never met."

"She was a great talent." It's the only nice thing I can think to say.

He seems to want to say more but bows his head instead. "Let's get that coffee soon, maybe tomorrow? Free around two?"

He has more to say but doesn't want to say it in front of the camera. That's strange, unsettling.

"I'd like that. It's a date."

"Good night, lovely Rosie," he says sweetly. And then he's gone.

There isn't much time to puzzle over the conversation; it's getting late, and I have to get downtown for Chad's final performance in his play. Inside, I hustle into a tight black dress and heels, grab my coat and head out the rear door again to the service elevator.

As I step back into the gray hallway, I swear I hear Charles and Ella's door open and close. But there's no one there when I peek my head around the corner.

Downstairs, the lobby is empty. Moving quickly, I slip behind the doorman station and knock on the door to the office. No answer. The door is heavy, and the brushed nickel scroll handle is locked tight.

I take out the ring of keys I got when we inherited the apartment and try using the first one, which opened the storage cage, but it's far too small.

I don't even know what I'm looking for—proof that Abi lied? Some insight into how the surveillance, the intercom, works? Abi said that the surveillance equipment doesn't record. But what if it does? Is there footage stored of Abi carrying the box down? For those reasons, and for something else I can't name, I just really want to get into that room.

I'm about to try the other key.

"Rosie?"

I spin to see Charles standing behind me. He's changed from his crisp cream suit into a black turtleneck and jeans. I see the shadow of the younger man he must have been, virile, handsome.

"Oh," I say, trying to cover with a smile. "I was just—looking for a package I thought was left."

Charles frowns. "George would have brought it to you, no?"

I clear my throat, step away from the door. "I received a notification that it was delivered, but I didn't get it. So I just wondered if it was down here."

"I'm sure Abi can look around for you in the morning. George is—not always reliable. Not like Abi."

There's something odd about the way he says it. He keeps his eyes on me.

"George said you were looking for a package earlier, too."

He squints, then gives a slow nod. "I was. Bad day for deliveries, I guess."

"Are you looking for it now?"

"Oh, no," he says. "I just thought I'd come man the door for a while. Some of the residents are still out."

I'm about to bid him good-night when I remember the chat forum. I tell him that I was on earlier, just reading up on issues in the building.

"I noticed a chat called 'Ghosts of the Windermere.' But it looked like it had been deleted."

Charles gives a subtle shake of his head. "Now, you don't believe in ghosts, do you, Rosie?"

"No," I say with a smile. "But I'm always curious about energies. Or what people think might be ghosts."

I wonder if he'll mention Miles, the son he lost. But he doesn't.

"Is this part of your research?" he asks, taking his seat behind the desk. He rubs at his shoulder as if it's causing him pain.

"I'm more interested as a resident. Why was the forum deleted?"

"Because it's silliness," he says stiffly. "And in this market, we don't need anything else lowering our property values."

"You're not a believer?"

"I wouldn't say that. I've always had a curiosity about the *mystical*, shall we say? But we can't have potential buyers scared away by the idea that the Windermere is haunted. It isn't. I assure you."

I can see we're not going to get any further with this tonight and I'm late, so I turn toward the door, waving good-night.

"Chad said you'd be meeting him," he says, rising. "Can I hail you a cab? I hate to think of you out on the street flagging down a cab by yourself."

I smile at that, the chivalry that smacks up hard against sexism, the attention that's kind and weirdly controlling, infantilizing all at once.

"I'm good," I tell him. "Thank you. I think I'll take the subway."

"Oh, don't do that—not in your—" He brings himself up short. And I know in that second that Chad told them. He told Charles and Ella that I'm pregnant, that Ella told Miranda. I feel a wash of anger, betrayal. That this thing that is mine, *ours*, has been shared and gossiped about.

Gossip can be toxic.

"Good night, Charles," I say.

I don't wait for him to answer, just rush out the door and jog down the street.

twenty-four

"How long are you going to stay mad at me?" Chad asks in the cab.

The city rushes by us in strands of light. I've been to his performance, the cast party afterward, playing the loving and supportive wife. But by the time we left, I couldn't contain it any longer. And then we had a big fight on the street outside the theater. We walked it uptown, finally got tired and hailed a cab.

I don't answer, because I'm not mad. I'm furious.

"Rosie."

I explode, nearly yelling. "I haven't even *tried it on yet*, gotten my head around it, seen a doctor. I wasn't ready to share this. Not with anyone."

"You didn't tell *Max*?" he asks, as if it's a foregone conclusion that I did.

"I didn't tell *anyone*."

He looks out his window and I look out mine. Our cab driver is on his own call, speaking softly, words muffled through the thick barrier between us. How many fights have there been in the back of this cab? I wonder.

"I'm sorry," Chad says finally after the barrage of excuses he gave me about family, and wanting to share joy and how they've been there for us. "I shouldn't have done that. I see how it was a betrayal."

I sigh. He senses me softening. "Is it so bad? To share our joy?"

Is it so bad? I don't know. It just feels so fragile, so tentative. And I asked him not to tell; he promised he wouldn't. But then he broke his promise. That hurts more than anything. Trust is our foundation. But maybe a part of me gets it. I would have loved nothing more than to tell Max. I only didn't because he's struggling. The truth is that I'm practically busting with it myself.

"I guess not," I admit grudgingly.

"You gotta get out here," says the cabbie.

"No," says Chad. "One more block."

The cab driver points ahead, and we see that Park is blocked at Thirty-Sixth Street both ways.

I sigh, so tired, still not feeling so well, feet throbbing in my heels; the extra block seems like a mile. We pay and exit the cab, walk toward our building.

Chad spins and blocks my way.

"Have I been a dick lately?" he asks. "I feel like I'm always asking for your forgiveness. First with the apartment, then Dana, now this."

I search his face and for a second when I look into his eyes, I feel a chill, like I'm staring into a void. Dana's accusations ring back. *A dark heart beneath a beautiful mask.*

Then it's just Chad again, gaze warm and loving. No. He's wonderful. The first safe place I've found in my life. My rock. Nobody's perfect. We all make mistakes, especially in intense times like these. Explosive changes, that's what Miranda said. These are growing pains, part of living a life together.

"No, you haven't," I say, touching his arm. "It's just that we're our own thing, okay? We make decisions as a couple, then honor those choices. Not say one thing and do another."

He kisses me, then puts a hand to either side of my face. "I'm just so fucking happy, Rosie. I couldn't keep it in. But not another word until you've seen the doctor. Did Ella give you the name of their friend?"

"I made an appointment with Hilary's doctor. I see her next week."

He hesitates, then nods. "Whatever you think."

That's right. Whatever *I* think. Because it may be our child, but it's my body and I'll say how this pregnancy and delivery go. I feel a little of my mother's strength, her fire, her knowledge, and I'm glad for it.

He drapes an arm around me, and we keep walking, our pace slowing as we draw near and see a crowd. As we grow closer it's clear that from the crowd, the ambulance and police cars gathered, that something has happened at our building. We start pushing through the throng, earning annoyed comments from the onlookers.

"Excuse me. We live here. What's happened?" I hear Chad saying.

My heart is pounding as we push to the front of the gathering. I draw back with a hand to my mouth, a scream lodged in my throat.

I see the man, his body ruined on the sidewalk, arms akimbo, legs twisted as if he's fallen from a great height. Eyes staring at me.

Xavier.

The world starts to spin and someone's screaming. It's me. I fall back into Chad, who catches me with strong arms. There's a brutal, sharp pain in my abdomen that doubles me over. Then the city, the crowd, my husband—everything including me—fades to black.

ACT III

ghosts and gargoyles

The hawk is in the air and I hear its screech. The hawk flies about me, then I can feel its talons on my scalp. It lets go and faces me. I look into its eyes. The hawk is ancient, yet I seem to know who he is. The hawk speaks, "I am the spirits from the past, and I come to you because it is difficult for you to come to us."

James Hollis
Hauntings: Dispelling the Ghosts Who Run Our Lives

twenty-five

The room is dim, though it's past noon, light blocked by the milky drapes pulled against the daylight. And I can't move. My limbs are filled with sand, and my head is heavy on the pillow. I can hear Chad's voice in the other room, low and serious. He's worried about me. There's a part of me that wants to get up. She's in there, the real me, the strong one, screaming, *pull yourself together!*

But no. A heavy despair sits on my back, crushing me into the mattress. Even my phone session with Dr. Black has done nothing to dispel the pall that has settled. He's called in a prescription for antidepressants; Chad will pick them up later. I haven't decided whether I'll start taking them or not.

My abdomen aches, my period heavy. I don't suppose you could call it a miscarriage just days after a positive pregnancy test. But it's a miscarriage of hope, of joy.

It's a loss, Rosie, said Dr. Black. *You're allowed to grieve that.*

The buzzer rings. Chad's voice rumbles, then Abi's over the

intercom. After a moment, Chad pushes in through the closed door, sits on the bed beside me and puts a hand on my hip.

"Detective Crowe is here. Olivia is on her way."

"I can't."

"We don't have a choice. It's this or go down to the station." The fatigue and the sadness I see on his face is a mirror of my own heart.

"I just keep seeing him there," I say, tearing up again.

"I know," he says, covering his eyes.

"The medium, Miranda, said that he was going to find love. She told me that our family was growing."

Of course, it's all a fraud; no one knows the future. I know that better than anyone. But still, I was happy to hear her words. Maybe that's when we cling to predictions and fortune telling, when the words are deeply what we want to hear.

"It just wasn't our time," Chad says when I say nothing more, stay still under the covers. "It will happen, Rosie. Lots of couples struggle with this. Our family *will* grow."

His optimism and strength give me some energy. He's right. Plenty of people have trouble getting pregnant. Plenty of people miscarry. They go on to have healthy babies.

The doorbell rings.

"I'll be right out," I tell him.

He watches me a moment and then goes to get the door. I lie still, listening to Detective Crowe's baritone. Olivia is here, too, her voice strident and high. It's with herculean effort that I push myself from the bed, pad across the floor and enter the living room where they're all waiting.

When I join them, a wreck in sweats and one of Chad's old sweaters, hair up in a messy bun, all eyes turn to me. Detective Crowe frowns. Olivia is pressed and put together, her ink-black bob tidy, suit clinging to her shapely frame. She comes to embrace me.

She's perfect; her skin dewy, her makeup flawless, nails painted a deep red.

"It's going to be okay," she whispers. I take in her lilac scent, then pull away. I sit on the couch, curling my legs up beneath me, wrapping my arms around my middle.

I know how I look—pale, exhausted, hair wild. I want to scream. It's lodged in my throat.

"So," says the detective, taking a seat across from me. "I have two deaths in a week. And what do they have in common?"

I stare at him. He, too, is sporting the purple shiners of fatigue, with uneven stubble at his jaw; his thick, dark hair is tousled. He keeps on his brown leather jacket, which he wears over a gray T-shirt. Jeans, work boots. He looks more like a construction worker than a detective.

"You," he says when I don't answer.

"You're reaching," says Olivia. She sits in one of the chairs facing the couch, and he sits in the other. Chad sits right beside me, a protective hand on my leg.

"Am I?" says Detective Crowe. "Dana Lowan is related to Chad Lowan. They were in a dispute over this apartment, among other things, apparently. She was blackmailing your client, by his own admission. And now she's dead. Xavier Young fell from the roof deck of this building. Did he jump? Was he pushed? It's too soon to tell, but here you are again, Rosie and Chad. It's odd, don't you think?"

Olivia is cool, easy. She offers a dramatic shrug, lifting her palms. "Many people in this building knew both Xavier and Dana. The Aldridges, right? The doorman Abi. Who knows who else?"

"There are cameras everywhere," I say. "In the basement, in all the hallways, on the roof, I'm sure."

"Yes," says Crowe. "There are cameras but no recordings. And your doorman Abi was, apparently, off. In fact, there was no doorman on duty that evening, so no one watching the monitor."

"He's a liar," I say. It just comes out and even I'm surprised at how angry I sound. Olivia and Chad both look at me.

"Is this about the box?" asks Detective Crowe.

"What box?" asks Olivia.

I repeat the story that I've told Chad and Detective Crowe.

"So the doorman has a history of deception," says Olivia, seizing on this piece of information. "Why don't you start your investigation there?"

"I'm still waiting on that box," says Crowe.

"Take it," I say.

I want the box gone. In fact, *I* want to be gone. We're selling this place. Nothing has been right since we moved in. Sure, lots of good things have happened. But way more bad things are piling up. Dead bodies. A miscarriage. I think about the history of suicides and violent deaths at the Windermere. Max was right. There's a bad energy here. We never should have come.

"Absolutely not," says Olivia. "Do you have a warrant to search the Lowan residence?"

Detective Crowe lifts his palms.

Olivia gives a curt nod of understanding. "There's no warrant because there's no evidence that the Lowans were involved in either incident. No judge would issue one at this point."

"When was the last time you saw Xavier Young?" he asks.

"Last night," I answer. "There was a gathering at the Aldridge apartment. Astrology night."

"Astrology night?" he asks with a smirk.

"There's a medium in the building. She does horoscopes, reads cards. She told Xavier that he was about to find love."

He gives me a look as if this is the stupidest thing he's ever heard, and maybe it is.

"Did he seem depressed, unsettled in any way?"

I remember laughing with him about the escort. "Not at all. But I didn't know him that well."

"Another resident said that you two left the gathering together. That he came into your apartment afterward."

Again, all eyes on me. Who could have known that? Only Abi, watching on the camera. But he wasn't here last night, or so George said. Or someone was watching through the peephole of Charles and Ella's. Or someone was listening.

"He wanted to come through our place to use the service elevator."

"Why?"

"He said he was trying to avoid Abi."

"Who wasn't working."

"That's what he told me," I say with a shrug. He could have used Ella's exit. He needed to use the service elevator in any case because George was gone. "Maybe he just wanted to see the apartment."

"What did you talk about?"

"We talked about Abi, and about how I shouldn't tell him anything I don't want the whole building to know. I asked him about the box, if he'd seen it in the elevator that day."

"And?"

"He said he didn't, but I think he was being careful about what he said. We planned to have coffee tomorrow. I think he had more to tell me."

Detective Crowe seems to take that in. If you're planning to kill yourself, maybe you don't make plans for the next day.

"Funny how Abi's name comes up again and again," says Olivia.

I hear the crackle that the intercom makes and now I get it.

"He's listening," I say. "Right now."

Crowe's face goes from hard suspicion to concern. Chad puts an arm around me.

"The intercom," I say. "Hey, Abi."

Everyone's looking at me and the silence expands. "Hey, Abi," I say again, this time louder. But he doesn't respond.

"Rosie," says Olivia, looking concerned about my sanity.

"The intercom," says Chad, clarifying. "It's voice activated. He's supposed to answer when you say 'Hey, Abi.'"

"Wow," says Olivia, looking toward the foyer. "That's creepy."

"Right?" I answer. "I think he might be listening right now. There's a weird crackle that comes from the speaker sometimes."

Chad's arm tightens around me. "Rosie has a thing about privacy. She's not a fan of the voice-activated intercom. We plan to disable it."

"I wouldn't be comfortable with that, either," says Crowe, Olivia nodding her agreement.

"So," she says, bringing us back to point. "Since this doorman's name keeps coming up, maybe you should be paying more attention to him," suggests Olivia again.

"I've spoken to him," says Crowe, eyes on me. "He tells a different version of your encounter with the box."

I blow out a breath. "I'm sure."

"And he claims that he doesn't have access to your apartment and wouldn't have been able to return the box, as you claim."

I don't say anything because it's just my word against Abi's. And now that Xavier is gone, there's no hope that he will be able to corroborate my version of events.

"But," says Crowe, "I went the extra mile on this and looked into your doorman. Mr. Abi Bekiri immigrated to America from Albania with his family in 1950. Mr. Bekiri has no criminal record. He graduated high school, became a US citizen. When his father died of a heart attack, Mr. Bekiri dropped out of school to work and help his mother take care of his two siblings. He has been working at the Windermere since 1962."

We all exchange looks. It seems impossible. What is that? More than sixty years? It's an eon.

"He is seventy-eight years old, claims that he loves his job here and has no intention of retiring. Meanwhile, he cares for his ninety-eight-year-old mother, who is in assisted living up in Queens."

Abi doesn't look a day over sixty. I conjure his straight posture, unlined face, quick movements, the cool intelligence of his gaze.

"Yoga," says Detective Crowe, as if reading my thoughts. "He has a daily yoga practice, which he claims keeps him so fit and young-looking."

"Impressive," says Chad. I can see him making a mental note to take up yoga.

"Meanwhile, his alibi for the day of Dana Lowan's murder checks out. He'd been on duty since 6:00 a.m. He left at noon to spend the afternoon with his mother in Queens. It was her ninety-eighth birthday. The records at the nursing home, as well as video surveillance, confirm his visit.

"He's a model citizen and family man, hardworking, dedicated," Crowe concludes.

I find myself shaking my head but say nothing.

"Your movements that day are well-documented, as well, Ms. Lowan."

Olivia's phone is chiming and beeping. But she keeps her focus on Detective Crowe.

"Mr. Lowan on the other hand—"

I feel Chad stiffen.

"You claimed that you were at an audition that morning and then at rehearsal for your play until you went up to Dana's studio."

"That's right," says Chad. Do he and Olivia exchange a look? It's quick if they do.

"Except that I've learned that you weren't at rehearsal," says the detective.

Chad clears his throat, shakes his head. "I was."

"Your director says that you were there for a while, then had to leave suddenly for a family emergency."

"Right," Chad says. "When I realized that Rosie was heading up to Dana's."

"You said around two?"

"Correct."

"He says around ten."

Chad shakes his head, emphatic. "He's wrong."

Olivia isn't chiming in, which strikes me as odd because they arrived at the studio together. His location services were off that day, I remember now. When I glance over at Chad, he's the picture of concerned innocence.

"It will be easy enough to confirm with your cell phone data."

"Not going to happen," says Olivia.

"I don't have anything to hide," says Chad.

"No way," says Olivia. "You want the box, his cell phone records—you need a warrant. You can't get one and you know it. Because you're just speculating, reaching, trying to get my clients to give away their rights."

"We just need to verify Mr. Lowan's story. And then we can cross him off our list of suspects."

List of suspects? The phrase fills me with dread, and I push into Chad. Do they think Chad could have killed Dana?

"My clients are upstanding citizens, professional creatives with no criminal history. They're artists, not murderers. They had no motive to harm either of the deceased."

Olivia's right. Maybe everyone does need a lawyer. She's a bulldog and thank God. We'd be turning everything over to the police if not for her.

"People have been killed for less than a five-million-dollar apartment."

"They have no reason to *kill* for it," she says sharply. "It belongs to them."

"Except that Dana Lowan told her ex-husband that she believed Chad manipulated her drug-addled father into changing his will. That he was on such powerful painkillers toward the end that he wasn't of sound mind. Apparently, there was a nurse who said she overheard something to corroborate this. Dana was about to sue for her inheritance."

No. None of that can be true.

"What nurse?" I ask.

"A Ms. Betty Cartwright."

"Did you talk to her?" asks Olivia. "What does she claim she heard exactly?"

"That's the thing. I can't seem to locate her. She hasn't returned my calls. And yesterday, apparently, she didn't turn up to work."

"Betty was flaky," says Chad. "Unreliable. She almost gave Ivan the wrong dose of pain meds one time. If I hadn't been there, she could have killed him."

I stare at Chad, his presidential profile and golden curls. I don't recall that, or Betty as being unreliable. There were several hospice nurses toward the end—all of them kind, competent, present. I always think of hospice workers the same way I do midwives. They are standing on the portals of life and death, ushering souls in and out. I have found almost without fail that there is a powerful wisdom to those people, usually women, who do that kind of work. Betty was one of those—always on time, never impatient with any of us, dedicated to easing Ivan's passing.

"Do you agree with that?" Detective Crowe is directing his question to me. "That Ms. Cartwright was flaky?"

"I don't remember," I say, not wanting to contradict Chad.

I feel the heat of the detective's gaze.

"Ivan loved us. And we loved him. That's why we took care of him, and I think that's why he left us the apartment," says Chad. "Dana was nowhere to be found as he lay dying. She never even came to say goodbye. She can't know if he was of sound mind or not."

Chad dumps his head in his hand then, shoulders starting to shake. I hold on to him tight.

"This conversation is over," says Olivia. "Your callousness is shocking."

Detective Crowe rolls his eyes, releases a sigh, then stands.

"One more thing," he says. "You say that your clients have no criminal records."

My shoulders tense and I feel Chad go very still.

"But that's not the whole truth, is it?"

Olivia has risen, as well, her face blank. She stays silent.

"But that's not true," he says again. "Is it, Mr. Lowan?"

twenty-six

Willa
1963

I am bold enough, cold enough, to have him in our apartment. With Paul away I remember what it's like to feel free—young and with no concerns except your own pleasure. We go out to clubs and the movies. We dance until the morning and wander home through the park as the sun rises, sleep during the day. Paul always calls after dinner, and I make sure that I am alone to receive him, sounding just lonely enough that he feels missed, not so despairing that he decides to come home.

It's so quiet here, so peaceful, he tells me. *I write all morning, then stroll through the woods, eat, write some more. All the chaos and noise and filth of the city seem so far away. I can't wait until we live like this all the time.*

Graveyards are peaceful, too, I think.

I am so happy you're happy, I tell him.

You sound so far away, he says worriedly.

I'm right here.

This morning in the mirror I saw the first sign of a real bump I think, though my body is still slim.

I look at the clock. Nearly eight. I'll be meeting my love soon. We'll go to a jazz club downtown, listen to music and smoke and drink and laugh. His skin is dark; his eyes darker, they sear into me and see my soul. He's never tired, never suggests that we stay in.

The buzzer rings and I startle.

Who's that? Paul asks, not in the least suspicious.

Probably just Ella. I'm late for game night with the girls. I am such an effortless liar. The lies just slip from my lips like so many butterflies.

Have fun, he says. *I love you.*

I love you. And I mean it; of course I do. *I'm sorry,* I want to say. *I wish I were the wife you deserved. But I'm not.*

I hang up and go to the apartment door. My lover is standing there.

I am shocked at, thrilled by, his boldness, to come up here this way. Usually, we sneak up through the service elevator.

Before I can protest, he puts a finger to my lips. *The Aldridges are out,* he says.

He's shifted out of his uniform and is dressed in crisp black slacks and a silk shirt, stylish loafers. He slips inside the apartment, shutting the door, and I let him take me in his arms, press his hot lips to my neck. I am helpless in the heat of his desire, in mine. I let him take me, right there in the foyer, knocking shamelessly against the wall.

Afterward, I pour him a glass of wine.

When will you leave him? he asks me. *We can't go on like this forever.*

He leans against the windowsill, looks out at the view.

Never, I think but don't say. Paul is my husband, and I will stay with him. I will move to the country and be a good wife. I thought he'd accepted this. Apparently not.

I don't know, I say. *Let's not think about it tonight.*

He frowns but then concedes with a nod. Neither of us is much for serious talk. We are about the city night and all its pleasures.

Slipping out the back door, we kiss, waiting for the service elevator.

That's when I see him.

That little monster, hiding behind the corner, watching us. I let out a little shriek and he turns and runs. I chase after him, but he's gone behind his apartment door, and I hear the latch turn.

I lean in close to the door and know he's right behind it. *You keep your mouth shut, you little brat. Or you know what.*

I hear little footsteps running away. He pulls me away from the door.

"He's just a child," he says easily. "No one will believe him."

"You said they were out."

"Charles and Ella," he clarifies. "The children are with a sitter."

"He saw us," I say.

"I'll handle it."

But the night is ruined. I ruminate at the jazz club. There's not enough gin to take away the image of that brat's mischievous little grin. He'll tell. He probably already has. I beg off early and though he's disappointed he escorts me home, ever the gentleman. I think he knows that it's over, by the sad way he looks at me when I let myself in the back door.

I must find a way to fix this, I think but don't say. I must dedicate myself to being a better wife. I just hope it's not too late.

But it seems he sees it on my face.

"I'll handle the boy," he tells me as I step inside. "I promise."

Upstairs, alone, I cry myself to sleep—saying goodbye to him, to the girl I hoped I would be, the young dancer living a glamourous life in Manhattan. The windows are open, and the city noise wafts up from below. I let it lull me into an uneasy sleep.

I dream of a terrible argument between Paul and me. He

calls me a whore and slaps my face. I fall to my knees begging him to forgive me. In the dream, I'm wailing in despair. I wake with a start, weak with relief that it wasn't real. The morning sun streams in the windows.

But then, there's a horrible keening wail and I wonder if I'm trapped—a dream within a dream.

But no, another shriek scatters the rest of my sleep and has me terrified on my feet, then running toward the door. I fumble with the locks, finally opening the front apartment door.

Ella is on her knees in our shared foyer, wailing in horror and misery. I try to understand the scene before me.

The elevator doors are open, but there's just a gaping black maw. The car is not there.

Ella, Ella, what's happened?

She turns and looks at me, her face a mask of horror and pain. *He fell*, she moans. *Miles fell down the elevator shaft. He's gone.*

twenty-seven

"There's something you should know about me."

Chad and I had been dating about a month, if you could call it dating, which implies something light and inconsequential. We had barely been apart since the night we met, both of us falling hard right away. I remember that time as a kind of hazy, heady rush—my days distilled into time with him or time away from him. He would be waiting for me outside my office, ready to whisk me away. We might do anything—run to see a friend in a show downtown, have a picnic in the park, walk the Brooklyn Bridge, spend hours over dim sum in Chinatown. It was all just foreplay, though, our night spent roaming each other's bodies. He was a drug; I couldn't get enough of him.

We spent most of our time in my East Village walk-up, which would later become our first home together, because he had roommates, and his place in Chelsea was a continuous party-slash-flophouse for all his actor friends. That time—it was light, free, glittery with new love.

"Oh," I said, feeling my heart stutter a little but playing it off. "That sounds very mysterious."

We'd walked up Third Avenue from the subway, on our way to meet his uncle Ivan for the first time at a little Indian place that he loved.

"Honestly, I'm surprised it hasn't come up already," said Chad, clearing his throat and not meeting my eyes.

He'd been subdued that evening, and I wondered if he was nervous about my meeting Ivan. Chad had said that Ivan was a bit of a curmudgeon and my internet search had revealed the extent of Ivan's renown as a war photographer. Also, he was Chad's only family. So I was nervous, too.

"Now I'm really intrigued."

He still wasn't looking at me, eyes on the sidewalk in front of us. "Most people find it when they google."

Slowing his pace, he finally came to a stop and moved to stand in front of me. I wasn't thrilled with what I saw on his face. That high-wattage smile was nowhere to be seen, a frown sitting on his forehead.

"I've, you know, lost people because of it."

People pushed past us on the avenue. It was late autumn, the night cool, both of us in jackets and scarves. I reached for him. "What is it?"

His eyes searched my face, then, "When I was in high school, my girlfriend—Bethany—was murdered." He stops a second, swallows hard.

"Oh," I said, his words landing like so many stones thrown. "That's horrible. I'm so sorry."

He took both of my hands. *Oh, there's more*, I thought. His words—that his girlfriend was murdered—twisted and snaked through my consciousness. I felt a deep pull of fear in my center.

"For a time, I was the main suspect. It went to trial."

Another blow, the breath leaving me. I stared at him, taking in all the details on his face—the sad wiggle to his eyebrows, the creases in his forehead. I saw his pain, a mirror of my own. The world around us disappeared. It was just us in a hum of the city noise, everything else falling away.

I'd purposely not searched him out on the web, wanting to get to know him in real time, allow him to reveal himself to me as he was ready. Just as I wanted to reveal myself to him, layer by layer. Now it felt like a mistake. Naivete. Me, the true-crime writer, the researcher, accustomed to digging deep to find out the truth. I never even googled his name.

Heat crawled up my neck into my cheeks.

How could he choose this time and place to bring it up? On the street, just minutes before meeting his uncle. Why now?

He gripped my arms, as if reading something on my face that indicated I would run from him. Maybe I should have. Maybe anyone else would have. But I didn't run. I stared deep into those faceted, heavily lidded eyes, took in the gold wisps of his curls tossed in the wind. All I saw there, despite his words, was goodness. I tried to imagine him on trial for murder; there was no way for me to cast him in that role.

"This is horrible timing. The worst," he said, reading my mind.

"I—don't know what to say." What *could* I say? Maybe if we'd been someplace quiet where I could process it, do research of my own. But we were on the street. Was it by design?

"It's just been weighing on me—so much. And I wanted you to know before you met Ivan, my only real family. And I'm falling hard for you, Rosie. I can't get in any deeper until you know this part of me, this ugly chapter in my life."

Since I'd known him, not very long, I'd never seen him look so sad. "Forgive me for telling you—like this."

"Okay," I said, releasing a breath. "So—what happened?"

We shifted over to an empty doorway for some modicum of privacy. So much of life plays out on the streets of NYC. It wasn't so unusual to have a potentially relationship-ending con-versation on the sidewalk.

I tried to open my mind, my heart, the way I do when I start researching, just listening to the facts as they are presented.

"The police thought that Bethany had tried to break up with me, and I killed her in a rage, then dumped her body in the woods behind her house."

I tried to imagine it—Chad enraged enough to kill, hurting someone, a young girl. I couldn't. I looked at the hands that had only ever touched me in tenderness. I'd never even seen him lose his temper or heard him say an unkind word about anyone.

"They thought I'd gone right from dumping her body to a football game, where I went on to win the game that would take us to the finals."

He bowed his head, and when he looked at me, his eyes had filled.

"Oh, my God," I breathed.

"She was missing a couple of days before they found her. The whole town was looking for her. After they found her body, they arrested me almost right away."

He batted away his tears as an ambulance screamed by and he paused, waiting for it to pass.

I wanted to comfort him but I stood frozen, listening for the notes of deception. If he was a killer, of course he'd also be a liar. A sociopath. Would I not have sensed that, seen other evi-dence of his darkness?

"I loved her," he said, voice breaking.

I'd seen some pictures of him as a teenager, lithe, athletic, that golden hair and megawatt smile. He was the all-American. Somehow, over the years, he'd grown even better-looking. He clasped my hands, his eyes searching me.

"I *never* hurt her. *Would* never. But they were sure it was me. We had made love that afternoon before the game. My DNA—it was everywhere."

"Oh, Chad."

I wished there was someplace we could sit down; I was about to suggest that we just go home, postpone dinner. But he went on.

"Ivan got me a great lawyer and paid for it. My parents couldn't afford any kind of real defense."

He paused a second, his breath a bit shallow.

"We were in the middle of the trial when her brother confessed to strangling her. He'd been a troubled person, struggling with behavioral and other problems. Apparently, he'd seen us together and they fought. Bethany—she was a firecracker, and she was always teasing him, giving him a hard time. She called him names, and he lost it. He killed her."

The words didn't do the story justice, stripped of all telling details and the raw emotions. A brother murdering his sister. Her boyfriend wrongly accused, standing trial. But I still felt the horror of it all, a tingle on my skin, a clenching in my center. That poor girl. Her parents. My God. I started crying then, too. "That is so—horrible," I said.

He just gave me a slow nod, paused a moment, seemed to search for words. "Later, her brother rescinded his confession, said he'd been coerced. Still, I was exonerated. His case went to trial and he was convicted. He's still in prison, but there's another appeal pending."

We stood facing each other, holding hands. "I was found innocent, Rosie. I *am* innocent. I need you to believe that."

A rowdy group of boys passed us. "Propose already!" one of them yelled, and the rest of them jeered. We ignored them.

I tried to imagine how it played out for him, how devastated he must have been, grief-stricken, terrified.

He bowed his head. "Then a year later—you know this much—my parents were killed in a car crash on Route 80. I barely made it, Rosie. I barely survived all that tragedy and loss, the terror of being wrongly accused. Then losing my mom and dad so suddenly. It almost crushed me."

I believed him. Right then and there on the street. I never doubted the truth of what he told me.

"Honestly, it was Ivan who saved me. He was there for me when no one else was."

I put my hand to his face, wiped at a tear.

"Some people in that town never believed me. Then when my folks died, there were all kinds of rumors about that. It was such a nightmare. On top of the grief and loss, there was the constant stress of living under the shroud of suspicion. I came here to start a new life and never went back."

We moved into each other, wrapping each other up. I knew his heart even then, even after such a short time. He was no killer. Maybe someone else would have needed more to convince them. But I didn't. I could feel his innocence, his goodness, with every cell in my body. We stood like that awhile.

"I'll let you google it, do your research. I know you'll need to do that, and you should. But I need you to know that I would never hurt another human being. That you are safe with me."

"I don't need to research it," I whispered, clinging to him. "I believe you. Of course I do."

He kissed me long and deep.

"I love you, Rosie," he said, his eyes boring into mine. It was the first time he'd said it.

"I love you, too. And I believe you."

But of course, I did research it. I probably know more about that crime than any other person except the cop who investigated Bethany's murder. The one who still believes Chad did it and that the wrong person is in prison. I wanted to write about it. But Chad was dead against it. "Please, let's not unearth the past. You never know what comes crawling out of the dirt."

Now, in our new apartment, the past has unearthed itself despite our best efforts. Olivia has placed herself between Chad and Detective Crowe. "My client was exonerated. Found innocent. And another man confessed and is in prison as we speak."

Detective Crowe bobbles his head side to side; it's kind of an obnoxious gesture, smart, know-it-all. "And yet, there are plenty of people who believe Mr. Lowan was guilty of that murder."

"Plenty of people believe there's a Santa Claus," says Olivia. "That doesn't make it true."

"Including the investigating detective," Crowe goes on, ignoring her quip. "There are allegations that someone, hired by Mr. Lowan's lawyer, coerced a confession out of Bethany Wright's mentally challenged brother."

Chad has gone sickly pale, and I grab on to him.

"Rumor, conjecture," says Olivia. "My client was innocent and found so by a jury."

"A murdered girlfriend. Parents killed in a suspicious car accident. Allegations of manipulating a dying man into willing his apartment. A cousin who hangs herself after blackmailing him. Now a neighbor falls to his death. That's quite a catalog."

We all stay silent. Chad's face is weirdly blank—not angry, not sad, not terrified. I, on the other hand, am all those things.

"That's a lot for one lifetime," says Crowe. "Let alone the span of ten years."

He's right. So much darkness, its tendrils snaking around his life, ours.

"Exactly," says Olivia, unfazed. "My clients have endured enough grief. Don't contact us again without a warrant."

Detective Crowe casts one more worried frown in my direction and then leaves, door slamming behind him. Chad sinks into the couch, and Olivia and I regard each other grimly. The city noise wafts up, the familiar and weirdly comforting cacophony of horns, construction, shouts.

"I can't—I can't go through something like this again," he says. I drop next to him, wrap my arms around him and he leans heavily into me, dumps his head in his hands.

"*Nothing* like that is going to happen," says Olivia, emphatic. She has her hands on her hips, Wonder Woman. "They have nothing on you, or they would have already arrested you."

Chad groans. "If they want to find something, they will. That's how they operate. They develop a theory and then try to prove it right. That's what they did when Bethany died. Nothing could have convinced them that I was innocent."

He's right. I've seen it myself in my research for my last book. The police constructed a narrative, nabbing the wrong man, and even evidence that would have pointed them toward Matthew Pantel, evidence that later proved him guilty, was ignored.

"That is *not* how it's going to go," Olivia says. "Not on my watch."

Olivia stands before us, looking powerful, certain of her position. I've always envied her confidence, the sureness of her voice and actions.

"I've got this," she says, gathering up her things. "Do not speak to him again. Not if he comes here, not if he stops you on the street. Not even if he arrests you—which he won't."

I release Chad, and he rises to embrace Olivia, thanking her for being here. When he looks back at me, the despair I saw earlier seems to be gone, as if she's transferred some of her confidence to him.

I, on the other hand, am still shaken to the core.

"Just—go about your lives as normal," says Olivia in the hallway by the service elevator. "I'll handle Detective Crowe. He has no evidence, just suspicions. So just keep your heads down, work, live and stay out of trouble."

Stay out of trouble? Easy enough when trouble doesn't seem to be waiting around every corner.

Back in the apartment, I pad into the dim bedroom and climb between the covers again, the world too heavy, my sadness too total. I think about those antidepressants and wonder if I need to take them. I can already feel it tugging at me, that undertow of darkness. It swallows all your ambition, joy, power. I can't slip down into that pool again.

It's the building, something whispers. *The pain, sorrow, fear, mur-*

der, death trapped within its walls is like a poison, like arsenic in Victorian wallpaper, making everyone sick.

No. Stop that.

Chad follows me into the room, lies beside me and wraps me up in his arms from behind.

"Olivia said to go about as normal," he says softly.

"I'll try."

"We start the table reading tomorrow," he continues. "Are you going to be all right on your own?"

"I'm fine," I lie. "Everything's fine."

twenty-eight

Harsh and insistent, the buzzer wrests me from sleep. I fumble for my phone, screen filled with message bubbles.

It's ten.

Shit. The room is still dim with the blinds pulled. It's been days since Xavier's death and Detective Crowe's visit, and my miscarriage. The slim bottle of antidepressants Dr. Black prescribed sits by the bathroom sink, untouched, waiting like a good soldier. Chad's been gone since the day before yesterday. And I've barely moved.

The buzzer. It won't stop.

I pad into the hallway wearing Chad's oversize T-shirt and press the button. "What *is it*, Abi?"

I can barely be civil to him after everything that's happened.

"You have a visitor, Ms. Lowan," he says, ever polite and professional, even though he must know that I'm the reason the police questioned him, poor, hardworking Abi, who takes care of his elderly mother.

"A Mr. Maxwell Collins."

"Excuse me, can I talk to her, please?" Max's voice comes over the intercom. "Rosie, let me up."

I sigh. "Okay, Abi, bring him up, please."

I run into the bedroom to pull on some jeans, drag a brush through my hair, shut the door to my office, which is a chaos of notes from my research and photos spread out all over—and which I haven't touched or looked at or thought about in days. Nor have I answered an email from my new editor—a twenty-something, I'm assuming, named Sebastian of all things. I googled him; he's edited precisely nothing, just very recently promoted from assistant to editor in the new shift around at the company. I have an interview with Arthur Alpern scheduled for this afternoon, which I was planning on canceling.

When I open the door, Max is standing there, getting ready to knock, his hand risen. Abi has already left. Max gives me this kind, loving, sympathetic look and I rush in to hug him; he holds me tight, and we stand there awhile; I don't know how long.

"Chad called me," he says. "He's worried about you. He can't focus unless he knows you're okay."

Chad is upstate in the town where they'll be filming his new series—*The Hollows*, the place that inspired the story. There's an energy vortex up there, according to Chad, and it's home to all kinds of strange happenings and a community of psychics. Which intrigues me, or would, under other circumstances. I'm supposed to meet him this weekend, but I don't even have the energy to leave the apartment, let alone get on a train.

Max and I head inside, and I walk him into the kitchen where I've determined Abi can't hear me because it's around two corners. And I tell him everything—about Xavier, Detective Crowe's visit, how he knew about Chad's past, the deleted chat room entry on the Windermere website, astrology night, Abi's secret room, how I haven't worked on my book in days.

It feels like a purge, and when I'm done there's a sense of release. Max leans against the counter, regarding me worriedly through his thick glasses. He looks around. It's kind of a mess with dishes piled in the stainless-steel sink; the marble counters need wiping; the scent of coffee left too long in the pot wafts on the air. The space is tiny, little more than a galley, wood cabinets in need of refinishing, tile floor begging to be updated.

"Why are we in the kitchen, Rosie?" he asks, edging toward the door.

I'm embarrassed to tell him, look down at my bare feet.

"Rosie?"

"Because he can't hear us in here."

That worried frown deepens.

"Abi," I whisper. "Over the intercom."

"Do you think he's *listening* to you?" he asks gently. Always the editor, skeptical, searching.

"I don't know," I answer. "I know he did something with that box and I think he stole the letter—who else, right? Dana told me not to trust anyone. And now Dana is dead. I spoke to Xavier about him by the service elevator and now Xavier is dead."

I expect for him, hope, that he's going to wave me off, offer some smart reason why I'm overreacting. Instead, he offers a careful nod. "That *is* weird."

I notice the deep circles under his eyes then, stubble on his jaw. He's rumpled—Bauhaus T-shirt wrinkled, jeans torn, leather jacket scuffed. He's got his own problems and here he is wrapped up in mine. Still, I go on.

"Detective Crowe made Abi sound like a model citizen, implied that I was the one with the problem."

Max rubs at his chin. "Okay, let's say he is watching and listening. Why? What would he want?"

I haven't thought about this, but I do now. "Maybe he's gathering information about the residents. Using it somehow?"

"Blackmail? To what end? Like any character, you need to figure out what he wants to understand him. What does he want that would be accomplished by listening in on the private lives of residents?"

It's a good question. "He's a voyeur?"

Max shrugs.

"Money? Power?" I say.

"Did you mention that his mother was in an assisted living home in Queens? That's not cheap. Way more than a doorman can afford, maybe?"

"Is that reason to spy, blackmail—maybe even kill?"

"Motive is personal," he says. "What makes sense to someone else won't always make sense to you or me."

I am swamped by the fog of confusion, my own sadness, the heaviness of all of it.

I lean back against the counter. "You were right. We shouldn't have come here."

"No," he says, shaking his head and looking at me with apology. "I shouldn't have said that. I don't really believe that, do you? That places are cursed?"

"I don't know what to believe."

He blows out a breath, lowers his voice to a whisper. "Are you safe here, Rosie?"

"I don't know," I answer truthfully.

"Then let's go." He sweeps an arm toward the door. "We'll go back to my place, call Chad and you stay with me until we've figured this out."

"It's tempting."

"Then pack," he says. "Let's get you out of here for a while."

I don't want to leave my home and stay with Max. Chad would not be thrilled with that move. And Max seems too eager for this option. It feels like defeat, like I'm slinking away, slipping out the back door and letting Abi win. Finally, I shake my head. "No. I can't."

"You can't or you won't?"

"Both."

Xavier's funeral is this afternoon. I plan to attend. I want to say goodbye, even though we'd barely come to know each other. And our encounters were all strange to say the least. But I'm also wondering what I can find out there.

Finally resigned, I guess, Max blows out a breath. "Then tell me—what can I do?"

I think about this a moment—about Detective Crowe out there, looking for reasons to arrest Chad—maybe he's even looking for reasons to arrest me. After all, I was the last person to talk to Dana. One of the last people to see Xavier alive. Crowe's words and phrases keep ringing back to me, about Chad, about Ivan, about all the dark events in Chad's past and present.

How long will it be before Crowe figures out that I come from a long line of con artists and fraudsters?

Maybe it's Max, or maybe it's the fact that I've managed to get out of bed for the first time in days. But I feel a sudden clarity. The truth is that *all of that* is out of my hands. I can't control Detective Crowe, and Olivia said to go about normal life. And that means pulling myself together, moving on from the pain of not being pregnant, returning to researching and writing. Because that's where I make sense of things—on the page. Maybe I won't cancel that appointment this afternoon, after all.

"Help me get back to work? It's the only thing I can control right now."

Max nods decisively. "Caffeine," he says. "That's the lifeblood of all writers."

I make some coffee, and he tells me about some of the projects he's working on freelance—a debut, a memoir, a young adult dystopian adventure.

"I can pay you," I say when he's done.

"No way."

"Max."

"Seriously? Offer again and I'm leaving. This is us. Some people share hobbies, maybe films, food, tennis. This is what we do, right? You and me. This is our thing."

Gratefully, I follow him into my office, sit on the floor and start sifting through my notes. We talk about Marc LeClerc. I tell him about my scheduled interview with Arthur Alpern, the man who writes about a haunted New York. Max comes up with some good questions—about the building, about energy and ghosts, the psychology of haunting.

But the past seems so far away, and the present so chaotic and strange. I can't stop thinking about Xavier, seeing him lying broken on the sidewalk. I imagine him now as one of the Windermere's ghosts.

What did you want to talk about?

But there are no answers from the spirit world. Maybe I need a Ouija board.

While Max is sifting through the Windermere detritus on my floor, I sit at my desk and log on to my computer to open Xavier's Instagram page.

The most recent image is of a white lily, the text obviously a message from his family. *We lay our beloved son Xavier to rest on Wednesday at 4. Join us at The Church of the Ascension to say good-bye and to celebrate his life.*

I scroll through the rest of his feed—a selfie with friends at a party, a colorful salad he was proud of making and having for his dinner, though the next picture is a decadent pile of brunch waffles covered in cream and syrupy fruit.

Two cocktail glasses clink against a sunset view that I recognize as a few floors up from my own—#paradisefound. I scroll and scroll at the snapshots of his life—which looked to be a happy one full of friends, and fine meals, travel—most recently a jaunt to Majorca in images of glittering blue water and tiny winding cobblestone streets lined with pink buildings; Xavier looking fit in tight black bathing suit briefs on a sunny beach.

I feel like we would have been friends. He was funny and smart, observant, kind to me. I would have liked to get to know him better. Detective Crowe must be doing the same thing, sifting through this record all of us keep of our lives, this curated and filtered diary that we post for everyone we know. I bet Crowe is looking for connections, suspects, theories. That's what I'm doing, I guess. But there's nothing really—just a handsome, urbane, forty-something man living his best life in Manhattan.

I keep scrolling until I come to an image that stops me.

Xavier is dressed in a tailored charcoal suit, behind him, large photographs. It looks like he's in a gallery, other chic, striking people around him, cocktails in hands, standing in small groups. He poses with a stunning redhead, her face pressed against his for the selfie, both smiling wildly.

It's Dana, looking joyful in a way she never was in our encounters.

Didn't he say they'd never met?

Clicking on the image and zooming in, around Xavier's neck there's a leather strap, and just the edge of the now familiar charm—the hand with a blue eye in its palm.

My breath quickens. Beneath the jolt of fear, there's a flash of that journalistic hunger. *Keep digging*, it demands.

Dana's Instagram feed is spare and grayscale, mostly just images of her work, many of the same striking photos from her gallery, those layered interesting faces, some cityscapes, some black-and-white shots of the woods. Scrolling down to the date of Xavier's post with her, I find one from the same event.

Opening night at the Great Jones Gallery! Dreams do come true!

The post has multiple images. Dana dressed in a dramatic black sleeveless shift with a plunging neckline, exposing her flawless décolletage and toned arms, obviously giving a speech, glass in hand, all eyes on her. Dana standing with two older men, who look at her adoringly. Group pictures with people I don't recognize. I scan the backgrounds, searching for familiar faces. I almost skip the final image, but then scroll again.

This one is taken from a distance. Dana stands in front of one of her portraits; she points at it. A young couple stands before her—he, tall and dark skinned, she, petite but full bodied, fair—clearly rapt by whatever it is Dana is saying.

I'm struck, as I often am looking at old photos, how life is captured, frozen in a single frame. Dana is gone, all her passion and joy, evident in these images, her talent, all gone with her. The couple listening—who are they? Where are they now?

I scan the rest of the people in the crowd around them. It takes a second, but I spot Lilian, Charles and Ella's daughter, her elegantly skeletal frame, big bangles on knobby wrists; a skintight, red, off-the-shoulder dress is painted on her body, her jet hair a striking contrast to her pale skin.

Of course I recognize the man she's with immediately, but it takes a second for the pain to travel to my heart. Those sandy curls, broad shoulders, the way other women in the room surreptitiously steal glances. It's not just his beauty that mesmerizes; it's his aura, his charm, his radiating kindness.

My husband.

Leaning into Lilian, a smile on his face.

Lilian looking up at him, with a gaze I know too well. Besotted.

Just six months ago or so. I recognize the shirt, one I bought him at Barneys, though we could ill-afford it. It was a soft blue oxford that I knew would make the blue flecks in his hazel eyes pop for his audition.

Where was *I* the night of this glitzy opening?

Here with Ivan probably, who was in steep decline, drawing close to the end of his life.

I struggle to fit this piece into the other lies and dishonesties and omissions Chad has offered me. It's creating a picture I don't quite understand. It feels like someone is squeezing my heart. Here he is at Dana's opening, when he claimed he couldn't reach her. Here he is, clearly with Lilian, when he claimed at our welcome party that they'd just met.

"What is it?" asks Max, maybe sensing a shift in my energy.

I minimize the window showing Dana's feed, click back over to Xavier's.

"Nothing," I say quickly, my heart still thudding painfully. "Just looking at Xavier's feed. He knew Dana."

I don't want him to know that Chad has been dishonest with me. As much as he tries to hide it now, Max's opinion of my husband is low. I don't want to offer this confirmation.

I search my memory. Where did I think Chad was that night? And other nights when I stayed behind to work or research, to care for Ivan, or just to be alone. He is the one who needs to go out, to party, to be the center of attention, the extrovert. Me, his opposite in that way, I'm the one who needs quiet, happier in the world of my ideas than in the real world. I thought we were honoring each other's differences. But maybe he was taking advantage.

Max comes up behind me and I show him the image of Dana and Xavier.

"He didn't mention that he knew her?"

"No. In fact, he said they'd never met."

"Why would he lie?"

I shrug, not knowing Dana or Xavier well enough to even guess.

"Did you see him at Dana's service?" Max asks.

"There hasn't been one. The police haven't released her body. The investigation is still ongoing."

He puts a comforting hand on my shoulder.

I drop my voice to a whisper. "Maybe that's one of the things that he wanted to talk to me about over coffee. Maybe he didn't want to say so in the building."

"Because someone is listening?"

We both look around to the intercom behind us in the hallway outside my office door. We each stay silent, wheels turning.

"So," he says, dropping the volume on his voice, too, "are you investigating Dana's death? Or writing your book?"

It's a very typical editor-type query—a question that's supposed to lead to the right answer, one which should already be known to you.

I look up at him.

"Both?"

I tell him my plans to go to Xavier's funeral after my interview with Arthur. I expect him to offer to go to both with me, but he doesn't, gives a glance at his watch.

"I'm all for a visit with Arthur. Stay grounded in the work, you know? But is a funeral a good idea?" he asks. "It doesn't seem like you're in the best place at the moment. A funeral isn't going to help that."

"I have to go. To pay my respects."

And who knows who might be there, what other connections I might uncover.

He looks at me, then down at his phone. "I have a meeting," he says quietly.

"Go," I say, swallowing my disappointment. "I'm fine. I'm good. Really."

"Rosie, just take care of yourself," he says. "Okay?"

I feel it then, a rift that's growing between us. We're not officially working together. There's the unspoken tension of his wanting more than I can give. All the things I haven't said about my miscarriage, about Chad. That's how friendships start to fray, and I feel the connection between us straining. Will our lives take us in separate directions now?

"Of course," I say. "I promise."

He hesitates again, looks back and forth between me and the door, trying to decide, I guess, between his life and mine. "Hey," he says. "Do you have an extra key to the back door?"

"Yeah, why?"

"Let me have it," he says. "You know, in case I need to get in and Abi won't let me up."

I hesitate a second, wondering how I would feel if Chad gave someone a key to our place.

"Just for now. Until Chad gets back, and things settle down," he says.

I head to the kitchen and fish the extra set out of the junk drawer, bring it back to him.

"Stay in touch with me today," he says. "Let me know how you're doing."

I give him a nod, not trusting my voice, not wanting to say goodbye to my friend, but knowing that I have no real right to ask him to stay. I flash as I sometimes do on that night we spent together. Where would we be right now if I hadn't left him before the sun came up, met Chad the following week?

Of course, there's no way to know the road not taken or where it would have led us. And I remind myself that I never wanted that anyway.

When he's gone, I try Chad again and leave a voice mail because of course he doesn't answer.

"Hey, look. We need to talk. It's urgent." But it feels like he's on the moon. And here I am on Earth, looking up, searching for him through the clouds.

I shower and pull on my simple black shift, heels and a blazer.

In the mirror, I look polished and put together. Inside, I'm pulling and fraying, coming apart, worried about my husband, his lies, our future, this building, its ugly history. The apartment, so beautiful with its crown molding and tall windows, the stunning wood floors and fireplace with original mantel, suddenly feels malicious.

Are you safe here, Rosie? Max asked.

The truth is I have no idea.

My phone rings as I am about to sneak out the back way. My body floods with relief when I see Chad's number on my screen.

But when I answer, there's only a thick static. I think I hear his voice.

"Rosie, Rosie, can you hear me?"

"Chad. Where are you? The connection is bad."

The static grows louder and louder, and then the call disconnects with those annoying beeps. I try him back, go straight to voice mail. Try again with the same results. I stand there, will the phone to ring again, but it doesn't.

I beat back a wave of despair, feeling like the lifeline between my husband and me has been brutally cut dead.

twenty-nine

Willa
1963

A pall has settled over the building since Miles's death. His accident was caused by a terrible malfunction. One that was foretold by strange noises and an occasional grinding and stuttering of the machinery, a topic that had apparently been on the agenda of the last board meeting. A service company had been called to diagnose and repair any problems but found no major issues. The elevator was serviced, old parts replaced, gears greased. The inspection found the old elevator in good order.

How it malfunctioned, fell to the bottom of the shaft, leaving a gaping hole through the open doors for Miles to walk through, is a mystery.

The funeral, held at the Church of the Ascension on Madison Avenue, is a misery, with mourners wailing as the priest tells us that all children are welcomed home personally by God. The day is dark with heavy rains and a wild thunderstorm as if the weather itself is railing against the accidental death of an innocent child.

He *was* innocent. A mean, angry little boy, but still, just a child. And I was so cruel to him. Nasty, treacherous me.

Suddenly, the building I have loved seems so cold, vibrating with malice. And the city feels ugly and dangerous. For the first time, I am eager to leave it all behind.

Paul came home right away, as soon as I shared the horrible news.

And now together we sit in the pew behind the family. Charles and Ella are nearly catatonic with grief, moving with a stiff slowness as if the very act of being upright is a chore. Lilian leans against an elderly woman whom I recognize as her grandmother from Greenwich, and whom I met at one of the Aldridges' famous Christmas parties.

I'll handle the boy.

No. No. That's not what he meant. Please, God. It was just an accident. A horrible accident.

Paul is right beside me, a strong arm around my shoulders. I lean into him. He's worried about me, the shock of this event and what it might do to the child inside me. It's true. I am shaken to the core. He's been attending to me since he rushed home, cooking and bringing me tea in bed. Thank God for him. I'll never betray him again.

We drive to the gravesite in Queens, part of the slow funeral procession, headlights glowing yellow, sodium light in the dark of the storm.

In the cemetery, we stand under umbrellas that barely keep us dry as Miles's little body is lowered into the ground. We line up to throw earth and flowers on his coffin. The tears won't stop when my turn comes. The white roses I've been carrying fall, scatter in the dirt below. The earth from my shovel lands on the wood below. The air smells of wet leaves and someone's heavy perfume.

When I turn, Paul is gone. I thought he was right behind me.

Making my way back through the crowd, I spot *him*. He's standing at the edge of the group, over by the trees. He makes his way to Charles, offers a bow and gives the other man an awkward embrace. When his eyes turn to me, there's an expression of profound sadness.

Quickly, I look away and find my husband. I see his gray felt hat, his head shaking as if in denial, and then I realize that Paul is speaking to someone, a woman, tall and slim.

As I approach, the woman turns to leave him.

It's Ella. I reach for her as she moves toward me, and we lock eyes. An unkind smile spreads across her face, but it's just a flash, soon swallowed by her mourner's mask of grief.

I try to grab her hand, to offer her my condolences. But she pushes past me without a word, her shoulder grazing mine roughly.

When I look back to Paul, his face is slack. In his eyes there's an ugly brew of sadness, betrayal, anger.

My heart nearly stops beating in my chest.

Ella knew my secret. And, I don't know why, here and now, but she's told my husband.

thirty

There are a few hours to kill before the funeral, and I find I can't stay at home another minute. I decide to keep my appointment with Arthur Alpern.

Alpern's place is not far, so I walk, slipping out the back, letting the city rhythm carry me through the streets. I realize that the farther I get from the Windermere, the lighter, more myself, I feel. And by the time I reach Alpern's Chelsea building, I have shed the darkness of my current life and disappeared into my writer-researcher mind. It's a relief to be admitted by his doorman and ride up his unmanned elevator. I am just a writer here, researching a book.

Arthur Alpern is a small man, elfin in trim pants and a velvet green vest. I like him right away when he swings his door open wide for me and lets me into the two-bedroom he's lived in since 1968.

"Ms. Lowan," he says warmly.

I ask him to call me Rosie. And he leads me into a small kitchen where he brews coffee, and we sit at a wooden table.

I take in the details. A folded dishrag by the sink, a single hydrangea in a glass vase on the windowsill, dishes neatly stacked behind glass cabinet doors. He tells me how he fell in love with the apartment when he was a young man and has never felt the urge to leave. It's a large, sparsely furnished space, a time capsule with Eames chairs and a leather sectional, a stereo and record player on a low credenza, photos of children and grandchildren on every surface, simple louver blinds, everything spotlessly clean and impeccably maintained.

"I've visited every grand building in the city, and I've never found a place I felt more at home," he said, rubbing at his snow-white goatee, when I asked him why he'd never moved.

"My late wife and I lived our life here, raised our son. She lives on in every nook and cranny. All our memories dwell here like ghosts. To leave here would be to leave her behind."

His words put a painful squeeze on my heart, thinking of Chad, our lost child, the darkness that has settled over our lives. Xavier's funeral looms like a storm cloud. But I try to stay here.

"And," he says, pushing up his thick glasses, peering at me, "I think that's all hauntings really are. Just memories lingering."

It snaps me back to the work.

"So the Windermere," I say.

Arthur settles in his chair with a nod. "It might have been unremarkable had its architect not leapt from the roof, ruined by the Great Depression."

"And since then, a number of horrible murders, accidents, suicides."

"Yes," he says, taking a sip of his coffee.

"You've visited so many buildings that some claim are haunted or cursed, populated by ghosts and demons, cults meeting in the basement to perform satanic rituals," I say, remembering my notes about him and his work. "In Brooklyn, there's even a building that is owned by a coven of witches. You've spent time at and written about all of these places. Have you ever experienced something you can't explain? Are there places you have felt are truly haunted?"

Arthur takes a deep breath, rubs at his beard.

"If you mean, have I seen wailing ghouls clanking chains, or felt cold spots, heard moaning in the walls? No."

"But…"

He leans forward, considers me. "But—I think buildings are like people," he says finally.

"Meaning?" I ask, though I think I know. The Windermere *is* like a person. Grand and mysterious, someone you want to love but who keeps you at a distance.

"They have memories. They dream. You know how when you meet someone there's a feeling—it's more than what they say, or what they're wearing, or how they do their hair? Without knowing why, you feel unsettled, uncomfortable?"

The basement where the lights go out, the howling draft in the back hallways, the residents who are friendly but aloof, unknowable.

"Some buildings just have bad personalities," he continues.

Dana's words to Chad ring back. A dark heart behind a beautiful mask.

"And maybe it attracts darkness. So if you're well and strong, and you see a place at the Windermere, something repels you, you decline to move in. But if you're vulnerable to sinister energies, if they speak to something going on inside you, maybe there's a strange attraction."

"Like a relationship," I say, and it makes a kind of sense to me. Was I ever repelled by the Windermere? Or was I drawn to its darkness, its mystery? Maybe all I ever do is chase ghosts, even though I judge my family harshly for their metaphysical practices. Maybe something about the Windermere seduced me.

But I didn't choose it. It was given, inherited. Through Chad's relationship to Ivan. So it wasn't just me or my choice. I check my phone again. Nothing. The funeral is in an hour. I don't have much time.

"Exactly," says Arthur. "A predator might initially be very attractive to his victim. She might be drawn to his darkness, his violence, without even realizing it because of some trauma in her past, some subconscious craving for pain."

I push away thoughts of how this theory might relate to me and my husband.

"A building is a living entity?" I say.

"In a way. This city is an untamed jungle of a place—alive with creativity, innovation, violence, tragedy, triumph, life, love, horror, death. Our buildings and homes grow from that energy, so how can they not be alive with everything we do and have done?"

I unconsciously tap at my phone again, the chaos of my life outside these walls rhythmic thumping on my psyche. Nothing. No one. Maybe I'm the ghost, lost and wandering.

Arthur goes on. "Primitive people believed that their memories were physically present. When you, a modern young woman, conjure someone who is no longer with us, you know that you're dwelling in memory. But early people externalized their thoughts. Ghosts and memories seemed to be visible outside the mind."

He doesn't know how close to the bone he's hitting. "And the Windermere?"

He offers a quick shrug, a wan smile. "Bad things have happened there, and I bet they will again. But the same could be said for lots of places. Maybe there are just echoes through time."

"Nothing special about it, then?" I want to believe that. That it's just a building like so many others, housing people who do wonderful things and horrible things—a microcosm of the world we live in. A body that we fill with our own souls.

"I wouldn't say that," he says. "Have you met the Aldridges?"

That he mentions them surprises me.

"They're our neighbors. Friends, really," I say. "Our apartment used to belong to them, but it was divided up and sold in the 1960s."

He nods, seems to wonder whether or not to go on. Then, "Did you know that Charles Aldridge comes from a long line of psychic mediums, magicians and astrologists?"

"I didn't."

It's surprising, Charles always seeming so down-to-earth. He and Ella used to own art galleries, were great patrons and avid collectors. Chad told me that they sold all their galleries and made a tidy sum, but that Charles and Ella both already came from money.

"His grandfather was an early investor in the building and one of the original owners. Charles Aldridge has lived there all his life. His grandmother was a medium, channeling the dead for the wealthy of New York, holding séances in that very apartment until she died."

Arthur gets up and returns with a book, flips through the pages, finds what he's looking for and then hands it to me.

It's heavy, leathery, in my hands. For some reason, I want to give it back to him. But I look down at the page he's opened to.

There's a grainy black-and-white image of a woman dressed all in black, flanked by a tall man with slicked-back hair and a powerful jaw, a young boy standing in front of them. The caption reads: *1940. Psychic Medium Esmerelda Aldridge, her husband, Charles, and their grandson Charles III.* They stand in front of the Windermere, the gargoyles looming above them. Fred and Ethel, I remember him telling me he'd named them later.

The photo emits a kind of raw energy, as if Esmerelda's gaze is reaching through time.

Young Charles, even then with that intense stare, the square jaw. It's striking how much he looks like my vision of Miles. I feel a chill work its way up the back of my neck, thinking of the boy in the basement, in my foyer.

Surely, Dr. Black would posit that somehow in my research, I'd already seen this photo, that it imprinted on my subconscious and rose to the surface due to my *stress levels*. But I know, little as I like to admit it, that there's more to it than that.

I saw Miles. And he looked like Charles before I had any inkling that Miles was his son.

Arthur goes on. "LeClerc's mother was a medium, as well. The families were friends. After LeClerc's mother passed, he consulted with Esmerelda, Charles's grandmother, for advice, guidance, to communicate with his dead mother."

I feel a strange agitation at this knowledge. I've run so far from this kind of thing, only to find it right next door. I think about what Arthur just said, about the Windermere attracting people who are vulnerable.

I remind myself that I didn't choose the Windermere. It chose me.

A cool certainty moves through me. We need to get out before the Windermere poison works its way into our system. Or maybe it's way too late.

He sips at his coffee, then breaks the thoughtful silence that has fallen. "You know how abuse runs in families, how the abused becomes an abuser, and so on down the line until someone breaks the chain?"

I nod, considering this.

"People can heal," he says. "They can change. So I think it's true with buildings. Just because there's darkness in the past, doesn't mean there must always be that. It just takes one person to break the chain, to heal the whole system and to let the light in."

He's looking at me pointedly, his gaze kind and deep. The gaze of a person who sees without judging, who cares without clinging, who has spent a lifetime exploring and questioning, not attached to the answers. There's an energy to his company, to this space. I feel safe here, my chaotic reality far away.

"Do you think the Windermere can heal?"

He shrugs, gives me a smile. "Sometimes it just takes fresh blood."

thirty-one

The Church of the Ascension on Madison Avenue is packed with well-dressed mourners, and outside, a light drizzle falls. Rushing from my appointment with Arthur, his words still ringing in my ears, I hurry inside just as the doors are closing and find a spot to stand in the back. The sad tones of an organ fill the space and incense is thick in the air. Above, the vaulted ceiling boasts an elaborate fresco.

Anna, Charles and Ella sit near the front in a group of the other neighbors, including Jasmine, the escort from astrology night, who weeps quietly.

Ella seems to sense me, turns and waves me toward her. I slip into the empty seat next to her at the edge of the pew.

"Isn't this a nightmare?" she whispers, taking my hand. "Our poor Xavier. Such a dear, lovely man."

Her eyes are red, face drawn. When she takes my hand, she's shaking a little. I look down the row to Charles, who gives me a smile that doesn't quite reach his eyes. It makes me think of Miles, of the picture in the book when Charles was a young boy, the image of the son he would later lose. I wonder how they could stay there, ride that elevator day after day.

I have a thousand questions for them—about the past, the present, about Dana, Xavier, Lilian and Chad, the necklace. But this is clearly not the time or place.

"I can't believe it," I whisper instead, keeping her frail hand in mine for a while before she pulls it away gently.

The priest speaks for a while, then a friend, then a brother, each sharing memories of Xavier—his kindness, his love of life, his passion for art and food, travel and fashion. I try to be present for the passing of this soul through the world, but I can't stop thinking about Chad—who I can't reach, about Dana. About Lilian.

The service drones on, the music, the soft sobs from mourners echoing from the vaulted ceilings. The casket, closed, rests in the aisle beneath a spray of white lilies.

My abdomen still aches, my heart. I close my eyes against the pain of it all.

When I open them again, something—someone—catches my eye over by the flickering candles to my right. The air seems foggy with incense, and the sound of the room begins to go distant.

A woman, dressed in a slim pencil skirt and white silk blouse, a wide-brimmed hat hiding her face, her dark hair in an elegant chignon, stands in the shadows. She wrings her hands, moves back deeper into the shadows. She's an image that won't come into focus.

My heart rate rising, my breath growing tight, I strain to get a closer look.

When she finally turns her face to me, our eyes lock. They're dark and swirling, like a galaxy. I'm pulled in, drawn to her. Who is she?

It takes a second, my mind grappling with where I've seen her before.

In photographs.

When I recognize her, a gasp escapes my lips. Ella pats my leg to comfort me, assuming that I'm in the throes of grief.

It's Willa Winter.

No.

Impossible.

She shuttles away.

"Excuse me," I say, slipping out of the pew to follow the sound of her footfalls on marble.

"Are you all right, Rosie?" whispers Ella.

But I've already left her, chasing the slender form down a long hallway, past rows of doors, the voices of the next speaker ringing after me.

Ahead of me, a door opens and closes. By the time I turn the corner, the hallway is empty.

I push through the door at the end of the hallway and hear the delicate staccato of footfalls on the steps, heading toward a lower level.

"Wait," I call. "Please wait."

I find myself at the bottom of the stairwell, another door to push through.

Now I'm in the basement surrounded by chairs stacked, old tables, shelves of bibles, a dusty organ. I follow the sound of her steps deep through the winding passageways.

The door behind me opens and closes then.

Someone has followed me into the basement.

Here, the first notch of fear, realizing that I'm trapped.

I move quietly, and finally, when I turn the corner, she's there, backed against a wall, still hiding her face behind that wide brim.

"Please. Who are you?"

When she tilts her head up, I let out a cry, almost a shriek— her neck is ruined, swollen purple, blue, black. Her eyes bulge like Dana's, a tear of blood down her face. She moves toward me, hand outstretched, causing me to back away, terror pulsing through my nerves and veins.

I hear my father's voice. *They're just pictures. They have a story they want to tell you. You're one of the few who can hear what they have to say.*

She moves closer and I continue to back away.

She's whispering something over and over. Finally, she's close enough for me to hear.

They're watching. Be careful. You're—in danger.

And then she's rushing past me, *through* me, and I'm knocked to the floor where I lie stunned as she disappears into nothing.

I stay still in the dim, the concrete cold beneath me, struggling with what just happened. Every nerve ending zinging like guitar strings. Pain—in my abdomen, my shoulder where I struck the floor. Shuddering as I used to when I was little, unable to make sense of either world—the one I saw that no one else could see, and the real world, which was equally unpredictable and unsafe. The familiar taste of shame and anger coats the back of my throat.

Then another set of footfalls approaches. Slowly.

I scramble to my feet, breathless with fear, adrenaline still pulsing.

Maybe I'm next, whoever killed Dana, or pushed Xavier, right around the corner.

Trapped, I prepare to fight whoever has come down here after me. I won't go easily or without doing some damage.

I reach for my cell phone. No signal. Of course.

I hammer out a text to Detective Crowe, hope it will send once it reaches a place where there's service, even if I never do.

I'm in trouble. Trapped in the basement of the Church of the Ascension on Madison Avenue. Dana, then Xavier, wanted to tell me something. Now they're dead. I think I'm next. Abi is a liar. Xavier and Dana knew each other; check her Instagram feed. My husband—

But I don't finish because whoever is down here with me is turning the corner. I hit Send.

I wait, my breath thick.

But the woman who comes into view is small, wearing an oversize coat and Converse sneakers. Her golden curls and up-turned nose, blushed cheeks, make her look like a doll. For a moment, I feel like I'm imagining her, conjuring her.

When she speaks, her Ozarks accent is twangy, pure country. And the sound of it brings me right back to the childhood bed-room we shared, the smell of my mother's kitchen, the whisper-ing willow in the yard. Another ghost? A vision? A memory?

No.

"Hey," my sister, Sarah, says with a sad smile. She's so changed, and yet exactly the same. "You look like you've seen a ghost."

thirty-two

"What are you doing here?" I ask, wondering again if she's here at all or if I've just gone full-tilt and this is it, time to get carted off to the place they take you when reality departs.

She still looks like a girl, not a married woman carrying a child. It's been years since I've seen my sister, but it might as well be minutes. The urge to run and take her into my arms is powerful, almost irresistible, but I keep my distance. My family is quicksand; get too close and they pull you under.

She shakes her head of golden curls. "I dreamed that you were in trouble."

"So what? You just got on a bus and came here—after all this time?"

She looks down at her feet, like maybe she's not sure why she came, either. "I dreamed that you needed me."

"You're pregnant. You left your home and your husband, came to a city you've never visited, because of a dream."

She gives me that stare-down she's perfected since childhood;

it radiates a surprising mettle, a knowledge of her own right-ness. Just like our father.

"Daddy said it was time one of us came looking," she says, jutting out her chin.

"That you couldn't run forever. That you need to remember who you are. Who *we* are. I am here to bring you home."

Her accent, so sharp and twangy on the vowels, the sound of my childhood and something I've worked hard to lose. It felt to me like my family, that life, was so far away. But she's crossed the distance and I am pulled back, a rip current in my life.

"That's—ridiculous," I say. There's that familiar lash of anger, of arguing with someone who won't hear reason.

"No." I pull back my shoulders, stand up taller. Organ music drifts down from upstairs. "I'm fine."

"Really."

Sisters. How they know your heart and your secrets, all the masks you put on to make yourself braver. Time apart doesn't diminish the bond, even if you want it to.

"How did you find me here?" My voice is sharp, angry. Her face wrinkles with hurt, but then she straightens up taller, too. We come from a family of strong and powerful women who don't back down.

"I've been standing outside that fancy building you live in now, waiting. I followed when everyone came walking here."

"Can't ring up like a normal person?"

She raises an eyebrow at me, a thing she could always do that I never could. Her smirk presses a dimple into her cheek. "Would you have let me in?"

"Of course," I say. "No. I don't know."

"Well, here we are. What did you see?"

I shake my head, still shivering, heart still pounding. "Nothing."

"Rosie."

It's no use—something about her gaze, her voice, her knowledge of all the parts of me I seek to bury. The dam bursts.

I tell her. Everything.

When I'm done, she just offers a knowing nod as if none of it is surprising. "Rosie, let me help," she says. I don't see what she can do, but then she opens her arms and I walk to her. Everything about her evokes my childhood, which brings comfort and pain in equal measure.

We return to the service just as the main eulogy begins. I look around the room for the ghost of Willa Winter, but she's gone.

You're in danger.

Her words knock around my head.

The man at the podium was featured prominently on Xavier's Instagram feed—traveling together, at dinners, parties. Standing in the back, we listen as he paints a picture of Xavier—a life-loving world traveler, a compassionate and devoted friend, a foodie, a bit of a party animal, a hero in his work as an EMT, a careful and dedicated health professional, committed to doing his job well. He wanted to serve. To help people in need. And when the life of the EMT became too much and burnout set in, he changed fields.

"What he loved most about his job is that he could save people from pain. That he made it so that doctors could save lives while their patients slept. Some people, in this life, are pain givers. Xavier only ever wanted to ease suffering."

Sarah stares around at the ornate church, the towering, vaulted ceiling with its elaborate fresco, the gleaming wooden pews, the marble floors. She must be comparing it to my father's church, the run-down old barn open to the sky. My father never called himself a Christian or a Catholic. *Religion was created for man by man. Call yourself what you want. Pray to Jesus or Buddha or Allah or whoever. But God's only name is Love,* he used to say. *The sky is our fresco. The stars, our angels, looking down.*

I remember believing that when I was small. That each point

of light in the night sky was a soul watching over us here on Earth. In school I learned the truth, that the stars were large incandescent bodies like the sun, living and dying, exploding and imploding light-years away. That was the moment I began questioning the things my father taught me. I hated him for lying to me about the world. About myself.

The mass continues and the mourners take Communion.

I see Abi standing off to the side, erect beside a pillar. He wears a simple black suit, is elegant with his dark hair slicked back. He looks every bit the sentry. Our eyes meet, and he holds my gaze, gives me a slight nod. Who is he? What is he hiding? What did Xavier want to tell me?

I say a silent goodbye to Xavier. Then I grab Sarah by the hand.

"Come on," I whisper, and pull her outside.

We hustle the few blocks home and I let us in the front door with my key.

No Abi.

No George.

Everyone else is at the funeral.

"This is very *worldly*," she says when we're inside, her voice tight.

Worldly. That's straight from my father's lips. To be worldly means to be concerned more with life on earth than you are with matters of the spirit. Wealth, travel, entertainment, indulgence of the senses. It's not a compliment.

She goes on. "This whole place. The city, the building, it's a monument to man, to ego."

"You sound like Dad." I dig deep for patience, remember what Dr. Black said about how she's still in my father's thrall, living inside his lies. But searching for compassion, I find only more anger. Annoyance.

"What are you doing?" she asks.

I've slipped behind the doorman station. I have one more key from the ring Ivan left us to try.

I turn it in the lock and a thrill moves through me as the door opens. It's like a little gift from Ivan. I wonder why he had a key to this room.

I hesitate and then head inside with Sarah at my heels.

thirty-three

Willa
1963

Since the funeral, things have been strained between Paul and me. He's started drinking, a thing he rarely does, and it makes him surly, cruel. I haven't asked him what Ella told him at the burial. I am too afraid.

If she's told him what Miles saw, or something she has seen, he hasn't confronted me. And I won't force that confrontation. I won't lie to him if he asks me. If I have to tell him the truth, I don't think he'll ever forgive me. So maybe we're at a standoff—where he doesn't want to ask, and I hope to never have to tell him what an unfaithful wife I've been. Still, it's as if we're both breathing the same toxic air, getting sicker and sicker.

Miles is dead. Ella and Charles look like ghosts in their grief, pale and fragile. Whatever tentative friendship existed between our families has perished.

I've had my first doctor's visit, where Paul sat stone-faced and grim the whole time. The doctor says I'm healthy and well and we should expect our first child to be the same.

"Let's see a smile, kids," the doctor said when we were both silent. Dr. Jackson is older, warm and comforting the way a physician should be. "Trust me, this is the good stuff. A baby will enrich your lives in a thousand ways."

I chattered nervously all the way home and Paul barely said a word.

Now Paul is working, still in the room that will be the baby's nursery until we find a house. I slip downstairs to do the laundry, sit with my book as the washer *swish, swish, swishes.* I'm so engrossed in *The Group* by Mary McCarthy that I startle when someone clears his throat.

My heart leaps when I lift my eyes. I can't help it, even though Paul is just a few flights away. I run to him, my love. He takes me in his strong arms, lifts and spins me and holds me tight.

Paul hasn't touched me since before Miles's burial, and I've been so terribly lonely in my skin. We don't go out, and I've promised myself to be good. So I've been the dutiful wife and helpmate—proofreading and making some of his calls, mailing his letters. But I'd be lying if it didn't feel like part of me has been dying inside. At night I dream of dancing on stage, my body light, moving effortlessly and joyfully, the music entering through my pores and pulsing through my blood.

And then I wake in the mornings and even though I can feel the life growing inside me and I'm so happy for that, part of me is lost. Despair tugs at my heart with dark fingers. Is this it? Is this all? Wasn't there meant to be bright lights and dancing, music and laughter, endless joyful parties, passion?

His strong arms, his kiss deep and passionate, his hunger, speaking to every hunger in me.

"Is it mine?" he whispers, taking me against one of the storage cages. "The baby. Is it mine?"

"No," I say emphatically.

"Are you sure?"

His gaze is so deep and true.

"No," I admit. "I'm not sure."

His lips on my neck, his strong arm around my waist. My whole body aches for him. We're tearing at our clothes then. He unzips his pants, and he enters me under my skirt. Oh, God, the joy, the pleasure.

"I can't live without you, Willa," he says, his voice taut with desire. "Leave him. He can't make you happy. You'll die living the quiet life he wants from you."

I'm lost in the pleasure as the washer keeps swishing.

"Oh, my love, my love," he whispers. The smell of him, the heat of him. I'm such a wicked girl and I've never felt better. I press my mouth against his shoulder as we climax powerfully, keeping silent as best we can.

A sound. A slamming door. I startle, nearly shriek. Oh, what are we doing? Shamefully, we pull ourselves together. He zips his pants and I smooth my skirt. Is someone here?

But when he goes around the corner to look, he shakes his head.

"No, no," he says. "There's no one. There are always strange sounds in this basement."

"This—" I say, shame burning at my cheeks "—can't happen again."

How weak it sounds, even to my own ears, a promise broken again and again.

"This," he echoes. "I can't live without it—without you."

I rush over to the laundry, hoping the act of changing the clothes into the dryer will help me to remember my duties, all the vows I've made.

"Willa," he says close behind me. "Please."

I need to ask; it's been torturing me. "Did you? Did you hurt that boy to keep him quiet? Did you—kill him?"

He draws back as if stricken. "No, no. Of course not. It was an accident. A terrible accident."

I want to believe him. I must—otherwise, I'm as guilty as he is. I don't see how the elevator could have malfunctioned that way. But what do I know?

His eyes plead. "It wasn't me. I wouldn't. Never. Not even for you."

He's so earnest. He seems to want to say more, but finally he just raises his palms in hopeless surrender.

I stand to face him, but when he reaches for me I step away.

"I love you," I tell him. "Maybe I always will. But please let me go."

"Willa." He looks so sad.

"I'm so sorry," I whisper. "Abi."

My beloved Abi. His smooth brown skin and shining dark hair; his deep, dark gaze. I'll never forget him. But I will be a better woman. A wife. A mother.

"This is goodbye."

I run from him, take the service elevator up to our floor. All these months as we ride in the elevator, as he opens the door for us, as he brings us our mail. Every day I pretend not to know him. His uniform a barrier; as if he's only mine when he's dressed for a night out, a different person altogether during our shared days. I can't wait to leave this building, this city, all the dreams that keep me tethered to the worst parts of myself.

In the kitchen I take a moment to collect myself, dry my tears, calm my breath. The apartment is dark and silent.

Paul must still be working, closed inside his office.

But when I enter the dining room, he's there, sitting at the table. It was a gift from his parents on our marriage, a beautifully made thing that we have cherished and by far the nicest piece of furniture we own. He has a bottle of whiskey on the wood and an empty glass; I worry for the varnish until I see that he's weeping.

"Paul." My voice is just a rasp. "What is it?"

When he looks at me, I see all the pain, confusion, rage I saw at the graveyard.

"Ella told me that you were being unfaithful. Running around with another man. I didn't want to believe her."

I shake my head, all words dying in my throat, only a sob can escape.

"She says that her little boy saw you and she didn't believe him. But then she saw you, too, coming in late at night. With him. Of all people."

"She's lying."

"I thought so, too. I couldn't believe it about you. And all these weeks I've been watching. I was starting to think that Ella was crazed with her grief. Mistaken, at least."

I stay silent, remember the slamming door downstairs.

"I saw you. Just now. With him."

His voice sizzles with rage, with despair. The words grind from his throat, and he staggers to his feet. The whiskey bottle is half-empty. How much has he had to drink? His staggering tells me that it's a lot, too much. He brings the glass and his fist down hard. It shatters and I see that he's chipped the table, left a deep groove.

Part of me wants to drop to my knees and beg him to forgive me. But there she is, that wicked girl who wants to be free, who wants to stay out partying, and dance across stages, and sing and act and be alive in this great city.

And she won't let me kneel.

The words come from another place inside me. A secret place, the real me.

"I can't be the wife you want me to be. I can't live this dull, bookish life with you," the bad girl inside me says. "I want to be free."

And even though I'm weeping, I'm rejoicing inside because yes, yes, it's true. And she's right, that terrible, selfish, wild girl my mother was always chastising and punishing. I can't be this person. I can't live this life.

His face. I've never seen the expression that settles there. Blank with rage.

And then he's on me, my sweet, gentle husband.

He hits me so hard across the face that I stumble backward, trip over a dining room chair, fall heavily to the floor. My ears ring, jaw and neck vibrating with pain.

No, no. It can't be. He would never hurt me. Other men, like my father, they yell and slap, grab your arm and say cruel things when you don't give them what they want. But not Paul; not kind, lovely Paul.

My child, I think too late, wrapping my arms around my middle.

I see the gun on the dining room table then, but not before his hands are around my throat and he's on top of me.

He's so impossibly strong for such a slight man.

I choke and claw, my fingernails digging into the skin of his hand, but he doesn't even seem to feel it. His eyes are black with hatred, and there's no air, so I have no voice. My limbs flail now, useless as butterfly wings. Panic is a siren and my vision fades to stars, a galaxy before my eyes. I swing my arms at him, but slowly all the strength drains from me. And it's like those dreams where you can't fight back, no strength, no air. Then like a miracle, the pain subsides, and after all, I *am* free.

I float above my poor body, which is pinned beneath him. I see my thin limbs gone motionless.

"How could you? I loved you," he roars.

I might say the same, but I have no voice.

I am nothing and no one, floating above us as he collapses over my silent, still body, wailing my name in all his rage and misery and wretchedness.

I rise higher and higher, and he crawls over to the table, sinks into the seat at the head, reaching for the gun. He doesn't hesitate but puts it to his temple and squeezes the trigger.

The sound, from this far distance, is just like the pop from a champagne cork, and I think about all those wonderful nights with my love, not my husband. The lovely, genteel Abi, so good to me, so full of life. A doorman by day, proper, slim, vigilant. And by night, my lover, my dance partner, a creature like me who comes alive after the sun sets and the music starts to play.

Higher, higher.

The ceilings are made from fog and I can see all my neighbors, living their lives. The actor is sleeping fitfully. And the model is entertaining a man; they linger over dinner. The young mother tucks her children into their beds. I see her, then—Ella, as she presses her ear against the wall between our apartments.

Her smile is pure evil.

Down below, at his doorman's station, Abi has his head in his hands.

Is he crying? Does he miss me already? I wish I could say a better goodbye and tell him that I made a horrible mistake, that we should have run off together, damn the consequences.

And the child inside me. It belonged to him.

thirty-four

The door to the office behind the doorman station swings open and I step inside, Sarah right behind me.

"Shut the door and lock it," I say, turning on the light.

"What are you doing, Rosie?" she asks, petulant and young just like when we were kids, but does what I say.

The room is disappointingly spare—a desk with several monitors, a tidily made cot, a shelf of books, a system of cubbies, with packages in some. There's a rack for hanging the dry-cleaning deliveries. There are some plastic-covered collections of clothing on the metal rod, awaiting delivery.

I sit at the desk and start rifling through the drawers. What am I looking for? I'll know it when I see it. Maybe the stolen letter to Dana? But the drawers are organized collections of pens and Post-it Notes, the pink message slips Abi might slide under the door for this or that.

"Rosie." Sarah is staring at me, confused.

"He's hiding something," I tell her. "He lied about the box. He's listening over the intercom."

Do I sound like someone clinging to edges of sanity? From the look on Sarah's face, I'm guessing yes.

I touch the keyboard and the screens come to life, all three of them, but the login is password protected.

"The Windermere" in bold purple type floats in the black background.

What password would he use? Most people use important dates or the nicknames of loved ones. But I don't know Abi well enough to have that kind of intimate detail about his life.

Rather than guess, I open the drawer beneath the keyboard. When it comes to passwords, it's also true that people don't go to the trouble of memorizing them, especially older people. I rifle around a bit and finally find a folded notecard buried in the back. It's filled with Abi's precise handwriting, smudged pencil, a list of characters and numbers, each one crossed off until the back of the card where a final collection of characters is scribbled into the remaining space.

I enter it carefully, Sarah standing over my shoulder. She still smells of home, laundry detergent and lilac soap, grass and sunshine.

I press Enter after putting in the password and am nothing short of amazed when it works and the black screen fades away.

I draw in a breath as the screen reveals rows of boxes, each one containing an image projected from one of the surveillance cameras.

Various views from the basement, the elevator foyer on each floor, the service hallways and garbage chutes, the back alley where the dumpsters sit, the mailboxes.

But scrolling through each one, it's just as Abi said, common spaces, dark places, entry points. I tap on each and notice that the operator can toggle the camera to get a different view of the room. There's a speaker icon in the corner of each image. Touching the curser to the laundry room, I hear the washing machine swishing.

How does the intercom work? I thought there would be

some kind of box or switchboard. There's nothing like that in the sparsely furnished room, nothing on the computers. There must be something. Where is it?

Feeling the ticking of the clock, I glance around the small space. Behind the dry-cleaning rack, there's another door.

It's locked, of course. I push and jiggle the knob, try my extra keys in the lock, but they don't fit. And I'm all out of secret keys.

Sarah moves over toward the other door, peers outside, and I go back to the computer keyboard. My hands are shaking, from nerves, from frustration.

When I move my finger over the track pad, a menu comes up in the right-hand corner. I click on the tab that says, "Other Views."

But a window pops up, asking for another password.

What *other views* and why is there another password for those?

The next tab is "Archives."

But when I click on that, there's just an empty page. Abi told me, and Detective Crowe, that nothing was recorded and if it is, it's not accessible to me here.

"There's someone coming," says Sarah urgently.

A quick glance at the lobby view reveals Abi walking in the front door.

I quickly log off the computer and grab a bag of dry-cleaning from the rack, feeling Sarah's gaze as the door to the office opens.

Abi is clearly startled, taking a step back.

"Ms. Lowan," he says tightly, keeping his composure. "Can I help?"

"Oh," I say, giving an embarrassed laugh. "I was just grabbing our dry-cleaning. Sorry to intrude. The door was open, and I knew you were out at the funeral. I just got back myself."

He looks to the door, which clearly, he thought was locked, then to my sister, taking in her obviously-from-out-of-town demeanor, then to me holding the pile of dry-cleaning that is not actually mine.

"I believe that belongs to the Aldridges," he says stiffly.

I make a show of checking the tag. "Oh," I say. "You're right. Thank you, Abi."

My cheeks are burning, my heart racing, as I hang the bag back up.

"Did you send out dry-cleaning this week?" he asks, knowing full well that I did not.

"I thought so?" I say, and start pushing my sister, who has stayed silent, out the door to the lobby.

He follows us and then opens the elevator door, still in his suit. He's fit and virile for a man nearing eighty, only the streaks of gray in his hair and the deep wrinkles around his eyes give him away.

We all climb inside and take the awkward ride up to five.

"My sister Sarah is visiting, Abi. Sarah, this is Abi, our doorman and elevator man."

"Nice to meet you, miss." He gives her a light bow and she smiles uncertainly.

When we arrive at my floor, Sarah exits the elevator first and I stay behind a second.

"What were you looking for, Mrs. Lowan?" he asks. "Really."

I am about to lie again. But then find I don't have the energy. "The truth, Abi. About you. About what's going on in this building."

We lock eyes.

"I'm sure I have no idea what you mean," he says, gaze darkly direct, almost menacing.

"Don't you?"

"Have a good day, Ms. Lowan."

And then he's gone behind the closing doors, and I am alone in the foyer with Sarah, who looks around, taking in every detail.

"This place has bad energy," she says.

On that, at least, we can agree.

thirty-five

It's awkward, having Sarah here. She's the past, one I've fled and have tried to forget, and the apartment is my present, one to which I'm trying desperately to hold on. Previously, these have been two different planets. Though my childhood home is just a short flight away, it might as well have been on the moon.

Sarah sits at my dining room table. I make us grilled cheese sandwiches, just like I used to. I try Chad again and again, no answer. His location services are off.

Where is my husband? I keep flashing on Detective Crowe's suspicious frown. What did he see when he looked at Chad? What have I been seeing? And which one of us is right?

The Instagram images of him with Lilian, the nightclub vision I had at the Aldridges, they swirl in my mind, mingling. Who are they to each other? How long has he known her? And why didn't he tell me?

The sun has tentatively come out and is gleaming off the Chrysler Building, that Art-Deco monument to old New York. Built in 1930, at 1068 feet, it is still the eleventh tallest building in New York, sitting at the intersection of Forty-Second and Lexington in the heart of Turtle Bay. Though there are certainly grander, taller, more dramatic buildings in this city, it remains my favorite, like a glittering dancing girl, joyful among more serious grand dames.

We eat in silence, neither of us knowing quite what to say or how to say it to each other. Finally, she just starts talking. About my mother, who's still reading cards all day, every day, with people coming from all over the county. How Brian is taking over the shop from his father, restoring old cars. And Daddy, well he's still Daddy.

"But…"

"But what?"

"He doesn't want me to tell you. But he's not well, Rosie."

"Not well how?"

"You know he won't see a doctor," she says with a rueful shake of her head.

"Thinks they're all crooks looking to profit off the sick and dying."

I almost guffaw at this, but the strained look of sadness on her face keeps me quiet. "He's wasting away, tired all the time. He thinks he doesn't have long."

I search for feeling. But it's buried deep, way beneath the chaos of everything else that's happening to me right now, and, honestly, I resent having this added on. I wish she hadn't come.

"I'm sorry," I say, trying not to sound cold. But I know it does—my voice ringing back tight and distant even to my own ears.

She looks down at her sandwich. "You should come home. Just for a visit."

I don't answer her, and she doesn't press.

Sarah finishes her meal. Mine sits mostly untouched, my stomach in knots, my hand reaching reflexively to check my phone over and over. Sarah stares at me a moment, then finally she rifles through her tattered duffel bag, fishing out a deck of tarot cards I recognize as belonging to my mother.

"No," I say, putting my hand on the purple-and-gold cardboard box. There's an undeniable energy, but I don't have time for games.

"It might help us, Rosie."

"Our fates are not predetermined, Sarah. There's no road-map to the future."

She shakes her head and looks me straight in the eye. "Then why are you so afraid of the cards? You've been running from us, from yourself, since we were kids."

I push back a rise of defensive anger, say nothing. I know there's no use arguing with them. They are set in their beliefs, have built a universe around them. To unstick from those beliefs now would have their whole world threatened.

She goes on. "Then you come here to this place, and all you do is talk to the dead."

I shake my head at her. "What does that even mean?"

"Your book, I read it—about the women who died, the man who killed them. And the one you're writing about this build-ing, its dark history. All you *do* is hunt for ghosts."

I bristle at this. "That's ridiculous. I am a journalist, a writer. I'm telling the stories of people and places. It's history. And if anything, with this book, I'm trying to prove that there is no such thing as hauntings or ghosts or cursed buildings."

I push away the images of Miles and Willa. Imaginings; noth-ing more. Dr. Black would surely agree.

"And you're so sure?" She starts shuffling the cards. "You're so sure you know the way of the world and what's true and what's real, and what isn't? You're that wise, that gifted, that in tune?"

Sarcasm doesn't suit her and I'm not even going to answer.

"You know what?" she says when I say nothing. "You're just like Dad. So certain that you're right that you never see all the shades of it, all the possibilities."

Just like Dad. If we were kids, I'd pull her hair and scream that she was stupid and to shut her stupid mouth. Instead, I seethe, silent.

"Just a simple past, present and future. What do you have to lose?" she asks, fanning out the cards.

Only everything. My integrity, my grip on reality.

But she's closed her eyes and the cards are shifting through her delicate fingers. And yes, there's something soothing, hypnotic about it. The cards are old and worn, edges soft and darkened from years of fortune telling. The whisper of the cardboard, the delicacy of my sister's hands. It reminds me of my mother, how much comfort she takes in thinking the answers are all there in the deck.

"Your past is represented by The Fool," says Sarah, laying down the card softly.

The image is of a young man, blithely headed off down a path, eyes to the stars, a knapsack over one shoulder, a white rose representing his purity of spirit. If only he would look down, he'd see he was about to step off a cliff. I touch my finger to the familiar image.

"The Fool heads off on his great adventure," says Sarah. "He is daring and carefree, ready to walk into new things, new places. That sounds like you, Rosie. You walked away from the only home you knew, to start a new life."

I think I hear something behind me and turn, but there's nothing there.

"But The Fool is also reckless, lacking foresight, taking wild risks," Sarah goes on. "Every card has two meanings—the upright and the reverse. The Fool is joyful, playful, ready to explore. Reversed it might mean you were careless, taking too many chances without wisdom. But we all need a little bit of The Fool in us, or we would just stand still, paralyzed by worry, dread and self-doubt."

Her voice has gone soft and sad. Then, "I envied you, Rosie. Leaving, going to school. I was never that brave."

I look at her really for the first time since she's come. Suddenly, she's not the girl from my past but the woman she has become. Older, wiser, more like my mother than my father. With the cards in her hand, a calm knowing radiates from her. I see her mettle, her staid reliability. The good daughter.

"I thought you *wanted* to stay there," I say.

"I'm not sure I ever thought about what *I* wanted," she says easily, softly. There's no resentment or anger, just an observation. "Your leaving caused them so much pain. I knew I could never do that to them."

Guilt and resentment are like heartburn, acid up my gullet. "I had to go. I couldn't stay there with them."

"I know," she says.

She reaches for my hand, and it rests cool and soft in mine for a moment.

"Your present," she goes on, taking up the deck again and flipping out another card, "is represented by The Lovers in reverse."

Reflexively, I check my phone. Chad is still out of contact. The sun is setting now, and the omnipresent skein of worry and fear deepens. I shouldn't be sitting here, looking at cards with my crazy sister. I should be out there, heading upstate to find my husband and demand some answers. Yes, I decide, that's what I'm going to do. As soon as I can get rid of Sarah.

"The Lovers means that you have a deep soul connection to someone in your life," says Sarah. "But it also represents the relationship you have with yourself, that you are choosing who you want to be, how you want to love, your values in a way that is true to who you are."

I hear a wailing horn in the distance, soft and mournful at this height, like the howling of a ghost.

"In reverse, it could mean that you are out of sync with yourself, the people in your life. It might mean that you are at war with yourself, that you might be punishing yourself. The Lovers in reverse suggests that you seek spiritual counsel."

I think about this a moment and realize that it's true. I have always warred with the teachings of my past, and the knowledge of my mind. Now, in this moment, I feel out of sync with Chad, with myself, with what I believe.

I feel so far away from my husband right now. Where is he? Who is he?

Sarah doesn't say anything more, but lays out the future card, and we both stare.

A skeleton in dark armor rides a white horse. He carries a flag with a white rose.

Death.

"Rosie," says Sarah. "It only means change, transition, sometimes painful but necessary. It's about endings and new beginnings. Birth and rebirth."

"I know what it means," I say, too sharp.

My middle still aches with my loss; I see Dana hanging. Xavier fallen. I think about Bethany, Chad's murdered girlfriend lying alone in the woods. Ivan in his final moments. Miles. Willa Winter.

Death is a part of life. We rail and resist, deny it. But there's a beauty in truth, a terrible, dark beauty.

In the background of the card, a boat floats on a river, carrying souls into the afterlife. And on the horizon the sun sets between two towers to represent death and rebirth, as the sun sets each night, and rises each morning.

Sarah opens her mouth to speak, but at that moment the buzzer rings loud and long, startling us both.

I rise quickly, eager to walk away from Sarah and her cards. "Yes, Abi."

"Ms. Lowan, Detective Crowe is here to see you."

I am exhausted, the weight of everything just too much for me. Can I turn him away?

"He says it's urgent."

"Does he have a warrant?" I ask. Already looking up Olivia's number on the phone in my hand.

"Yes, Ms. Lowan. He does."

There's a dump of dread in my stomach; a shaking starts deep in my core. I fumble for Olivia's number and call her. But it goes straight to voice mail, and I hang up. I send a quick text, and it just hangs. No pulsing dots to say she's typing on the other end.

"Okay," I say, sounding calmer than I feel. "Send him up."

When he comes to the door, Detective Crowe looks grim and exhausted. He has two uniformed officers with him. A tall, lanky woman, blond hair pulled back tight, and a stocky, older man. Chests thick with their Kevlar vests, belts heavy with gun and billy club, radios squawking.

"Is your husband home?" asks Crowe.

I shake my head, not trusting my voice.

"This afternoon we found the body of Betty Cartwright. She washed up downtown from the East River. Her skull was bashed in."

The world tilts a little. Chad is missing. Now Betty is dead. Panic is a siren in the back of my head. The horrific possibilities swirl.

I draw in a deep breath, to steady myself, lean against the wall.

Betty, the nurse who helped us take care of Ivan. Always kind, warm, efficient. Not flaky, as Chad described her. A mother of two, grandmother of five. She was always knitting, loved mystery novels, had a tattoo of a butterfly on her wrist that was a reminder that life is fleeting but beautiful. I don't want to think of her floating in the East River, broken, discarded.

Detective Crowe is saying something, but I'm lost in a fog of fear.

Behind the officers, and the detective, I see Willa and Miles. They stand stock-still and unseeing. I will them away, but they stay, standing sentry by the elevator with Abi between them.

"Will you be all right, Ms. Lowan?" asks Abi. Do I see a slight smile on his face?

"Yes, thank you."

The elevator doors slide closed.

Detective Crowe hands me two pieces of paper.

"Your husband was the last person to see Ms. Cartwright. According to her sister, he'd been harassing her. A witness saw him yelling at her on the street in front of her apartment."

The information doesn't compute. My husband doesn't harass women. He doesn't yell. He doesn't hurt people. He doesn't. More lies about my husband. "What? No."

My voice is a rasp; I grip the paper he's handed me.

"Meanwhile, he was supposed to report to work yesterday in a town upstate called the Hollows. Is that right?"

"Yes," I say, the word sticking in my closing throat. I feel Sarah come up behind me.

"He did not arrive or call to say that he wouldn't be there."

Another piece of information that doesn't compute. His big break, the role he's been working toward all his adult life. He just didn't show up?

What could ever keep him from that? Fear grips my stomach and twists.

"That's—impossible," I stammer.

Dread is a finger down my spine. A micro expression of compassion fleets across Crowe's face but it disappears quickly.

"Ms. Lowan, when did you last see your husband?" His voice is cold and flat.

"When he left yesterday morning after breakfast. I was supposed to meet him this weekend."

"When did you last speak to him?"

"He called last night to check in on me and say good-night."

"Did he say where he was?"

"No," I say. "I assumed at the hotel where he was booked. An inn, like a bed-and-breakfast place. I have the address because that's where I was meeting him."

"The Blue Hen Inn?" he asks.

"Yes, that's right," I answer, remembering.

"He's not there, Ms. Lowan. He never checked in," says Detective Crowe. "We have a warrant for his arrest. And to search this apartment."

"Who's this?" he asks, nodding toward Sarah, who regards him with naked suspicion.

"My sister is visiting from out of town." She gives him a curt nod, grabs my hand and pulls me back away from the detective. She's always been protective, even when she was too small to protect anyone.

When we step inside the apartment, I'm grateful to see that she's cleared the cards and put them back in her bag.

I stand by helpless as the police fan out in our apartment, our dream home, the place where I thought we'd conceive our first child. Every footfall takes me further away from the future I imagined here.

When I look back in the elevator foyer, Miles and Willa fade before my eyes, absorbed into the walls of this cursed place.

Two, three calls to Olivia go straight to voice mail and don't get returned. Not like her at all. Why can't I reach either of them? Are they together?

My head is spinning, fear and anger dueling in my chest. The police take their time. Ivan's box is removed. They take my computer, which luckily is backed up to the cloud. All I'll need is another device to access my work. I fight for my research papers and lose as they, too, are boxed up and taken away.

"This is my work," I protest to Detective Crowe. "It has nothing to do with anything."

"I can't know that until I've looked at it all," he says. "I'm sorry."

He's not. He's not sorry at all. It's just like Chad said. He has an idea, a theory, and he'll do anything he can to prove it.

Luckily, we have very little else for them to rifle through, a closet of clothes, a filing cabinet with personal documents beside my desk.

"I just saw your text," he says when I try to leave the room.

"What text?" I ask.

He holds up the phone and I see with dismay the panicked message I fired off in the church basement when I thought I was trapped. I had forgotten all about it.

"My husband—what?" he asks. "You didn't finish. What about your husband, Ms. Lowan?"

"I was scared," I say. "I followed someone down into the basement of the church. Then I thought someone was after me, that I was trapped. I panicked, sent you that text."

"Who were you following?"

Oh, you know, just the ghost of one of the people I'm researching for my book. Yeah, she died here in this building—she was murdered, actually, by her husband. She was trying to tell me something. That I was in danger. So, yeah.

"No one. I made a mistake."

"And who was following you?"

"My sister. My sister came after me, to see if I was all right."

He squints at me—part concern, part suspicion. "Let me read it back for you."

"That's not necessary."

"*I'm in trouble. Trapped in the basement of the Church of the Ascension on Madison Avenue. Dana, then Xavier wanted to tell me something. Now they're dead. I think I'm next. Abi is a liar. Xavier and Dana knew each other; check her Instagram feed. My husband—*"

"I know what I wrote. Did you know? That Dana and Xavier knew each other? Is that a connection you're exploring?"

He shakes his head slowly, not answering me. "What did you want me to know about your husband?"

"Nothing," I say. "I don't remember—like I said, I was panicking. I don't think we should talk anymore, Detective. Not without my lawyer."

We lock eyes. It's a standoff.

"It doesn't seem like it, I know. But I'm trying to help you, Rosie."

I shake my head at him. "You're right. It *doesn't* seem like that. And I need my lawyer."

The staring contest continues. And finally, I lose, walk away into the living room, feeling the heat of his gaze on my back.

thirty-six

Sarah sits beside me on the couch, and I remember how she used to climb into my bed during thunderstorms because she was afraid, but her nearness comforted me, as well. I lean into her, and she pushes back.

"What will you do?" she whispers.

The phone feels like a dead weight in my hand, none of my calls returned.

I give her the truthful answer. "I don't know."

"Let's go," she says. "Let's go home. Where you belong."

Why doesn't she understand that I don't belong there anymore? I look around the apartment. I'm not sure I belong here, either. Where do I belong?

"You go," I say. "I have to stay."

"You don't," she says. Her eyes are wide with worry. She tugs at my arm. "It's not safe here. You're not safe."

"This is my home," I tell her, sounding defensive and tense even to my own ears. "I can't just leave. Chad is *missing*."

The phrase hurts to utter, opens that gully of worry and fear.

He didn't turn up on set. That's unthinkable. Never checked in to his hotel. His location services are off; he still hasn't answered my calls. My husband is *missing*.

"Chad," she says. "I googled him."

I draw in and release a breath, say nothing. I always think of her living as we did—no internet, of course, no television, radio, newspapers, a place utterly apart from the chaos my father perceived in the world. And here she is googling my husband.

"Rosie," she whispers. "He's surrounded by death. *He's* the monster. The one who's drinking your blood."

"Stop it," I say sharply, holding up a palm.

"I saw him," she whispers fiercely. "In my dreams, he had his teeth in your neck and you weren't even fighting him."

"Sarah."

She stands and starts pulling at me. "I came here for you, to save you, to take you away from this place, from him. To bring you home where you'll be safe. Daddy wants you to come home. We need you."

I try to imagine the urgency, the fear, that made her travel from home to this urban jungle, to brave the strange world to find me. She loves me. I know this. But I'm not going with her.

"I *am* home," I say, standing. "I'm not going with you. I'm never going back there, Sarah. Ever."

The look of hurt on her face twists my heart.

"Can't you feel it? The danger here," she says. "There's been nothing but death here. You lost your *child*. You said so."

I draw in a breath against the anger I feel. She can't help it. She's been brainwashed, like I was, to believe that her imaginings and fantasies are real. She believes she's here to help me, that she can take me away from this life and save me from whatever is happening. But she can't.

"Sarah," I say calmly. "Please go. Go home to your husband, to Dad, to your dreams. I can handle my own life."

She blows out a breath, looks around. "I can see that."

"Just—go."

She stares at me a moment, then walks over to the table and grabs her duffel. She gives me a sad look, then leaves through the back door. I hear the fire door to the stairs open and close. Faintly, her footfalls echo off the concrete. I fight back tears as I listen to her disappear from my life, probably for good. Part of me wants to chase after—to follow her away, or to bring her back. But the truth is that we belong to different worlds and it's better if we part before we hurt each other any more than we already have.

I walk next door to Charles and Ella's, knock softly. I have a thousand questions for them.

But there's no answer as I wait in the foyer.

I've never felt so totally alone. Not since I left home and came to the city by myself to go to school. I remember lying on my dorm room bed, staring at the ceiling, listening to the city noise, and thinking I might as well be on the moon so far away was I from everything I had known. I had a new roommate, a girl named Noel, but she was a stranger sleeping on the other bed. The loneliness was almost unbearable.

"Ms. Lowan?"

I spin to see Detective Crowe standing before me. In his gloved hands, he holds a gun, a flat black menace across his palms.

"*What* is that?"

"Is it yours?"

"No," I say, frowning. "Of course not."

A gun. In our house. How could I not have known about it? What else am I not seeing that's right in front of me?

"It was in the kitchen, sitting on top of the cabinets."

"We don't have a gun," I say, staring at it. "Maybe it was Ivan's."

I follow him back inside my apartment and he slips the gun into a plastic evidence bag, hands it to a waiting officer. It looks so foreign. I'm not sure I've ever seen a real gun. Even from where I'm sitting, it looks old, dusty. Maybe it's been up there for decades, untouched? I hope.

I sink onto the couch, and he sits across from me. He steeples his fingers in that way that he does and looks up at the ceiling as if wondering how to say what he wants to say.

Then, "I spent a lot of time talking to the cop who investigated Bethany Wright's murder. You know what he said about your husband?"

I've read every word Detective Marlo Graves has to say about my husband. He is a vocal and passionate believer that Chad got away with murder and the wrong person is in jail. He'll tell anyone who will listen. I say nothing.

"That he's a sociopath and a stone-cold killer. Graves believes that your husband killed his girlfriend Bethany, then somehow menaced her mentally challenged brother into confessing. He also believes, though he can't prove and has no evidence, that Chad Lowan tampered with his parents' car and was responsible for their deaths, as well."

This does not surprise me. I've heard all these things before.

"It's not true. None of that is true."

"I know you want to believe that," he says with a careful nod, and for a moment he almost seems like he cares about me, about us. "We always want to believe that the people we love are who we think they are."

Again, I opt for silence, willing my phone to ring. It stays dark and heavy in my hand. I feel like my lifeline to Chad has been cut, that he's floating further and further away from me.

"Do you know what I think?" he asks into the silence.

"I have a feeling you're going to tell me."

"I think your husband is a very talented actor, and he's been playing a role for you, wearing a mask."

I flash on the image of him in his horrible witch costume on stage, hear Dana's words that he shared with me that so closely echo what the detective is saying.

I close my eyes and try to feel Chad's energy. His love. His kindness. His arms around me. I don't know where he is, but I can feel him. My husband. My love.

"You're wrong."

He stares at me long, then, "I hope I am."

When he rises, I stay on the couch, the room, my world spinning.

What next? What should I do?

I can't just sit here, waiting for the next horrible event or piece of terrible news.

Should I call Max? No, because then I'll have to tell him all these things about Chad.

After our argument, I can't take Sarah up on her offer and I don't want to anyway, have no way to reach her now. I twist at my wedding ring, as the police continue to rummage through my things.

Do I have to stay here? Should I? Where is Olivia?

Sometimes when your world falls apart, you just have to take action. Sitting helpless is not a good option. So finally, I grab my bag and leave out the back door before anyone can stop me.

thirty-seven

I hail a cab and head uptown, the city foreign and strange, a blurry photo. This feeling of floating, of being alone, it's familiar. I felt it as a child in the world my father created, one I always sensed on some level was not quite true. Then, when I left it all behind to pursue an education, the truth about the world and myself, I remember wondering if *anything* was real, anything was true. Or if every place, every reality, was just another story that you choose to believe.

For the first few months in school, I felt like a ghost in this city, invisible. Until my life started to take root. I made friends, earned good grades, started learning and living—going to clubs and movies, picnics in Central Park. The city became my universe—worldly, as Sarah would say—solid and undeniably real.

When the cab comes to a stop, I swipe my card. The driver doesn't say a word as I exit and as he pulls swiftly away. I never see his face except on the ID tag posted on the thick plastic divider between us. How strange this city must seem to Sarah who's never been out of our town. There's a twinge of sadness, of sorrow, about the way we parted. Maybe I'll never see her again. Another loss, another person drifting further and further away. How will she get home? I suppose the same way she arrived. She's a grown woman, not the child I left behind.

I have no place else to go, so I've come to see if I can find Olivia. It's after five, so she's not in court. Her towering, gleaming apartment building looms above me—all metal and glass and amenities. I'm going to wait for her at her apartment until she comes home. I approach her building.

The truth is I've always been a little jealous of Olivia. She seems so much more adult, more together, than I could ever hope to be. But Chad always described their relationship as difficult. An early spark of passion, but then in the end they were too different— she too regimented for him, he too laid back for her. She wanted more—to move in, to get engaged. He wasn't ready for any of that, still reeling from his losses and trauma—not with her, not with anyone. In the end, their friendship worked better than their love affair. That's what he always told me.

And it's true that Olivia and I are opposites. She's tough and hard-bodied, spending much of her free time in physical activity— running marathons or taking climbing trips to this mountain or that. I'm bookish and small, more at home at the library than the gym. *We're so different*, I thought when I first met her. How could he be attracted to her once, and now to me? Don't most people have a type? Floppy-haired creatives, that's my thing.

Olivia's doorman is reading *The Post* as I approach, but he puts it down as soon as he sees me.

"Hey, Rosie," he says. We've been here a million times. And her muscle-bound, bald-headed doorman, Brando, knows us well. "I'm not sure she's home. Have a pile of packages here for her."

"Hey, Brando. She's not," I say. "She asked me to stop by and feed the cat."

He frowns, looking at the computer screen in front of him. "Oh...she didn't leave word."

I match his frown. "Oh, really. I'll call her."

I make a show of calling her and getting her voice mail, hanging up.

"Poor Truman," I say.

Truman is Olivia's ancient cat who only likes Chad and me. So we're her go-to cat sitters when she's away, often dropping by to take care of him when she's working late, or tied up with a big trial.

He waves me off. "Nah, it's okay. Don't bother her. Just go on up. You have the key?"

"I do."

He frowns at me before going back to his paper. "Tell her next time she needs to let me know, though?"

I toss him a smile. Some of Chad's acting skills must be rubbing off on me. I drop the happy, carefree act as soon as the elevator doors close and see my frazzled reflection in the mirrored doors. I'm a wreck in jeans and Converse, Chad's old leather jacket and a gray T-shirt.

People have died. There's a warrant out for my husband's arrest. He's missing. Olivia, my lawyer, is not returning my calls, or the call from Detective Crowe. I know that's not right—she *would* have called. Should have.

Something's very wrong.

I knock on the door in case she's in there, but there's no answer. So I use my key to press inside. The apartment is dark, blinds pulled.

"Olivia."

Nothing. I pause, breathing deep. What am I doing exactly? I guess I'm just going to sit on her couch until she comes home. I have no place else to go.

I wander from her minimalist living room with its low sectional and hanging orb lights, large-screen television mounted on the wall. Huge windows provide stunning views of downtown. In her white bedroom, there's a platform bed and simple dresser, touch lamps on each side table. Everything simple, elegant. Curated.

The apartment smells like her, the Armani cologne she favors. Her bathroom is pristine, surfaces clean, electric toothbrush stowed in a cabinet. Expensive makeup neatly organized in a drawer.

Her closet is a showroom of gorgeous suits and silk blouses, a collection of shoes that probably cost more over time than a used car, built-in drawers lined with designer workout clothes, jewelry displayed in lit glass cases, rows of stunning lingerie.

I run my fingers along the beautiful fabric of her clothes, think of our own messy closet at home, Chad's side even more chaotic than mine. No wonder they didn't make it. They don't fit. Chad couldn't fit into this perfect space; maybe no one could. Suddenly, I feel lonely for Olivia. Life and love, people, are complicated and messy. That's part of the beauty of life, that nothing fits perfectly into a little box.

A noise from the bedroom startles me, and I freeze, listening.

A shuffle of the bedclothes, the sound of something falling to the floor with a thud.

My heart leaps into my throat. Who's here?

I move quietly from the closet, mouth and throat gone dry, fingers shaking against the drywall. I pause in the hallway, listening. Nothing.

Slowly, I peer into the bedroom.

He comes from nowhere, a shadow leaping from the dim of the room with a horrifying yowl. I am knocked back against the wall, issuing a scream as he runs past me toward the kitchen, disappearing around the corner.

My heart hammers, my knees weak beneath. I lean on the wall for a second, trying to catch my breath.

Truman. The cat.

We terrified each other.

"Truman," I say, steadying myself, following. "I'm so sorry, buddy."

In the kitchen he forgives me, walking figure eights around my ankles as I clean his water bowl and open a can of food for him, fill his second dish with kibble. I pet him on his head, and he deigns to let me scratch him behind his ears, his purr a furry engine running in overdrive.

"I'm so, so sorry, buddy," I tell him again, my heart still racing, hands shaking.

He goes to his bowl and starts eating as if he hasn't been fed in days. When was Olivia home last? The place is spotless, not a speck of dust, not a dish in the sink, or any evidence that the stove has been used—ever.

Another sound, this one coming from the bedroom. A low buzzing, over and over.

I follow the tone into the bedroom and sit on her tightly made bed. This is wrong, how totally I am invading her space. Still, guiltily, I open the drawer in the side table. There, a buzzing cell phone.

But that's not the first thing I see.

The only other thing in the drawer is a picture of Olivia with Chad.

They stand on the beach; he's wearing white linen pants and an open linen shirt, exposing his muscular abs and chest, hair wet with seawater.

She wears a stunning sarong, brightly colored in reds and purples. Her smile as she looks up at him, pure joy and love. He has his arms around her waist. I can't help but notice that he doesn't look at her the same way, his gaze drifting off into the distance. I know they were together. But somehow this still hurts, feels like a betrayal. Does she lie in bed at night staring at this image of their past couplehood? How long ago was this? They both look younger, fresher. I have never seen Olivia smile that way; it brightens her face and makes her seem girlish, even more beautiful.

I hold the framed picture, stare at the gorgeous sky and blue-green water lapping the shore. The image could be in a magazine—an ad for beachwear or some sunny destination. It reminds me that my husband and I have never had a honeymoon. And I feel a dump of fear and despair so total it nearly buckles me over.

Chad. Where are you?

The phone in the drawer rings again, drawing my attention. I noticed right away that Olivia's laptop and the phone she uses for work are nowhere in the apartment. That makes sense; she's never separated from those things. She never stops working. This is another device.

I hesitate, again shocked that I would commit such a horrible, dishonest invasion. The circumstances are extreme, but this is not cool. Still, when it buzzes again, I pick it up. I breathe, terrified now that I'll find messages from my husband, learn that he and Olivia have been having an affair. That they've run off together. She was with him when he came to Dana's. Maybe this has been happening under my nose all this time.

Everybody's words about Chad—Max's, Dana's, Detective Crowe's, crowd my thoughts.

He's a player.

A dark heart beneath a beautiful mask.

A stone-cold killer.

I hit the home screen. Her phone is as curated as her life, the home screen not a chaos of widgets like my own.

I click the text icon and scroll through the only chain I find there, heat rushing to my cheeks as I do.

It's risqué, complete with pictures and raunchy talk. I shamelessly read, face burning, hand shaking, until I get to the missives at the end.

At midnight last night: Good night. Sweet dreams.

There's no answer from Olivia.

This morning at 9:03: Hey, good morning. Late night last night? See you for lunch.

12:40: Hey, I'm here. Running late?

1:00: Okay, I'm officially worried. Call me?

I see a few attempts at calls. And then the most recent text.

Are you ghosting me? There's a ghost emoji. Was it something I said? With the quizzical face emoji.

I put the phone down, look out at her expansive view, the Brooklyn Bridge off in the distance. I am buffeted by a rush of complicated emotions.

It's not Chad who's been having an affair with Olivia.

It's Max.

thirty-eight

It's not a betrayal, not at all, but it feels like one. It's a secret kept by a friend, and I wonder why he never told me. It hurts. From the text chain it looks as if this has been going on for weeks. Maybe it's new, maybe they agreed not to share unless they were sure things were going to get serious. But things seem pretty serious to me. I think about calling Max, confronting him, but what right do I have? I am an intruder, rifling through Olivia's things, looking in her private spaces. I'm in the wrong here, not them. They're adults and what they do is up to them.

Still, something stings.

When my phone pings, I nearly jump out of my skin. My heart lurches with hope but it's Detective Crowe.

Where did you go, Ms. Lowan?

I don't answer.

I still have questions.

I stare at the little pulsing dots that tell me he's still typing.

People around your husband turn up dead. You're not safe, Ms. Lowan. Rosie. Let me help you.

I still don't answer, my hand shaking, my eyes filling.

Come to the station with your lawyer tomorrow at 9 a.m. It's not a request. I don't want to have to issue a warrant for your arrest, too.

Truman leaps nimbly into my lap, settles in. I put my hand on his back and stroke his soft fur. Outside, the sky is growing dark, a gray cloud cover blocking out the sun.

"What are we going to do, buddy?"

He starts to purr. I lie back on her bed, keeping my shoes off the snowy-white comforter and cuddle with Truman for a while, waiting. I must doze off, because I wake with a start and Truman is gone. I'm guessing that Olivia is not coming home.

Okay. Okay. What are my options here? Go back to the Windermere? Face my apartment being torn apart by the police, confront Abi—again, try to talk my way into that secret room? Go to Max, ask him about his affair with Chad's ex? Go upstate to try to track down my husband, who could be anywhere, his location services still off, my calls to him unreturned?

I linger awhile longer, make sure Truman has enough food and water, then leave, no idea where I'm going.

thirty-nine

But the truth is that I have no place else to go. So I return home.

Abi is not at his station as I let myself in through the locked front door. The lobby is silent, smelling of furniture polish and wood.

I use my opportunity to try the door again but this time my key doesn't fit. How could he have changed the lock so quickly? Something is going on behind those doors, and someone is clearly trying to hide it.

Exhaustion pulls at my limbs, my eyelids.

I walk through the lobby, the mailroom and into the back of the building to ride the service elevator up to my floor.

All the way up, I pray that when I walk inside, Chad will be there. His phone lost or broken. An explanation for why he wasn't where he was supposed to be, where he told me he'd be, ready on his lips.

I'll believe him. I just need him to—correct the tilt of our world, put us back on the axis of our happy, hustling life where everything—my book deal, his new role, our quest to grow our family—is moving in the right direction.

But no.

As I enter quietly and walk through my empty apartment, it doesn't seem like ours anymore. Images of death, the tarot card Sarah pulled, the horrible things I've seen, are on a loop in my mind, mingling with what Arthur told me about the Aldridges, their lost child falling down the elevator shaft. What a horror.

"Chad?" I venture.

But silence is the only answer.

The space feels violated—items moved or taken, things not left as they were. The dining room chairs stand askew. The magazines seem swept from the coffee table, lie open and scattered on the floor. The area rug is flipped up. The drawers of my desk are open, emptied. My computer, the Windermere box gone, books tossed from shelves. I try to straighten things.

We'll make it right again, I tell myself, when all of this is over. We'll make it our home again. We'll heal this place. Maybe it's us—our new energy, a future child that will finally heal the Windermere, release Willa and Miles and every other dark thing trapped here.

When my phone rings, I frantically dig it from my pocket.

Max.

I decline the call, don't know what to say to him. He calls again, then texts.

Did you decline my call? I need to talk. Call me.

I can't bring myself to call him back. Then there's a soft knock at the door.

When I open it, Ella is there, stylish even in her sleepwear— black silk pajamas and a cashmere robe. Without her makeup she looks her age, tired tonight, wrung out. Her gray hair is tousled, eyes worried. Charles stands behind her, expression similarly concerned.

Whatever Ella sees in me makes her face go soft with compassion.

"Oh, my dear girl," she says. "What's happened?"

She opens her arms and I let her take me into her fragrant embrace, leading me into their apartment.

At their kitchen table, I tell them everything that's happened. They both lean into me with concern, Ella holding my hand and Charles making all the right affirming noises.

"There must be some terrible misunderstanding," says Ella firmly when I'm done. I've left out the part about Dana's gallery showing, how they were all there, while I was home with Ivan, how Chad seemed to be too intimate with their daughter, Lilian.

"Chad would never do anything to you or anyone," says Ella. "You must know that. He's a good man who adores you, Rosie. Anyone can see that."

"Then where is he? Betty Cartwright is dead, and he was seen arguing with her. Her sister said he was harassing Betty. Now he's missing—didn't show up on set."

Ella has risen and taken a pot from the refrigerator and put it on the stove. It's her famous chicken soup. Just the smell of it warming gives me comfort.

"You must be starving. When did you eat last?" she asks.

"I think the only logical thing for us to do," says Charles, rubbing at his forehead, "is get in the car and go up north and find Chad."

He's echoing my own earlier thoughts. But it seems like a fool's errand. And what if Chad is in trouble, comes back here and finds me gone?

"The detective said he's not there. Not at the hotel. Not on set."

"Well," says Charles, jutting out his chin, determined. "We'll just have to see that for ourselves."

"Rosie needs to rest," says Ella. "Look at her. She's been through too much."

They both look at me and whatever they see has Charles nodding his head.

"I'll go, then," says Charles.

"No," I say. He's an old man—fit and in good shape but no. "I can't ask you to do that."

"You didn't ask me. And what else? Just sit around here frantic with worry, calling and calling? If Chad has disappeared, hasn't called you or returned your call, he must be in trouble. Maybe he needs our help."

What help can you give him? I wonder but don't say.

Ella puts the soup in front of me and I eat it. It's so good. Savory and hearty, filling my senses with its aroma and heat. She serves it with buttery crusty bread, and I eat with gusto, as if I haven't eaten in days.

"Charles, don't be silly," says Ella. "Chad will call. There must be some good explanation for all of this."

But her mouth is pressed into a tight, grim line. She's trying to stay positive, but the situation is not good; we can all see that. Since Chad and I met we have never been out of communication for more than a few hours. Maybe he's left me—for Olivia, for Lilian.

"I was on Xavier's Instagram feed," I say, finally. "The night of Dana's art opening, Xavier was there. So was Chad—with your daughter, Lilian. You were there, too."

Ella smiles thinly, shakes her head.

"No," she says. "I don't think so. You must be mistaken. We didn't know Dana well enough to be invited to her events."

That gives me pause. I know what I saw. They were there.

"I saw the photos. Chad and Lilian—they seemed intimate."

I flash on that image. Of the waking dream I had here in this apartment of the man and woman in the nightclub.

Ella leans toward me, puts a comforting hand on my arm.

"I assure you whatever interest there is, it's strictly professional.

Lilian is very much the devoted wife to her Robert. Besides—
Chad's a good-looking man but Robert has something he doesn't."

"What's that?"

"Money and power," says Ella simply. "That's what Lilian
cares about. There's little she cares about more."

Charles offers a little chuckle. "That is true."

The room grows overwarm, and my cheeks start to flame.
My vision stutters, and a ringing starts in my head.

There he is. Miles. He stands in the corner, watching me,
shaking his head, eyes wide.

"I didn't know you lost a child," I say to Ella. The words escape my lips before I can stop them. She draws back, surprised.

"Who told you that?" She looks so stricken. I wish I could
take it back but it's out there now.

"In my research. I read about it. I'm so sorry."

The room tilts, and I feel sweat come up on my brow. My
throat feels tight, and my breath comes raspy.

"It was a lifetime ago," says Charles sadly. Ella looks at him
through squinted eyes, and I can see years of resentment and
anger in that stare, sharp as knives.

"It was *yesterday*," she says. "Just like yesterday. For me."

"Life and death go hand in hand," he says easily, like all the
ways of the world are known to him. "Light is always followed
by darkness."

"Shut up, Charles," she says. "Spare me the philosophizing.
Our son *died*."

And I almost laugh even though it's the furthest thing from
funny because it's so unlike her and suddenly, my vision starts to
go fuzzy. It's getting hotter, and their voices are growing fainter.
And suddenly, the world turns upside down.

I hit the floor heavily, feeling my head knock against the
hard tile.

No.

The soup. Oh no, the soup.

I remember with a cold dawning now the terrible nausea that followed the last time I had it. How, that night, I lost our baby. Oh, my God. What's happening?

I'm on the cold floor, looking up at Charles and Ella, who are peering down at me like two doves, craning their necks toward each other.

"You gave her too much," he says, his voice pulled long and slow like taffy.

"And last time it wasn't enough, was it?" Hers is high and fast. Willa is there. And Miles, too, both watching sadly.

"Just help me get her out of here," says Ella. I try to fight them, but my arms are weak, useless.

"What are you doing?" I ask but it comes out slurred in a voice nothing like mine.

"Rest now, Rosie. Just rest. You're not well," says Ella kindly, but her eyes are hard.

Before everything goes totally black, I see him, standing tall and staring by the doorway into the kitchen with his crisp uniform and perfect posture.

"Don't just stand there," barks Ella. "Help us."

Abi.

ACT IV

resurrection

I stood as a pupil of death: stood before death's boundless knowledge and let myself be educated.

Rainer Maria Rilke

forty

"Didn't I tell you, little girl, that the world out there is dangerous, with predators lurking around every corner?"

I sit beside my father in the first pew of his church, which is just a long bench, rickety and threatening to splinter apart. Above us the sky moves fast, thick gray clouds ready to storm visible through the wide holes in the roof. I can smell the rain coming, feel my sinuses swell. I don't like to admit that I loved that place, its run-down beauty, its undeniable energy. I don't like to admit that deep down I loved my father, even with all his flaws, all his lies.

"You lied," I say. "About so many things."

He bows his head, long salt-and-pepper hair obscuring his face.

"Are you so sure that *I* am the liar? And those teachers, those books, the world out there, that those stories they tell you are any truer?"

"Science, Dad."

He laughs, a big chuckle that always makes me laugh, too, even when I'm angry. And I *am* angry at him. I carry it with me always, this seething resentment for all the ways he failed me. *At some point we can choose to find ways to forgive our family,* Dr. Black always says. *If they hurt you, chances are someone hurt them, too. To accept that is a release.* So far, it hasn't happened for me. Or I haven't allowed it.

"Science is infallible?" asks my father.

I don't even answer him because he'll never convince me that he can heal the sick with his touch and he'll never believe that he can't. So what's the point?

"So what will you do now, rose petal? Your sister came to help you and you pushed her away. Now what?"

My wrists ache and I look down to see them bound. I get up and start to run but then I fall to the ground, my ankles bound, as well.

This isn't happening, I think, as I lie on the ground. It's just a dream.

He stands over me, looks down, pitying. "We bind ourselves, rose petal. This world is a kind of prison, and we can only free ourselves."

I wake with a start and find myself in my own bed, the shades pulled, the room darkened. I reach for my phone but I can't move and my phone is not on the bedside table. I fall back heavily onto my pillows and try to piece together reality.

What time is it? The clock is gone. There's no light coming in through the drapes.

There's a terrible ache in my wrists and my ankles. I realize with a shock that my wrists and ankles are, in fact, bound. That part was no dream.

"What the fuck?" I struggle, arms behind my back.

"You've been sleeping a long time, dear. You must have needed it. You young women today, you work yourselves so hard."

The light flips on and Ella sits in the chair over by the window. She looks pale and ghoulish. Has she just been sitting there in the dark, watching me sleep? Did she tie me up? Those final moments in her kitchen come back—Charles was there, Abi. What is happening?

My mind grapples with this bizarre reality.

With Chad missing, who will wonder where I am? Max? Detective Crowe—I am supposed to meet him at nine. Will he come for me, bust inside here?

"Me?" Ella goes on, as if we're just chatting over coffee. "I only ever wanted a husband and children. I never had any grand ambitions. Not like you and my Lilian. So *driven*."

"Ella," I manage. "*What* are you doing? *Why* are you doing this?"

She shakes her head, puts a finger to her lips.

"This apartment," she says. "It's *ours*. Did you know that it belonged to Charles's family, that we divided and sold half of the space in 1960?"

"Yes, I knew that," I say, trying to keep my voice even. Slowly under the covers, I start working on my bindings. "To Paul and Willa Winter."

"Horrible people," she says with a disgusted shake of her head. "It nearly killed Charles to put up that wall and sell off half of his family legacy. His grandfather was one of the original investors in this building. A great friend of Marc LeClerc, the architect."

I decide to play along with the whole chatting easily over coffee vibe despite the fact that I've been drugged and bound, am clinging to consciousness.

"Why did you sell it?" I ask, keeping my voice light, still working my bindings.

She rolls her eyes, shifts in her seat. "Why does anyone sell something that's important to them, dear? We needed the money."

My head is a jackhammer of pain, stomach roiling. What did she give me? What was in that soup? I will myself to be strong, solid. I have to find a way out of here. She's an old woman; if I can undo my bindings, she won't be any match for me. I have no idea how close Charles and Abi are; maybe they're just outside the bedroom door.

"Charles wasn't much of a provider," she goes on. "The gallery we owned for years lost as much as it earned. His inheritance was dwindling. He was burning through mine, as well. We had no choice, really, if we wanted to stay on at the Windermere. So we sold this half."

The bindings at my wrists are loosening, I think. I keep working them slowly beneath the covers.

"He wrote terrible novels, you know," says Ella. "Paul Winter? He fancied himself a literary star, but he was just a hack. And her—running around on him behind his back, out at all hours. With our Abi, can you imagine? She broke so many hearts. A dancer with dreams of Broadway, but a middling talent at best, little more than a stripper."

"Willa Winter had an affair with Abi?"

I try to imagine Abi young and in love. But I can't see him as anything but what he is now. Some kind of sentry for the Windermere, doing the bidding of the Aldridges.

"The Winters were about to sell it again, wanting to move to the country like most people then, someplace safe for their children. We hoped at that time to buy it back but, even then, we couldn't afford it. Charles always had this scheme and that grand plan, spending money like there was an endless supply of it, and already the proceeds from the first sale were dwindling."

She's lost in memory. I try to bring her back to this moment.

"Ella, what did you give me? Please—let me go."

She lowers her voice, leans closer and whispers. "I can't, Rosie. I'm sorry."

"Is it really just the apartment you want? I mean—it's yours." That can't be it, can it? All of this just for a two-bedroom apartment. I remember what Max said about motive. It's personal.

She stays silent, watching me.

"Ella, where's Chad?" I try again when she doesn't speak. "Please. Do you know where he is?"

But she's not listening.

"When Miles died, I was so distraught, so tortured by my pain. I thought that maybe Willa had something to do with Miles's death. He saw them, you know, Abi and Willa, fooling around in the basement. But he was always a little troublemaker, telling lies and making up stories. So I didn't believe him."

"I'm so sorry, Ella," I say and mean it. "That loss must have been crushing."

"You can't understand," she says. "Because you don't have a child."

I take the blow, try not to let it show how much it hurts.

"But the police ruled Miles's death an accident," she continues. "The elevator malfunctioned. And the truth was I wasn't watching. The doors opened and he just ran, assuming the elevator was waiting for him. It was my fault, a failure to protect my darling boy."

"It was an accident."

She shakes her head. "I sank into darkness. I wanted to die with him. But I couldn't—because of our Lilian."

There. I work one of my hands free, sliding it slowly from the loosened binding. I start wiggling at my ankles, slowly.

"I lashed out in my grief. I told Paul what Miles saw. That she threatened my little boy, made him swear to keep her dirty secret."

She pauses, draws in and releases a slow breath. "I was in so much pain, I guess I just wanted to cause others pain, as well. I didn't imagine what he would do. I hope you can believe that. I just wanted them to divorce and leave."

"I'm so sorry, Ella," I say again. "You must have been in so much pain."

This time she looks at me surprised, then closes her eyes.

"Ella."

She goes on, "And the apartment went into probate—since

there was no one to inherit it. Finally, it went to an estate auction and Ivan bought it out from under us."

Ivan told me that it languished on the market for years, no one willing to buy it because of the murder-suicide, that he got it for a fraction of its worth because he wasn't concerned about death and dying, and all the ways people hurt each other. He'd seen it all. He never mentioned an auction or that he'd outbid the Aldridges. Memory is tricky, though. Which of them is right? Does it even matter? The fact is that the Aldridges lost the apartment again.

"Then Ivan moved in, and he was so often gone, so quiet when he was here. It was almost like there was no one next door. We had a key to his place so that we could check on things and bring mail in for him. And he didn't mind if Charles spent time there once in a while. So it was almost like we had the place back."

She goes quiet a moment, and I stop moving, afraid that she'll know I'm trying to get loose.

"When Lilian befriended Dana a few years ago, the two of them struck a deal. We knew the apartment would come to Dana in her inheritance—someday. It was agreed that Lilian and Robert would buy it from her because Dana had no interest in living there, and she needed the money. Artists always need money."

Her gaze is blank and distant, as if she's ever more lost in her reverie. I stay quiet, working the bindings, feeling some blood flow come back to my hands and my feet.

"And, finally, finally, it would be back in our family. You're too young to understand legacy, what you want to leave behind for your children, what you want to survive after you're gone. This building, this apartment, it's ours, always has been.

"What a joy it was to imagine Lilian right next door when she was in town. And when we died, we'd leave our place to her and finally she could put the two units back together. We could *know* that, even if it didn't happen in our lifetime."

It's just an apartment. Just floor and walls and windows. But no, it's not just that. Not to her, not even to me.

Ella looks at me coldly.

"And Miles would always have a home here. There would always be family for him. He wouldn't be alone after we were gone."

I wonder what Dr. Black would say about this, or Arthur Alpern. We cling to things we've lost, don't we? To the people who've left us. It's that clinging I think that forces us to do horrible things.

"It was settled," she says. "And not long after then Ivan fell ill. We were sorry for poor Ivan, of course. We never wished him harm. But it seemed like the place was back within reach."

I have a horrible thought. Chad said that Betty Cartwright almost gave Ivan an incorrect pain dose. Ella was watching Ivan the night he died. Could Ella have done that, to speed his passing?

"Did you kill Ivan, Ella?" I ask.

She blinks at me. "Ivan died from his illness. You know that."

As if she'd admit it.

She lifts her gaze to me, continues on as if I didn't interrupt her. "Then you and Chad swept in."

I shake my head. "We didn't *sweep* in, Ella. We cared for Ivan while he was dying."

I might as well not even be there; she doesn't even acknowledge me.

"And somehow your Chad manipulated Ivan into leaving *him* the apartment. Both of you, actually. It's in both of your names."

I remember Dana's rage and how I felt sorry for her. I thought she was grieving her father. But maybe she was really grieving that windfall of money.

"It was Ivan's idea to leave us the apartment," I say. "Chad wanted it to go to Dana."

Ella smiles. "You really believe that, don't you? You really believe that your husband is a good man. He's not. He's an operator, an opportunist. And now this place is yours."

"Where is he, Ella?" I ask. Because it's clear now, if they've taken me, they must also have taken him. "What have you done with him?"

"This building," she says, looking around the room. "It's not for everyone. Not everyone deserves to live here. Marc LeClerc only sold to true believers."

"True believers?"

The bindings around my ankles finally grow loose enough that I get one foot, then the other, free. I lie still, waiting. But I'm free. I glance at the door, wonder who might be outside.

She keeps talking. "People who understand that there's more to life than what we see before us. That there's energy, and spirits, other planes. This building is special and the people who live here need to be special, too. Slowly over the years, there have been less and less of those kinds of people. And the Windermere's power has been diminishing."

"Its *power*?" Ella is clearly losing her grip, or she lost it long ago.

"Like so many buildings in this city, it's a grand place that attracts artists and actors, mediums, authors. Like you and Chad. This building is a dream maker—or it used to be. If you come here with your dreams, its energy helps you make them come true. Think about it. How long after you moved here did Chad get his big break? Days."

That's ridiculous. Talent, hard work, tenacity—those are the only dream makers in this life. Success is not magic—its blood, sweat and tears. But I don't bother. That's the thing with true believers—their minds are closed. I've known enough of them in my life to know that.

"Ella, just tell me what you want me to do."

She lifts a stack of paper. "Your friend Olivia drew this up to save Chad. And Chad signed it to save you. And now all we need is your signature and we'll bring you to your husband."

I'm grappling with the twisted logic of this. So they have Chad and Olivia somewhere? They coerced Olivia to create a document, Chad to sign. And if I sign, then they'll bring me to Chad, and we all go free? No.

"What is it?" I ask, voice shaking.

"It's a quick claim deed, a document that you will sign, giving us the apartment to thank us for all we've done for you, for Ivan. Because over the years, we've become like family. Haven't we, Rosie? Both of you alone in the world, we took you under our wing."

"And then what happens to us?" I ask stupidly.

"We all go about our lives. You and Chad, far from here. You don't tell a soul. And we won't share what we know about Dana's death. Your husband with his terrible history, who will believe he didn't kill her when the evidence points to his guilt?"

The room is spinning as I process all of this.

"You're just going to let us walk away if I sign over the apartment."

She gives me a pitying look. "We don't want to hurt you, dear. We always liked you both so much."

"You know, Ella," I say. "I don't believe you."

She smiles that smile, shakes her head. Her snow-white bob frames her gaunt face. She steeples her long, bejeweled fingers.

"The soul is infinite, Rosie. We might shift off this body, but we live forever. Like our Miles. You've seen him. You know. We can never leave this building, even after everything, because I can never leave my son behind."

It echoes what Arthur Alpern said about the memories of his life with his wife that still lingered in the apartment.

"And Paul and Willa," she says. "Sometimes I hear his typewriter. He used to write in the same room where you work now, Rosie. Sometimes I hear the gunshot we heard that night. Maybe when you and Chad are gone, we'll hear you laughing, or making love."

I don't wait to hear more. As quickly as I can, I throw back the covers, get up and start to run with all the strength I have left.

forty-one

I stumble at the bedroom door, my legs weak beneath me, catch myself on the frame, keep running, crashing through the door and into my empty apartment. Ella screeches after me, as I race through the dining room, into the kitchen.

Grabbing a knife from the block on the counter as I pass, I slam out the back door, head down the fire stairs toward the street, screaming for help. Someone will hear me, won't they? Call the police?

Everything tilts and my head is hammering, the concrete stairs hard beneath my bare feet. I am almost at the bottom, when I hear the exit door to the ground floor open and close.

"Ms. Lowan."

It's Abi. His voice carries up, soothing and mellifluous. "Ms. Lowan," he says. "I know you're upset. But everything is okay. Let us help you."

"Help me?" I scream. "*What* are you doing? Why are you helping them?"

I turn and run back up the stairs, with Abi coming up, foot-falls heavy, echoing behind me.

I run with everything I have, the world shuddering. I fall, knocking my knees hard against the steps, get up, keep going. A stitch in my side, my heart working double time, breath ragged.

Up and up and up, his footsteps coming faster. My mind is blank with terror, no time to think about Chad or Olivia or where they are and if they're okay. I can't go there; it will double me over with fear. All I can do is try to survive this.

I pass my floor, expecting to see Ella come from the door, but she doesn't. Then I'm on six, then seven.

My lungs burn, leg muscles on fire. I'm going to be sick, but I will myself to be solid, to keep moving. If I stop, they have me and I won't get away from them again.

Abi's still behind me. I can hear his labored breathing, gain-ing, as I pass nine, ten. I turn around to see him still coming as I burst out through the door to the roof, the cold night air hitting me like a wall, the tar rough beneath my feet. The stars above obscured by city light, and the wind whips.

I slam the door hard and realize, too late, that I'm trapped. I have no phone to call for help. And no one will hear me scream-ing up here. There's no other exit off this roof.

Except for one.

I remember Xavier's ruined body on the sidewalk. What was he trying to tell me? Did it get him killed like it did Dana?

I run for the shadows and crouch in the darkness of the far corner of the roof, behind a huge air vent, listening. Curled up, I wrap my arms around my legs and wait, clutching the knife I grabbed from the kitchen. Something sparkling catches my eye.

When I look down, I find its one of those stupid necklaces, pick it up and hold it in my hand. The tiny palm with an eye in its center, a protection from evil. How many of these did Ella give to people, and how have they fared? Was it a charm, or a curse? I never wore the one she gave to me.

I've seen one on Chad, on Dana, on Xavier.

Xavier and Dana are dead. Chad is missing.

I realize then that I must be near the edge where Xavier fell. Or was he pushed, as he, too, ran up here to get away from people chasing him?

Why? Who? What do they want? Not just the apartment, surely. I shiver, holding the charm in one hand, knife in the other. I'm all alone in the middle of the most populated city on earth, trapped. No way out.

I close my eyes and do a thing I never do. I pray. To the Universe. My father always said to ask when things seemed hopeless: What is possible? Will you show me the way?

I repeat those two sentences like a mantra as the door to the roof opens and closes hard.

"Ms. Lowan," says Abi. "It's not safe up here. Not safe at all."

I stay quiet, using the dark and my hiding space to my advantage. I won't go without a fight. I will create as much damage as possible. The door opens and closes again.

"Rosie." It's Ella. "You're distraught. You've been through so much. The loss of Ivan, finding Dana's body, Xavier, your miscarriages. Just come inside and we'll call your doctor, talk this all through."

If they need my signature on that paper, they won't get it.

I decide that I'll jump myself before I give it to them. But then what? What story will they write about me? Will they say I was prone to depression, unstable? People would believe that I killed myself. And will they somehow get the apartment anyway?

"The truth is, dear, that our artist friend Anna is also an accomplished forger. Your signature will be easy for her to copy. We'd like your signature. Should there be scrutiny, it would be best to have it. But we don't need it."

So then, what *do* they want from me? It dawns on me then that Chad must be dead. They got his signature and he's gone. The thought opens a black hole of despair inside me. I don't want to live this life without him. I choke back sobs.

Olivia, too. Like Dana, Xavier, Betty.

Because of the apartment? Because of the Windermere?

Maybe I'm the only one left. It feels like it, like I am the only one left in the world.

I stay quiet, shaking. What else is possible? What is left for me to do now? I ask a god I don't even believe in. Not surprisingly, there's no answer.

I hear a muffled cry. A note that sounds familiar.

"But if you do sign," Ella says. "We'll let your little sister and her baby go home."

My blood runs cold, and it takes everything I have to stay silent.

They're lying. Sarah left, hours ago. She's long gone, heading back to her country life, rightly giving up on her sister who is never coming home.

"She never left the building, Ms. Lowan," says Abi, reading my thoughts. "We took her as she tried to leave. She's well, I assure you. For now."

There's a shuffle and a murmur. I rise from my hiding place, keeping the knife behind my back. It's not just Abi and Ella. Charles is there, too, holding Sarah. Her mouth is gagged, and arms bound behind her back. Her face is streaked with tears as she struggles. She's such a tiny woman, like a child next to Charles, who towers over her as he holds her tight.

"Let her go," I say, voice strained with anger and fear.

My whole body is shivering, weak from whatever they gave me, cold, terrified. The palm that holds the knife is clammy and shaking.

"We'll happily release her," says Ella, level, unruffled as ever. "She'll go back to her life because she wants to save her baby, and we all heard over the intercom how badly you have treated your family. So why would she care what happens to you after we release her? All you have to do is sign."

Right.

All I have to do is sign—and die.

forty-two

The world is fading. I don't have much time, I think, before I pass out again. I can feel the drug—whatever it was—still pulsing through my veins, making things foggy and vague.

And isn't there some kind of relief in that thought? That it's over, that I've lost? After all the fighting and hustling and reaching for this brass ring, and all the blood and grasping after things just out of reach, that you're just falling and falling, the ground rising up fast to greet you. We never belonged here. We were never going to stay at the Windermere.

Chad and Olivia are probably already gone.

I look at the ledge and remember Xavier's choice. It's tempting. If Chad's gone, what's left? Or maybe it wasn't a choice, and he was pushed.

"What's it going to be, lovey? We don't have all night," says Ella with an annoyed sigh.

My sister makes some kind of panicked noise, and we lock eyes. I feel the jolt of our connection.

Maybe I can broker my sister's safety, send her and her baby home. At least my life can be worth that much.

"Okay," I say finally. "I'll sign."

Sarah starts to scream behind her gag and struggles against Charles, who holds her firm, his face blank and impassive like he couldn't care less about any of it.

"That's a good girl," says Ella. "I always knew you were smart."

Abi grabs me and easily wrests the knife from my weak grip, tosses it out of reach. So much for putting up a fight.

I think I see the flicker of apology in his eyes, but it quickly fades to coldness.

"Why are you helping them?" I think back to my conversation with Max about what he could want. "What is in this for you?"

But he doesn't answer. He doesn't even look at me again—like I'm the package he's delivering, the luggage he's hauling out to the curb.

Sarah struggles and yells all the way down the stairs, earning strained grunts from Charles. She's saying the same thing over, and over, but I can't understand her words.

Finally, I get it: *Rosie, don't you dare sign.*

We keep going down, all the way to the basement, through the maze of passageways, past the laundry room, past the storage cages and finally into another locked room, which Ella opens with a key. I don't fight at all, weak and fading fast.

"What are they paying you?" I ask Abi. I remember that his mother is in assisted living and maybe that's it. Just money. The simplest of all motives. "*How much* could they be paying you that you would do this for them?"

"Be quiet, Ms. Lowan." I notice then that he's also wearing one of those necklaces, the little silver palm glinting at his neck. In fact, they are all wearing it. I think about Arthur Alpern's books, about Charles's family of mystics. Dana wore one. And Xavier. And Chad. Not me, though. I never put mine on. Maybe that's a good sign.

"I mean, what is in it for you? Or are you just their servant? You've been waiting on the rich, mad people in this building so long that you've lost all your self-determination."

He gives me a dark look, and pushes me roughly through the door.

It's a huge space that I never knew was here. On the wall, mounted monitors, with a window into every single apartment in the Windermere.

Miranda is meditating, peaceful upon a floor cushion. Anna watches television, her face blank and washed blue in the light of the screen. Ogadinmah Mgbajah is cooking his dinner, chopping vegetables while listening to classical music.

Our apartment is empty, dark, waiting.

I knew it. All the apartments are being watched.

"Hey, Abi?" The voice seems to come from nowhere. I realize it's coming from one of the apartments.

Abi clasps his hand hard over my mouth and drags me over to the computer, where he clicks a few keys.

"Yes, Mr. Donofrio."

I scan the monitors and see the older man who I've only met in passing. He and his wife live on ten, owning the entire floor.

"I think I heard something on the roof."

"Hmm, that's odd. I'll check the cameras." Then, "No, nothing up there that I can see. I'll take a run up and have a look."

"Good man, Abi."

That's when I see them, Olivia and Chad, lying bound and gagged, back to back, in another storage cage, both of them stone still, heads tilted, unmoving.

I scream his name but he doesn't respond. He seems so helpless. My heart floods with fear, legs buckle with it and I can't stand that I lost faith in him, thought he was having an affair with Lilian. Wondered if he'd run off. All this time, he's been here, captive in the basement of this cursed apartment building.

"Just let them out," I beg. "We'll give you everything we have. We'll never say a word. Just let us go."

I'm desperate now, begging on my knees on the cold concrete. I don't care. All pride goes out the window when you're fighting for the people you love.

Ella has taken a seat at the long table in front of the monitors and spread out the paperwork.

"Just sign, Rosie," she says. "And it's done."

I look at the signature line, the pen. Abi has a tight grip on my shoulder.

"Rosie?"

We all startle. "Rosie, where the fuck are you?"

Max. In my apartment.

I remember then that I gave him the keys to the street door, and the back entrance to my apartment, because he was worried about me and wanted a way in while Chad was away.

"Goddammit," he says to no one, walking helplessly from room to room, his footfalls echoing. "What the fuck is going on?"

He's holding his phone, must dial my number because I hear my ringtone. He finds the phone on the dining room table, looks at it with a worried frown.

"Oh, my God, Rosie. Where are you?"

Something about Max's voice, his despair, it reminds me of who I am. That's what friends do; they connect you to your best, strongest self.

"Tie her up and go manage him," Charles barks at Abi, unlocking the storage cage and trying to push Sarah inside. But she starts struggling again, yelling against her gag, and then suddenly she uses all of her strength to charge the door he's trying to close, knocking him hard against the wall. I hear his head hit with a horrible smack. He looks stunned, starts to slide down the wall.

Ella screams his name, racing to him, papers forgotten. And as hard as I can, I wrest free from Abi, push him back and then move in to punch him with everything I have, my fist landing right at the bridge of his nose. His hands fly to his face, stumbling back as blood gushes down his shirt.

I tackle him and bring him to the ground. Rage overtakes me and I punch him again, again, until he lifts his arms to block my blows.

"Please, please," he begs, and I draw back, shocked at myself, my violence. Oh, my God, who am I?

Sarah is yelling, and finally I climb off Abi to untie her. When her arms are free, she wraps them around me.

Charles has sunk to the floor and Ella is wailing his name—all of us forgotten.

I press the button to the intercom and yell, "Max, it's Rosie!"

He jumps, startled, and looks around, terrified. "Rosie!"

"Max, I'm in the basement. Chad and Olivia are hurt. Call the police."

I hear his voice as he fumbles for the phone and dials.

I listen to the chorus of voices, people talking, televisions, music playing—all sounds from the apartments of the Windermere. And now, Abi's weeping on the ground.

"You *were* listening," I say. "Watching—everyone."

But Abi doesn't answer, struggles to get to his feet, but falters, lies back weeping. He is not as powerful and strong as he seemed to me. He is old and frail and beaten. And Ella is still wailing over Charles's still form, Sarah standing over them in a stance that says she's ready to fight.

I puzzle a moment over the three of them, what sickness, what agenda, bound these three people together. But then I rush over to Chad, rest my head against his lifeless body.

With a rush of joy, I realize that he's still breathing. He's alive. Relief floods like a tsunami. I press my finger to Olivia's throat. She's alive, too.

Quickly, I move to untie them, and Chad rouses.

"Rosie, what happened?" he murmurs. His eyes are glassy, lips parchment dry. He reaches for me and pulls me tight.

"Charles and Ella," he whispers, disoriented. "I think they're trying to hurt us. They're watching us. You were right about Abi. He's like their henchman. You're not safe."

It's a strange echo of Willa Winter's ghostly warning. And once again I wonder at the way of things, the world, how mysterious and strange it all is.

"We're okay," I tell him, working his bindings free. "We're all going to be okay."

I almost believe it. He loses consciousness again, falling heavy in my arms. I try to wake him, but he's out cold.

"Why did you do this?" I ask Ella.

But she's gone nearly catatonic, rocking.

"You killed him," she says over and over. I look at Charles in horror. He's pale and so still, but I think I see him breathing. I leave Chad to approach them, then I bend down beside him and feel his throat. There's a weak pulse.

"He's alive, Ella," I say. But she doesn't seem to hear.

Suddenly, I am overcome with sadness that money could bring people so low. People who I thought were our friends, were plotting against us all along.

And then there are voices, shouting. Footsteps coming loudly down the stairs.

"Rosie! Rosie Lowan!"

"We're over here," I yell, running for the door.

I never thought I'd be glad to see Detective Crowe, but I am. Max is right behind him looking frantic.

"Rosie," says Max, grabbing me. "*What* happened?"

I'm still piecing that together. He holds me a moment and heads over to Olivia. I watch as he lifts her into his arms and rocks her until the paramedics come racing through the door. Sarah drops beside me and wraps me in her arms. I sink into her and start to cry.

"Please," says Max, desperate. "Tell me what is happening here."

But I don't have any answers, only a million questions. They all jam up in my throat.

forty-three

Later, I sit in the quiet dark beside Chad's hospital bed, trying not to think about the fact that we don't have medical insurance.

He's received a dose of Narcan, is on IV fluids and has yet to regain consciousness. He's severely dehydrated, but he'll be okay, the doctor says.

We'll be okay. That's what matters now.

Olivia, too.

Charles sustained a head injury, but he, too, will survive this nightmare. Abi and Ella have been taken into custody. There's no comfort in that, somehow.

There are still a thousand questions. Like how Chad and Olivia both wound up in the basement of our building, how long they'd been there.

I wait, glad for the quiet and the night. My nerves are still tingling, a terrible ringing in my ears. My sister sleeps fitfully, uncomfortably, in the chair beside me. Max is with Olivia somewhere in the same hospital. The heart monitor beeps, a beautiful reminder that Chad is alive and well. We survived this, whatever it was. Where there is life, there is hope.

A shadow in the doorway draws my attention. Detective Crowe.

I get up and follow him out into the hallway.

He takes an evidence baggie out of his pocket. "We found this in the Aldridges' kitchen."

"What is it?"

He shakes the bottle of pills. "It's fentanyl, a powerful opioid, about eighty times stronger than morphine."

I stare at it.

"That's what she put in my soup?" I say.

He keeps his eyes on me. "She says she put it in Chad's coffee, as well. According to Abi, he stopped to see the Aldridges on his way out of town. Once Chad was unconscious, they bound him and put him in the basement. You're lucky. It could have easily killed you."

"And Olivia?"

"They coerced your husband to call her, under threat of harm to you. Chad told Olivia that it was an emergency, to please come. She did. Apparently, Abi took her to the basement where he and Charles accosted her, held her captive. They convinced her to draw up the paperwork they needed, promising they'd let her, and Chad, go. Once she'd done the work, they put a fentanyl patch on her, bound her and put her in the basement with him."

"They were going to kill us all," I say, releasing a breath.

"That was the plan. They were going to make it look like a murder-suicide, a mimic of the way Paul and Willa Winter died. As if the place was cursed."

The writer is at a rare loss for words.

"And your apartment would have belonged to them again, finally," he says. "This, according to Mr. Bekiri, who is cooperating freely with police. He claims that they were paying for his mother's assisted living, and threatened to stop, effectively putting her on the street. That he had no choice but to do their bidding."

He gives me a look. If he wants to say "I told you so," that people might kill for a five-million-dollar apartment, he has the grace to stay quiet.

All of this for seventeen hundred square feet in a Park Avenue elevator building.

"Where did she get those powerful drugs?" I ask.

"Abi claims Xavier was getting it for her," says Crowe. "Stealing from the hospital where he worked."

"Why would he do that?"

"The three of them—Charles, Ella and Abi, they were spying on everyone in the building. They knew everyone's secrets. Apparently, Xavier had been stealing narcotics and selling them out of his home."

"So they blackmailed him."

"Abi claims that the Aldridges threatened to turn him in to the police, and he killed himself."

"But…"

He bows his head. "But security footage shows Abi following him up to the roof."

"I thought there was no recording."

Crowe's phone pings, and he looks at it quickly, then back to me. "We found the archives on a computer monitor in the basement. The footage from the roof however had been deleted. We're having our tech team see what they can retrieve. I thought you'd like to know, though, that you did bring that box down with you that day. He never loaded it into the cab."

I smile at him. It's a small thing. But it's nice to know you can trust your own memories. I wonder about the letter and ask him if he found it. But he shakes his head.

"Lots of questions, still," he says. It's cryptic. His eyes drift over to Chad.

"Such as?"

"I mean, what was the endgame? They stage a murder-suicide scene, kill Olivia, and then think there wouldn't have been questions about the sudden quick claim deed? It's just a big job, so many moving parts, so many things could go wrong. And—they're all so old. All of this for an apartment."

"People have killed for less. You said so yourself," I remind him. "And maybe it's about legacy, about the building. They all seemed to be attached to it in a strange way, like it cast a spell on them."

"The building," he says flatly, gives me an NYPD smirk. "The building cast a spell on them. They'd kill for it."

I think about my conversation with Arthur Alpern.

Some buildings just have bad personalities. And I think maybe it attracts darkness. If you're vulnerable to dark energies, if they speak to something going on inside you, maybe there's a strange attraction, a lure to that dark part inside you.

"People act in their own self-interest only," says the detective when I don't answer. "I assure you that their motives were entirely worldly. Money, legacy, control."

"And Abi. I still don't get why he would be involved with them."

"Abi, it turns out, was deeply in debt. And, like I said, the Aldridges were paying for his mother's care. He was beholden to them."

But it was more than that, wasn't it? There was something that kept them tied together. He wore the necklace, too. Maybe Ella was right about the building having some kind of power.

"That's motive enough in my experience," says the detective, maybe reading my expression.

"You might be right."

He nods, satisfied. "Well, you and your husband, your friends, your sister—you're safe now. That's the important thing. The rest of the pieces will fall into place."

"What will happen to them?" I ask. "To Ella and Charles, to Abi?"

It's strange that I still care about Charles and Ella. So many years of thinking of them as friends, a kind of surrogate family, leaning on them while Ivan was dying. Was it Ella who bumped his dosage, sped his passing? I guess it will all come out.

"We've arrested Ella Aldridge and Abi Bekiri for abduction and attempted murder. More charges are pending based on the outcomes of the investigations into the deaths of Dana Lowan, Xavier Young and Betty Cartwright."

I think about what Ella said, about evidence that linked Chad to Dana's murder. Naturally, I say nothing. I try to put the pieces together, imagine what could mean so much to me in this world that I would scheme like that and kill for it.

I can't think of anything, not even love.

"Ella said that the building has a kind of power. That it's a dream maker—or it was. And that only a certain type of person should be allowed to live there, otherwise it loses its energy, becomes less."

Detective Crowe gives me the look that has become familiar, a kind of knowing, seen-it-all smirk. "You believe that?"

I shake my head, thinking about it. "There's more in heaven and earth, Horatio, than dreamt of in your philosophies."

"When people start quoting Shakespeare, that's my cue to leave. Stay easy for me to find, Ms. Lowan. I still have lots of questions for you—and your husband."

"Rosie?" I turn to see Chad trying to sit up and move over to him quickly. When I look back at Detective Crowe, he's gone.

"I'm sorry," says Chad, reaching for me. "I'm so sorry you were in danger, Rosie. I trusted them. I thought they were our friends. How could I have been so wrong?"

"I trusted them, too," I say, putting my hand to his cheek. "None of that matters now. We're safe and well."

"I'll never forgive myself," he says, pulling me close. "We almost lost everything, each other, our lives, because I couldn't see what was right in front of me."

I climb up on the bed and lie beside him. "There was no way to imagine any of this, Chad."

"I should have," he says. His tone has gone dark. "I know what people will do."

When I look at him his eyes are angry and sad, something I rarely see in him, even after all he's lost and been through.

"No more darkness," I whisper. "Now we move into the light."

I think about what Arthur Alpern said about breaking the chain, about healing.

It will be us. I know that in my heart. We'll be the ones to heal whatever ails the Windermere. We've rooted out the sickness, and now we'll bring wellness into those walls. We'll stay. We'll work; we'll make love. We'll grow our family.

No more spying and secrets, blackmail and murder. And definitely no more game night.

I look over to my sister. They've never met—Chad and Sarah. But she's gone.

I find her outside by the vending machine, trying to get a wrinkled dollar into the slot. I take it from her, smooth it out on my leg and then slide it in. She chooses a bag of cookies, sits on a nearby bench. We share it in silence.

"I think I need to go home," she says. "I don't like it here."

I laugh a little. "I can understand why."

"This city, that building. It's not safe."

She's right, of course. But then again, the world isn't safe.

"This is my home," I tell her.

She shakes her head.

"I thought they were going to kill us." She looks down at her small baby bump. Instinctively, I put my hand on it and she puts her hand over mine. She's well. They didn't drug her; small and innocent, she was easy enough to overwhelm and lock away. They baby is healthy inside her, unharmed. My niece or nephew. My connection to my sister is strong, but not strong enough to bring me home.

"I'm sorry this happened to you."

"Rosie," she says. "Please, just come with me."

"I can't," I say. "I belong here with Chad."

She looks back toward the room and shakes her head, then she rises, shouldering her duffel. I remember the tarot cards, how she fought in the basement, how she used to curl up beside me in bed when we were children. She's kind and sweet, but strong and wise. My sister. I'll always love her, but we dwell in different worlds now.

I don't tell her that she can't go home, that the police will need her for their investigation, that if there's a trial, she'll probably have to testify.

I don't say any of that, but she seems to read my thoughts, gives me a sad nod. When she turns to walk down the hallway toward the exit, I don't try to stop her.

Then I return to my husband and lie beside him on his bed, listen to the sound of his breath. My body aches, my head swims. When I close my eyes, I quickly fall asleep and dream of Willa. *Rosie,* she says, eyes red with blood, throat bruised, *you're in danger.*

SIX MONTHS LATER

forty-four

"It's great, Rosie," says Max. "It's truly great."

Max and I are sitting on a bench in Madison Square Park, eating hefty burgers and crispy fries from the Shake Shack, talking about my finished manuscript.

"Really?" It's all we ever want to hear. Unqualified raves. Writers are a fragile bunch.

"I mean it needs another pass," he says, always the editor. "There are some things that need clarifying, flushing out. But yeah, it's fantastic. And I love how you used your own story, your childhood, your questioning about the supernatural, your experiences at the Windermere, as the thread that ties the whole narrative together. It reads like fiction. I couldn't put it down."

An older man walks by us, carrying a copy of *The Post*. It features a courtroom shot of Ella looking pale and severe. "Cultist Asserts Her Innocence," the headline reads. "Jury Deliberates."

Charles and Abi have already been convicted of conspiracy, drug dealing and the murders of Xavier Young and Dana Lowan.

Those evil eye charms were a major piece of evidence linking the two murders.

Other charges pending include blackmail, attempted murder and kidnapping. They each await sentencing—Charles apparently the mastermind, and Abi in the role of henchman.

As Detective Crowe said, Abi was deeply in debt, and the Aldridges were paying for the care of his elderly mother. He was in their thrall completely.

And the story has become one of those New York curiosities, a major topic of news, gossip, dominating headlines and morning show banter, late night television bits.

Reporters have picked up on the fact that Marc LeClerc and Charles Aldridge had mediums for mothers. Astrology night has morphed into cult meetings where residents asked the Universe for the things they wanted. And Miranda, our resident psychic, is not helping by giving interview after interview about how the Windermere is an energy vortex attracting powerful good and terrible events. The board has asked her to stop. But she keeps putting herself out there. And now there's no one to delete her posts on the Windermere chat forum.

"And I love how you worked in the current events, even the questions that are still open," Max goes on. "I'm guessing there's time to add an appendix when all the court trials are done."

I nod. "Sebastian is waiting for that. Hopefully, Ella's trial will end today or tomorrow. And then it will be over."

I can't wait. It's been exhausting—the researching, writing, testifying in court, metabolizing all the trauma, pain, still living at the Windermere.

"Are you staying? At the Windermere?" Max asks.

I nod. "It's home. Anyway—who's going to buy it now? With all the bad press?"

Max shrugs. "There's always someone looking for a haunted house."

The air is cool, and leaves fall around us. I draw in a breath and release it.

"How's Chad doing?" he asks.

"Getting back into town today." I glance at my phone, realize it's almost time to meet him back at the apartment. He's been up in the Hollows filming. I've been using the time to do another draft on my book. Vision and revision. We're both in the zone, in spite of everything, working hard and honing our crafts. So far, no news on the baby front. But we're enjoying working on it.

"You guys really got past this, didn't you?" he asks, dropping a hand on my leg. "I'm happy for you."

"It hasn't been easy," I admit. "But yeah, I think we have."

He looks off over at the playground, where shouts and laughter ring out and leaves fall.

"Any word from Olivia?" I ask gently.

He shakes his head. "I just follow her on Instagram now."

After her abduction, Olivia decided she needed to take a break. She admitted to Max that she'd never stopped loving Chad. She never wanted to practice law, was only doing it to please her family. So she quit her big job, sold her apartment and left the city to go on a "vision quest" as she put it on social media. The last I saw, she was helping to build a school in rural Guatemala. The smile on her face reminded me of the one she wore in the picture I saw in her drawer. I'm glad she's happy, and I'm sad for Max, who clearly cared for her. He's been meeting girls on Torch, the popular dating app. But so far, no love connection.

I give him a peck on the cheek. "Love is right around the corner," I tell him.

"Is that a prophecy? Did you read my cards?"

I smile at him. "Just a guess."

"I'll take it."

I'm walking the short distance home, hustling up Park Avenue, when the phone rings. I'm surprised to see it's Chad's agent, who never calls me unless he can't reach Chad and something big is happening.

"Hey," I say.

"Hey, Rosie, sorry to trouble you but are you with Chad?"

"No," I say. "But I'm on my way to meet him at home."

"I've been trying to reach him, but my calls go straight to voice mail. The showrunner needs to talk to him and hasn't been able to get him since he left the set yesterday."

"Oh," I say. Yesterday?

I feel a familiar flutter of unease.

"When you see him, can you have him give me a call?"

"Of course," I say. As far as I knew, Chad was still on set yesterday.

I check the location app now and see that he's at home. I pick up my pace.

Chuck, the new doorman, is not at the desk when I enter the building. I check the mail and press the button to call the new self-operated elevator and press the button for floor five. We'll be paying off the assessment for years, and I miss the romance of that old elevator. But the privacy is worth it.

The doors open, and I take a quick step back.

Lilian, looking gaunt and angular, angry.

We face each other for a moment. She tried to buy us out of the apartment, but we declined. Now Charles and Ella's place is languishing on the market.

I expect her to glare at me, but instead she offers an unkind smile that reminds me of her mother. I flash on Lilian at the theater, in the photos with my husband. Chad admits now that he met her before he told me, but swears that he has always been faithful. It's something we're working on in therapy—honesty. How omissions are lies.

Needless to say, Lilian never called my agent for film rights, nor did her husband offer Chad a role in his new film. He still claims she was only there on his opening night to scout him for her husband. Whatever she saw didn't impress. I look forward to the day when I won't run into her in this building again.

"Rosie," she says, eyes lidded with dislike.

"Lilian."

I brush past her, and catch the whiff of her cologne. The elevator reeks of it as the doors close.

Chad's waiting for me at the apartment door, looking sexily tousled. His hair is longer, and he's a bit beefier with the weight he's gained for the role of Detective Jones Cooper. And I'm so happy to see him after our days apart that I forget all about the call and his agent.

I'm about to tell him about my encounter with Lilian. But he sweeps me off my feet the moment I cross the threshold and kisses me deep. It quickly heats up, and then we're tearing at each other's clothes. It's our window for baby making, and nothing keeps us from it. Soon, we are a tangle of limbs, and I lose myself to love and pleasure, and my still-fervent desire to have a child with my husband, every dark thing forgotten.

It's nearing dusk when we're spent and lying side by side. I listen to the beating of his heart, and relish the warmth of his skin.

"I missed you," he whispers. "Now that the book is done, come with me next time we're on location."

I nod. "Yes, I'd like that. Oh."

"What?"

"I'm sorry," I say. "Your agent called, said he couldn't reach you? The showrunner needs to talk to you. He said that you left the set yesterday."

I feel that whisper of unease—Chad not where he's supposed to be. Lilian in the elevator lobby.

Chad frowns and shakes his head. "No. That's weird."

He takes his phone from the bedside table and scrolls through the calls. "Oh, wow. I did miss some calls. Service up there is wonky."

"Huh," I say.

"Well, let me call Sean. That guy is a total flake. I'm not sure he's the best choice for a showrunner. Doesn't even know who's on set."

Something about the phrasing makes me think of Betty Cartwright.

Chad called her flaky when the detective told us about her claims that she overheard him manipulating Ivan into willing us the apartment. She wasn't flaky. She was competent and kind. I look up at Chad, who's already got the phone to his ear.

"Sorry I missed you, Sean," he says. "Service is bad up there."

I don't hear the response because I get up and go into the living room, pulling on Chad's shirt. The television is already tuned into the news, volume muted.

I push away the uneasy feeling. I get weekly calls from Detective Crowe, who even though he has three people in custody, two convicted and one with the jury deliberating, still doesn't feel like he has all the pieces. He still has questions for Chad about Dana's murder, about Betty Cartwright's. But he has no evidence against my husband, just questions. I think Detective Marlo Graves, the one who still thinks Chad killed Bethany, has poisoned his mind against my husband.

Sarah calls often, too. She's still having her dreams about a monster drinking my blood. My father is getting worse and when will I come home. Lately, I'm starting to think it's time to make amends with my past. I try to be as gentle with her as possible when I tell her that I am already home, that I don't know when or if I'll visit, but it will be in my time, on my terms.

I settle onto the plush sofa, pull the blanket around me. All the surveillance cameras and audio monitoring have been removed from our apartments. And our new main doorman, Chuck, is a retired cop. I finally feel safe in this apartment, like it's ours.

A headline on the screen has me turning up the volume on the television. A young, blonde female reporter stands in front of a prison, the sky gray and moody behind her, her hair whipping about in the breeze.

"Nolan Wright, who was convicted of murdering his sister Bethany in 2015, and whose upcoming retrial based on newly acquired evidence was set to start tomorrow, killed himself in prison today."

A picture of the young and beautiful Bethany appears on the screen, beside another image of her brother in a prison jumpsuit. My heart starts to thump, and my throat goes dry.

"Authorities say that he took a lethal dose of fentanyl. But have no idea how he obtained the narcotic. An investigation is pending."

The reporter goes on, voice grim.

"Wright left a suicide note confessing once again to the murder of his sister and apologizing to his parents and to everyone who loved Bethany. He claimed not to have deserved a new trial and didn't want to cause his family any more suffering."

I sit, staring, my skin tingling.

"A terrible end to a tragic story. This is Rachel Jones, reporting from Union Penitentiary."

Some of the pieces click into place then, and I feel the bottom fall out of my universe. Fentanyl was the drug Ella and Charles gave me. Did Chad have access to it, too? Detective Crowe's lingering questions echo. My husband, according to his agent, was not where he claimed to be, once again. A dark heart behind a beautiful mask. Was Dana right?

"Rosie."

I turn and there he is in the doorway. My husband. My love.

And I see him for the first time. I see what Detective Crowe sees. What Marlow Graves saw. My sister.

The boy who murdered his girlfriend in a jealous rage.

Who tampered somehow with his parents' vehicle and caused their deaths, inheriting all their money, far less than he imagined.

Who manipulated a dying man into willing him an apartment that should have gone to Dana.

The man who killed Dana to keep her from telling me the truth about him.

The man who bashed in Betty Cartwright's skull to keep her quiet.

The man drinking my blood until I'm too weak, too blind, to see what's in front of me.

A monster.

"Rosie," he says, with a confused smile. "What is it?"

But then his eyes drift to the television screen and he sees what I see. His body freezes.

"Oh, God," he says, coming to sit beside me. "I can't believe it."

He sinks his head into his hands. His shoulders shake but I know he's not crying. I put a comforting hand on his back, my mind spinning.

I look up to see Willa standing in the corner of the room. Her eyes are wide. When she opens her mouth, I hear her terrible scream.

Run!

forty-five

"That's horrible," I hear myself say gently. "But I'm glad there won't be another trial. One less thing to worry about."

He doesn't look up.

I rise and go into our bedroom, pull on my jeans slowly.

I dropped my bag by the door; I'll grab it on the way out. I'll say I'm heading out to get groceries for dinner. Time seems to slow and warp. Chad keeps his place on the couch, head still bowed.

As I'm pulling up my jeans the phone falls from my pocket. I pick it up and see a text from Detective Crowe.

> I shouldn't be doing this. But we're coming for your husband. If you can get away from him, do it.

I shove it in my pocket, paste a smile on my face.

When I leave the bedroom, he's not on the couch anymore.

He's by the front door.

"Rosie," he says, lifting a palm. "Don't."

"What?" I say, giving a light chuckle.

"I can explain."

"Explain what?" It's one of the things Chad taught me about acting. Believe it. "I want to make us a nice dinner. Steak. I'm just going to pop out to the store."

He shakes his head. "Not right now."

"O-kaaay," I say, drawing out the syllables. "You're being weird."

A vein throbs in my throat.

I move back toward the living room, and he grabs for and catches my wrist. I turn back to him.

He's not smiling. And when I look into his eyes, I see his darkness. It swirls and twists like a black hole, sucking in light and time.

"Let me go, Chad," I say, still playing confused.

"I can't do that, Rosie. I love you."

Far in the distance, I think I hear sirens. Too far. Too late.

Am I going to die in this apartment like Willa Winter, at the hands of my husband?

Will the Windermere win after all?

The buzzer rings then, long and loud, startling us both. I turn quickly and start to run.

But he's on me fast, taking me down to the floor hard, putting a strong hand over my mouth as the buzzer keeps ringing.

"Did you call the police?" he asks sadly.

I shake my head. Then I bring up my knee hard into his groin. His eyes go wide with pain, and he issues an agonized groan, falls off to the side. I get up and start to run again.

Through the living room and the narrow dining room, the tiny kitchen. He's up quickly, right behind me, roaring my name.

I get out the back door and slam it hard, listen to him fumbling with the latch as I bust through the fire door, which now, with recent updates, sounds an alarm.

Bells start ringing, loud and chaotic. I turn to race down the stairs.

But there's Miles, looking wicked and wearing a terrible, toothy smile.

I back away from him, heading up and up and up, when Chad bursts out the fire door and is pounding up the stairs after me.

Finally, I make it to the roof, bursting outside to find it snowing. The lights all around the building are a blanket of stars, and everything seems so quiet, the street noise and sirens so distant, the tar roof dark. The air is frigid.

Suddenly, everything just feels too heavy. All the running we do. The hustling, the fighting. Clinging to faith that things will turn out all right, even when all evidence points to the contrary. Believing the lies told by people we love. Trying to figure it all out. Do the right things. Acquire. Achieve.

My husband, the monster, exits the roof door. With brute strength, he breaks the handle off and lets the door close behind him. We're trapped up here now, together.

"I thought we could make a life apart from all the things I've done wrong, you know?"

I am up against the edge of the building and he's coming closer.

"There's a light that comes from within you, Rosie. Something bright and right and true. Pure goodness. And I thought if someone like you could love me, then I must—on some level—be okay."

He looks so sad, so broken. My heart still aches for him. My instinct is to comfort him, to hold him. But I stay where I am.

"I know," I say, softly.

"I thought if I could get this place for us, it would be like our little oasis. And we could build a life, a good one."

"I thought so, too."

"I did pressure Ivan to give us the apartment. It wasn't hard. I just reminded him that we were the ones caring for him. That Dana abandoned him. He was so weak. I don't know if he wanted to sign those papers. But he did."

Poor Ivan. He was barely clinging to reality at the end. In my heart, I always knew he wanted the place to go to Dana.

"She didn't deserve it," Chad says. "We did. And I thought if we could have it, then everything wrong and bad—I would just leave that part of myself in the past."

"I know," I say, trying to stay solid.

"But they just kept coming for me. They just kept hounding me. Dana with her threats. She was going to tell you that I was having an affair with Lilian—which I wasn't."

He shakes his head.

"The Aldridges kept trying to convince me to sell the place to Lilian. Lilian always turning up, telling me that she was scouting for Robert. Abi always watching, watching. Detective Graves with his constant suspicions. Detective Crowe lurking. Nolan's new trial. They wouldn't let me be."

"Did you kill Dana?" I ask.

"You know, I think she was the only person who ever truly saw me. The real me. She was so angry that we got the apartment. She was going to tell you everything, about her plan with the Aldridges, how I screwed her out of her inheritance. I was just trying to reason with her, get her to shut up. She wouldn't."

He's crying. "She would *not* shut up about how I was a bad person, a monster, that once you knew you'd hate me. I *did* manipulate Ivan. It was the least he could do, after all we did for him."

"The letter," I say. "You took it."

He glances up at the sky, snow gathering in his curls, offers a slow nod.

"It was Ivan's apology to Dana, written long ago, saying how he hoped that the inheriting of the apartment took care of her and her children in a way he never had. If she'd seen that, she'd know her suspicions about me were true. She'd have grounds for her claim that I manipulated a dying, drug-addled old man."

"And Betty?"

"She overheard me pushing Ivan to change his will."

All of it—such a waste. So many lives ruined, ended, because of an apartment.

"We never needed it," I choke out between sobs. "I never did. I just needed you. *Us.*"

He gives me the loving smile that has been the joy of my life with him. "I know that. Because you're good—the only good thing in my life. And that bad person, the person that I was, I thought he was gone. I'm not that person with you, Rosie. I'm better. *You* make me better."

I am weeping now because I know he's right. The man I love is not the one capable of doing all those terrible things. He's someone else, someone who only exists with me, for me. I reach for him, but he stays back.

They're pounding at the door. A rhythmic thumping echoes in the night as they try to break it down.

What if they can't? What if they stay out there, and we stay here forever? A kind of limbo where the world outside, the real world, can't touch us. Above me, I see the stars. It reminds me of my father and his run-down barn church. Daddy always said that you couldn't see the stars in the city. But he's wrong. They're up there, twinkling dimly against all the light we create down here.

"I can't go back there," he says, looking behind at the door where they are still pounding. He keeps creeping toward me, his hand outstretched. "I can't face the world that's waiting for us, Rosie."

"Please," I whisper.

But he's so fast and lithe—he's on the ledge before I can stop him. He teeters there, back to the city, facing me.

I drop to my knees and put my hands in prayer to my chest. My voice, I don't even recognize it.

"Don't. Don't do this. It doesn't have to be this way."

"I think love makes you a better person, you know?" he says, balancing there. "People *can* change. You changed me. Not just because you loved me, Rosie. But because *I* loved *you*. You made me see that there was more to life than just my own appetites, emotions, rages, desires. Thank you for that."

"Come down. Come back to me. We'll be okay." I'm still clinging to hope, my mind grappling for a way out. But my voice is just a wail in the night, in the sirens wafting up from down below.

The door bursts open then, Detective Crowe coming through.

And Chad turns, with me screaming, racing to the edge, slow motion, time warping, my fingers just grazing his shirt. I almost made it to him. Almost.

It doesn't seem like he jumped as much as he took flight, spreading his arms like wings, never making a sound and disappearing into the city lights.

epilogue

My niece, little Rosie, is in my arms.

It's a beautiful spring day in the Ozarks with the wind blowing and trees bowing and flowers blooming.

The congregation has gathered in my father's church to celebrate the arrival of this new little spirit. Sarah and Brian stand on either side of me and I hand little Rosie, who is quiet and sweet, off to her mother, as my father anoints her with water from the river on our property, saying words about nature and God and how every new soul in this world is a blessing, no matter what path they take through this life.

And I am here, home again. And not.

Just a visit, a trip into the past. I don't know how long my father has. But he looks happy as Sarah hands little Rosie to him, and he lifts her up to the congregation and everyone oohs and aahs and cheers. It's joyful, and above, through the holes in the roof, I see the bright blue sky and the high, towering clouds.

I have sold our apartment at the Windermere. There was a bidding war, despite all the horror that has taken place between its walls. The buyer, as rumor has it, is a renowned psychic who claims that it was his calling to live there, that the Windermere beckoned him. He's welcome to it. He outbid Lilian, who still seems to want to reclaim that piece of her family's legacy. Then finally, she sold the adjoining apartment to him, which he will put back together into one apartment.

I never did find out what Lilian was to my husband, if anything, or if it was just one more Aldridge scheming to reclaim apartment 5B. It doesn't matter now.

My book is in its fifth week on the *New York Times* bestseller list, due in part, I think, to the real-time scandal, the trial, my husband's suicide. The Windermere has no more secrets to keep. It's all out in the light now. Arthur Alpern says that he believes I've healed it. Fresh blood. Maybe he's right. Maybe not. Time will tell.

And I have no idea where I will go next.

Sadness, grief, loss. I carry it all with me. But I accept this as a part of my life, as a part of all life. And in this moment, I don't let that darkness rob me of the joy at the birth of my niece, and the happiness of my sister. We can be both. Dark and light. Sadness and joy. They dwell side by side in everything. And Chad, my Chad, the man he might have been, is still with me. I still hear his voice, and catch his scent on the breeze. The man in the news—the one who lied and murdered—that's not the man I loved. I don't even recognize him as the same person.

Now Max sits beside me, awed by the place where I grew up.

He leans in close. "You have to write about this," he says.

"Maybe someday."

He wraps an arm around me, and I move in closer. He remains the most true and loyal friend a person can ever have. I smile at him, grateful that he's come with me on this trip home. Friendship, such an underrated relationship. And yet, sometimes friends are the family we choose. Without him, his support, I might have been crushed by the weeks after Chad's death. He was there. The rock.

Later, after celebration and food, I find my way back to the river where Sarah and I used to play for hours as children. It's full and rushing with the spring thaw, filling its banks.

My father joins me, coming to stand beside me. For a while we are silent, watching the water flow and hawks circle overhead, the bees visiting the wildflowers.

"So do you still think I lied about the world out there?" he asks. His voice is gentle and raspy.

I smile and take his hand. It's frail in mine and I look into his eyes and see how old he's grown. I stop short of quoting Shakespeare again but get close.

"I think there's more in heaven and earth, Dad, than either one of us will ever know."

He's quiet for a moment, and then he gives me an assenting nod. "Fair enough, rose petal."

Together, we walk back toward the barn, which glows white against the gloaming.

★ ★ ★ ★ ★

acknowledgments

Fiction is a strange beast. It's true, you know—*all* of it. And, of course, none of it is true. Every novel is a confabulation, a flight of imagination, a warped twist of memory, a waking dream. Still, there are *so many* true pieces in this pack of lies I call a novel.

Let me explain.

My late aunt, Phyllis Davidson, was a complicated, urbane and stylish Manhattanite. As a child, I thought the life she occupied in New York City was glamorous and enviable. There was more to it, and to her, than that, of course. But for most of my life she dwelled at 55 Park Avenue in a two-bedroom apartment that was very much my dream of what it would be like to live in Manhattan. The apartment that Rosie and Chad inherit in this book is inspired by her place in Murray Hill. My aunt has passed, and that apartment has sold, but it's still vivid in my memory and brought to life here. Longtime readers might also recognize a version of the East Village walk-up where I lived while I attended Eugene Lang College of Liberal Arts at The

New School. This apartment first appeared in *Beautiful Lies* and wanted a visit in this novel, nearly twenty years later.

Rosemary's Baby by the late, great Ira Levin was a source of inspiration for this book, and fans of the classic horror novel will see an homage here and there. I've had a lifelong love affair with New York City and the buildings that line its streets. There's an energy and a personality to its various neighborhoods, to the architecture of individual buildings. Some buildings are as famous as their residents. While the novel *Rosemary's Baby* was inspired by the Alwyn Court apartments on Fifty-Eighth Street, and the movie adaptation was filmed at The Dakota, an iconic residence, home to stars of stage, screen, page and vinyl, I wanted something smaller and less recognizable, the kind of building that epitomizes my New York, the one I hold in my memory and imagination. So, it had to be 55 Park Avenue, my late aunt's Murray Hill prewar gem.

Other books were significant to my research: *New York's Fabulous Luxury Apartments: with Original Floor Plans from the Dakota, River House, Olympic Tower and Other Great Buildings* by Andrew Alpern; *The Dakota: A History of the World's Best-Known Apartment Building* by Andrew Alpern; *The Big Book of New York Ghost Stories* by Cheri Farnsworth. An article in *New York* magazine by Wendy Goodman about architectural historian Andrew Alpern was the inspiration for Rosie's visit to Arthur's Chelsea apartment. I also used an imagined version of Mr. Alpern as the inspiration for the character Arthur Alpern.

More truth melding with fiction below.

The literary agent in this book is named Amy, and I assure you that this was a totally unconscious inclusion, though, in fact, my real agent is Amy Berkower of the sterling Writers House. My depiction of Rosie's agent led mine to write me a note of apology for texting while she was talking to me on the phone! Which of course she doesn't do! Anyway, only the good things were inspired by Amy—champion, rock, therapist and navigator of the big waters of the writing life. I'd be lost without her and am so grateful for her wisdom and support. Huge thanks also to her intrepid assistant, Celeste Montano, and to the international rights group that put my books in the hands of people around the globe.

Likewise, some of the conversations between Rosie and her editor, Max, led my (esteemed and brilliant) editor, Erika Imranyi of Park Row Books, to write some comments in my Track Changes like, *Hey! Is that me?* or *I feel like that's a dig!* (No, it's *not* her—except, again, for all the good things.) And no, I would not make unflattering fictional observations about my editor in a book that she would be the first to read. Let me state for the record that Erika is the kindest, wisest, most insightful and OMG *patient* editor a writer could ever have. Every book that we've worked on together is undeniably better for her collaboration. I feel blessed by her presence in my life.

My grandmother who was born in Little Italy on Mulberry Street moved to Bay Ridge as a child and then lived there until her passing at one hundred years old. She taught me (and many years later, my daughter) how to play Rummikub, and now, weirdly, I play it with my friends. The copy editor Kathleen Mancini said that Rummikub was invented in Romania in 1944 and didn't come to the US until 1977. Because copy editors *just know* these things. I don't know if this is something my Italian immigrant family brought over with them, but I'm sure my family was playing it in the US long before then. You know what they say: *To write is human. To (copy)edit is divine.* So, I have removed its mention from the 1963 sections of the book. Thank goodness for copy editors (with special thanks on this outing to Kathleen Mancini) who save us from our worst mistakes—or try to!

The bestselling and award-winning true-crime writer, *New York Times* book reviewer, and all-around lovely human Sarah Weinman was so helpful in talking to me about the different ways nonfiction writers do their research and all the resources available in New York City. Her "Before, and After, the Jogger" article in *New York* magazine was one of the finest pieces of crime journalism I have read, and it inspired the subject matter of Rosie's first book. I'm so grateful for Sarah's candor and generosity.

Now some totally true things.

I say this every year, but the teams at HarperCollins, Harlequin and Park Row Books are a writer's dream. In everything from copyediting to marketing and publicity, from art to sales, they are exemplary. I can't say enough good things about the people who devote themselves to publishing my books in the most thoughtful possible ways. Special thanks to executive vice president and publisher Loriana Sacilotto and vice president of Editorial Margaret Marbury for their wise leadership and endless creativity. Publicist extraordinaire Emer Flounders tirelessly works to spread the word about my novels and launches me (kicking and screaming) out onto the road with endless patience and organizational genius. Lindsey Reeder and the fabulous social media team help me to stay on the bleeding edge of what's happening in the virtual world. Much gratitude to Rachel Haller, marketing maven, Randy Chan, independent-bookstore and library whisperer, and Nicole Luongo, editorial assistant, for her organization and good cheer.

How could a writer survive without her friends? Mine cheer me through the good days and drag me through the challenging ones. They are forced to attend book signings year after year, read early drafts of my work and endure my social media posts. But they still love me! And I love them! Erin Mitchell is an early reader, tireless promoter, inbox tamer, voice of wisdom and pal. Heather Mikesell has been a longtime early reader, eagle-eyed editor and bestie. Jennifer Manfrey is always on standby to dig in deep to some obscure topic over which I'm obsessing. Her support, friendship and wisdom are foundational in my life. And honestly, I think she buys more of my books than anyone else on the planet! Lifelong friends Tara Popick and Marion Chartoff have had the pleasure of dealing with me since college and grade school, respectively. They still answer my calls! A big shout-out to Team Waterside—Kathy Bernhardt, Colleen Chappell, Marie Chinicci-Everitt, Rhea Echols, Karen Poinelli, Tim Flight, Bill Woodrow and Jennifer Outze, Celeste Van Auken, Cathy Kimber, and Heidi Ackers, to name just a few—for being my home team, reading, supporting, showing up at events and being there in every way possible. The Laymans—Andrea, Bill and Ayers—have shared every chapter of our lives and are so often the loving faces I see first when I look out into a crowd.

My mom, Virginia Miscione, former librarian and avid reader, gave me the gift of loving story in all forms—books, film, television and theater. She remains one of my earliest and most important readers. I don't usually give my dad, Joseph Miscione, much of a shout-out. In fact, I mainly just give him a hard time for being the guy who told me *not* to pursue my writing dreams but to get a "real job." I usually do this onstage and it always gets lots of laughs—especially when he's there! (It's not bad advice, though. I have succeeded against all odds!) But he and my mom have been the safety net beneath me as I walk that tightrope we call life. Thanks, Mom and Dad, for always being there. And of course, along with my brother, Joe, for shamelessly bragging, facing out books in stores and always spreading the word.

I usually begin these acknowledgments with my husband, Jeffrey, and our daughter, Ocean Rae, because they are the rock-solid foundation of my life. Every word I write is for them. Jeff, you're the love of my life, my partner in crime, and my best and truest friend. Good job running "the corporation"—and taking care of us in every other way possible. Ocean, you are by far my greatest accomplishment and deepest source of pride and joy; you're a light bringer, a joy maker, our North Star. Our beloved labradoodle, Jak Jak, is my faithful writing buddy and foot warmer, and a constant reminder to finish up work so we can play.

And finally, a writer is nothing without her readers. Some of you have been with me from the very beginning. Thank you for all of your support—for connecting, reviewing, turning up at events, engaging in social media and generally making this writing life more fun. It means so much to me to know that my stories, characters and words have found a home in your minds and hearts. Thank you for reading!